JAKOB'S

LEGACY

STAN PARKS

Dedication

This book is dedicated to the lady of my life who had faith in me and encouraged me to write this book:
My Lady Norie, my First Mate and Only Mate.

Prologue

The marriage ceremony between Jakob Miller and Geraldine Landry Widacker was one of the biggest Sheridan had ever seen. Delayed by circumstances beyond their control, the trials the couple had faced gave them strength and resolve, which brought them together at St. Ignatius church that day. Reverend John Binotti performed the service and Doc Kelly, dressed in his new suit, was best man. Eleanor, Geraldine's sister, stood as maid of honor. Jakob's daughter, BethAnn, proudly walked down the aisle carrying a small bouquet of flowers.

People packed the church to overflowing and stood crowded together along the sides. Others gathered outside, hoping to see and maybe hear the goings-on through the open doors. Harry Morgan, the honky-tonk piano player from the Lucky Lady saloon, was decked out in a tuxedo and played soft music on the church piano.

The crowd hushed when the bride arrived, escorted by Dr. Bob Miller, Jakob's dad. She was beautiful—tall and slender, wearing a pale blue, floor-length wedding dress that was simple yet elegant. The neckline was scooped low, adorned by pearls Jakob gave her as a wedding gift, and the bodice was a slightly darker blue lace over the dress. Her brown hair was set in an updo, and a short light blue veil reached her waist. Her brown eyes glistened as she smiled. Harry began the wedding march Bob Miller, Jakob's dad, slowly walked her down the aisle. As they approached the altar and Jakob, he lifted her veil and kissed her on the cheek. Bob shook his son's hand, wished them God's blessing, and then took a seat next to his wife.

The ceremony was simple, and John Binotti directed the words to Jakob, who he knew really well, and to Geraldine. When it came to putting on the wedding rings, Doc Kelly had a problem finding them, but Jakob saw him put them in his right upper vest pocket and was able to come up with them. This caused the church to laugh and stopped the ceremony until John Binotti got them to quiet down. When he finished the ceremony and told Jakob he could kiss the bride, BethAnn came up to them and put her arms around them, and kissed them both. It put a final tie in the marriage. They were now married and had officially become a family. It brought tears to the eyes of those who realized

BethAnn now had a living mother, something she had prayed for.

A seemingly endless receiving line preceded a reception at the Sheridan Inn. It appeared the entire community had come out for the wedding, underlining the fact that Jakob was a popular man in Sheridan. Lady Geraldine had experienced little contact with the people in Sheridan. Still, she was heartily accepted by Sheridan as Jakob's wife.

Chapter 1
The Honeymoon

Sunlight crept through the edges of the draperies in the bedroom, and Jakob opened his eyes. He could feel Geraldine's soft, warm body lying next to him. Lifting his head, he watched her as she continued to slumber.

There was a chill in the room. The fire in the fireplace had almost gone out. Jakob tried not to disturb his wife as he laid his head back on the pillow. His thoughts were of the night before. They had arrived from Sheridan after their magnificent wedding reception at the Sheridan Inn on the day before. They will be spending their honeymoon at Geraldine's Oliver Henry Ranch.

Jakob had wanted to take the train to Chicago and spend their honeymoon in one of the fancy hotels. It was October, and the weather would still be Indian summer in Chicago. Still, Geraldine felt she needed to be at the ranch. She had been absent since April and felt she needed to look after the business. Jakob decided they could take the Chicago trip sometime later. Geraldine promised him she would give him all her time while they were there. Even though her sister Eleanor took care of things while she and Jakob were in England, there was still much for her to do when she came back. He decided being at Oliver Henry Ranch wouldn't be too bad for a honeymoon. There would be no patients or other people to bother them there. He snuggled closer to her, and his thoughts were about their night before. They made love freely, and there were no misgivings now because they were married.

He was beginning to hear some movement out in the hall. *Eleanor and Roger must be about, but there's no reason for us to get up,* he thought. Then he felt Geraldine start to move, and she moaned a little. *Oh, she's waking.* Geraldine lifted her head and turned to him, kissing his forehead.

"You're awake," Jakob said quietly. She smiled and nodded. "Sleep well?"

"Hmm, and why not? I'm with you next to me. Why has it taken us so long to be together? I love you, Jakob Miller," and she snuggled closer to him and held him tightly. They laid there quietly as she softly kissed him.

"You know we could do this all day if you'd like," remarked Jakob.

"Oh yes. Could we? I'd love that. I'll ring for Little Deer. She can bring up our breakfast, and we can spend the rest of the day doing...."

"But I thought you said you had other things to do here. Eleanor and Roger are up already. They'll be wondering why we're not."

"Spoilsport," she teased. "All right, we'll get up too. You'll be sorry when I'm with the cowboys, and you're here alone."

Jakob laughed. Putting his robe on, he went to the fireplace and stirred the glowing embers, then added some wood. "Okay, sleepyhead, you can get out of bed now."

Geraldine moved her naked body to Jakob; opening his robe, she put her arms around him and kissed him passionately.

"All right now, remember, you said you had to also meet with the foreman."

"But you're my favorite cowboy and foreman."

"I'm not a cowboy. I'm a dentist."

"Oh, so you are and such a good one. But I guess I will have to wait for an appointment with you to make love." She laughed and started to dress as Jakob pulled on his trousers and tucked in his shirt.

"I see you're almost ready," Geraldine said. "You can go ahead, and I'll be down as soon as I can."

Jakob left and went down the ranch's magnificent staircase to the dining room. Eleanor and Roger were already seated and having their tea while Little Deer served their breakfast.

"Good morning, Jakob." Eleanor smiled. " Did you have a good sleep? You must have been tired after that long ride out here."

"We were both very tired after the wedding and reception, then the long ride. I hope Little Deer made some coffee. I really need it."

"I'm sure she has remembered you drink coffee since the last time you were here. Oh, here she is now."

"I have coffee for you, Mister Doc. Lady Geraldine, she coming?"

Geraldine arrived, gave Jakob a quick hug and kiss, and bestowed a kiss on the cheek to Eleanor and then Roger. Looking out the window, she exclaimed, "Oh look!: what a beautiful morning we have. I guess I must have overslept." Looking at Jakob, she added, "My husband woke me up. We've been on the run so much, I guess it's starting to catch up with me. But I promise, from now on, I'll be up on time." She laughed.

Eleanor went on to tell her, "George Roberts, your foreman, was here a while ago, but I told him you were still sleeping. He said he'd be back later. Said something about moving some stock today. I guess he has some other things he wants to talk about."

They chatted at breakfast. Eleanor asking how long they would be staying at the ranch. Geraldine shrugged. After breakfast, Jakob visited with Roger and Eleanor. At the same time, Geraldine left to finish getting ready for her meeting with her foreman, who arrived soon. He congratulated Geraldine and Jakob on their marriage and shook Jakob's hand. There was some small talk, and then he began to inform Geraldine of the problems which had to be taken care of that day. Jakob sat back and listened as the boss lady answered George's queries.

"We're going to move some of the stock from the west grazing ground closer in for the winter. Do you want to go and take a look? Be nice if the men saw you were around now. Maybe Doc would like to come along. You still going to be the boss here now that you're married?"

"That won't change things here, George." Geraldine bristled at the remark.

"Oh, no, I didn't mean anything by that remark. I know you be the boss here," countered George.

Jakob saw George was uncomfortable and remarked, "Hey George, she may be my wife, but she knows what she's doing here. My business is in Sheridan. You know I'd like to go along with you guys and see how you do things here."

George nodded and smiled.

Geraldine added, "Good idea, Jakob. George, get the horses ready for us to leave right after lunch."

"Might be a good idea to go tomorrow. It's a long ride up there unless you plan on staying overnight."

"You're right, George. We'll get an early start tomorrow, and then we can come back here before dark. There are some other things we can do here on your list today."

George left, and Jakob looked at Geraldine. "And what have you got for me to do, Boss?" She came up to Jakob, put her arms around him, and kissed him. "I suggested it this morning, but you seemed to think I should get up and get to work. Nothing saying, though; that later on we couldn't take the horses and go for a ride up to the Buffalo springs."

"I'm just kidding. You go ahead and do what you have to do, and if there's time, we can go for a ride. I wonder if the horse I rode when I was here last time will remember me."

Geraldine left, and Jakob sat on the porch and watched her as she walked toward the corral. His thoughts sifted through his head as he gazed at the barn. It was the first time he was alone since they came to the ranch. *Our wedding was really something,* he thought. *I guess I didn't realize I had so many friends. I'm glad Geraldine had some of hers there. Too bad her mother couldn't be here. I hope things will work out for her. I know Geraldine must miss her. I really liked Lady Mary, but she will be isolated at Landry Manor. There really is no hope for Sir Gerald's recovery. But, he could live a long time and then, maybe not. I wonder if he would have accepted me for his son-in-law?* Jakob's thoughts rambled. Then he remembered getting married to Liz. *That was a nice affair too. We were younger then and so much in love.* His thoughts ended suddenly.

Roger came out to be with Jakob. Jakob wasn't sure he wanted to chat with Roger, but he was there, and conversation was inevitable.

"Nice to be here at the ranch, isn't it?" Roger began.

Jakob agreed, and Roger continued. "You haven't really spent too much time here, have you?"

Jakob replied he had been there only twice: once when Oliver Henry had his grandiose birthday party and again when he and BethAnn visited. Geraldine had given BethAnn instructions in horseback riding, and Jakob had enjoyed their visit.

"We've been here for five or six years," Roger went on. "It's beautiful with the mountains in the background, and working the ranch is interesting. We've enjoyed it, but it can get pretty lonesome. We've had guests come by on a few occasions. I'm glad Geraldine is back; it will be good for Eleanor. When we first came out, we thought it would be adventuresome, and it has been, but those cold winters we've had can be trying."

Jakob kept up the conversation on a positive note but felt Roger was not satisfied with ranch life. He wondered if Eleanor felt the same. Roger was younger than Jakob and probably came from a family who never experienced life such as this. He doubted Roger made much effort to work with the hired hands. Oliver Henry was often out with the men—taking part in the roundup, moving the herds, and branding the calves. The thought came to mind that maybe the rustic life was not for Roger, and perhaps not for Eleanor, either.

The conversation came to a close when Geraldine rode up on her white stallion, Sir Richard. She was excited about her day and the things she accomplished and said she felt the ranch hands really missed her while she had been gone. The men insisted she and Jakob have supper with them that evening. "Roger, you and Eleanor can join us. We'll have their fare for dinner. Hector is really a good cook. A little overbearing and temperamental, but a good cook. The men will entertain us. I guess they really missed me."

Jakob agreed and thought it was a good idea. He knew a few of them because they had been patients in his office.

"Then it's all set. Some of them are already with the herd, but we can eat supper with the rest. Little Deer should have a lunch ready for us now, and then we can go for our ride to Buffalo Springs. Roger, why don't you and Eleanor come with us?"

Roger was rather non-committal but went in for lunch with them. They met with Eleanor and had a pleasant lunch. Still, they declined to accept the invitation to go riding with Jakob and Geraldine. Eleanor begged off as not feeling well.

It had been a long time since Jakob and Geraldine had ridden together. It was back in England in those last days at Landry Manor. One of the men brought Sir Richard, and the chestnut mare Jakob would ride. Jakob was amazed the mare remembered him. They trotted off toward the northwest, where the foothills to the Bighorns began.

As they rode, they chatted and enjoyed the fall scenery. Geraldine led the way. It was hilly but not difficult. Jakob had gained enough experience to be a good rider. Considering he was a city boy, he became quite proficient at riding. Geraldine was an expert horsewoman. She said she was born on a horse. They enjoyed this time together. Geraldine once mentioned her former husband didn't enjoy riding a horse. Thus, this was one thing Geraldine lacked in her marriage with James. They would seldom go riding together.

They paused from time to time to view the pleasant fall landscape and arrived at the springs, a picturesque stop. There was only one spring, but it was met with a creek that had become dammed to cause a small pond. Willows edged the pond, and ducks flew in and out. They got off their horses and led them to the water. They laid down in the grass, looking up at the clouds as they passed by.

Geraldine rolled close to Jakob, then lifted herself and kissed him. "Jakob, I love you. You have made me so happy. The thought just passed my mind about the time back at Landry Manor, and we laid like this over-looking the estuary. I felt so low. I saw no way out of our predicament, and you said of the dark cloud we were under that it would pass, and the sun would shine again. We are so fortunate to have each other.

"You know, maybe we better get back to the ranch now so we can have supper with the men. This is the first time I've been asked. When Oliver Henry had the ranch, they used to ask him and Abby to come over several times a year. James felt we should not fraternize with them, and consequently, we were seldom asked to do it. I guess that's the difference between the English way and the American way."

The ride back got them to the ranch just as the dinner bell rang. Still dusty from the ride, they quickly cleaned up and joined the men for supper at the bunkhouse. Several of the hands came up to them and welcomed the couple. Geraldine officially introduced Jakob as her partner in the ranch. However, she told them she would still be managing the operation. Roger and Eleanor would be responsible when Geraldine was not there. She explained she would be spending much of her time in Sheridan with her husband. A few men joshed her and told her Jakob would make a good hand, and they would be happy to teach him the job.

Jakob laughed and said, "I don't do horses and cows. They just don't fit in my chair."

They broke into loud laughter. This was a good relationship between the owner and the workers. Geraldine had felt they didn't respect her, but the fact was they didn't know how to approach her as the boss. After the sumptuous barbeque put on by Hector, Geraldine gave him the praise he richly needed.

Hector responded, "I keep telling these clods they git the best cookin' they ever had. But all they do is gripe."

The others started shouting him down as Geraldine laughed and brought them to silence. Harold, one of the older cowboys, brought his fiddle out and started playing "Let Me Call You Sweetheart," which they sang to Geraldine and Jakob. Another brought out a guitar, and the guys did some singing. The party lasted till almost ten. Geraldine thanked them for the pleasant evening and announced they would be leaving and she would be riding out with them in the morning to the west grazing area.

They walked back to the ranch mulling over the evening.

Jakob spoke, "I have to hand it to you, Honey. You know how to handle those men. I didn't realize you were so capable of management. This is another side of you I have discovered. You don't act like an English aristocrat in dealing with them."

Geraldine laughed, "And how am I supposed to act in dealing with my hands?"

"Well..."

"Well, tell me how I should act. No, don't. First of all, I'm really glad you were with me. You gave me the courage to do what I knew I should do. Back in England…"

"Yes, I remember back in England how you took charge of Landry Manor."

"I guess I learned much from my papa. He was concerned for his tenants and did everything he could for them, and they respected him. No, he wouldn't sit down with them for supper. The way I see it, those men make it possible for me to have a successful ranch. Without them, I couldn't do their job. I need every one of them, and if they stay with me and work hard, they should be rewarded. Spending the evening once in a while is not too great a price to pay for their loyalty."

Jakob smiled, put his arms around her, and kissed her. "I'm in full agreement with you, Honey. What time do I get up tomorrow, boss?"

Chapter 2
On the Trail

It was an early start for Jakob and Geraldine, and they were on the trail at dawn to the western grazing grounds. There was a chill in the air, but it was exhilarating. They stayed even with the cowboys, as there was no real trail, so the riding was slower, but they made it to the western grazing grounds by mid-morning. The men there had already started rounding up the herd.

October weather in Wyoming had been dry, so there was a great deal of dust. Geraldine motioned Jakob to move his bandana to cover his nose. She rode up to him, told him to stay put and watch while they got the steers together, then left to join the cowboys. Jakob watched as they rounded up the cattle and was almost horrified when he saw Geraldine as she cut in and out and approached wayward animals and edged them back into the herd. At first, he was frightened for her safety, but he marveled at her skill as he watched. *If that didn't change the men's minds about the aristocratic lady's ability, nothing would.* Jakob was well aware of Geraldine's horsemanship but never realized she could do the work of the cowboys. He observed her for some time. Eventually, she left the herd and returned to Jakob. She was dusty and breathless as she slowed to his speed.

"Want to join us?" she laughed. "This will give you a thrill."

Jakob laughed and shook his head.

"Are you kidding? I'll keep my job. Where did you learn to ride like that? Bet you couldn't do that side-saddle. By the way, where is Sir Richard? I thought you'd be riding him."

"You don't understand. We use quarter horses, bred for this kind of work. They are our specialty at Oliver Henry. I've been sending some of them back to England, where they like my horses as well as the local ranchers here in Wyoming. I'm even starting to get orders and inquiries for them in other countries. The Oliver Henry Ranch breed is becoming well known."

They slowed down and were now walking their mounts as the herd and riders moved ahead. A couple of cowboys laid back and directed the strays.

"Oh Jakob, you're funny. We are working and training our horses, which I learned to do by watching the men. They are skillful in their riding and do not take chances, even if they make it look like they do. They understand the actions of the cattle and outwit them. Also, their mounts are agile and can sense what to do. Reining and cutting are their business. I really enjoy doing this. Oh, don't get me wrong, I wouldn't want to do it all the time, but it sure has sharpened my riding skills. Maybe later, I'll let you join in on the fun. Let's get going because we're falling behind."

They both started to catch up with the herd, with Geraldine heading off a steer that was going off on a tangent. They stopped near a stream and dismounted.

Geraldine pulled down her bandana as well as Jakob's and kissed him on his dusty lips. She drank from her canteen and then handed it to Jakob. "You need some water, too. I don't like to kiss dusty lips."

They both sat down, and Geraldine brought out some lunch she had prepared and carried in saddlebags. Finishing their lunch with a long drink of water, Geraldine gathered the leftovers.

"Well, that should hold us until we get back to the ranch. Let's get back to the herd."

They mounted and rode on until they caught up to the herd. Geraldine went up to the foreman and told him they would be leaving soon. He tipped his hat. She and Jakob followed along for a while, and Geraldine rounded up some of the strays. Eventually, she decided it was time to go back. It wasn't too long before the herd was far behind, and only the dust could be seen.

They arrived back as the sun was starting to go down. One of the men took their horses, and they climbed the stairs to the ranch.

Geraldine looked at Jakob. "How was that for a day's work?"

Jakob laughed. "I didn't exactly do any work. I just went along. Although I must say, I feel tired from the ride. Let's clean up first and then have dinner. I'll make you Jakob's special martini before we eat."

"That would be fine, but we have to get rid of this dust first."

Maria prepared baths for both of them, and they dressed and were ready for dinner. Roger and Eleanor were already having cocktails when they went down. Jakob, using his bartending skills, made the martinis. They met in the great room by the fireplace and talked.

Eleanor was the first to speak. "Well, how was your day? I guess it was a long one for you. You must have left before we got up."

Geraldine told them about the roundup, and Jakob described how she joined in with the men and helped them put together the herd.

Eleanor remarked, "Geraldine, you were always a good horsewoman. I could never do that. Remember the time I fell off my horse and broke my arm? The doctor scolded me and said I shouldn't ride."

"Yes, I remember when you took the fall, but you did ride after that, didn't you?"

"Papa insisted I ride, but I never really enjoyed it. I did it for him."

Jakob held up his glass, and they toasted the evening. It was a short while later when Little Deer called them in for dinner. The table was adorned with shiny silver and glass and burning candles. Maria served them a fine meal, including roast duck that Little Deer prepared.

After dinner, Roger said, "Jakob, I could go for a glass of Port. How about you? If you wish to have a cigar go ahead, but I don't like the horrible things."

Jakob laughed and agreed to have the Port and just chat. Roger did most of the talking, and Jakob listened. Roger talked mostly about his life in England. Jakob got the feeling Roger was homesick, and the thought passed his mind that his friend might be thinking of going back. They had a good conversation, and Jakob was impressed with his friend's background.

He was not sure what sort of arrangement Geraldine had with Roger and Eleanor. From the conversation, he got the idea perhaps they were losing interest in ranching. Maybe it wasn't what they thought it would be. If they moved back to England, Geraldine would need to run the day-by-day operations. Jakob had hoped Geraldine would spend most of her time in Sheridan and leave the ranching to them. BethAnn needed a mother, and Jakob needed a wife. The evening was pleasantly spent, and Jakob learned much about Roger and Eleanor. Still, with the long day and the roundup, both Geraldine and Jakob were tired.

They bid goodnight and went up to their bedroom. Both were tired, but Jakob felt he should approach Geraldine with what he had learned from Roger. "Honey, what sort of arrangement do you have with Eleanor and Roger? I thought you told me they were interested in running the ranch."

"Yes, that's right. The couple came here because they were interested. Roger had no skills other than his Cambridge education. He will not share in his family's inheritance, and he didn't want to join the army and have a military career. Roger also did not want to go into the ministry or practice law. When he married Eleanor, they both craved a different lifestyle and thought they would like to take up ranching. Papa had the idea they could eventually buy the spread, and I could come back to England." Geraldine smiled and cuddled up to Jakob. "But then I met you." The conversation didn't last too long, and they were soon asleep.

Little Deer came by and awakened Geraldine at sunup.

Jakob was not quite ready to face the day. "Honey, is this your usual time to get up?"

"Jakob, you can stay in bed, but I have to get together with George this morning. There are still things we have to work on. I'll be back in an hour, and we can have breakfast together." She kissed him and went into the dressing room.

Jakob pulled on the covers and closed his eyes. He heard Geraldine quietly scurrying about until she left. Much as he tried, Jakob couldn't fall back asleep. His thoughts invaded his mind and kept him awake until he finally gave in and got up, dressed, and went downstairs.

"Good morning, Mister Doc. I have coffee for you." Sure enough, Little Deer had it ready for him.

"You make good coffee, Little Deer." This gave her a boost, and she related that Geraldine had left with George and would be back soon. Then they would have breakfast.

Jakob took his cup and sat on the porch behind the kitchen. Roger and Eleanor would soon arrive. Jakob noticed that since Geraldine and he had come, she took over the ranch's operations. Roger and Eleanor seemed to do nothing.

They all waited for breakfast until Geraldine came back, which was just a short time later. Geraldine talked about what she had done and discussed it with Roger and Eleanor. After breakfast, Geraldine and Jakob left and went to their bedroom.

Jakob took his wife into his arms and kissed her. "There are some things I'd like to talk over with you." He proceeded to tell her about the conversation he had with Roger. "I wonder if they are getting bored with the ranch. What's your feeling.?"

Geraldine felt he may have misinterpreted Roger. "I believe they can take over the operation."

"Then, why don't you let Roger take over? You are assuming all the work. Roger should have been at the roundup—maybe not filling in with the cowboys like you did—but being there just the same."

"You are probably right. I have taken over, but I am the owner."

"If you'd like them to eventually buy you out, it might be a good idea to let them assume some ownership now. That would give them more incentive to contribute to the ranch's success."

During the following days, Roger worked with Geraldine and George, and she was satisfied with his performance.

Geraldine and Jakob were having their cocktails on the verandah when they noticed a rider in the distance. He finally arrived, tied up, climbed the steps, and approached Jakob. It was Harold, one of the boys from the Lucky Lady.

"Hey Doc, glad I could find you. Doc Kelly sent me over to tell you he has a guy in the hospital who needs you, and you better come back and take care of him."

"What's the problem?"

"I dunno. He jes tole me ta get ya."

Jakob turned to Geraldine. "When are we going back? We've been here over a week, and I've been thinking about it. I miss my BethAnn. What do you think?" And then turning to Harold, "Harold, why don't you go over to the bunkhouse and introduce yourself. Henry will find you a place to bunk for the night, and you can chow with them. I'll talk it over with my missus and let you know tomorrow."

Geraldine was the first to speak. "You want to go back, don't you? I could use a few days more, but we could leave the day after tomorrow. I miss my daughter too. I don't know about you, but this has been a nice honeymoon for me. Now, I have a home I have to get started on. Let's go back the day after tomorrow. Is it all right with you?"

"I don't know what Kelly has in mind for me, but maybe we should get back. The day after would be good with me. These cows and horses don't need me."

Chapter 3
Geraldine Takes over

Geraldine asked Raymond, her straw boss, to take them back to Sheridan. The day was overcast and threatened rain. She took some of the clothes she would need and a few other items from the ranch. Her horse and Raymond's would be trailed behind the wagon. They hadn't gone very far when the winds increased, and it started to rain. Jakob and Geraldine went inside the covered wagon to prevent getting wet, but it was a long ride. The horses were constantly spooked by the rain, lightning flashes, and thunder. Geraldine decided to ride her horse and help control the horses during the journey and got thoroughly drenched. The rain stopped periodically, and she was able to dry off some.

They entered Sheridan as it started to get dark and were wet and tired. The wagon pulled in next to Jakob's home on Loucks Street. They could hear Skippy barking up a storm as they exited the wagon. BethAnn opened the door and literally bounced out of the house, followed by Chucha. BethAnn flew into Jakob's arms, flooding him with kisses. She repeated the same with Geraldine.

"Oh Daddy, I'm so happy you're back. I was hoping you might be home today." She divided her attention between Jakob and Geraldine. Chucha following up with a hug and kiss for both of them. They quickly emptied the wagon of their possessions. Raymond would stay at the Commercial Hotel and would ride back the next day with supplies. Skippy added to the welcome by jumping and moaning.

They entered the kitchen, and Chucha started putting food on the table for the hungry travelers. She brought a bottle of wine from the cellar and opened it, pouring glasses for Jakob and Geraldine. They toasted their return. BethAnn was filling in as waitress, and all were seated. The newlyweds had their first real dinner at home, and it was toasted with wine. Everyone excitedly talked, including Chucha. They had to know what Jakob and Geraldine did while at the ranch. BethAnn became excited when Jakob told her about how Geraldine helped during the roundup. When everyone was talked out, BethAnn invited them into the living room and sat down at the piano. She played them a little ditty Harry taught her while they were away. They applauded and laughed as she got up and bowed.

It had been a long day for Jakob and Geraldine, and the hour grew late. Excited as she was, BethAnn would be going to school the next day. She helped Chucha, and they had the kitchen cleaned up. Jakob let Skippy out for his comfort stop.

BethAnn left for her room, with Geraldine following. She noticed how her room was neat and clean; the covers laid back and her pictures on the wall. BethAnn turned around and saw Geraldine, who hugged and kissed her.

"Does this mean I will get hugged and kissed by you and tucked in by daddy too?"

Geraldine smiled. "Maybe sometime I will get to tuck you in too."

BethAnn beamed and said, "Sure, you're my mother."

"Yes, I am." Tears flowed down Geraldine's cheeks. She took her in her arms and held her, and kissed her. "Yes, I will be your mother."

Jakob came into the bedroom. "What are you two doing up here? I came up to tuck BethAnn in bed."

BethAnn laughed, "All right. Who's going to do it today? But first, I have to brush my teeth. Okay?"

Geraldine laughed. "Your dad can do it today, but maybe I can do it tomorrow." She left the room and sat in the parlor to wait for Jakob. Skippy sat on the seat next to her. Skippy took a liking to Geraldine, and she gave him her attention. It wasn't too long, and Jakob was sitting on the other side of her.

"Well, we're finally home. This is our home now, yours and mine. Have you seen our bedroom yet?"

Geraldine smiled. "Yes, I did."

"I had it redecorated for you. I hope you like it." Jakob had made the arrangements before they left. There were too many memories, and he had to make this a new start. He worried that Geraldine might find it difficult to take second place in his and Liz's home. She got up, took his hand, and led him to the bedroom. Opening the door, Jakob picked her up and carried her inside, placing her on the bed. She had already unbuttoned his shirt as they kissed passionately. Clothes were scattered as they laid together in each other's arms.

Jakob's eyes opened. He felt the cold nose of Skippy rubbing against his backside. *Oh no, how did Skippy get into the room? I can't get up for that dog.*

Skippy continued to pester him, then moaned. It was so comfortable lying ever so close to Geraldine, but Jakob realized the dog wouldn't give up. He slipped out of bed, found his robe, and followed Skippy to the back door. *Oh, that dumb dog. This has to stop.* Jakob slid back into the bed next to Geraldine, but it was too late. Geraldine was now awake.

"Honey, what time is it? Do we have to get up?"

Jakob put his arms around her. "No, we don't have to get up, and yes, it is too early. I don't know what I can do with that dog. When he wants to go out, he is uncontrollable. I will not let it interfere with our lovemaking."

Cuddling up to Jakob, she kissed him and held him close. Before letting him go, she asked, "Jakob, don't you have to see someone in the hospital? Doc Kelly sent Harold to get you. Remember? I wouldn't want to interfere with your job."

"Okay, I remember. So I'm being paid back." Geraldine laughed and snuggled up to him until they heard Skippy barking and scratching at the kitchen door.

"I guess I have to get up. Skippy wins again." Jakob put his robe on and went to the back door.

Chucha was already there. "I let Skippy in and make coffee."

Jakob turned around and went back to the bedroom but was met by Geraldine coming out.

"Might as well make some coffee," she said, and both went back to the kitchen laughing as Chucha was putting cups on the table.

"Coffee take a while. I got berries for you," Chucha announced.

Skippy was now licking Jakob's hand. "Get away from me, you dumb dog. You ruined our sleep."

Geraldine laughed as he pushed the dog away. They both stepped out the back door and stood on the porch, but it was cold and windy. The sun was now up, and patches of fog covered the backyard.

Jakob mentioned, "I guess there is no doubt that winter is on its way," and they went back into the house. Chucha poured them hot coffee. BethAnn soon arrived, rubbing her eyes. She kissed Geraldine and went to Jakob, who hugged and kissed her. Chucha quickly had breakfast on the table for her.

"I'm glad I did my homework before you came. Miss Smothers says we are going to have a test today." She was then off to get ready for school. Geraldine told her to dress warmly as it was cold outside, then followed her up the stairs to her room.

Jakob's first stop for the day was at Doc Kelly's. Kelly already had a room full of people waiting for him. Opening the door for Jakob, he said loud enough for everyone to hear, "Well, look who's here. It's the newlywed dentist."

Everyone in the room started to laugh.

"Nice to have you come back to take care of your patients."

Somewhat embarrassed, Jakob answered. "Why doctor, I thought I was to take care of your patient, and you needed my able assistance."

The laughing in the room continued.

"Never mind Jake, there's a guy in the hospital who got pretty roughed up with a broken jaw and a bunch of broken teeth. We got to fix him up. I'll meet you over there at noon. Now, I got work to do, so get out of here so I can take care of these people."

Jakob tipped his hat and started to leave, but some of the people in the office recognized him and congratulated him. Jakob left and decided to go to his office first; to check things out. Sure enough, there were a couple of people waiting for him. *Now how would they know that I'd be here?*

"Hi Doc, I heard you was back in town. I have this ..."

And thus began Jakob's day. This patient was followed by several others, and by the time noon was approaching, he realized he didn't have time to do other things he was planning to do.

Jakob left his office to meet Doc Kelly at the hospital. The Wyoming General Hospital was built in 1905. It was the jewel Sheridan needed and had forty-five beds to care for its patients. The location was near the railroad in northeast Sheridan. Doc Kelly insisted Jakob be staffed there. He had already worked on patients at the hospital because they used general anesthesia. Up to now, anesthesia was difficult in dentistry. The pain had to be tolerated by patients who were given whiskey to sedate them. It didn't help much, and sometimes they had to be held down while he removed their teeth. Later, cocaine was used, but it was limited, so working under general anesthesia in the new hospital was a successful alternative. Dental surgery was very painful. Now he could remove teeth painlessly as the patients slept.

He entered the hospital, signed in, and found the room where the patient was staying. Doc Kelly hadn't arrived yet. *Kelly said this guy was worked over,* Jakob thought. *This guy has been rolled over.* He introduced himself to the man whose face was completely bruised. He evidently had a broken arm and leg that were already in a cast. Kelly had put a scarf around his head and jaw, so he couldn't open it. This was to prevent him from opening and moving the fractured jaw. The patient told Jakob his name, but he couldn't understand it because his jaw was shut tightly.

"What do you think, Jake?" Kelly came in with a nurse and was behind Jakob. "We got an x-ray of his head."

Jakob looked back at Kelly. "I think I... I think I'd like to see it."

"Let's go, then."

The patient, who had been silent, moaned and grunted, but they couldn't understand him. In the room, they brought out about four x-rays before there was a distinct one, so a fracture showed.

"It's fractured between the lower right cuspid and the first bicuspid, and there is no apparent displacement. We're lucky. But there are also at least six busted teeth too."

"Okay, let's get it fixed."

"Hold on, Kelly. We got two different things to take care of. The busted teeth and the jaw fracture. Luckily, we have good teeth on either side of the fracture, so we don't have to perform an open reduction. We'll put him to sleep and get the broken teeth taken out, and then I have to figure out how to do the jaw. I've been studying up on a new procedure to deal with the fracture."

Kelly looked at Jakob. "I got to hand it to you, kid. I think you got this under control. When do we get started?"

"Right now if you want. We'll get those broken teeth out first. Oh, shucks. I forgot. I have to get the instruments from my office. They don't have any here. You know I probably should get some instruments together and leave them here. That way, I'll have them when I need them. Let's set it up at 4:00. Will that work for you?"

Kelly agreed to meet then. Working in the hospital had its drawbacks. Jakob always had to bring his own instruments with him because it was not set up for dental work. He went back to his office, gathered the ones he needed, and took them to be sterilized there.

At 4:00, he was ready to work. He started by going into the scrub room to do the surgical scrub, hospital style. The nurse then gowned and gloved him and put on a mask. His patient had been prepped for anesthesia, and a nurse would be giving it. He looked for Kelly, but he hadn't arrived. In the meantime, the operating room filled up with student nurses who wanted to observe what he was doing, and one of them asked Jakob if she could assist him. Jakob was a little flabbergasted. He never had a nurse help him, but Kelly wasn't there.

"Well, yes, you can assist me," he said. "The instruments are laid out, and I will name them for you as I pick them up. Later, I will ask you to pick them up and hand them to me as you become familiar with them."

She was also gowned and gloved, and excited to help. He nodded to the nurse to start the anesthesia.

Jakob had taken off the scarf holding the jaw in place and first packed the throat with sponges before starting the surgery. His assisting nurse wasn't much help at first, but she learned fast and did assist some. The surgery was routine, and Jakob removed the broken teeth and roots. He noted the area of the fractured jaw before he sutured things together. He would work on the fracture the next day and ended the operation by removing the sponges.

The students were excited with what they saw, and the student who assisted thanked Jakob for allowing her to help. Others asked questions, which he answered. Jakob realized he had been teaching as he worked and felt he liked doing it.

As he was getting ready to leave, Doc Kelly walked in. "How'd you do, Jake? I got tied up in the office, but I knew you'd do fine. Did the students like the experience? I figured it would be good for them."

"Oh, it was good for them, and one assisted me. Maybe I could do a class sometime, and they could all learn to assist."

"When are you going to do the jaw?"

"I have to get a few things together, probably tomorrow. I'll tell you later what I'm going to do. Right now, I have to go home to my family for dinner."

Kelly laughed and told him he would see him tomorrow and help him. Jakob signed out and left for home. It was later than he usually worked, but he felt it was a good day.

Jakob walked in on his new family. He was greeted, and they wanted to know what he had done. BethAnn related she had gotten a good grade on her test, and Geraldine unpacked and became familiar with the home.

"I am making plans for things I want to do," she said. "Chucha and I had a long talk, and she told me all about what she was doing in the house. I know we will get along really well. After BethAnn got home from school, we went out for a short time with the horses, and BethAnn showed me around town. I can't believe she is so well acquainted with Sheridan. Everyone knows her, and she introduced me to the ones we saw. We stopped at Elmer Findley's general store, and I got a chance to see what he carries in food and supplies. I understand Chucha does the buying, and that's fine with me. This really has been a fun day."

Geraldine also mentioned she would like to start BethAnn learning more about equestrian events. "You know, we can do some exercises right here in the yard. We may have to enlarge the barn. It's pretty tight.

BethAnn told me there were no equestrian events in Sheridan other than horse races. Maybe I can get some started. We might even do them in conjunction with the Sheridan Fair."

Jakob was happy for Geraldine. He was concerned she might find it boring not being involved in the ranch or in Landry Manor. They had dinner on a high note, and BethAnn was off to do her homework while Jakob and Geraldine made plans for their home. He put Geraldine in charge and told her to do as she wished. They made a pact; both would concur on things they wanted.

Jakob told Geraldine about his current patient in the hospital. He was extending the scope of the practice and felt he might want to advance his education. Jakob had already been in touch with his father to get his equipment modernized. He decided to buy an x-ray machine to help him diagnose dental problems. His father had sent a promising new local anesthetic agent, so Jakob could prevent pain in the surgical procedures right in his office. It had been developed by a German scientist and was called Novocain. The first full day in Sheridan was a full one for Jakob, and he was back doing what he felt the people needed.

Jakob held Geraldine in his arms as they sat next to the fireplace. Outside, the rain played a staccato on the windows as they quietly shared their thoughts for their life together. He was especially happy because Geraldine was accepting her role as a wife and mother.

Chapter 4
Geraldine Brings English Culture to Sheridan

Jakob met with Doc Kelly in the hospital. He had prepared two silver bars which he bent in the shape of an arch in his laboratory. Each would be wired to the teeth of the patient's upper and lower jaw. Then he would put the patient's jaws together and wire the arch bars together. This would keep the mouth from opening and make it possible for the broken bones to heal together. This was a technique an eastern dentist developed. It prevented the lower jaw from moving so it could heal. It was not easy to live with because food could not be chewed during the healing process. All food had to be liquified to pass through a straw. John Ross, the cowboy patient, would have a period of four to six weeks to live that way before the jaw would be healed and the wires could be taken off, so he would be able to open his mouth. The bone will have healed by then, and he will be able to chew his food again. However, John also had his broken arm and leg in casts, so his future for the next four to six weeks was bleak. His doctors would be seeing him regularly to monitor his progress.

Jakob left the hospital for his office, satisfied he did a good job. There was a group of Indians waiting for him in front of the office. Luckily for him, one of Liz's Indian students was with them, and she could speak some English for the little Indian girl whose face was swollen. The poor child was crying in pain. Jakob immediately felt sorry for her. He could see she had a baby tooth badly decayed, and it would have to be removed. Jakob took her in his arms and softly talked to her. She couldn't understand him, but he mesmerized her and gained her confidence. She even started to talk to him. He slowly sat her in his chair while talking. Jakob was trying to talk to her using Little Flower, Liz's student, as his interpreter. It took a while before they had the little girl under control since she was in pain and not very happy.

Jakob thought he'd try the new anesthetic solution his father had recently sent him. His father was very impressed with its results. Out of sight of the child, he filled a syringe with the solution and managed to inject her. She only whimpered a little, and in a matter of minutes, she started to smile and even laughed as she jabbered. He tested the area for pain, but there was none. Now all Jakob had to do was take the tooth out. They kept her distracted as Jakob quickly removed it. She started to cry again, but Jakob kept some trinkets in his office for children, and he gave her one of them. That changed her mood. Jakob had a way with children, and they usually cooperated. Jakob was excited that the Novocain worked to obtund the pain. For the first time ever, he removed a tooth painlessly without putting the patient to sleep. Jakob picked up the child, hugged her, and even kissed her before handing her back to her mother, who turned and hugged Jakob. The child jabbered something, and Little Flower said she thanked Jakob and the Indians left the office talking and acting happy.

It wasn't but a few minutes later that several townspeople walked in.

"Doc, did you take care of those savages?" asked one.

"Yes, I did. That poor little girl was in terrible pain. I had to help her just as I would help your little girl."

"Doc, don't you realize you are just encouraging them to come into town?"

"So what's wrong with that? They don't bother you, do they? They are here, and we have to get along with them. I will certainly take care of anyone who needs me. They cause no more trouble than the rest of our population. The wars are long over. Now, if you'll excuse me, I have work to do." Jakob was irritated and concerned by the man and his remarks. This was 1907, and there was still animosity toward the indigents.

As he cleaned up his operatory, another patient walked in. He finished his other patients as they came, and he finally left the office. As he walked over to the Lucky Lady, the crowd welcomed him.

Andy Meeks put glass and bottle in front of him. "Welcome back, Doc. Good to see you back from your honeymoon. I heard you were working already. Have this one on me."

The crowd came by and congratulated him on his marriage. Some chided him in a friendly manner. "How's it feel to be married again, Doc?" said one of the group.

Just about this time, Kelly came in. "I looked in on our patient, Jake. He looked pretty good. Didn't complain about anything. If he did, I wouldn't understand him anyway with his jaw wired shut the way you have it. That's interesting how you stabilized the jaw. Where did you learn that?"

"After we did the other broken jaw, I was in touch with one of the profs at my old school. He does them that way. He offered to teach me a lot of new things I would find useful out here. What do you think?"

"Well now, maybe it would be a good idea. There's no one around other than you to handle those kinds of injuries, and Sheridan is growing. We have the hospital now. These new guys who have come in lately can't handle them. There will be other times when we need to take care of those people." The conversation ended as Mayor Burns came by.

"That was some wedding you had, Doc. That's one good-looking woman you have for a wife. She should make you happy. You aren't thinking of moving out to the ranch, are you.? We need you around here."

"Now, Mayor, I wouldn't want to leave you. You know that."

"I figured so. Well, Doc, we got some things to bring up at the next commissioner meeting, and I want you there. I've come to depend on your input."

"You can count on me, Mayor. I'll be there. Now, if you folks don't mind, I'm going home to have dinner with my family." That, of course, got a lot of commentary, as some of the men joshed Jakob for being a dutiful husband. Jakob laughed and told them they should treat their wives well and they would have good marriages.

As he arrived home, he saw BethAnn and Geraldine in the backyard working on some of the things she would need to do in equestrian trials. Geraldine rode over to Jakob and told him how well BethAnn was doing. "We are working the simplest dressage exercises. I'm glad I gave her Nelly. She's gentle and smart." Geraldine smiled. "Jakob, there is some land nearby I saw which we should be able to buy. It would be a better training ground than the backyard. If we bought it, we could set it up for BethAnn's training. It might also be a good investment we could resell later if we wanted to."

Jakob scratched his head, nodded, and said, "That might be a good idea. Land here is a good investment, and if it could be used by BethAnn for her horse training, I would go the route. We can take a look at it. Are you just about finished with your teaching? I'll get Jenny in the barn and meet you in the house." He put his horse in the barn, watered and fed it, and noted the barn was tight on space with the three horses.

In the house, he encountered Chucha working in the kitchen. She told him what they would be having for dinner. He entered the dining-room to find the table set fancy with linens, glassware, and silver, and the candelabra ready for lighting.

Chucha followed Jakob into the room. "You like how I set table? Lady Geraldine want me set table in dining room like she have back home."

Jakob nodded approval and smiled. *Looks like a bit of old England right here in Sheridan.* He went to his room, cleaned up, and started to dress. *I wonder if she wants me to put on my evening-ware.*

Geraldine came in after taking care of the horses, and he could hear BethAnn race up the stairs to her room. Geraldine came up to him and kissed him, all excited about her time with BethAnn.

"I wasn't sure if I should wear my evening-ware with the dining-room set up for dinner."

"Oh, you silly! I just thought it would be fun to do it like home once in a while. You don't have to dress special." She laughed and hugged him as she began to get ready for dinner.

Jakob went outside and sat on the swing. He reflected on his day and was satisfied with the things he accomplished. BethAnn was the first to arrive and was wearing her birthday dress for dinner. Surprised, Jakob said she looked cute. She was followed by Geraldine in a yellow-flowered ankle-length dress with a string of pearls adorning her neck. Jakob was flabbergasted by their dinner dress, and they all laughed. Chucha followed and announced dinner was being served. They all sat down at the table, which showed the elegance of Landry Manor.

"I thought we could maybe do this once a week. I hope you don't mind. It does make our dinner something special," Geraldine remarked.

In the meantime, Chucha served wine and followed it with an excellent dinner of baked chicken, an array of vegetables, and a dessert. BethAnn talked about her time with Geraldine and what she had learned to do. "Geraldine said she will teach me how to jump. I can't wait until we start."

Geraldine then added she was satisfied with BethAnn's progress but felt the backyard was not really big enough to do the things BethAnn had to learn. She thought Jakob should consider buying the property she had seen.

Chucha chimed in that the dinner table reminded her of how they set tables for Christmas and Easter holidays back in the old country. She left and came back with Kolachi (a pastry) for dessert. With dinner over, BethAnn asked to be excused to do some homework and went off to her room, leaving Jakob and Geraldine.

"I asked Chucha to bring in some port, and we can have it in the drawing room. I don't think you want a cigar. Or do you?" Geraldine said as she laughed. A silver tray with a couple of port wine glasses and a decanter sat on a table near the fireplace. They toasted and sat close, with Jakob's arms around her.

Geraldine talked about the things she hoped to do. "Having BethAnn around is so enjoyable. She talks incessantly, and I like being a part of her life. She's so inquisitive and has an imagination. She is also doing well on the piano. Her day is full. We share the love of horses. I really believe she will do well with her equestrian endeavors. It will be fun for her, and we'll enjoy her accomplishments.

They heard BethAnn coming down the stairs; her schoolwork finished. She sat on the floor with Skippy and told them of her friends and the happenings at school. Chucha announced the milk and snack were ready for her. When BethAnn finished, she informed them she was going to bed.

"Who is going to tuck her in bed tonight?" asked Geraldine.

"Why don't you go first, and I'll make sure you did it right," said Jakob.

With BethAnn bedded down, Jakob and Geraldine talked of things they felt had to be done. Geraldine again spoke about the need for a training area for BethAnn. "If we find a place, I could buy it for us."

Jakob felt he could do it, and she didn't have to. They would go out looking at various properties and then decide how to handle the details.

"Did you enjoy dining English style?" Jakob asked and laughed. "Isn't it going to be more work for Chucha?"

"I guess it will be, but I think we'll need some help for her. I noticed she seems to be moving slower. How old is she?"

Jakob shrugged his shoulders. "I don't know. She was an old lady when we hired her back in 1897. Yes, I noticed she moves slower, but she does all her work. Maybe we should get her some help. There is more housekeeping now that our family has grown. I wouldn't want to lose her. She has become part of the family."

Geraldine agreed and felt maybe they should get a housekeeper and leave the cooking to her. They decided to give the idea a little thought because they had no one in mind.

Jakob realized his lifestyle would be changing now that Geraldine was his wife. However, he was now aware he was happier than he had ever been since Liz, who would still come up in his thoughts. Seeing

BethAnn with Geraldine gave him much happiness for his daughter. She now had a mother who would guide her into womanhood. This is what he dreamed about.

The next weeks were productive for him, and he was satisfied with the direction his practice was taking. There were now more new dentists in Sheridan, but Jakob seemed to be as busy as ever. Of course, Sheridan was growing, and it meant new people. The idea of extending his education was always in the back of his mind, and he mentioned it to Geraldine. She was all for it, but when he told her he would have to go to Chicago, she would say she didn't want him to leave.

Geraldine contacted the ranch when someone would come to Sheridan for supplies or pick up something needed. Eleanor would write a report from time to time. Geraldine tried to stay abreast of what was happening, although she had not been back to the ranch since the honeymoon. The weather was now getting progressively colder.

"Jakob, Raymond will be coming in within the week. I should really get back to check things out before the snows come. I believe the Allens are doing fine, but I should look in on them. I'd ask you to come with me if you can, but I know you're busy. I really should go. December and Christmas will be on us soon."

Jakob had wondered when she would want to go back. He hated to see her go and especially without him. He remembered how last year she wasn't able to get back to Sheridan until March because of the heavy snow and severe cold. His experience of leaving Buffalo in a snowstorm back in 1897 was something he would never want to experience again. Sheridan winters were not to be reckoned with. "Do you really have to go? If there are things you want to communicate to them, you could write them down and send them with Raymond."

"No, I really must go. I won't stay but a few days. I'll be back before the first of December."

The day was dreary and cold. Geraldine was dressed in woolens and furs. Raymond had the wagon filled with staples for the ranch but with just enough room for Geraldine to squeeze in the wagon. They said their farewells, and the wagon lumbered off. Jakob, BethAnn, and Chucha saw her off with misgivings.

Chapter 5
Geraldine's Brush with Winter

Jakob had just let Skippy out. The sun was up, but the sky was heavily overcast. It was a cold day, and the wind blew flurries of snow. He started the coffee on the stove and, while waiting, looked out the window, watching Skippy.

Geraldine had left yesterday for the ranch and should be there by now. *Why did I let her go? It looks like we're going to get some real heavy snow. She could be up there for the rest of the winter. The hell with the ranch! She's my wife.* Jakob was truly concerned about Geraldine. *Dammit, why didn't I try harder to dissuade her?*

Skippy was barking to come in, so Jakob opened the door and, with a blast of cold air, Skippy ran past. The coffee was now ready. He poured himself a cup and thought about Geraldine. *I should have realized she would want to look after the ranch and go out there, but not in this weather. It can be dangerous. I remember that trip from Buffalo.*

Chucha entered the kitchen, looked at Jakob, and said, "What matter, Pan? You look sad. You worry Lady Geraldine? She be all right."

"I know, but I can't help being concerned. She'll be all right at the ranch, but she'll be coming back into weather that could lead to heavy snow, and that wouldn't be good for travel."

"She got big cowboys. They take care of her, Pan."

Jakob smiled. "Thanks for your concern, but she's my wife, and I love her dearly. I waited a long time to get her." He heard soft footsteps coming down the stairs.

BethAnn arrived and kissed Jakob. "You know, Daddy, Geraldine has only been gone one day, and I miss her already. When will she be coming back?"

"I'm not sure. She said she would be gone only three or four days. I'm worried about the possibility of heavy snow. It's a long day's travel from the ranch in good weather. In snow, it could be much longer, and there are no places to stop overnight. But she has Raymond as her driver, and he makes the trip to Sheridan regularly. I suppose I shouldn't worry, but I can't help it."

They had their breakfast, and BethAnn went to her room to dress.

Jakob got ready for the office and hitched up the buggy. He would take BethAnn to school first. It was a long walk for her, so he dropped her off and decided to stop at the Weather Bureau. Maybe they could fill him in on the details of the latest conditions. He spoke with several of the people there who gave him their local weather predictions and those for the Bighorn foothills. Snow was already falling in the north and far west mountains, but they didn't expect any locally for some time. There was nothing conclusive about the Bighorns and Sheridan. He left somewhat satisfied but still worried.

Jakob hadn't seen his patient in the hospital for several days. Doc Kelly was visiting him and his other patients regularly, but Jakob thought he would look in on him anyway. He stopped at the hospital, signed in, and went up to see him.

A nurse had just left his room, and Jakob queried her. "How is our patient doing?"

"He seems to be doing as well as can be expected, Doctor. He has no fever. His leg is hurting him a lot, so I gave him morphine. His jaw doesn't seem to be bothering him, and the swelling is down, but it's hard for him to take his food through a straw. It plugs up. He's doing as well as can be expected."

Jakob examined the man's jaw and had to adjust a few wires that were sticking into his cheek. He seemed to be doing well enough. Jakob told him he realized it was difficult to eat, but he had to try hard under the circumstances. He left the hospital satisfied the broken jaw was healing as expected.

Approaching his office, he saw someone waiting for him.

"I thought you'd be in today, Doc. Shore is cold out here, but I figured I'd better see you fore this tooth gets worse."

Jakob took care of him, and then there was Mrs. Johnson, who came in with her boy. "Doctor, my boy has been crying. His tooth hurts. It's only his baby tooth and will fall out. No use doing anything."

"Mrs. Johnson, it will not fall out, but I will have to take it out. Right now, he has an abscess I have to treat first. I'm sure the poor boy is in pain." He took the boy into his operatory and asked the mother to wait outside. He'll be fine, won't you, Herby?"

Mrs. Johnson wasn't happy about that. "I can't see why I can't be with my boy!" However, she acquiesced to Jakob's suggestion. Little Herby sat in the chair and was very cooperative. Jakob carefully opened up the abscess, with the boy hardly feeling any pain. He gave the mother instructions for his care and told her he must see the boy the next day to take the tooth out. The rest of the morning was light for him. It was cold, and people in Sheridan stayed in unless they absolutely had to go out.

The next week Jakob spent much of his time home. However, he had stopped at the Commercial Bank to see Jozef, his friend and the nephew of Chucha, Jalob's housekeeper for many years.

"Jozef, I have been more than satisfied with Chucha all these years. I don't know what I would have done without her. But I think she may need some help. She moves slower now. I wonder how old she is."

"Well, she is older than my mother, and my mother must be over seventy. There is even a brother in between the sisters. Chucha is the oldest. I know she loves working for you. You are her family. Even though she misses my mother, she seldom wants to go home."

"She has more work to do now that Geraldine and I are married and BethAnn is older. I think I should get her some help. Do you have any ideas?"

"Hmm. Not really. Getting someone from Acme would mean they would have to live with you. Do you have room for another? Wait, I have an idea that might solve your problem. My wife, Wanda, talks of getting a job. She doesn't like staying at home, and we don't have any children yet. I don't know if she would be interested, but I can ask her. What would she have to do?"

"It would mainly be housework during the day helping Chucha and being a personal maid for Geraldine. See what she says, and maybe I could talk to her." Jozef agreed to talk to his wife, and he would report back.

Jakob had some of his patients come in for extended dental work. Some people would treat themselves with new dentures to eat better and show a better smile during the holidays; what with the Christmas season approaching.

It was now two weeks since Geraldine had left, and he still had not heard from her. There was some snow on the ground which would interfere with travel, but the big storm he had predicted had not arrived. No one from the ranch had made it to town. Jakob was even beginning to think about trying to go to her, but he was not sure of the trail. The times he went, one of the men from there did the driving.

Sheridan was now getting ready for Christmas. There were decorations and holiday displays everywhere, and people were making preparations. Christmas cards were now arriving, and letters from England for Geraldine had come. Jakob was distraught. BethAnn and Chucha shared his concern. He could not even begin to think of Christmas or prepare for the holiday.

It was the twenty-first of December, and Jakob had not seen or heard from Geraldine for a month. He was home from the office, and Chucha had prepared and was serving their dinner. Skippy was the first to hear something outside, and he ran to the door barking. Jakob got up and went to see who was there. He turned on the porch light and opened the door. Skippy rushed out, and Jakob followed. Snow was lightly falling, and then there was the sight of a sleigh with Geraldine and Raymond. They had arrived. She was wrapped in furs, and he could see her smiling. Tears came to his eyes as he picked her up out of the sleigh.

"Oh, Geraldine, I was so worried about you." He carried her out of the sleigh, up the stairs, and into the house, placing her on the couch. Everybody was talking at once, welcoming her home. There was joy beyond belief.

She spoke quietly with tears in her eyes. "I'm so glad to be home."

Jakob started to unwrap her furs. Her face seemed so white that it frightened Jakob.

Then Raymond spoke up. "Lady Geraldine has been sick in bed since we got to the ranch. She's much better now, and I picked yesterday when it wasn't snowing much and not so windy, and we started out. I knew of a small ranch off the trail, and we stopped there for the night. Jeremy Homerding and his wife Rhonda took us in. They gave up their bed for Lady Geraldine, fed us a good meal, and put up the horses. I tried to pay for our keep, but they wouldn't have any part of it. They said they were Christians and that the Lord brought us to them so they could help. I shore thanked them for their kindness. I kept her bundled, and today was not so cold. And it stopped snowing. She's much better now and insisted on coming back."

Jakob held her in his arms and kept kissing her, with BethAnn holding her hands. Chucha made her a cup of hot tea and put honey in it. She handed her the cup, and Jakob helped her hold it. She then got a cup of coffee for Raymond and offered a whiskey to him, which he gladly accepted.

The color came back to Geraldine's skin, and she smiled. "You can't have any idea how happy I am to be back. I'm so sorry I put you all through this."

Chucha went off to the kitchen to get dinner for Geraldine and Raymond. Jakob thanked Raymond for the special care he gave her.

"No problem Doc. She's my boss and a special lady."

Jakob helped Geraldine to the table. He poured her a glass of brandy which she sipped. They finished their dinner and sat by the fireplace. Jakob instructed Raymond to go to the Commercial Hotel and bring the horses over to Wilbur's livery for the night. The warmth of the fire gave them a mellow feeling. Geraldine arrived safe and was with them. Skippy laid in front of Geraldine. After a while, the dog got up and placed his paw on her lap, moaning his welcome to her. BethAnn left for bed, and Chucha cleaned up. Jakob and Geraldine talked for a while, and then Jakob helped her to bed. They laid close together before falling asleep.

Jakob didn't sleep well that night. He worried about Geraldine. She said she felt well, but she looked pale. She evidently had tonsillitis, but it had lasted longer than he thought it should. *She should see Kelly in the morning.*

Jakob woke up early while she was still sleeping. Skippy met him at the door. While waiting for his coffee, he thought about Geraldine. He was happy she was home because he had worried she might not return in time for the holiday. Now that she was back, he was anxious to get the house decorated and a tree put up to make it a great holiday.

Chucha came down in time to pour Jakob's coffee. "Pan, you happy Lady Geraldine come back. Now we have big Christmas holiday."

"Chucha, you will be going back to visit your family, won't you?"

"No, I stay and help you. You maybe need me."

"I would hate to see you miss being with them, and I know your family will miss you. We can get by. You used to make your Christmas Eve dinner; you know you called it Wigilia. That would be fine for us. We have been invited out for the big dinner at the Findlay's, so that will take care of Christmas. We'll go to the Sheridan Inn for their big Christmas breakfast. I'd feel bad if you missed Christmas with your family."

"Pan, you my family. Maybe, I go see my sister and brother. I talk to Jozef."

BethAnn arrived and sat on Jakob's lap. "Daddy, I'm so happy Geraldine is back. I missed her so. She will now be with us for Christmas. Are you going to get a tree for us to decorate?"

"Yes, I'm going to get a tree today. We'll go after school and pick one out."

Geraldine entered the kitchen, and all welcomed her. "Looks like I'm the last one up. I did sleep well, and I do feel good. I didn't tell you much last night, but I have to tell you about the Homerdings where we stayed the other night." She picked up her coffee and took a sip. "It was starting to get dark and snowing hard. Raymond told me he knew of a small spread about a mile off the trail, where he thought we could stay for the night. He said he had met the young man some time ago and thought he was very nice. I don't know how he knew where to turn off the trail because it was very dark. We went some distance, and then we came up to the house. It was now snowing harder. We saw the lights, and suddenly a dog started barking. A door opened up, and a man stepped out holding a rifle in one hand and a lantern in the other. Raymond told him who he was, and the man immediately recognized him. He invited Raymond and me to come in. I was so cold by then.

"The lady inside helped me to the fireplace where she had a rocker and sat me down. Oh, the warmth felt so good. She brought me some coffee and introduced herself as Rhonda Homerding, and invited us to stay. She immediately brought out two plates for our dinners and placed them on the table. They hadn't eaten yet. I took off my coat and boots, and she put a shawl around me and invited us to their table. We held hands, and Jeremy, her husband, gave thanks for the food and for us being there with them. We had such a good supper, and we talked late into the night. I learned so much about them. They insisted I take their bed while they slept on the floor. I felt so good with them. I can't explain it. Raymond tried to pay them, but they wouldn't take it. Rhonda said the Lord had sent us. I have never experienced such hospitality. I must do something for them."

Everyone was quiet; then Jakob spoke. "Father John Binotti would have an explanation. He would say it was God's will. And you are now with us and safe."

No one talked much as they ate their breakfast. BethAnn went up to Geraldine and hugged and kissed her; told her how happy she was that she was home; then went up to get ready for school. Jakob did likewise. He hugged and kissed Geraldine. "I want you to see Kelly today. I'll be back and take you after I get through at the office."

Chapter 6
Preparing for Christmas

After leaving his home, Jakob's first stop was at Doc Kelly's office. Kelly had a couple of people waiting for him, so Jakob knocked on his door. Kelly answered, and Jakob told him he was bringing Geraldine in to see him.

"She has been sick for nearly a month at her ranch and came back yesterday. Says she feels okay but, I'd like to have you check her and see if she's all right. To me, she seems like she's weak."

"Sure, bring her in, Jake, and I'll take a look."

"Thanks, we'll be back later, probably in the afternoon."

Sheridan's weather was very cold, and light snow was falling. Not too many people were on the streets, and some of the stores had not opened yet. Jakob stopped at his office, and it was really cold, so he started a fire in the stove, put on a coffee pot, and started cleaning.

Sitting at his desk, he looked through his mail, and thoughts about Geraldine returning came to mind. *It has taken a lot of worry off me,* he thought. *Now she'll be with us for the holidays. I'll take BethAnn with me later in the day to get the Christmas tree, and then they can decorate it. We'll have a great Christmas.* Then it dawned on him. *I haven't gotten any Christmas presents and today is the 22nd. Oh my gosh, what am I going to do? I have to get Geraldine something nice, but what can I get for her? She has everything,; clothes, jewelry; the closet in our bedroom is full and the one on the second floor is almost filled. So what can I get her?* Then his thoughts of Liz crept in; he *remembered making her the gold hearts in his lab that first Christmas they were married. She was so thrilled with them. The women over at Findley's Christmas party seemed almost envious of Liz. She was so happy, but I can't do the same thing for Geraldine. I just can't. I loved Liz so much but... It just wouldn't be right. It was for her. She was special, but so is Geraldine. But what can I get her? I don't have time to make her something. I know. I'll stop over at the New York store. I should be able to get something nice for her there. Oh, then there's BethAnn. I have to get her something too. She has been so cute. BethAnn and Geraldine seem to be really getting along so well. I guess I'm just one lucky guy that things have worked out for us.*

The door to the office opened and jogged Jakob's mind to the here and now. It was Harry from the Lucky Lady.

"Hey, Doc. I just thought I'd stop by to tell you how your daughter was doing on the piano. You know, I think she's doing pretty good. I hope she's practicing enough, but she's only been on it for less than three months. I've been giving her little ditties to play. That should keep her interested. She said she played one for you, and you guys applauded her. That's good. We have to keep her interested and not just teach her scales. Practicing should be fun. Being winter now, her outside activities are less, giving her more time in the house to practice. She sure is one smart kid, and I enjoy teaching her."

"I'm glad to hear that, Harry. She does the piano on her own. No one has to pressure or remind her. I sure want to thank you for helping her out, and I don't want you to do this for nothing. You keep tabs on what you want, and we'll settle up."

"Doc, I enjoy doing this. It's something I like to do. Haven't done it in years. As long as she's interested, I will give her lessons. You don't owe me anything. Why can't I do this for a friend? Well, I gotta go. I have to relieve Andy for lunch. See you later."

Jakob was pleased with what Harry told him, and he knew BethAnn was doing her piano practice. Thinking about BethAnn, he wondered if he was showing her enough attention now. *She and I used to do a lot of things together, but with Geraldine around now, she spends time with her, and that's good. I'm happy about that because she's very much the lady, and she'll pass it on to BethAnn. I have to get BethAnn something special too.*

Jakob left his office and went to the New York Store over on Main Street. It moved from Broadway and was one of the first stores in Sheridan to have a bricked front. Emma, the owner, greeted him and laughed when he told her he was looking for a Christmas present for Geraldine.

"Doc, do you realize Christmas is just three days away? You sure do your Christmas shopping late."

Jakob felt embarrassed and told her he worried Geraldine wouldn't get back from the ranch for Christmas and completely forgot about Christmas presents.

"Well, Doc, you sure are lucky. I still have some fine merchandise left. I've had a lot of shoppers come through this season, but let me show you a few things I'm sure your lady would like. I know she dresses well, and many of her clothes come from England. But I have some things that come from New York. They are the latest styles in the East, and I got them just a few weeks ago. These are styles that are big in New York and Boston. The fancy ladies there are wearing them." She took Jakob to the woman's dress section of the store, sat him down, and started bringing out some mighty fancy dresses. She showed him a long black velvet dress with a big red sash. The gown almost reached the floor. The neck dipped low. "Now, this would look great at the Sheridan Inn's New Year's Eve party."

Jakob got up and felt the material. "Wow! I bet she would look great in this with the long pearls and earrings I bought her. Do you think it will fit her?"

"Don't you worry, Doc. I have the very best seamstress in the west working for me. I guarantee it will fit. And, I have just the hat. Let me show it to you." Emma came out with a large brimmed hat with a similar sash trim and white feathers. "I bet she has a boa or a fur. If not, I have something else to go with it. I also have the slippers to wear and don't forget the gloves to match. She will be the belle of the ball in Sheridan or New York City or Boston."

One of the clerks came over and held the gown next to her and put on the hat.

Jakob just smiled and nodded his head. "You are right, Emma. She'll be the belle of the ball. I'll take them."

"And I'll wrap them special for you," said Emma.

"That's great. Now, if you can come up with something special for my BethAnn, it will make my Christmas giving list almost complete.

"You're in luck, Doc. Let's go to the young ladies' department, and I'll find just the outfit for her." There were quite a few people in the store, and some of them ogled at the gown Jakob bought for Geraldine. Emma came out with two dresses that looked perfect for BethAnn. Jakob couldn't make up his mind.

"Take them both, Doc. If you don't want to keep them both, you can bring one back."

"That's fine with me. I still want to get her some new riding boots from the Bighorn Boot store. Okay, just one more gift for Chucha, my housekeeper. You know her. She likes to wear a shawl when she goes out. A good warm one."

"You came to the right store. I have just the kind you want. Those ladies from over in Acme just love them." She brought several out for Jakob to pick, and he found one he thought she would like. Jakob was happy that he found the gifts he would need.

"Well, Doc, you came to the right place. The New York Store filled your Christmas list. Now, how about a present for you? Harvey can show you some nice things, especially for you, when you take your wife to the New Year's party at the Sheridan Inn."

Jakob laughed, "I'm all set, Emma, but I thank you for all your help. You saved my day. When can I pick up my wrapped presents?"

Emma said they would be available the next day and thanked Jakob for the business.

Jakob left the New York Store happy to have his Christmas presents bought. He stopped by the Lucky Lady to see his friend Andy Meeks. Andy put a bottle and glass in front of him.

"Not yet, Andy. I still have to go back to the office. My day isn't finished. I did get all my Christmas presents bought except one more for BethAnn, which I still have to get."

"Glad to hear Geraldine finally got back from the ranch. I guess you were worried she'd get snowed in out there."

"I guess I'm lucky we didn't get the big snow, or she wouldn't be back."

"I remember that year you almost didn't make it back from Buffalo. Wyoming winters are not to be reckoned with," said Andy.

Mayor Burns came in and stood next to Jakob. "Glad to hear your wife got back in town. I expect you'll be over to the Findleys' for the Christmas dinner. I always look forward to it. I haven't sent out the letters yet, but I want to alert you to the commissioner meeting after the first. We got a lot of planning to do for the next year, and I need you there."

"Yes, I expect we'll be at the dinner, and I plan on making the meeting after the first. Sorry I have to leave now, but I must get back to work."

Jakob left for his office, but it was already mid-afternoon, and he had no patients for the day. He still had to get BethAnn her boots, so he stopped at the Bighorn store. He found the ones he wanted for BethAnn and completed his shopping.

Geraldine was waiting for him when he got home, though she felt it was unnecessary for her to see Doc Kelly. "I'm feeling just fine now. You shouldn't worry."

Jakob convinced her to see Kelly and let him look her over. They entered his office, and Kelly had her come in. "Jake, why don't you just wait outside while I do my examination."

At first, Jakob balked, but Kelly felt he could do better without him. He nervously waited as Kelly looked her over. It seemed like it took a long time, and he wondered why.

Finally, Kelly opened the door and invited Jakob in. "Jake, your wife seems to be pretty much over her tonsilitis. Her throat is still a little red, but her heart and lungs are pretty clear. I'd like for her to get a chest x-ray anyway. She can go over to the hospital and get it. She also said something to me about wanting to have a baby, and if you don't know how to accomplish that, come and see me. What are you laughing for? I'm a doctor, and I know about such things."

"Kelly, you dog!" Jakob laughed. "I can take care of that department."

Poor Geraldine blushed. "You guys sure know how to embarrass a lady." She thanked Kelly for the exam and told him she felt Jakob could handle the other situation perfectly. They left, and Geraldine told Jakob that Kelly had done the best physical exam she ever had.

At home, BethAnn was waiting for Jakob to take her out to find a Christmas tree. The snow was not so deep, so they could use the buggy. Jakob knew of a stand of trees out on the trail to Bighorn, where BethAnn picked out a nice one Jakob was able to cut down. She was thrilled and hugged and kissed him.

"I found the decorations. Geraldine and I will dress it up just beautiful. I made some ornaments to put on it at school. This will be a great Christmas, Daddy. We have Geraldine to celebrate with us. I didn't tell you, but I have a surprise for you at church on Christmas day."

"You do? What is it, Honey?"

"I can't tell you because it is a surprise. You have to wait until Christmas."

Jakob took her into his arms and kissed her. "I know it will be a wonderful surprise because you will do it for me. I will patiently wait and look forward to it." Jakob thought about BethAnn. *How blessed I am to have such a sweet daughter. It will be our first Christmas with Geraldine.* They came home and had dinner. BethAnn was anxious for Jakob to put the tree on a stand and bring it into the house to decorate.

Jakob placed the tree in the living room, near the window on the other side of the fireplace, which already had a log burning. As Geraldine helped BethAnn decorate the tree, she told her of Christmas in England. She sang some of the carols she remembered from her childhood. The bond between BethAnn and Geraldine was strengthening. BethAnn now had the mother she waited for.

After her bedtime snack, Geraldine accompanied her to her bedroom to help her get ready for sleep. Jakob anxiously waited to finally tuck her in. Returning to the living room, Geraldine and Jakob sat on the couch facing the fireplace. They sipped a glass of port and spoke softly. They could hear the wind in the trees as the fireplace crackled and warmed them.

Geraldine kissed Jakob. "I'm going to get ready for bed, but I'll be back out and finish my drink."

A mellow feeling came over Jakob. He was happy and content. He had a beautiful daughter that he loved and a wife he was deeply in love with. What more could he want?

"What are you thinking about?" Geraldine asked. She had changed her clothes and wore a silken robe. He noticed her fragrance and her hair, which was down over her shoulder. She sat close to him and kissed his cheek.

"Hmm, you smell so good," Jakob said. "I have a question to ask you. I didn't quite understand what Kelly meant when he said something about you having a baby."

"Oh, I guess he was just kidding because I asked him if I was too old to have a baby. You know I'm in my thirties now, and I want us to have a baby. He said he didn't see any reason why I shouldn't. He also said I should see Dr. Ross. He takes care of many of the younger women, and I should talk with him. Should I go and see him?"

Jakob smiled, then laughed and kissed her. "You do know I love you very much, and I want to make you happy. Sure, I think it might be a good idea to see Dr. Ross. I want what you want. BethAnn needs a brother or sister."

With that, she kissed him and held him tightly. Then she got up and took his hand, leading him into the bedroom.

Chapter 7
Geraldine's First Sheridan Christmas

Preparations for the Christmas holiday were now in full swing at the Miller home. Chucha was getting her Polish Christmas Eve dinner ready before she left to visit her family in Acme. She insisted on making her traditional *Wigilia* before she left.

Geraldine became interested when Chucha mentioned it. "I was in Poland as a child with my father," she said. "He was a member of the House of Lords when he made an official visit there. It sparked my interest in the country, so I am excited to learn more about your Christmas customs, Chucha."

A patient stopped by the Miller house in a lot of pain. Jakob told him to go to the office, and he would meet him there. December 23rd was a typically cold day in Sheridan, with snow on the blowing around, as he tied up his horse, Jenny, in front of the office. His patient was nervously waiting for him. The office was cold, not much warmer than the outside, so Jakob quickly started a fire in the stove.

"Doc, it feels like the top of my head is getting ready to explode. Ya gotta do somthin, or I'll go nuts. But, it's crazy, Doc. Ya know, it hurts less now since I left the house. When I put ma frozen glove against the side of my face, it almost stopped hurtin', but now it startin' up agin. I must be going nuts."

"No, you're not, Harley," Jakob said. He put on a pot of coffee, which would slowly perk while waiting for the office to warm up enough for him to take care of the man. "You got an infected tooth, and your face is starting to swell. The cold decreases the swelling and the pain that goes with it. I have to open up the tooth and establish drainage. It will feel better then, but first I have to give you something to numb the nerves to the tooth. Don't worry; you'll hardly feel it."

Jakob anesthetized the tooth with Novocain and then drilled a hole in it. Opening up the nerve, he cleaned it out, drained the tooth, and put in a loose medicated dressing.

"Gee Doc, I feel good already. Am I gonna be all right now?"

"Not exactly, Harley. You might still have some pain, but it shouldn't be bad. If you do hurt some, I want you to put something cold on the side of your face. Just use a cold pack for about fifteen minutes. I got some pills you can take if you need them. One of these pills every three or four hours should control it. I'll see you in the office tomorrow at about noon. It's Christmas Eve, so I will be in the office only in the morning. I'll probably take out the tooth then."

"Sure feels good now, Doc, but I'll see ya tomorra."

In the meantime, several other people entered Jakob's office for dental treatments. Others stopped by to leave treats of freshly baked bread, cakes, cookies, and other goodies. They brought treats from the hearth and heart for Jakob and his family. He had a full day of patients and visitors, the last being Josef.

"I thought I'd stop by, Doc, and let you know about my wife Wanda's decision. She would like to talk with you and Geraldine. Wanda told me she thinks she would like to work with Chucha for you. They know each other, and she likes her. I'll be taking Chucha to Acme tomorrow for the Christmas holiday. I know she will be happy to spend it with her sister and family, but she worries about leaving you. I told her I thought you would do all right without her, and she's informed me about the *Wigilia* she would do for you. She just loves being with your family."

"Yes, I know, and we really have made her the mother of our house. Don't mention anything to her about your wife. I want to tell her myself so she won't get the idea we are not satisfied with her."

"Good idea. See you tomorrow when I pick her up. And have a Merry Christmas."

Jakob was happy Jozef's wife was interested in working with Chucha. It would take some load off Chucha, and Geraldine would like the extra help to keep up the house. He closed the office and went over to the New York Store to pick up his wrapped gifts.

Emma had them ready to take out to the buggy and thanked Jakob for the business. "Now, you be sure she brings the gown over to the store to have my seamstress make any necessary adjustments. I want her to be able to tell anyone who compliments her for the gown that you bought it at my New York Store."

Jakob laughed, "She'll be the most expensive model you will ever have."

Emma thought a moment and then laughed with Jakob. She took the packages to the buggy and wished Jakob a Merry Christmas.

He left the store and stopped at the Post Office, just as it was closing, to get his mail and some parcels they had. With his buggy now filled with packages, Jakob pulled up next to the house.

Skippy greeted him as he entered with his arms full. He put the presents under the Christmas tree. But, his weren't the first, as he noted many others, finely wrapped and placed there before his. Taking in a deep breath, his nostrils were greeted with pleasant aromas that came from the busy kitchen, and he heard the voices of ladies and their laughter. *That's strange; they haven't noticed I came in.*

He placed the patients' gifts on the dining room table, which had already been set with special white linens, shining silver, and glass. Two silver candelabra with red candles adorned it. *Aha, this has to be the work of Geraldine!* He opened the door to the kitchen. Chucha, Geraldine, and BethAnn, with aprons on, greeted him. BethAnn was the first to encircle him in her arms and kiss him.

"Pan, I have *bardza* (lots of) help today." Chucha smiled.

"Dinner will be ready soon. Just wait until you see what we made for you," said Geraldine. "You can clean up and get ready for dinner, and I expect a special cocktail before dinner for my work."

After he had cleaned up and changed, he met Geraldine in the living room.

She waited for him to serve her a martini and sit next to her. They clicked their glasses. "It looks like Santa Claus came by when we were in the kitchen and put all those presents under the tree."

"To me, it looks like he made two trips," said Jakob, and they both laughed. Geraldine kissed him, and they sipped their drinks.

"Jakob, this day has been so much fun for me being with Chucha and BethAnn. I never had the enjoyment of preparing for Christmas as I'm experiencing here. Back home, the staff did everything. They decorated Landry Manor and made all the special foods. Oh, we did enjoy the holiday, but the excitement of doing the preparations has been such a wonderful experience for me. Our English Christmas was fun, but I can't tell you how much I liked being with my daughter and that nice lady, Chucha."

BethAnn came in and sat on the floor in front of them. Skippy came to her and laid his head on her lap. "Daddy, I just can't wait for Christmas. I see all the boxes wrapped so pretty. I have a present for you. I hope you will like it. Do you think we can sing carols tonight?

That will be fun."

"Of course, we'll sing Christmas carols, and I know I will like your present."

Chucha came in and invited the Millers to dinner. She then brought out a browned baked chicken, potatoes mashed with turnips, a bowl of gravy: buttered carrots, beets, creamed cauliflower and, *chleb* (a white bread). The dessert was an apple pie.

The candles burned brightly. Jakob invited Chucha to eat with them, and when all were seated, they bowed their heads as Jakob gave thanks for the food they were about to receive. Chucha asked Jakob if he would like to cut and serve the chicken. It was a perfect meal.

Geraldine talked about Christmas at Landry Manor. She missed her mother, her father, and her peers. "I received letters from my mother and sister. It was sad because my father still lays stricken in bed on the second floor. Mama would have some family and very close friends for the holiday and was sorry Jakob and I couldn't be with them. She mentioned Lord Oliver Henry had been invited and said he asked about us. My brother is now home, and he is engaged to Jenny Lynn."

The news from England was not all happy, and Jakob felt empathy for his in-laws. He had spent some time with them when he went to England with Geraldine, so he knew them.

The tone of the evening lightened when the conversation shifted to the present, and everyone retired to the living room. Jakob and Geraldine had their customary after-dinner port wine.

BethAnn sat with them and told them about the holiday happenings at school. "I have a special surprise for you, Daddy," she announced. "I was going to do it tomorrow, but I will do it today." She got up and went to the piano, went through some of her sheet music, and came upon the one she would play. Everyone became quiet, and she began *Silent Night*. She played it slowly and most correctly. Then she repeated it as she sang the words in a good voice.

"BethAnn, that's beautiful, said Geraldine. "Can you do it again while we all sing?"

Everyone sang as she played. Geraldine then sat next to her and began the English song, *Green Sleeves,* as she sang its haunting words and then played some traditional carols that they all sang. Everyone was in the Christmas mood.

Chucha suggested they all have a bedtime snack. She had baked fresh *kolacky*, a type of biscuit which she had made with plum filling.

"Chucha, your baked goods are so special. You must teach me how to do it."

Chucha laughed. "I learn you how Lady Geraldine. You be good cook for husband. You be good wife."

They had their *kolacky* and sipped hot tea. Jakob looked up at the clock.

"Yes, Daddy. I know it's past my bedtime, and I'll go just as soon as I finish my snack. It's my mother's turn to tuck me in bed."

Jakob and Geraldine looked at each other and smiled as BethAnn left for her bedroom.

Chucha cleared the table and said, "*Dobra noc (good night)."*

They replied, "*Dobra noc."*

Geraldine went up to tuck in BethAnn. Jakob put another log on the fire and sat waiting for her. Skippy took his turn and jumped up next to Jakob until Geraldine returned and sat next to him.

"I'll be right back," said Jakob as he left to see BethAnn. Her eyes were closed, and he bent down to kiss her. She opened her eyes and smiled. "I can't let you go to sleep without kissing you."

"Night, Daddy."

Jakob awakened early. He thought he heard the wind and looked out the window to see what looked like a maelstrom. He opened the door for Skippy, but Skippy was reluctant to go out, so he closed it quickly because the snow was blowing into the kitchen. Looking at Skippy, he said, "When you're ready, dog. I'm not going to hold the door open for you until you make up your mind." Skippy looked quizzically at Jakob, who filled the coffee pot and put it on the stove.

Looking out the window, he saw darkness. He heard the shrill sound of the wind and could hardly see the tree near the house, for the blowing snow. *Wow, that doesn't look good. I wonder if Jozef will chance the trip to Acme?*

Skippy finally made up his mind to go out, and Jakob quickly opened the door for him. He wasn't gone more than a few minutes before he was at the door barking.

Jakob was pouring his coffee when Chucha arrived in the kitchen.

She had a bewildered look on her face. "No look good. Pan doctor, bardza snow."

Jakob smiled, "I'm not sure it will be safe to leave for Acme. We'll have to wait for Jozef."

She just shook her head and agreed.

Geraldine came in and asked, "What's going on? I heard you both talking."

"Well, we have a bad snow storm going on out there. I'm not sure

Chucha will be able to leave for Acme. Jozef will have to make that decision."

Chucha started to get breakfast together, and BethAnn arrived.

"Oh great, we are getting a lot of snow. Maybe we can make a snowman?"

Jakob laughed, "I'm not sure anyone will want to go out there in this snow and make a snowman. Going out to the barn to take care of the horses will be enough of a task."

They convinced BethAnn not to do the snowman until the next day, maybe, and they had a leisurely breakfast.

Josef pounded on the door around mid-morning. He told Chucha he thought the snow was too heavy to chance a trip to Acme. "We'll see about going tomorrow, but even then, I doubt it would be wise to go," he said.

Jakob thought about the patient he said he would see and decided he better go to the office. Geraldine and BethAnn would look after the horses.

He met his patient at the office despite the storm and took care of him. After he returned, he took care of his horse before he returned to a warm home. Jakob wasn't sure Chucha was all that disappointed she wasn't going to Acme to be with her family. She happily hummed as she got ready for the *Wigelia*. The storm continued with snow drifting. BethAnn stayed in the kitchen helping Chucha.

Chucha's Christmas Eve supper was about to begin. She came out in traditional Polish garb—an ornate red skirt with embroidered designs and a white puffed blouse with laces and embroidery. She spoke of the reasons for the traditions carried on for over a millennium in the old country and what they meant to her. There would be thirteen different courses to the meal: signifying Christ and his twelve apostles. Pickled herring, mushroom soup, trout, sauerkraut, pierogi (a dumpling), noodles with poppy seed and honey, fruit compote, poppy-seed rolls, and a honey liqueur comprised the traditional dishes. An empty chair was at the table for an uninvited guest.

Before the feast was to begin, she gave each one a thin wafer. They were to share some of it and ask forgiveness for any transgressions they may have subjected them to during the past year. Chucha directed each in this moment of peacemaking.

Now the dinner. Jakob filled up on the gourmet delights. Geraldine tried them all, as did BethAnn. They finished the feast with a special honey liqueur Chucha had made. BethAnn turned her nose up at the taste of the liqueur, but Geraldine slowly sipped it after they left the table.

Jakob held his glass up high. "Chucha, we thank you and toast you for sharing this custom with us and making this delicious dinner possible. We love you."

"Chucha, what a beautiful custom you shared with us. We thank you," said Geraldine.

BethAnn went to the smiling lady and hugged her, and placed a kiss on her cheek. She was so thrilled with the response that she forgot and answered in her native tongue, *dziekuje* (thank you.). Skippy followed with a woof as he partook of the leftovers.

They left the table after spending almost two hours. The candles were put out, and they started singing Christmas carols. BethAnn played *Silent Night* and kissed Jakob and Geraldine before going up to her room.

"Who is going to tuck me in tonight?"

Jakob and Geraldine looked at each other and smiled. "It will be a surprise," they answered. They held each other and kissed before they went up to tuck her in bed.

With the lights out and the glow from the fireplace, they sat closely and slowly finished the liqueur.

"Jakob, I am so happy. This will be a memorable Christmas Eve."

Skippy's moaning and bumping the door were enough to wake Jakob. He could still hear the wind blowing and the scratch of the tree limb close to the house. He got up, put his robe on, and opened the door for Skippy, only to find a wall of snow facing him. He moved back and said, "Let's try the front door, Skip."

Sure enough, the dog got on the porch and down the stairs but was back in a matter of minutes. The storm continued in full force. Skippy came in shaking the snow from his coat and lay down near the fireplace.

"What's the matter, Skip? Can't take it, huh?" The dog just raised his head and put it down.

Jakob went back to the kitchen, but Chucha was already making the coffee. "It's still snowing hard. Looks like you're here to stay, Chucha."

"So right, Pan."

BethAnn came downstairs. "Are we going to open up presents now, Daddy?"

"Of course, we were just waiting for you."

She smiled, pulled out a box, and handed it to Jakob. It was her present to Jakob, and it was a colorful scarf.

He thanked her and kissed her. "It's beautiful, and I really need it."

Each present was opened with oohs and aahs. BethAnn was thrilled with her dress and fancy riding boots.

Geraldine loved the gown Jakob had picked out for her. Jakob opened the largest box to find a fur-collared winter coat that had been made in England. It was dark blue with a black fur collar. Everyone received several gifts.

Chucha put out several of the cakes and breads that patients had brought to Jakob's office.

"Daddy, will we be going to church for the Christmas service? It looks like the snow has stopped."

"Let me go out and take a look. The temperature is five degrees above zero, and it's a half-hour drive there. The sun has come out some, but we have warm furs and coats."

"I go with you, Pan," said Chucha.

The sleigh ride was cold, but they were dressed warmly. The church was filled with people, but even though there were stoves for warmth, it was cold inside. Father Binottti prepared a proper but short sermon.

Jakob noticed that BethAnn took a seat with the choir, who sang Christmas carols, then BethAnn sang *Silent Night* as a solo. Her voice was beautiful. The church was quiet, and her voice was so clear one could almost feel the silence of that night so long ago. Jakob looked at Geraldine and noticed a tear course down her cheek. Then he remembered that BethAnn had a surprise for him.

They left the church slowly, wishing each other a Merry Christmas. When BethAnn joined them, Jakob put his arms around her and kissed her. He felt so proud of her. "I'll remember that present for as long as I live. Now I know how sweet angels sing," said Jakob.

Father John recognized them and thanked BethAnn for contributing to the service. They returned home and sat by the fireplace.

The holiday was not over yet. They were invited to the Findlay Christmas party. It was an annual event, but this would be the first time Geraldine would be going. BethAnn would stay home with Chucha. She said she would write thank you notes for gifts she received from her grandparents.

Jakob noticed that she had received a gift and letter from the Jensens in Iowa, which brought back memories of Liz. *I guess I've forgotten those fine people. They haven't seen BethAnn since that last day after Liz's funeral. Maybe this summer she can visit them. They, too, lost Liz, and BethAnn is theirs, too.* For the moment, he felt like he had betrayed them for not sharing BethAnn with them.

They both dressed for the grand event. Jakob would dress in the suit that Geraldine bought for him in Ipswich, and he would wear the coat she bought for him for Christmas. Geraldine wore a magenta calf-length velvet gown and a single strand of pearls—elegant, to say the least, with her gray squirrel coat, hat, and muff.

Jakob had the sled ready, and they were at the Findley's gracious home in less than half an hour. The Findlay home was on Clarendon Avenue with all the other big homes but not too far from Loucks Street. The snow had stopped, but the cold lingered.

Elmer welcomed them with a cheery Merry Christmas. He led them into the large living room and introduced them to the group. Jakob was known by all, but Lady Geraldine was new to the group, although most had been to the wedding. They received their eggnogs laced with brandy.

As Jakob walked through the crowd with her, they briefly chatted. She looked exquisite. But, all the ladies were well dressed. There were all kinds of conversations, and most were anxious to know how she liked Sheridan. Few had the opportunity to meet her socially. Standing next to the spirits table was a familiar figure, Buffalo Bill Cody, a most prominent and suave figure.

"I was wondering when I would get to meet this lovely and charming lady," Bill remarked.

Geraldine was stopped and, with a demure look, said, "And you must be the famous Colonel Cody. I have heard so much about you."

Bill Cody had met his match but, even though he was flustered, he held his own. "Lady Geraldine, you must be from England, a country that holds a special place in my heart. I have many fond memories of England. You may remember it was on your Queen Victoria's Jubilee that my group performed for her. The first time was in...ah, 1887 or 8. She is perhaps the most gracious ruler I have ever met. And, I have met many. And then, I was invited back in 1892 for my command performance. Your Prince of Wales set up that first performance. So, I must have been good because I was invited back."

"Colonel Cody, never in my fondest dreams would I ever thought I would meet you personally. I attended that performance in 1887. My Papa, Sir Gerald, a member of the House of Lords, took me to it. I was so excited about your performance."

"You were there?" said Cody.

"Oh yes," said Geraldine.

Cody smiled and said, " I remember the large group of children that attended."

"Thank you for the compliment, Colonel, but I wasn't with the children."

"Well, my dear, with your beauty, you could have well been."

"You're making me blush, Colonel, thank you." Geraldine loved talking with him. He admitted he thought the queen might knight him but was happy to perform for her, which gave him notoriety throughout Europe. As she and Jakob moved on, he would revel in his European trips of Buffalo Bill's Wild West to the others.

Geraldine was well received by the group. Jakob was glad they had come. They had not been out socially since their wedding. The dinner was outstanding, and Harry brought his concertina and played for everyone. When the party was ending, Little Henry from the livery brought out the horses and rigs. The ride back was a cold, short one, but the evening out was pleasant.

Chapter 8
The Beginning of a New Year

The last day of the year was cold and dreary. The remnants of Christmas Eve's crippling snowfall were still visible in the piled-up snow and streets with ruts and ice. Sheridan was difficult to move around in.

At the Miller house, Chucha had breakfast on the table. Jakob had not planned to go to the office until a patient came to his home before he even got up.

"Doc, I got me lots of pain. Can you help me?"

Jakob recognized him as a former patient and told him he would meet him at his office at 10:00.

There were no other plans for the day other than prepare for the New Year's Eve party at the Sheridan Inn that night. After breakfast, Geraldine and BethAnn were going to feed and water the horses, which had to be done no matter the weather. A stove in the barn, which kept the drafty building warm enough for the animals, needed to be tended as well.

Jakob hitched a horse to the buggy and left for the office. His patient was already waiting for him when he arrived. Snow had piled up against the door during the night, which had to be cleared before they could get into the cold office. He immediately started a fire in the stove. It didn't take too long before the office was warm enough to take their coats off. The patient was in pain, and Jakob had to remove the offending tooth.

As he was finishing up, Doc Kelly walked into the office. "Wasn't sure you'd be in today, but I see even you have to take care of people who are in need. I was in the hospital yesterday. Got a patient with pneumonia over there. Bad shape. I don't think he can make it. Anyhow, I looked in on our fracture patient. It's been a month since we put him together. I had them take x-rays of his broken bones. I was surprised, Jake. He's doing damn good. The broken jaw looks healed to me. Both the leg and arm bones are also on the mend. Why don't we go over, and you can see the x-ray of the jaw for yourself? If he's healed, maybe you can take off them wires. Felt sorry for the poor guy. He looks like he has lost a lot of weight and looks miserable. Maybe we can make it possible for the poor guy to get a decent meal for New Year's Eve."

"It's four weeks, huh? Little early, but maybe. Well, there was no post-operative infection, so maybe he could be healed," said Jakob. "I'll be through here in about 15 to 20 minutes, and we can go take a look at him." Jakob finished his patient, gave him instructions, and dismissed him.

"Jake, I'll take my rig, and we can go together. I may not take the cast off the leg yet. Give it a little more time to heal, but at least he can get around on crutches. We can take the arm cast off and, if necessary, put a splint on the arm for a couple of weeks."

The drive to the hospital took a while. The streets were rutted with snow, and it was very cold. They stopped by the hospital, signed in, went to the doctors' room, and had a hot cup of coffee. There were only a couple of doctors there, and they talked with them for a while.

"Let's take a look at the x-rays first, "said Kelly.

Jakob studied the films. "You know, Kelly, it might be a good idea if we got one of the nurses some extra training in x-rays. These pictures are not that good, but it does look like the jaw is healed. Let's take a look at him first." The nurse had the patient sitting in a chair with his leg up on a stool. He didn't look too happy and had lost some weight. He mumbled something to them, but they didn't understand what he said. Jakob examined his mouth and thought a bit.

"I think we can take the wires off. Four weeks just might be enough. It does look healed."

He looked at the patient and smiled. "John, I'm going to take the wires off. Your jaw looks healed to me."

John's eyes opened up wide. He started to grin, and he mumbled something.

The nurse set up a tray. Jakob had brought some of his wire cutters with him. He carefully went around the teeth in the lower jaw, cutting the wires and taking them out. He slowly removed the arch bar. The lower jaw was now free to move. Jakob felt the break. It seemed firm, and the patient felt no pain.

He slowly opened his mouth a little and began to smile. "Doc, it feels good. It don't hurt. Look, I can open my mouth!"

Jakob handed him some water and told him to rinse.

"Kin I drink some?" the man asked.

"Sure, go ahead. Then I'll get the upper wires cut."

As Jakob cut the wires, Doc said, "You know Jake, that's quite a contraption you got there. It sure kept the jaw from moving so it could heal."

"And it looks like we got a good heal," said Jakob. I want to get a final x-ray with the wires off." Taking a syringe filled with water, he cleaned out all the accumulated debris from the mouth, and there was plenty. "I'll clean your teeth good in my office next week," he said as he gave him more water to rinse with. "Well, John, they'll give you something substantial to eat for lunch today. I'd start with soft stuff for a couple of days."

John was excited and couldn't thank Jakob enough.

"Stick around, Jake," said Kelly. "I'm going to take off the arm cast." The nurse had a tray of instruments, and she handed them to Kelly as he cut the cast off. They cleaned up the arm, and Kelly checked it. They took x-rays of the arm and a final head plate of the jaw.

John got his Christmas present on New Year's Eve. He said he couldn't wait until Kelly removed the leg cast but would wait a while longer to be sure it was healed.

"No sense goin' back to the office now," said Jakob.

"Let's stop over at the Lady and have us a drink to celebrate John's good fortune," said Kelly. Arriving at the Lady, the celebrating had already begun.

Andy came up and smiled. "Well, gents, what will it be?" he said as he placed glasses and a bottle in front of them. "Didn't expect you here so early. But it's New Year's Eve, and this one's on the house."

"Andy, we do have to take care of people at all hours, and today was no exception."

They all laughed and downed their whiskeys.

"Kelly, I got to get back to my office now to clean up, so you can play cards if you want to." Jakob left for his office. He finished sterilizing his instruments and was getting ready to close up when Jozef stopped by to talk with him.

"Doc, if you have time today, I can bring my wife over to meet you folks, and you can decide if you would like to hire her to help Chucha."

Jakob suggested they meet at the office in the afternoon, and he would bring Geraldine.

Jozef introduced his wife, Wanda, to the Millers. She was an attractive blond-haired young lady who freely talked. She had a nice personality.

"Jozef and I haven't been married too long, and I would like some work so we could save enough money to buy a home. I was born in Acme and lived with my parents until we married. Then I moved here, but I need some work to help with our needs."

Jakob explained why he was interested in hiring someone to help Chucha. He just felt she was older now, and her workload had increased considerably since Geraldine and he were married. Getting someone to help Chucha with the housework would make it easier for her. He asked Wanda if she minded doing housework and some personal maid duties for Geraldine. She said she thought she would like to take care of the house and do the personal maid work.

Wanda was pleasant, neat, and looked like she would be able to do the job. "I could even help Chucha with the kitchen work if needed. I learned how to cook and bake."

Jakob told her the work hours would start at 8:00, and she had to work until 5:00. That way, she could go home and be with her husband. Jakob made her aware Geraldine had things to do other than the housework. They would give her time to think about the job if she wanted and talk to Chucha about hiring her.

After they left, they both agreed she looked like she would work out. Geraldine never did any housework while living in England or at the ranch. The aristocracy always had sufficient help to take care of the manor and the family. At the Oliver Henry, she had a cook, housekeeper, and maid. Geraldine thought of having a personal maid, and they were happy to find someone who could do it.

When they came home, they sat down with Chucha and told her what they planned.

"Chucha, you have been doing more work since Geraldine came here, and we have decided to get you some help."

"Oh no, Pan, I happy Lady Geraldine come. She not more work for me."

Jakob laughed, "I know you can do the extra work, but I want to get someone to help you. She can take care of the housework while you do all the cooking and take care of the garden in the summer. You aren't as young as you were when you came here and you have too much to do. BethAnn is older now and requires more help. I have found a lady that would like to help you, and you know her. It's Wanda, Jozef's wife."

"Oh, she young. She no work like me."

"I'm sure you're right, but she can help, and maybe you can teach her."

Chucha laughed and shrugged. "Maybe you right. She nice lady. I like her. She mother my cousin Anna."

Jakob and Geraldine dressed for the New Year's Eve party at the Sheridan Inn. Geraldine put on the dress he bought her for Christmas, and she looked stunning. He dressed in the formal wear he had in England.

They were greeted by Henry Clayton when they arrived. "Haven't seen you folks for a long time. We're sure glad to see you here today. Now that you're married, I guess you don't get out much."

"Henry, we miss doing some of the things we used to do, but the next year it may be different."

"Annabelle is expecting you, and Lukas has some specials for tonight."

As they walked into the dining room, Annabelle was waiting for them. "I have a good table for you, Doc. I'm really happy to see you two. It's been a long time since you've been here. Lukas will be happy you came in, and I remember what you and Lady Geraldine like. William will have his special martini for you."

They smiled at the greeting they received.

"How could you remember that we liked martinis?" asked Geraldine.

"Oh, that's easy, Ma'am. You are the only folks that drink them." Annabelle laughed as she walked away.

Geraldine held Jakob's hands. "She's right. We haven't gone out much. This winter weather has been keeping us in. We should come here more frequently."

Annabelle served them their martinis and left a menu with them. They toasted and sipped the ambrosia as Lukas came by.

"Lady Geraldine, Doc, I shore am glad to see you folks. Been a while since you've been in. Married life must be good for you since you don't go out. But I'm glad you're here tonight. I got your special duck, Doc. Lady Geraldine, I think you'd like it too. I do it with a chokeberry sauce. But, I got the other items you like, too. Or, how about steak Diane? You make your choice, and I'll make it for you. Annabelle will take your order when you're ready. Bon Appetites." Lukas left, and Jakob and Geraldine laughed and looked at the menu.

"He sure aims to please you, Jakob. But, he is a good cook."

Jakob reached over the table and kissed her. "It's nice to be able to sit together and have dinner by ourselves. Just like when we were falling in love. Remember?"

"I never believed I would be able to find someone like you to give my love to. I'm so happy, Jakob."

They sipped their martinis and talked, interrupted only by people they knew who would wish them a happy new year. The noisy room didn't bother them. The floor was filled with dancers as a band played for the occasion. Some of the men came in tuxedos and the ladies in fancy dresses. Jakob and Geraldine danced some and sat and listened to Jozef play his violin. Both ordered Lukas's special duck and toasted with champagne when the orchestra played Auld Lang Syne. They stood on the floor in each other's arms and kissed as the clock turned to 1909.

"Whatever this New Year brings, I will make it a happy one for you," said Geraldine.

Jakob kissed her softly. "We have each other, and we'll work together."

They moved together to the music and stopped to wish their friends a happy new year. Finally, they sat at their table and finished the champagne.

"I have an idea," said Jakob. "You've never been in the Lucky Lady. Let's go over and see some of my friends. You know, Doc Kelly and Andy Meeks, Mayor Burns and some others. It's not as fancy as the Sheridan Inn, but you can take it. I remember you taking me to the Great White Horse over in Ipswich. Remember, even Sampson didn't think you should go there. I think you'll like the Lucky Lady."

"Jakob, you know I'm not one of those bluenoses you talk about. Let's go. I may even have one of those shots you drink." Jakob laughed, and they left the rollicking dining room. They put on their coats—Geraldine in a fur coat and the hat tied under her chin that Jakob bought her for Christmas and Jakob in the winter coat with a fur collar Geraldine had bought him.

As soon as they opened the door of the inn, they caught a rush of cold wind. They started across the street, carefully avoiding ruts and ice. There were a few people out and just a couple of horse-drawn sleds moving along the road. They could hear the Lucky Lady as soon as they walked out.

Opening the door, they walked into the raucous crowd. Jakob followed Geraldine. It seemed like time stood still when the group first saw Geraldine as she walked into the room. When Jakob appeared, everything continued at the previous tempo. Geraldine saw Andy Meeks at the bar and worked her way through the crowd, Jakob following. Heads and bodies turned as she passed through.

"Lady Geraldine, Happy New Year, and welcome to the Lucky

Lady," said Andy. Two less than ordinary clods opened up space for her and Jakob when they saw her. One politely tipped his hat, and the other gave a big toothless smile and a howdy. Andy placed the whiskey and glass in front of Jakob and looked at Geraldine.

"And for you, Lady?"

"Same as my friend."

Andy's mouth opened, and he didn't utter a word. He shook his head, placed a glass in front of her, and filled it as he looked silently at Geraldine. She picked up the glass and tasted it, looked at Jakob, and downed it. Everyone at the bar silently watched.

She put the glass down as tears came to her eyes. "Andy, do you have some water to go with that?" she gasped.

He nodded, placed a glass in front of her, and waited as she sipped some. The bar went into an uproar as Jakob put his arms around her, kissed her, and followed with his whiskey.

Andy shook his head, and looking at her, he said, "Lady Geraldine, you're some lady!"

Everyone was laughing and joking, and Jakob was the most astonished.

"Let's go over to the poker table and say hello to Kelly," said Jakob.

They started toward the card game, and as Geraldine moved, the way opened up with smiles, tipped hats, and remarks. There was Kelly playing poker with the mayor and four others.

"Well, look who's here! Lady Geraldine," said Doc Kelly, "would you like to play a few hands with this gentlemanly group? Special invite just for you. Don't ordinally give them to just anyone who comes in here. I'll even split my poke with you. How's that for an invite?"

Geraldine laughed and gave that inimitable smile. "Why doctor, I couldn't do that. Just because I trust my health to you doesn't mean I would trust my gambling with you. Besides, I just might win the pot."

There was laughter, and Kelly got a lot of ribbing. Kelly looked at Jakob and asked, "Jake, is that true? Is she that good a gambler?"

"She sure is. She won me."

The crowd broke out in laughter.

Geraldine continued, "I thank you, gentlemen, for the invitation, but I'm going to take my winnings and go home with him. Happy New Year to you all."

The crowd clapped and laughed, and she and Jakob left the Lucky Lady. It was bitter cold as they walked through the snow and ice to the livery. Little Henry took them to their home.

The house was warm. Chucha smiled as they walked in. "Good night, Pani e Pan," she said as she walked up the stairs to her room. The fire felt warm as they removed their coats. Skippy came up to Geraldine as she sat next to Jakob, snuggling. She petted him and kissed Jakob passionately. He smiled, and they got up and moved to the bedroom. Jakob closed the door behind him, picked Geraldine up, and placed her on the bed.

Chapter 9
Jakob Faces a Difficult Result

Jakob's eyes opened when he heard Chucha in the kitchen making breakfast. He could feel the closeness of Geraldine laying next to him, and he smiled. It was New Year's Day, and an overwhelming feeling came over him. He was happy beyond words. The previous night at the Sheridan Inn's New Year's Eve party and the stopover at the Lucky Lady were a real treat. Then, when they arrived back home, they completed the night with their lovemaking.

Life had been good to him. He remembered how he almost gave up when he came back from England without Geraldine. He hadn't been sure she could or would return. He loved her, and he missed her terribly. Then when she returned, his life took on a new meaning. BethAnn finally had the mother she yearned for, and he had the wife he needed to complete his life. Geraldine slept soundly, but he felt fully awake. He slipped out of bed, put on his robe, and went into the kitchen, where Skippy jumped up and greeted him.

Smiling, Chucha handed him his coffee. "Good morning, Pan. Is new year today. You sleep good?"

"Good morning, Chucha. Yes, I did. I slept just great. You're certainly wide awake."

"I go see my family today. Jozef, he take me today, remember? We not go on Christmas because bad snow, but I go today, and I be back Sunday. I fix breakfast for you and make *chleb* and *kielbasa* for you. There be plenty to eat. I see my sister and her family. Maria, she have eight children. Someday, maybe you see her. My *bratchek*. I forget. My brother Johanek, he older than me and not well. I see him."

"I'm glad you will be able to be with your family. It's too bad you couldn't make it for Christmas. But this should make up for not being with them on Christmas. Don't you worry about us. We'll be fine."

With that said, BethAnn entered the kitchen and gave Jakob a hug and kiss.

"Don't worry, Daddy. Chucha taught me how to make breakfast and lots of other things. Chucha made a big pot of soup and chicken we can heat up."

Jakob had his coffee and was sitting down when Geraldine came into the kitchen. "Good morning, everyone." Geraldine was radiant as she entered the conversation. "You have forgotten I am a capable cook, and so no one will go hungry."

The conversation went on as Chucha gave everyone their breakfast. There was a loud knock on the front door, and Chucha let Jozef in. Jakob offered him breakfast and coffee.

"No, thanks. I've come over to get Chucha. We have to leave for Acme. It will take some time to get there."

Chucha left the kitchen and quickly came down from her room with her bag. She seemed anxious to leave but was concerned for the Millers. Both Jakob and Geraldine tried to assure her they would be all right and she should enjoy being with her family. The day was cold, but the sun was up, and it looked like it would be a nice day for their trip to Acme.

They finished their breakfast, and BethAnn cleaned up the kitchen. Jakob said he had some things to do.

Before he left, Geraldine suggested, "Father John said there would be a church service at noon today. Why don't we ride the horses over to the church? I haven't been on a horse in a couple of months. They could use some exercise. I saw the temperature was 25 degrees, so we could handle that for a short time. I remember back home, on New Year's Day, we used to always ride. Sometimes, we even followed the hounds. Then after church, we can stop at the inn for a bite to eat. What do you say?"

"That's a great idea, Mama. I miss riding my Nelly. Daddy, let's go. Okay?"

"I guess I'm outvoted. I was going to stop at the Lucky Lady, see some of my friends, and then come home for a nap."

"Oh no, Daddy. Let's do what Mama suggested."

"Okay, you ladies win. Get yourselves ready and dress warm. We should leave soon because we have to get the horses ready."

They readied themselves. BethAnn wore her new boots, hat, and gloves, and the horses were prepared for the ride to the church. Although it was cold, the ride was refreshing. They followed a trail free of ruts and ice and made it to the church on time.

Surprised to see the church filled with people, Father John welcomed them. The church was heated by the two stoves, and the sun had warmed the day some. BethAnn joined the choir, and Father John gave an appropriate sermon for New Year's Day. He wished them health and happiness and to be grateful for the gifts God gave to them. As they were leaving, Jakob asked Father John to have lunch with them at the inn.

"Good idea, Jakob. I'd love to do it, but I will be doing a service at Acme, and I have to leave just as soon as the church is empty. Those people out there really want me there today. Most of them are Catholics from the old country, you know. I've got to be there for them, but thanks. We'll do it another day."

The horses snorted as they mounted. They weren't used to standing and waiting in the cold weather. There were now a few people on the trail, and they soon arrived at the Sheridan Inn.

"You know, maybe we should take the horses to the livery. We may be here for quite a while. Little Henry can bring us back. The horses have been out long enough." They got the horses undercover, and Little Henry brought them back to the inn.

"Happy New Year, Doc. Glad to see you folks," said Clayton. Lukas has a great spread out there for New Year's Day."

Annabelle had a table ready for them. "Looks like you folks need something to warm you up. Those rosy cheeks mean you were out of doors for a while. I'll get the little lady a hot chocolate. How about a brandy for you folks?"

The dining room was almost filled, and considering the party the night before, it had been cleaned up quite well. They spent the time eating and talking with their friends. It was time for Little Henry to bring the horses over for them, and they left for home.

The fire in the fireplace warmed their home. The Christmas decorations were still up. BethAnn sat at the piano and played some things she had learned.

"I'm so glad I got her the piano for her birthday. She's really doing quite well," said Jakob.

Geraldine agreed and complimented BethAnn. "There are some things we should discuss, Jakob. One of them is I think we should hire Little Henry to take care of our horses. BethAnn has learned how, but I would rather see her at the piano than in the barn tending the horses. She would do better with her time at her studies and the piano, and I certainly don't want to do that work. I'll pay Little Henry to tend to them."

"I agree because I don't want to do the work either. I'll let Little Henry know," said Jakob. "Wanda will be starting to help Chucha when they get back from Acme. We'll be able to do the things we want to do as a family."

"Daddy, I'll still be able to go to the barn and be with Nelly and help take care of her, won't I?"

"Oh, it's just that Little Henry will do most of the barn work."

The rest of the day was spent in a card game, and Jakob and Geraldine had letters to write. In the following days, they would take care of the household needs until Chucha came back.

That evening they were invited to a neighbor's home for dinner. BethAnn's playmate was there to entertain her. They had received several invitations to other neighbors to which they would be going, and Geraldine mentioned she was planning to do an English-style dinner party.

Jozef brought Chucha back from her holiday visit along with her sister, Maria Grabowski. Chucha insisted Maria see Jakob because she was having a serious dental problem. Jakob welcomed her and said he would see her the next day at his office. Her concern was quite serious, and he said it required a great deal of work for Jakob to do. They decided she could stay in Chucha's room because traveling back and forth to Acme would be difficult. Unfortunately, there was no dentist in Acme, and the people there often neglected to get treatment.

The Miller house was filled. Wanda helped Chucha, and Maria even pitched in. Wanda became Geraldine's personal maid, and she had also started doing the housework. The house was filled with people, mainly women. This was nothing new to Geraldine, who was used to having guests in the big Landry Manor and a large staff working. Jakob and Geraldine laughed at the antics of Chucha and Maria. They were sisters, and each had her own personality.

Jakob had to remove many of Maria's teeth, leaving her partially edentulous. She would need partial dentures but would have to wait for healing to take place. Jozef would take her home and then bring her back in about six weeks. Life was back to normal for the time being. The house took on a shine with Wanda doing the housework.

Geraldine bought new pieces of furniture, and a telephone was installed. Jakob made his first call to Milwaukee to his parents. It felt good to be able to talk with them. Geraldine was also able to make a transatlantic phone call to Landry Manor and spoke to her mother and brother. Her father showed no improvement, so it was a bittersweet conversation, but her mother was happy to hear from her. The biggest problem with transatlantic calls was the time difference. Late evening calls from England came the next day early in the morning.

Geraldine would have her first dinner party before Maria came back for the rest of her dental work. She decided to have Elmer Findley and his wife, who invited them to their Christmas party, and four other couples that she wanted to have as friends. She was excited to make it a grand affair. It would be a bit of old England in Sheridan. She would let Chucha make some of her English specialties. Invitations were sent saying the evening would be a bit of old England.

Jakob was experiencing the effect of Geraldine on his household. With Wanda helping Chucha, Geraldine was also using her as a personal maid. Wanda was talented, and Geraldine was starting to look the part of a titled lady. She was a very beautiful woman, and Wanda helped with her couture. She became a good customer of the New York store.

Jakob also noticed the changes in BethAnn. Geraldine bought her dresses and had Wanda help the girl with her hair. He also saw changes in her manners and speech. She was starting to be the little lady BethAnn. She spent more time at the piano. Harry, her teacher, was satisfied with her progress and started her on more complicated pieces.

Geraldine's dinner party was set for the fifth of March, and it was a success. She was the perfect hostess. The beef roast was done in the English style, but Chucha made other items in her own style. The table was covered in bright white linens, sparkling glassware, and shining silver. Two silver candelabra cast a warm glow on the table. Chucha and Wanda served with new uniforms, and place cards indicated where guests were to be seated. Wines were offered with different courses. Dinner had the guests participating in lively conversations. When finished, the party split and the men went into Jakob's library, which Geraldine had updated from what was once Liz's sewing and craft room. Port was served, and cigars were available, but the men chose the bar whiskey.

Ella Findlay noticed all the changes that Geraldine had made. "Lady Geraldine, I do believe you are making this house into an English manor."

"Ella, my name is Geraldine to my dear friends, and you ladies are my dear friends. I have enjoyed making the changes. They are part of my former life, just as you are part of my new life here in Sheridan."

The ladies were thrilled with Geraldine, and the evening became a grand success. It broke up with fond goodbyes that lasted longer than one might expect. BethAnn had spent the evening with Amy Schroeder, and Amy's father, George, brought her home.

"Geraldine, that was some dinner party you put on. This has to be a first for Sheridan," said Jakob.

"I really enjoyed doing it. I think our guests enjoyed it too," she said, "because they joined in with interesting conversations. Martha Schroeder said she would like to visit England and some of the others did likewise." She hugged Jakob. "But, I'm tired. We can talk more about it tomorrow." She led Jakob into the bedroom.

A banging on the front door awakened Jakob as well as the whole household. Jakob answered, and Doc Kelly entered the house. "Jake, we got a guy in the hospital in bad shape. There was a gunfight in the Broadway Saloon. Two are dead, but one is still breathing. At least he was an hour ago. Lost an eye besides a bunch of teeth and maybe a broken jaw. I need you now."

"Okay, let me get some clothes on." Jakob quickly dressed while an anxious Kelly waited. "What happened?" said Jakob.

"I don't know. I think it was a card game that went bad. They hauled three of them over to the hospital and called me. The living one was pronounced dead at first, but now they tell me he's still breathing."

They arrived at the hospital. There was a lot of commotion until Doc Kelly kicked them all out except for the nurses. Digger O'Brian had already wrapped up two of the bodies and was getting ready to haul them off. Kelly was right. The third one was breathing but unconscious.

"What do we do, Kelly?"

The patient's face was lacerated. All his front teeth were fractured as well as some others. His nose was broken, pushed to the left side, and bleeding, and one eye was hanging out. As Kelly started to move it, he began to moan and seemed to be coming to. He tried to talk but continued to moan.

"He's got a pulse, and his breathing is strong. Let's stop some of this bleeding," said Kelly, as he started to clean up the lacerations and stabilize the nose.

"I'll clean out the mouth so he doesn't aspirate any of those broken teeth. I can take out the roots later. I don't think the mandible is fractured, but the malar process (cheekbone) is pushed in."

It seemed the patient went in and out of consciousness, and they did the best they could. Kelly had been a battlefield surgeon during the Civil War. But for Jakob, it was a new experience he never had expected. He was glad he had Kelly next to him. They would wait and see how their patient progressed. He would remove the broken roots later and even lacerations in his mouth. They stopped the bleeding, and he appeared to be stabilized.

"Jake, I'm going to stick around, but you might as well go home. Why don't you come back about noon?" Kelly suggested.

It was still dark when he got home. Geraldine was in bed but wide awake.

"What happened, Honey? You left in such a hurry."

Jakob filled her in on the details and then cuddled next to her. It was an unnerving experience he had been through, and he felt he needed her support. They laid in each other's arms until they heard Chucha in the kitchen, and then they got up.

Chucha queried Jakob on what had happened and Jakob filled her in. She had been awake when she heard Doc Kelly banging on the door but left when she saw him.

Jakob decided to go back to bed. He was still stressed from the night in the hospital and would try to recover some lost sleep. Geraldine stayed up and would help get BethAnn ready for school. She had taken over much of the care of BethAnn and appeared to be the mother she needed.

Jakob slept soundly until a patient stopped at the house because he didn't find him in the office. He made arrangements to see him in the afternoon. Jakob would have his lunch and go to see his patient. Afterward, he would go to the hospital. He was in the middle of a procedure when Doc Kelly walked in.

"Jake, come out here. I have to talk to you."

"What's up, Kelly?"

"Bad news, Jake. The patient in the hospital we took care of died." Jakob was stunned.

"Kelly, what the hell happened? He was doing all right when I left."

"Don't exactly know. When I left the hospital, he seemed to be doing okay. He lost a lot of blood and was pale, but his breathing and heart seemed all right. Later in the morning, one of the nurses came to my office and told me he was having a hard time breathing. By the time I got to the hospital, he was gone. Must have had a heart attack."

Jakob sat down, speechless. He paled a little. "Kelly...Kelly, he was alive when I left. Could we have done something more for him?"

"I don't know. He did take a terrible beating. I'm going to do a post mortem on him. Want to stick around and help?"

"A post mortem exam? No, I'd rather not. That's not my thing."

"That's all right. I asked Ross to help me. He's done some. I'd like to know what happened. I know how you feel. We did the best we could. Why don't you stop at the Lady after you finish? I'll buy you one. That's the way it is, Kid. We can't save them all."

Jakob shook his head. "Yes. I guess you're right. I better get back to my other patient."

Kelly left, and Jakob went back inside, sober and quiet.

"What's the matter Doc? You don't look so good."

Jakob assured him he was all right, but the thought of the man dying just couldn't leave Jakob. He took care of several more people that afternoon, but the idea of the dead man dogged him. He closed his office and remembered he told Kelly he'd meet him. But he couldn't get himself to go. Halfway home, he turned around and went back to the Lucky Lady. Kelly was at the bar talking with the mayor and motioned him over.

Mayor Burns acknowledged Jakob's presence. "Doc, Kelly filled me in on the loss of that guy who got beat up at the Broadway Saloon. Too bad. I heard he was a decent guy. We got to do something about that place. There's always trouble there. Bad elements hang out there. Those are the first deaths we've had for a long time. Actually, there was just one a couple of years ago."

"I told the mayor that Ross and I did the post mortem. We found he had a ruptured spleen. He had a belly full of blood, and the heart stopped pumping. He must have taken a terrible beating."

Jakob hardly said anything. For him, it was an experience that he should never have had. He had a drink, chatted a while, and left for home. Geraldine greeted him, and he got his hug and kiss from BethAnn. Though he tried to put the thing aside, it continued to affect him.

Chapter 10
A Homecoming for Geraldine

After several months, Jakob still had the patient on his mind. He had become his usual self, and the loss was beyond his responsibility, but he learned something about the fragility of life. The roughnecks, or toughs as they were called, often ended up losing their lives or suffering irrefutable injuries to their bodies while trying to prove they were more manly.

Sheridan's weather moderated, and the snow started to melt off. Geraldine and BethAnn were riding more and began making plans for her horsemanship training. Geraldine felt she could train for equestrian shows and competitions. She found some property nearby to set it up for the different trials she would have to learn. They both loved working with the horses, and Geraldine was the teacher.

Geraldine did another dinner party with a different group of friends. They were invited to several other parties, and their social life was expanding. Geraldine was a people person and was invited to join the Woman's Club of Sheridan. She would take part in their various civic programs.

It was time for Maria to have her dental work finished. She came to stay with Chucha so Jakob could finish it. He made her partial dentures, replacing her lost front teeth, and she was thrilled with the change in her appearance. Initially, she seemed withdrawn, sober and avoided smiling or talking. She was embarrassed because of the loss of teeth. When she saw herself in the mirror, Maria saw a different person. Her personality blossomed, and she became animated and talkative. She hugged and kissed Jakob, thrilled with her change of appearance.

Like Chucha when she started living with Jakob and Liz, she spoke very little English. But Liz, the teacher, brought her into the world of the English-speaking. Living with Chucha, who took to prodding and teaching, Maria was beginning to understand and even speak enough English to get by with people. Jakob gave her some of Liz's books to help her learn more. She left for Acme with Jozef the next Saturday, a new person.

In the following months, Jakob had a rash of patients from Acme looking for dental care from Jakob. They had seen what he had done for Maria. Seeing the need, Jakob found one of the younger dentists who had come to Sheridan and encouraged him to open an office in Acme. This made it possible for more people in Acme to get dental care without traveling the distance to Sheridan.

Spring had arrived, and Geraldine was anxious to go to the ranch. Traveling there would be possible, and Geraldine was ready to go there to check it out. She had contacted one of her men—one who came to Sheridan for supplies several times since she got back in December—so she was kept abreast of the happenings there. Still, she felt the need to go back and see for herself. Raymond, one of her bosses, would be coming in the next week.

Jakob was not too happy about her going but realized she needed to make the trip. She said she would return as soon as possible. Geraldine was hoping Eleanor and Allen would eventually completely take over the ranch. Geraldine liked living in Sheridan and was happy to enter into the community affairs. She was immediately immersed in the works of the Women's Club.

Several weeks had passed since she left. Raymond returned to Sheridan for some supplies, but Geraldine did not come back. He told Jakob there were some problems with the herd in the winter. It seemed some of the stock had disappeared, and there was now concern it might have been rustled. They were now moving the grazing grounds closer to the ranch so the men could watch over them. He felt Geraldine would be back in a few weeks. Jakob thought about going with George, but he was very busy in his office. He also needed to attend a meeting of the city council. If she didn't return soon, he would go out to the ranch. BethAnn missed Geraldine. There was now no doubt she was her mother. While she was gone, Jakob took to riding with BethAnn whenever he could.

The mayor was anxious that all members of his council attend this meeting. "There is important business we have to take care of today," he said. "We have to make a decision regarding the streetcars. If you remember, we discussed the idea of having streetcars operating down our streets. Some thought they weren't necessary, but some felt it was a good idea. Cheyenne is a smaller city than Sheridan, and they now have them. We're growing, and times are changing. We have to keep up with the times," said the mayor.

David Johnson, a pharmacist, thought it was a good idea, as did some others.

"How much will this cost the city?" said Jakob.

"Nothing.," said the mayor. "The eastern car builder has asked for no money from us or any local investors. It's a good deal. It will create new jobs in town. The Sheridan County Electric Power Plant at Acme will provide the power. This will bring in the people from Acme, Monarch, and even Buffalo. Think about the business it will bring into town."

The mayor was sold on the idea as well as most of the council. Jakob was thinking about Maria, who depended on Jozef to bring her to Sheridan. It would solve the transportation problem in this part of the Goose Creek Valley.

Sheridan, as Jakob found it in 1895, had changed considerably. But it was still the kind of place he wanted to live in. The only thing it lacked, for now, was Geraldine. She had been gone a month, and he and BethAnn missed her terribly. He expected Raymond to come in that weekend. *If she doesn't return with him, I'm going back,* he thought. *I hope she hasn't had any other problems.* He was finishing up his day at the office when the door opened. *Oh no, not another patient,* he thought.

"Is the dentist still in?" a familiar voice called. It was Geraldine. She came home!

He rushed out and picked her up, and they kissed passionately. "Honey, I missed you so."

"I'm sorry it took so long, but I had to stay to get things straightened out."

"I missed you too. I was really getting ready to come out and get you. BethAnn really missed you, but you're back, and that's all that matters."

They left for home, and BethAnn had her homecoming gift for her mother. She had painted a picture of her from a photograph that was taken at the wedding. It was done very well, and Geraldine was moved by the thoughtfulness. Everyone was excited about Geraldine's return.

Wanda went into the bedroom with Geraldine to help her get ready for dinner. The large bedroom Jakob had occupied was now divided so that she had a dressing room. Wanda could help her with her hair and dress.

Chucha started to prepare the table for Geraldine's return. She would set it Landry Manor style as Geraldine had taught her. BethAnn went to her room to put on a special dress for the occasion. Jakob put on his dinner clothes with a white tie and went into the kitchen to make martinis. Elmer Findley's store now carried olives. Sure enough, Geraldine came out wearing an ankle-length beige dress with long pearls. The martinis were on a silver tray, and Jakob handed one to his wife.

"I made this especially for you, my Lady."

She tasted it and smiled. "Why, this is better than Robert's!" She put it down and put her arms around Jakob, and kissed him.

BethAnn walked into the room wearing a new calf-length powder blue dress, and her hair was coiffed. Wanda had taken care of it. She looked so cute.

"Hi folks, can I get in on the kisses?" she said as she approached them.

They held each other, and the three of them kissed.

"So you can join in with us now," Jakob said. "I got you that new soda drink, Coca-Cola. Elmer got some for me."

"Oh, like Grandfather Miller gave me."

They toasted together, and Geraldine told them about what had happened at the ranch. They had lost some cattle but not too many. They felt a rustler took them but possibly just a few at a time. They moved the rest closer to the lower grazing ground, and someone would check on the herd daily. She also related some of the other things going on. "I believe that Allen and Eleanor are showing more interest since they became part owners. They have some ideas I might consider taking on."

Chucha came in and announced dinner was ready. She had put on her new serving uniform. The table was set, and candles cast a warm glow.

"Chucha, you didn't have to be so elaborate with our table. It's fit for the Queen," said Geraldine.

Chucha laughed. "Not Queen. We have Lady Geraldine home now."

"How sweet, Chucha! It feels so good to be with you all. Thank you so much."

"That goes for us too. Right, Daddy?"

Jakob laughed. "We're happy to have Geraldine with us, and no one could make a better dinner than Chucha."

Chucha had fashioned a Coq au Vin, flat noodles, roasted vegetables, and bread pudding for dessert.

Jakob invited Chucha to sit with them for dinner. "Chucha, you are part of the family, and I want you to sit with us."

She thanked Jakob for his kindness and sat down. Everyone had a story to tell. BethAnn told about her school, and she had learned a new piece for her piano, which she promised to play for them after dinner.

Jakob related what had taken place at the mayor's meeting. "What do you think about that? Soon we will have electric streetcars on the streets of Sheridan."

It was exciting news, and all thought it was a good idea. Chucha had some very interesting information to tell about her sister Maria. "My sister, Maria, she very happy because Pan Jakob make her teeth. She look very nice. She tell me she have man friend. He bring her flowers, and they go to lodge dance. She tell me maybe they get married. Not right away. But maybe."

"Wow, Jakob! Did you hear that?" asked Geraldine. "How nice. She did have a lovely smile after you fixed her teeth. I'm happy for her because she is a beautiful lady."

Everyone was excited about the news of Maria. After finishing dinner, Geraldine asked BethAnn to play her new piano piece for them. Her playing didn't just end with one song, but she played others that she had learned.

Jakob commended her for her progress. "Harry is really doing a good job teaching you. Is he providing you with the music?"

"Yes, he is, Daddy. He's so funny. He told me that I will do a concert at the Cady Opera House someday and he will do a duet with me. Do you think he was kidding me?"

"No, I don't think so. And I will have a big party for you at the Sheridan Inn afterward."

"Now you're kidding me, Daddy."

"No, I'm not, Honey. I believe you will have the concert at the opera house."

"And I will be there too because I know you can do it," said Geraldine.

BethAnn smiled, "This has been a great day. I'm so glad you came back, Geraldine, because I really missed you."

"Now that the weather has gotten warmer, we can spend more time riding and practicing the equestrian trails."

BethAnn snuggled up to Geraldine. "I'm so glad you're my mother."

Tears came down Geraldine's cheeks, and she kissed her. "I am too," she said.

Chapter 11
A Surprise for Jakob

Jakob found himself becoming more involved in community life. Each mayoral meeting brought new problems the community faced. Sheridan wanted to be known as a town or city where families could live and raise children safely. There were churches of various denominations and schools for the children, fraternal organizations, clubs of all sorts. Andrew Carnegie blessed Sheridan with a library. Sports teams of all types provided recreation. Even an elaborate Natatorium was built, which made swimming in the summer available for all. But, like most growing cities, there was always that element you hoped would not be there. The railroads had paying customers as well as non-paying travelers. Those no-payers, or hoboes as they were called, often presented problems.

The Sheridan Ministerial Association protested the granting of saloon licenses on occasion. Hence, the mayoral council had to face the problem. Along with the drinking establishments were the ladies of the night, who often posed significant problems. For medical and dental care, practitioners found such ladies to be non-paying customers. They needed dental care, so Jakob was faced with making it available. However, many of these ladies carried various social diseases which had to be reckoned with.

One evening, Jakob finished up with his day at the office. He looked forward to dinner at the Sheridan Inn with Geraldine. The outside door to his office opened, and he heard a commotion in his waiting room. Opening the door, he saw the room filled with Indians and a lot of jabbering but no English. One of the squaws came forward, and Jakob recognized her as one of Liz's language students. She pushed forward a little girl who must have been about five. The left side of her face was quite swollen, and she was sobbing almost uncontrollably.

The woman, whose name he couldn't remember, managed to communicate that the little girl had been in considerable pain for several days. Evidently, their native witch doctor or shaman was treating her unsuccessfully. The woman insisted they bring her to Jakob.

Oh, boy! This isn't going to be easy. The poor child is really worked up. There has to be an abscess. I have to get her by herself or maybe with the woman and get rid of the rest of the tribe.

At that moment, Geraldine walked into the office and had a horrified look on her face when she saw all the Indians. She had never really dealt with them, other than Little Deer, who worked at the ranch.

Maybe she can assist me, Jakob thought, then said aloud, "Geraldine, will you come in here? Go into my operatory and stay in the corner. Maybe you can help." He then went to the stressed child and lightly touched her shoulder while motioning the woman to come with her. He then petted the child genially, picked her up into his arms, and carried her into the operatory while quietly talking to her in a soothing tone. The child sobbed and whimpered but was becoming more controllable.

He placed the child in his chair while quietly talking to her. She watched his lips move and listened as he repeated the words slowly over and over. He touched her gently and told her to open her mouth while opening his to show her what he wanted her to do. As she opened her mouth, he was able to see inside. There were several badly decayed teeth with a large bubble on the side and below one of them. This was the abscess. He had a clear liquid in a small jar and, using a cotton-covered wooden pick, moistened the cotton and gently painted the swollen area with it. All the while, he gently and softly talked to her and made eye contact. He kept talking and talking to her, softly repeating what he said. Taking a scalpel, he quickly pierced the abscess.

She moaned a little and but kept watching Jakob. Pus immediately oozed from the swollen area, and some of the swelling disappeared. He soaked up the puss in a gauze, pressed ever so gently, and then saw blood going forth. The little girl smiled at Jakob and mumbled some words. She evidently felt relief. He patted her on the head.

He gave the woman, who had accompanied the girl to the back, a gauze pad, told her to put it in warm water, then place it over the swelling and hold it there. Jakob demonstrated what he wanted done and communicated to her that she should repeat the process several times. She seemed to understand she was to do it frequently the next day and then bring her back so he could remove the rotten teeth. In the meantime, the little one was jabbering and laughing. Jakob had a box that looked like a treasure chest with trinkets for children, and let her take one. She smiled and hugged Jakob as he passed her to the woman. They all gathered and left the office, talking to one another. The little girl went with the others, apparently feeling little or no pain. She waved to Jakob as she left and smiled while she jabbered to him.

Geraldine came forward to Jakob with a look of surprise on her face and shook her head. "Jakob Miller! I almost can't believe what I saw. That child...you...how? You took that crying child and got her to let you stop her pain without her fussing. How did you do that?"

Jakob smiled a little. "I guess I was able to gain some control over her fears. I've been reading a book recently by a European doctor who tells about how to control someone's emotions. I guess several doctors are trying to understand minds and fear. This doctor was a psychiatrist and called what I had done hypnosis. I'm not sure I did it right, but I think I successfully got the child to let me help her. Actually, I wasn't sure what I would do at first. I just knew I had to gain her confidence to help her."

"I learned something I never knew about Doctor Miller today. He's an amazing guy. Now, doctor, that's over with; let's see if he will buy me dinner."

"You're on, my lady. And, I'll buy you a martini too."

They closed up and left the office for the short ride to the Sheridan Inn. The verandah was crowded with young people.

Jakob looked at Geraldine. "Looks like Bill Cody is in town. He must be having tryouts for his show. You want to say hello to him. I think I see him over there. He sure thought you were something special at the Findley's party last Christmas. Maybe he's looking for an English rider to join his troop. The way you were cutting steers at your ranch, I'm sure he could use you."

"Jakob, you silly! What would you do if I did join his group? You became frantic when I was gone for a month."

"Maybe you're right. Forget about Cody."

They entered the inn and got a rousing hello from Clayton. "Always glad to see you, folks. Were you watching Cody and his bunch?"

"Geraldine was, but I won't let her join his group."

Geraldine slapped Jakob on the back. "Liar! Clayton, does he always lie like that?"

"Well now, Ma'am. I've known him for quite a few years, but I will never get in the middle of folks having a difference of opinion, so we'll just drop it right there." He winked at Geraldine and started to laugh. "You two have a good dinner."

They moved to the dining room and were met by Annabelle. "I was expecting you might come in today, so I saved your special table. You don't mind if it's near Dr. Ross, do you? He's sitting with some new doctor."

Jakob turned around, and sure enough, Frederick Ross was sitting just ahead of them.

He saw Jakob and Geraldine and got up. "Lady Geraldine, how nice to see you. Jakob. I want you to meet a new doctor who will be coming to town—Doctor John Hudell. I finally talked him into moving to Sheridan to open a practice here. He has had some special training at the John Hopkins Medical School in taking care of patients with heart problems."

"Well, that sounds good. Nice to meet you, doctor."

"Jake, he graduated from The Chicago Medical School. Didn't you graduate from a Chicago dental school?"

"I sure did. His school was on the other side of Cook County Hospital. Good school. I'm sure glad we'll have a doctor who trained in Chicago."

"I'm sure you don't mean Philadelphia doctors aren't as well trained. If you remember, Dr. Benjamin Rush, who signed the Declaration of Independence, was a Philadelphia trained doctor."

"Now, Fred, I meant nothing of the kind. I have the greatest admiration for you Philadelphia doctors."

"Now that you doctors have finished, I do believe I will enjoy being in Sheridan," said Doctor Hudell. "Lady Geraldine, I'm also happy to meet you. I trust you folks will have a good dinner."

Annabelle was anxiously waiting to take their order, and Jakob sat down and ordered their martinis.

"Jakob, I'm so glad I saw you with that little Indian girl. I felt so sorry for her and that she was in so much pain. The poor child. She was so cute, and you did so well with her. I was amazed to see your work with her. Why did they wait so long to get her treatment? Couldn't something be done for her sooner?"

"Yes, there could have, but they chose to let their doctor make his attempts to treat her. You would call them witch doctors, and they prey on those people. It's part of their culture. Maybe someday, this will change. For now, I see them in my office as a last resort and usually for serious emergencies. They do have confidence in me. I've been invited to their Pow-Wows by their chief. But, enough of that. Let's talk about us."

The two doctors had finished dinner, got up to leave, and bid them goodbye.

"Well. Where do we start?" said Jakob.

"A toast to us," Geraldine said. They raised their glasses as Annabelle returned. "Oops. I better order my dinner. Yes, Annabelle, I'll order the duck."

"Good," Jakob said. "We'll both have the duck."

She nodded in approval and left.

"Did I ever tell you how much I love you? And I definitely want you to know that you can't join Bill Cody's group," said Jakob.

"Oh, you nut. Of course not. Besides, I belong to your group. Jakob, I have something I want to tell you. I went to see Dr. Ross the other day."

"Ross! How come? Weren't you feeling well?"

"Well, not exactly. Actually, I feel pretty good."

"So, why did you go to see him?"

"Because, Jakob, we are going to have a baby."

"BABY? Do you mean we are going to have a baby? A baby! You and I are going to have a baby! How do you know? Are you sure?"

"Yes, I'm sure. That's why I went to see Dr. Ross. He confirmed my suspicions. You realize that you are involved in this baby thing. You are the cause of it."

"I suppose I am, and why shouldn't I be? You are so beautiful and desirable; you drive me mad with passion for you. You're happy, aren't you? I know you always wanted a baby. That's why I tried so hard to help. I'm glad. I'm glad for both of us." He leaned across the table and tenderly kissed her.

"You're happy, aren't you? It's not just me," said Geraldine. "Does it matter if it's a boy or a girl? I bet you want a boy. Don't you?"

"Sure, I'd like a boy who would be a brother for BethAnn, but I love girls, and a sister for her would do just fine. What God gives us will be all right." He chuckled. "John Binotti would say that whatever it is, it is God's will." He saw tears streaming down her face. "Don't cry. I'm happy with you. You'll make me cry." He handed her his handkerchief as Annabelle came up with their order and placed it in front of them.

Annabelle noticed the tears. "Something wrong, Ma'am?"

"No, dear. Just happy."

They finished their dinner. Jakob grinned as they talked about the baby. "That will change our life some. Are you ready for this?" he said.

"I've thought about it a long time. I almost wondered if it would happen. I feared I might be too old, but Doctor Ross said I had many childbearing years ahead of me. He is so nice. I'd like to have him as my doctor. Do you think it might offend Doc Kelly if I did? It's not that I don't like him, but he is so much older. You know what I mean?"

"Of course. Kelly's not like that. In fact, I'm sure he would refer you to him. He didn't take care of Liz. Agnes Johnson, the midwife, took care of her. I get the feeling Kelly would like to cut back. I don't know how old he is, but he was a doctor during the Civil War, so he's no kid. If you like Ross, go ahead. I hear nothing but good things about him. We should get to know him better socially. He's married and has three kids. He doesn't come to the Lucky Lady, so maybe that's why I didn't get better acquainted with him. Why don't we invite him and his wife over for dinner sometime? By the way, when is thing going to happen?"

"Well, as far as we can count, it will be in October," said Geraldine.

"Wow, maybe we'll celebrate our anniversary at the same time. We can have a big party. Sort of a coming-out party, if you know what I mean."

"Jakob, you are incorrigible! I will be in no condition for a party. You're something else."

"Maybe you're right. No party. But we should get to know the Ross family better."

"Don't you have any professional groups that get together?" asked Geraldine.

"I guess there are, but I haven't gotten into them. Doctor Hudell seemed like he would be a good doctor, and he comes from Chicago."

They talked for some time. Lukas stopping by to chat and have dessert with them.

Before they left, Jakob asked, "When will we make it known to the others about the baby?"

Geraldine pondered a moment and said, "Maybe, we should wait a bit. I think I have to let BethAnn be the first to know. I'll find the right time with her. I wonder how she will take it? Oh, I'm sure she'll be thrilled. She once asked if she could take care of the Cleary youngster. I know she likes children because I've seen her with them. She will be happy even if we will have to spend time with the baby and less time with her."

They left the Sheridan Inn with Jakob smiling like the Cheshire Cat. Arriving home, they found BethAnn playing the piano. She told them she would have an arithmetic test the next day and thought she was ready for it. Chucha brought BethAnn her snack, and she was off to bed. Jakob followed to tuck her in.

Geraldine curled up on the couch, and Jakob sat next to her and spoke, "We have much to look forward to during the coming months. How are you feeling? You said you were fine, but pregnancy usually brings some discomforts. No morning sickness?"

"Not really. Oh, maybe some, but it hasn't really bothered me much. Maybe it will come a little later. I'm maybe in my third month. The doctor said I was in good shape and that riding is a good exercise if I didn't overdo it. He wants me to have a good diet but not to gain too much weight. Oh, he did say I should see a dentist to make sure my teeth were taken care of and that if I didn't have one, he would be happy to recommend one. Why are you looking at me that way? He did recommend you. You're laughing."

He took her in his arms, held her, and then kissed her. "I love you, my mother-to-be. I wonder what you have inside of you. Whatever. It will be God's will. I'm happy. Maybe we should call it a day. I have a full schedule tomorrow. I have a woman patient who has many badly decayed teeth I will remove under general anesthesia in the hospital. She has a pathological fear of having it done, and it has already affected her general health, so we have to put her to sleep to do it."

They moved off to the bedroom. He cuddled Geraldine but couldn't seem to fall asleep. Jakob heard her breathing softly, and his mind remained awake with thoughts of his Geraldine, his love for her, and the baby she carried. Would it be a boy? That would be just great. He remembered his father and how he had a relationship with him. The things they did together. Hunting birds in the cornfields surrounding Milwaukee. How his father taught him to swim in the lake: cold Lake Michigan in the summer. The big walleye he caught on Green Lake and the thrill his father had when he brought it in. He could see him in the stands, excited when he hit that double with the bases loaded, and they won the Wisconsin high school championship. He remembered the sense of pride his dad had when he walked across the stage of the dental school and was addressed as Doctor.

And then the thought came to him. What if it's a girl? He thought of his BethAnn and how much he loved her. How she pulled him through the loss of Liz. Sleep finally came to him as his mind came to rest.

Chapter 12
Doc Kelly Becomes the Patient

Jakob's day began with his thoughts of the baby Geraldine would give him. Of course, deep down, he was hoping it would be a boy. He told no one yet because BethAnn had to be the first to know, and Geraldine should be the one to tell her. Geraldine and BethAnn spent much time together, especially riding their horses. The weather was ideal for riding—not too warm but brisk.

Geraldine was teaching an eagerBethAnn how to jump. Being careful to not expose her to any danger, Geraldine did not want the young girl to fall and get injured. BethAnn's mustang, Nelly, was an ideal size for her but not bred for equestrian events. Nelly was a smart enough animal and could learn to do the jumps. Geraldine thought that as BethAnn got older, she would get her a bigger horse.

Chucha went home to visit her family in Acme for the Easter Sunday weekend. The Millers left for church services at St. Ignatius. Father John's sermon was on the meaning of the resurrection. BethAnn sang with the choir. She had a beautiful voice and had solo parts

After the service, they spent time chatting with their friends. Leaving the church, the three talked about the sermon while going to the Sheridan Inn for breakfast. The dining room was crowded with many friends.

While their order was being prepared, Geraldine thought this was the perfect moment to tell BethAnn the news. "BethAnn, we have something very special to tell you."

"What is it, Mother? Do you think I'm ready for a bigger horse?"

Geraldine laughed. "Oh no! This is something really, really special. BethAnn, I am going to have a baby."

BethAnn's eyes got big.

"We wanted you to be the first to know. It will happen sometime in October, and you will have a new brother or maybe a sister."

BethAnn thought quietly, then smiled. "You mean we're going to have a baby in our house? Wow, that's great! I may have a sister or maybe a brother. That's really great. Will I get to take care of him or her? Why do we have to wait so long?"

"Well, that's because he or she is growing inside of me and won't be ready to be born until then. I've told you how a mother horse has a baby horse, and she carries it inside her until it is big enough. Maybe when you go to the ranch, you might see a baby horse being born. Well, mothers carry a baby until it grows enough too. "

BethAnn was thrilled with the news but uncertain about the details.

"Gosh, it will be great to have a sister or a brother. Most of the kids in my class have brothers or sisters. Some have both. My friend Angie has two sisters and a brother."

"Whatever we have, you will be the big sister," said Geraldine.

BethAnn seemed thrilled about the idea, and they talked about it at the inn while they ate breakfast.

"BethAnn, I haven't told anyone else about this yet, so it's still kind of a secret. I will be telling some of our friends soon, so wait a while before you tell your friends that you will have a brother or sister."

"Will you be telling Chucha and Wanda?"

"Oh certainly, when they come back." The inn dining room was filled, and there was much conversation and laughter. Jakob saw Frederick Ross and his family and invited them to meet his family. They did stop by, and Jakob introduced them to Geraldine and BethAnn. The doctor's wife was Barbara, and the two boys were James and Mark. They also had a daughter named Sarah, but they called her Daisy. It was a nice meeting, and Geraldine mentioned she would be inviting them for dinner to get to know each other better.

They spent the day together with BethAnn, who asked and talked about the baby.

Later, Chucha came back from Acme and told them about her visit. She brought back with her some of the things that they had during their Easter celebration. They had traditional foods, and *kielbasa* (a sausage) was one of them. The various cakes and desserts would be served the next day. She told them John Binotti was there for their church service after the one in Sheridan. Chucha was happy to be back with her adopted family.

BethAnn was really excited about the baby. Later, Geraldine kissed her goodnight and told her how happy she was. BethAnn said to her that she was also pleased that she would soon have a sister or brother.

Jakob awoke to the smell of Chucha making a special breakfast. He was having his coffee when Geraldine and BethAnn arrived to have the sumptuous meal of eggs, sausage, and a potato pancake, which Chucha called *latke*.

Wanda had just arrived when BethAnn looked at Geraldine. "Geraldine, are you going to tell them? You know."

Chucha and Wanda were perplexed but said nothing.

Geraldine laughed and looked at Jakob. "Should I?"

He smiled, and BethAnn nodded.

"I suppose you're wondering what this is all about," Geraldine began.

Wanda and Chucha shrugged and nodded.

"Well, BethAnn wants me to tell you that I am going to have a baby."

Both of the ladies said, "What?"

Questions and laughter filled the kitchen. Chucha, with tears in her eyes, put her arms around Geraldine, hugged her, and kissed her while Wanda followed suit. Chucha, of course, had to hug and kiss Jakob as well. The approval was outstanding.

Geraldine was thrilled with their display. You could see they had both become fond of Geraldine. The production finally cooled down when BethAnn had to get ready for school. Jakob would be going to the office. They left, leaving Geraldine with the two excited women.

Jakob had a patient waiting for him at the office, and his day was busy. His friend Andy Meeks, from the Lucky Lady, stopped by to go for lunch with him. They went to their favorite Chinese restaurant, and Andy gabbed about the goings-on over the weekend.

Jakob pondered whether he should give him the good news. He was ready to burst with excitement and decided to tell him. "Hey Andy, I got some good news for you."

"Yes, Doc. What you got going for you? Gonna take some time off and go fishing?"

"No, Andy, better than that."

"What then?"

"Geraldine is going to have a baby."

"What? You're kidding!"

"No, she's going to have a baby."

"Well, that's great. I'm really happy for you. You got yourself a fine wife." He laughed. "You know, I can still remember her coming in with you on New Year's Eve and taking that shot with us. That was really funny. Well, that's great. What's it going to be, a boy?"

Jakob laughed. "I wish I knew. But does it really matter? My

BethAnn is a great kid. Another girl would be fine with me. Now, you don't have to broadcast this. You're the first one I've told. I'm leaving it to Geraldine to spread the news."

"Well, thanks Doc. I appreciate the confidence. Mum's the word."

They left, and Andy slapped him on the back. "You son of a gun. Lots of luck," he said as he walked toward the Lucky Lady.

Jakob was off to his office to take care of his patients.

In the next weeks, the news of Geraldine's pregnancy spread. She kept up with her schedule with BethAnn, who learned many of the things she had to know to enter equestrian competitions.

Jakob and Geraldine were having a leisurely Sunday morning breakfast with BethAnn, and, as Chucha poured his coffee, there was a pounding on the front door. Chucha left to answer. She informed Jakob it was Andy Meeks, and he wanted to see him.

Andy had followed her to the kitchen. "Doc, I thought I should let you know about Doc Kelly. He's in the hospital. It was about eleven last night, and he was playing cards with the usual guys when he won a big pot. He was laughing and making a big fuss when he grabbed his chest and cried out in pain. He passed out but kept holding his hand over his chest. Said it was burning and squeezing; then like choking. We laid him down, but he kept saying his chest felt like someone was sitting on it and wanted to sit up.

A couple of guys picked him up, loaded him in a buggy, and took him to the hospital. Some of the other guys went to get Doc Ross. Kelly was really in a lot of pain and sweatin'. The nurses took over and put him in bed. One of them gave him some oxygen, but he was really hurtin'.

"Doc Ross came and started examining him. He took out a bottle of pills from that black bag he carried and took out one and slipped it in his mouth under his tongue. It was just a little while, and Doc started feeling better. Ross was listening to his heart. He didn't say anything, but you could tell he felt better. Doc Ross told him he had an angina attack and said he should stay in the hospital. You know, like Doc Kelly, he was worried we didn't pick up his big pot. He wanted to go back to the Lady, but Doc Ross told him there was no way he would let him. We stayed up with him for a while until he fell asleep. I thought maybe you might want to go see him. He sure didn't look good. I almost thought he was a goner."

Jakob downed his coffee in one gulp, and they left. Coming into the hospital, they could hear Kelly shouting and arguing with the nurse. Andy's eyes looked up, and he smiled. Jakob gave a chuckle,

"That's Kelly, all right. He doesn't sound like he's sick," said Andy.

Kelly was shouting, "I want to go home!"

But the nurse wouldn't give him his pants. She kept telling him he had to wait for Doctor Ross, and he kept telling her he wanted his pants. Jakob and Andy walked into the room.

"Hey Kelly, what you doing here?" asked Jakob.

"I told this gol-dern nurse I'm okay and I should go home. But she won't let me go until Ross says it's okay."

"So what's wrong with that?" said Jakob.

"I'm a doctor, and I don't have to wait around for some other doctor to tell me I can go home."

"Well, Kelly, you may be a doctor, but you're Doctor Ross's patient, and he can tell you when you're ready to go. Besides, he's not here right now."

Kelly's eyes flashed, "Hey, who's side are you on, Jake? Me or Ross?"

"I'm on your side Kelly, but you had a bad night, and Ross is taking care of you. You're lucky he came down and gave you a nitroglycerin pill. You might still be holding your chest and screaming."

"Get off it, Jake. I'd have known enough to take the pill."

"So why didn't you?"

"Because I didn't have one with me to take."

Jakob laughed. "Kelly, where would you get one? Ross got out of bed and came down here to take care of you. Now behave yourself and wait for him to sign you out."

Kelly folded his arms and stared at Jakob. Turning to the nurse, Jakob asked her if he had his breakfast. She said he didn't, and she would get one for him if he behaved himself. Kelly just gave her a dirty look as the nurse left.

Returning shortly, she brought him breakfast. "Doctor Kelly, I think you should apologize for your behavior," said the nurse.

Kelly just grinned at her and laughed. "Okay, I'm sorry, nurse. Now can I have some coffee?"

She started to laugh, and laughter with the group prevailed. But Jakob looked at Kelly from a different perspective. *This is an old man. His face is ashen, and he looks sick, like a typical old man. The hospital gown doesn't help, but he is not the gregarious, all-knowing man I know so well.*

As Kelly finished his breakfast, Doctor Ross walked in.

"How are you feeling? The nurse tells me you want to go home. You sure do look better than when I first saw you last night."

"I'm fine, Ross. I'm okay, and I just want to go home."

Ross looked at Jakob. "Do you think I should let him go, Jake? He sure had a rough time of it last night."

Jakob shrugged. "You're the doctor."

"Kelly, I'll sign you out if you insist, but you should really stay here for a few days to rest. You know John Hudell, the doctor I introduced you to the other day? I think you should see him. He's going to be in my place until he finds an office, and he knows a lot more about hearts than I do. He even knows more than you do. He's had good training, and he may be able to help you more now that you have recovered from the angina attack."

"Sure, I'll go see him. Now can I leave?"

"I'm not kidding, Kelly. I want you to see him. He may have some good advice to help you. The thing I wonder about is why you didn't have some nitroglycerine tablets with you last night. You must know you have angina, and you must have had attacks before. Right?"

"Yes, I've had attacks before, but they didn't amount to much. I forgot to take my pills with me. Okay?"

"Enough said, Kelly. See Hudell, and if you go to the Lucky Lady for cards, cut out the spirits. They don't help the medical problem you're living with. Are you listening? Oh, and be sure to carry your pills with you."

"Okay. As Jake said, you're the doctor, I think. Now can I get my pants from the nurse?"

Ross just shook his head at the stubborn man. Then he smiled. "Well, now that I know you're on your way to recovering, I can leave. I have to take my family to church, and after that, we'll go to the inn for breakfast. You going over with the family, Jake?"

Jakob nodded in agreement. "Be sure to let me know if you have any problems, Kelly."

Doctor Ross left as the nurse cleared away the breakfast tray and handed him his pants, which he put on.

Jakob asked Kelly if he would be all right or if he thought he might need some help.

"Sure, I'll be all right. If I need some help, I can get my friend, Mary Daniels, to come over to my place."

"Oh, that's right. I almost forgot you two are friends. Kelly, you know a man does need a woman to help him once in a while, right?"

"Just once in a while, Jake. Just once in a while." He laughed and waved goodbye as Jakob and Andy left the room.

Outside the hospital, Andy said to Jakob, "You know, Doc, he doesn't look too good to me. I hope he'll be all right. He's not the old Doc Kelly I know. All of a sudden, he looks like one of the old geezers that come into the Lady. How old do you reckon he is?"

"I was thinking the same thing. You figure it out, Andy," Jakob said. "Let's see, if Kelly was 25 when he went to war, and the war ended about 48 years ago, that would make him about 73. He's no kid, Andy, and he's had a hard life. But that heart thing wears a guy down. If he takes care of himself, he'll recover. Will he take care of himself? You know Kelly as well as I do."

"Sure hope so, Doc. He's one great guy. Well, I got to open up the Lady. See you later."

Jakob got up in the buggy and headed for home.

Geraldine greeted him at the door. "Is Doc Kelly all right?"

Jakob assured her that he was better and that he was recovering from the angina attack. "Doctor Ross said he would be okay, but he has to take care of himself. Knowing Kelly, that might not happen. He's one of a kind and does what he wants to do."

It was time for them to go to church. Jakob thought a lot about Kelly, who meant more to him than just a friend.

Chapter 13
Surviving a Storm

Jakob was in the Lucky Lady talking with Mayor Burns when Doc Kelly walked in.

The mayor scrutinized Kelly. "Doc Kelly doesn't look good to me. Since he had that attack, he seems to have slowed down. He's pale. Not his old self. We play cards, and he's not winning the pots. Seems like he's not thinking. Do you know what I mean? I can't seem to describe his change. Not the spark. Understand, Jake?"

"Well, it's been a while since the angina attack, but I think he's coming around. You know it may be that it shook him up emotionally. He's had angina for a while, so he must have known he had it. This last attack was a bad one, and it probably got him thinking. You have to know Kelly. He wants us all to believe he's tough, but I believe deep down he's a softie. I've seen him in some situations which overcame the tough-guy image. I think he's coming back. You know, he's no kid. He'll never admit to his age, but he's up there, even though he's demonstrated that he's physically strong. Another thing, Doc Ross told him to lay off the booze and cigars. You've seen Kelly playing cards, chewing on a cigar, and a drink near his hand. He's trying to live just as he always has—two-fisted."

"Maybe I've misjudged him, but he's not his old self," said Burns.

"You may be right. I saw him at the hospital. The nurses had a hell of a time with him. But he simmered down when Ross came in, although he isn't exactly following his doctor's instructions. Nobody is going to tell Kelley what to do. Oops, here comes Kelly now. We better knock it off."

"Hey, guys. What are you talking about here? Not me, I hope."

"Why should anyone want to talk about a reprobate like you. Certainly not me," said Jakob.

"Oh well. Say, Jake, I got a guy who needs you. One of those old civil war vets. I forget his name, but you know who I mean. He's always marching with the vets at the fair. Got long hair and a big gray mustache.

He limped bad until they put him in a wheelchair. He's got a wooden leg. Had musket shot in it until I operated, but gangrene set in. We tried maggots, but it was too late and they couldn't eat enough, so I took the leg off. He's been in bad shape for a long time, but we got him fixed up. Had a crutch for a while, but then we got him a peg leg, and he does okay. Lots of rotten teeth. Maybe you can fix him up. Oh, now I remember his name—Howard. Yes, Howard, but I don't remember his last name. He'll let you know. Oh, now I know why I came over here. Heb, Rob, and Joe want to play cards, Burns. You won't make any money here talking with Jake. We'll be waiting for you. Don't forget that, Jake. Howard." Kelly went back to the card players, and Burns followed him while Jakob left out the swinging doors.

It was now generally known in Sheridan that Geraldine was going to have a baby. She was doing quite well with her pregnancy. She could do everything and continue riding her horse and teaching BethAnn what she needed to know to enter equestrian events. However, other people in Sheridan approached her to teach their children when they heard about her work with BethAnn. She thought it would be a good idea but rejected doing so at this time.

It had been some time since she visited the ranch, and she was planning on going there to check things out. Spring had arrived in Sheridan, and the weather was pleasant. Jakob decided to take some time off to go with her. They would be leaving BethAnn with Chucha because she still had school to attend.

Geraldine had an idea she had been thinking about for some time. A number of her friends from England had asked her if they could vacation at her ranch. Several of them had been her guests, but she now considered doing it on a paying basis. They could accommodate a few in the guest house, but she thought of adding an additional structure and serve more people. It would bring in more income. If it proved successful, they could add even more facilities. The Oliver Henry Ranch would also become a dude ranch. There was already one in the Goose Creek valley area that showed signs of success. Jakob thought it was a good idea. With the increase in railroads serving the area, easterners were coming out for vacations in the summers. A dude ranch would be an exciting event for them.

Raymond, the Oliver Henry's straw boss, was making a trip for supplies so he would take Geraldine and Jakob back with him. He came for them as dawn was breaking. They loaded their possessions in the back of the wagon, as well as a lunch basket Chucha made up for them. They sat next to him as the wagon moved away from their home. Main Street out of town was now paved to Ranchester, Monarch, and Acme, but they would be turning off long before they got there, and it was mostly a trail for the rest of the way.

Raymond was quiet as they moved along but finally turned to them and spoke. "I think we are going to have some rain ahead. Just feel it in my bones. I hope I'm wrong, and we make it to the ranch before it comes, but it shore don't look good.."

"Well, it's quiet now, Raymond. Not much wind, and the sky seems clear," said Jakob.

"I know, but if you look ahead, you can see the clouds building up."

"Maybe, but if we do get some rain, it won't be much," said Jakob.

"I sure hope so."

The trail was rough from the ravages of the past winter, so they moved slowly. Some hours into the trip, the sky darkened as it did when a storm was imminent. Geraldine suggested they stop and have lunch, but Raymond said they should continue as far as possible before it hit. They could eat in the wagon as they moved along. She took out the cold chicken, fixin's, and cold coffee.

They barely finished when the rain began, first lightly and then heavy, and flashes of lightning lit up the road ahead. By now, the sky turned colors and got as dark as night. Geraldine got in the back of the wagon under cover from the downpour. The wind had picked up considerably, and the flashes of lightning increased. The horses spooked as forks of bright light flashed, and the sound of thunder crashed. The deluge continued with no letup for what seemed like an eternity. The wind was cold, and the droplets pelted them like flying sand. Raymond had a difficult time with the horses, who reared up, stopped, and then tried to run.. They had to cross rivulets of rushing water. Each one got deeper. There was no place to shelter, so they had to continue. Jakob and Raymond were both soaked.

The wind and rain continued, and they had to shout to be heard. Then, lightning struck a tree ahead of them and fell across the trail. The horses reared up and stopped when they saw the tree catch fire. Jakob took the reins as Raymond got off the wagon to try to control the frightened animals. Geraldine also got off the wagon and took hold of one of them until they calmed down. The tree on fire quickly went out with the drenching downpour, but part of it still blocked the trail. Raymond and Geraldine coaxed the horses past the downed tree, but the storm continued as other trees crashing down nearby.

"Raymond, what can we do?" shouted Geraldine.

"Not too far ahead is a turnoff to the Homerding place. Maybe we can get shelter there until this storm passes. Right now, there's no tellin' when it will let up. We best stay with the horses and lead them. Otherwise, they won't go."

Raymond and Geraldine led and consoled the horses. Jakob came down off the wagon and assisted as they walked into even stronger winds and heavier rain. They turned off the trail which went to the higher ground toward the Homerding's ranch. The horses faced another difficult challenge as they slipped and got stuck in the mud in places.

After what seemed like hours, they saw lights ahead and the Homerding's cabin. Jakob left them and fought the wind to the door. He saw a barn next to the house that had lost some of its roof. He had difficulty standing because of the wind, but he continued pounding on the door until it opened. "We need help!" he shouted. "My wife and our man are behind me. Can you give us shelter?"

"Of course, of course, come in."

"No, I'm going back to help them bring up the wagon and horses."

The wagon had stopped, mired in mud. Homerding was behind Jakob, and together they managed to unhitch the frightened animals. They led them to the barn and sheltered them with the other horses. Raymond offered to take care of the horses and sent everyone else to the house. He said he would be in as soon as he had them fed and bedded down.

It was hard to walk as the wind gusted and carried the rain. Tree branches flew, and all kinds of debris pelted them. At last, Geraldine and Jakob entered the house with Mr. Homerding.

His wife instantly recognized Geraldine. "Please come in, you poor people. We have never seen such a storm. You must be drenched to the bone. Lady Geraldine, I'll help you with those wet clothes." She put her arms around Geraldine and embraced her, then looked at Jakob. "This must be your husband. I'm Rhonda Homerding, and this is my husband, Jeremiah. Welcome to our home. I pray this maelstrom will end soon".

Jeremiah handed Jakob a steaming hot cup of coffee and helped him to a chair. Jakob seemed un-nerved as he sipped the coffee and eventually gave it to Geraldine, who sipped some and then handed it back.

"Come, we have to get those wet clothes off, or you'll catch a death of cold," Rhonda said. She led Geraldine into the bedroom and got the wet clothes off her. Jeremiah helped Jakob remove his clothes and came back with dry clothes for him. They sat by the fireplace while the Homerdings put food on the table. The door opened, and Raymond stumbled in. Jeremiah went for more dry clothes and helped him change.

"I got the horses fed and bedded down," Raymond told Jeremiah. "I hope you don't mind, but I used your horse blankets for them. The poor animals must have suffered greatly. I don't believe I have ever been in such a storm."

Even from inside, they could hear the ferocity of the wind and rain. Flying debris hit the house. Lightning flashes could be seen in the windows. The roof had several leaks that filled buckets and pans with water, but it was warm inside. They ate the dinner the Homerdings provided, and Geraldine's eyes were closing when Rhonda told her they should take their bed.

"No, we don't want you to give up your bed. We can sleep out here," said Geraldine, and Jakob agreed.

"No, we'll be fine. We can sleep in the loft. I hope Raymond don't mind sleeping near the fireplace. He'll be warm there. The Lord brought you to us, and we are grateful to be able to help you during this terrible storm."

Geraldine went to Rhonda and put her arms around her. "It seems like you have come to my rescue before. How can I ever repay you for your kindness?"

"The Lord will repay me. What else do we need? Now, you and Jakob take to the bed and pray that this storm will end."

Jakob and Geraldine went into a comfortable bedroom and laid in bed.

"Jakob, those people are beautiful. We must repay them for this kindness. By the way, did you notice? I think she's pregnant."

"I can't tell with that dress she's wearing, but they sure are kind and generous to us. I wonder how well they do out here. We have to talk more with them. I doubt that we can leave tomorrow even if the storm is over. Maybe we can really do something for them." The talk soon ended. Both were exhausted and soon fell asleep.

There was a crash, and Jakob awoke. He heard Jeremiah moving about and opening the door to go outside. *I wonder if I should get up and go out. Oh, I guess he just returned.* Jakob laid there listening to the wind and rain and finally fell back asleep.

Jakob's eyes opened. He heard movement outside the bedroom.

Geraldine was still asleep. He thought about her and what they had been through the day before and became concerned. *She's pregnant. My God, I hope this hasn't been too hard for her. She strained, holding those horses. God... please look after her and our baby,* he thought. He carefully slipped out of bed, trying not to disturb her, and left the bedroom.

The Homerdings and Raymond were up and sipping coffee. Rhonda immediately filled a cup for Jakob and handed it to him. Quietly speaking, she said, "I hope we didn't wake you. We tried to be quiet."

"I haven't been out yet, but it has stopped raining, and the wind has quieted down," said Jeremiah, "I'm almost afraid to look outside and see the damage. I hardly slept after that tree crashed. Did you hear it? We've been here almost five years and never faced such a storm."

The sun was just starting to filter through the wet windows. All was quiet outside. "Yes, I heard it too. Geraldine is still sleeping," Jakob said.

Raymond picked up his still wet coat and put it on. "I guess we have to face the inevitable."

Jeremiah put his coat on, and they opened the door. The scene was one of destruction. Fallen trees were everywhere, including one that had spread a large limb over the shredded cover of the wagon. The corral was filled with water. The barn was largely intact except for one side of the roof, which lay next to it. As if to magnify the destruction, the sun rose in an almost cloudless sky with no wind.

"Thanks be to God we are all alive, and none of us are hurt," said Jeremiah.

"We can put things back together again," said Raymond, "but I don't know about the wagon. I hope that the back wheel isn't damaged. I'm going to look in on the horses. They should be all right, but it was a hard day for them."

"Looks like we all have our work cut out for us, so we better get our breakfast. Rhonda will be working on it. Let's figure out what we have to do first. I know you folks will be anxious to get going, so we'll check out the wagon after we have to get the limb off it. I'll get the axes and a bucksaw from the barn."

"I appreciate your concern for us, Jeremiah. I would like to get on, but I want you to know that I'll send two of our men back to help you get your place put back together. I know a good carpenter, so you can get the barn roof fixed too."

"Oh, you wouldn't have to do that," said Jeremiah.

"No, no, that's the least I could do for all you've done for us. We'll talk more later."

The tree limb was large and couldn't be moved, but fortunately, it didn't destroy the wagon bed. The wheels appeared to be intact. They worked until Geraldine came out to call them in for breakfast.

Rhonda made a sumptuous breakfast of bacon and eggs and fried potatoes. Raymond came in and informed them the horses were all doing well. He had fed and watered them.

"Looks like the wagon can make it to the ranch, but it will have to be rebuilt. The supplies and everything inside got soaked, but they can be dried out. We'll have to secure the load better for the rest of the trip. I think that if all goes well, we can probably leave tomorrow," said Jakob.

"Jakob, we can't just leave these people. We have to help them," said Geraldine.

"We won't just leave these people, Geraldine. I told Jeremiah we would send a couple of the men from the ranch back to help them."

"Oh, that's a good idea, Doc," said Raymond. "Harvey Jenkins is one good carpenter. He can fix that barn roof."

The Homerdings were happy to get help to rebuild after the storm. Sitting around the table. Jeremiah put his head down. "If you don't mind, folks, we should give thanks to the Lord for our being here together." He put his hand out to Jakob and held his other hand to Rhonda, and she took Raymond's, and he took Geraldine's, who took Jakob's.

"Thank you, Lord, for bringing us together and for saving us in that bad storm. Thank you for bringing the Millers here. We will help each other and put back what was broken and fix it. Thanks for the food Rhonda made for us, and thank you for the baby that she carries. In Jesus' name, Amen."

"Jeremiah, Rhonda is not the only one with a baby," said Jakob as he looked at his wife. "My Geraldine is going to have our baby."

"Then she gets included in my prayer, God."

They all laughed and partook of the breakfast.

Raymond excused himself and went out, followed by Jeremiah and Jakob, to repair the wagon. The limb was removed, and the load was secured. This took most of the day, and they were now ready to move on tomorrow. The warm sun dried the wet clothes.

Jakob spent some time talking with Geraldine. "Honey, these people are just wonderful. They're the kind of people you want to have as friends. I don't know their situation here, but I wonder if they could help us at the Oliver Henry. You talked about the idea of a dude ranch. We're going to need good help for an undertaking like that."

"Jakob, it's incredible how we think alike. That exact thought came to my mind. I just love Rhonda. We are so much alike. Yes, she is going to have a baby and is concerned as to who will help her. We will help when she's ready to deliver. She has to come into Sheridan and have one of the midwives take care of her. She could even stay with us."

"You're something else, Geraldine. You're way ahead of me. We'll talk to them after supper."

Rhonda made them a fine meal. When they finished eating, Raymond went to the barn to take care of the horses.

Jakob glanced at Geraldine. "My wife has an idea she wants to share with you. The Oliver Henry is her project. I just go along with her, so I'll let her tell you what she has been thinking about."

"Rhonda," Geraldine began, "we want you to come into Sheridan when you are ready to have your baby. We'd love to have you stay with us or, if you want, at the hospital. There are doctors and mid-wives there who can take care of you. Then when you are up to it, you could come to the ranch. I plan on taking guests in. I will need reliable help, and you and your husband could be in charge of the guest ranch. I know you have a nice place here, but this might be something you'd like to do, and we would pay well. You don't have to tell me now, but just give it some thought, and we can talk about it later."

The Homerdings were surprised at the idea and said they might be interested in such an arrangement. There was more talk, but the hour got late, and they all needed some sleep. Rhonda embraced Geraldine and thanked her for the idea of coming to Sheridan when her time to deliver her baby came due. It lifted the burden of the delivery of her baby.

Chapter 14
Cowboys and Rustlers

Jakob and Geraldine were getting ready to leave the Homerding place. Raymond had the horses hitched, and they were prepared to go. The weather was sunny, and the sky was clear.

"I've decided to go along with you part way, just in case you run into problems," said Jeremiah. "That storm did a lot of damage. The trail could be blocked by fallen trees, and you might need someone to help remove them. I'll take some axes and a bucksaw with me."

Jakob agreed, and they started off. There were a few trees downed and blocking the trail, which they removed. They passed through some standing water, along with more downed trees, and crossed a swollen Goose Creek. Fortunately, the bridge did not get damaged. Jeremiah stayed with them until they reached the gate, then he turned around and bid them goodbye.

There were some downed trees near the ranch, but they were able to bypass them. Fortunately, there didn't seem to be any significant damage to the buildings. Raymond removed their belongings from the wagon at the house and took the damaged wagon with the rest of the load to one of the barns. Eleanor and Allen were anxiously waiting for them.

"You must have gotten caught up in the storm from the looks of that wagon," said Allen. "We've never had such wind and rain. I'm surprised and grateful we didn't sustain much damage here. Whatever we had was minimal."

"We did get caught in the worst of it and were lucky enough to get shelter at the Homerding place," said Geraldine. "A large limb fell on the wagon and almost destroyed it. There was a lot of damage along the way—downed trees and lots of standing water."

Eleanore embraced her, and they entered the ranch house. Little Deer and Maria were happy to see them and were getting lunch ready. They each talked about the storm which had passed through. George, the ranch foreman, came and talked about some problems resulting from the storm. "There were some calves lost, and one of the steers was really mired down in the mud, but they were able to free it.

George then told them, "We've lost some more cattle. It seems there's a rustler at work, but he just takes a few head at a time. I'm thinking we should go out and try to find 'em. It all started in the upper grazing ground last fall. I'm for going up there to see if we can locate 'em. If we can find where the cattle are, we may be able to recover 'em. Could be just a couple of guys doing this. I doubt if we can get the sheriff to come out this far. We're going to handle this ourselves. Some of our men are good with their guns if necessary."

Geraldine looked concerned. "George, I don't want this to end up in a gunfight. You're sure the sheriff won't come out here?"

"No, Ma'am, but if we can find who's doing this, then maybe they'll send out some deputies to bring 'em in. I'm for leaving tomorrow and going to the upper grazing grounds where this started and take a good look around."

"Well, maybe that's the thing to do. Jakob, what do you think?"

"I think we should follow George's advice. We're going to have to face up to the problem sooner or later. We can follow along with them and see what we can. If we find the culprits, I'm sure I can get the sheriff to come up here."

"All right, George, you're right. The sooner we get on this, the better, and we'll tag along."

"It's a fer piece up there, so we'll leave at first light," said George, and he left.

Geraldine decided she and Allen could look over the ranch with George.

George had mentioned that one of the men was injured during the storm and wondered if Jakob could look in on him. Jakob headed for the bunkhouse. H found one of the men in his bunk with a large laceration on his arm, still oozing blood. Jakob stopped the bleeding and changed the bandage.

When Geraldine and Allen came back, it was time for supper. They had made a good inspection of the ranch, and Geraldine saw most of the men. She felt her ownership was well accepted by the men, and she was now comfortable dealing with them.

Little Deer and Maria had a fine dinner for them, and most of the talk was about the ranch. Allen decided to leave with Geraldine and Jakob in the morning to look for the rustled cows and maybe the rustlers.

Dawn came early. Little Deer had breakfast ready for them and put together some food for the trip, which would take all day. They followed behind George and two of his well-armed men. George made it known they were not looking for a gunfight, but they had to be prepared.

The idea was to find the cattle, so they had to look at the areas where they might be hidden. Most of the day was spent checking out the upper grazing area. They had hoped to find a trail the rustlers used, but the previous day's rain had made that impossible. They came on a small stream that led them to a pond, with a large grassy area. A perfect spot to keep cattle. Sure enough, there was a small herd of cattle grazing.

"Now what?" asked Jakob.

"Let's just wait a while here and see if anyone shows up," said George. "Frankie and Jim will sneak up and see if they can take a close look at the animals. They can check the brands and see if they're ours."

"Wouldn't they change the brands?" asked Jakob.

"Maybe, but they can tell." They waited as the two men approached the cattle. No one seemed to be around. The men went through the herd, checking the brands. When they returned, they reported the cattle were marked with Oliver Henry brands.

"These are our cattle," said Frankie.

"What do you plan to do, George?" asked Geraldine.

"Well, it's too late to try to move them, and we would need more men. We need to go home, now. I'll bring enough men back with me tomorrow to drive them back where they belong. There's about a hundred fifty head there, which is what we've lost. It will take a few days to bring them back if we don't run into trouble. There's no use trying now. Whoever did this is probably nearby, so we couldn't get very far. At least now we know where the cattle are. Let's leave now. It'll be dark soon." They rode away, and the sun was down when they saw the lights of the ranch ahead.

"I plan on getting enough men to bring those cattle home. We'll start early," said George.

Not used to being in the saddle so long, Jakob was ready to call it a day as he climbed up the steps of the house.

"I think I'll stay with dentistry and leave the ranching to your men."

"Poor boy. Can't take a little riding," laughed Geraldine.

Little Deer had dinner on the table for them, and they soon sat down. They talked about their day and the plan to take the cattle back. Allen said he would go with them.

"I don't think you should go with them, Hon. They can handle things for you," said Jakob.

"I feel I should, Jakob. If there is a problem, I want to be able to make the right decision. I don't want anyone to get hurt. You don't have to go."

"If you go, I'll go."

Allen also agreed.

"We all better get a good night's rest."

They were up before daylight and were on the trail following the men. It was cold, and they experienced a sharp wind. They passed the chuck wagon that started ahead of them, but George and the cowboys were still in front. With the sun up, it got somewhat warmer. The men arrived at the herd and started rounding them up to get ready to move. Geraldine joined in with them but did no cutting, and the cattle started moving ahead.

It was about noon when George rode up to Geraldine. "If you look back, you'll see two riders following us. They're staying pretty far back. I wouldn't be surprised if they're the rustlers. We'll just keep an eye on them." And he then rode away.

The rest of the day was one of keeping the cattle moving. With night coming, they stopped. Fires were lit, and George had guards posted, although the two riders had disappeared.

The men stopped by the chuck wagon for supper. It was a hard day's ride for Geraldine and Jakob, and they sat by the fire and ate with the men. One by one, the men put out their bedrolls and were soon asleep. Jakob and Geraldine sat by the fire until they decided to turn in, and they too put out their bedrolls, snuggled, and fell asleep.

Jakob awoke several times when one of the men added wood to the fire. The sounds of the cattle and horses, plus other sounds of the night, kept him awake. Some wind came up, and it was cold. He laid close to Geraldine and could feel her softly breathing. An occasional howl of a coyote could be heard.

His eyes opened when he heard sounds from the chuck wagon. The cook was up, and soon others could be heard milling around. It was still dark except for the light from the fire nearby. He dared not move, or Geraldine would wake up. His mind was a jumble of thoughts. *Never would I have ever dreamed of being here with a herd of cattle. This is a far cry from my life in Milwaukee. I wonder if those rustlers are still around. Would I ever have the guts to shoot one if I had to?. I hope they realized there are enough of us here and left. George said there were only two of them.*

Geraldine started to move. She whispered, "Jakob, are you awake? I can hear them moving around. Is it time to get up?"

"I've been awake, waiting for you," said Jakob.

"You have not. Have you? It's still dark. You have to get up and go with me. I have to go, and there is no chamber pot here."

"I'll call one of the men over to help you."

"Oh Jakob, you wouldn't."

Jakob laughed, got up, and walked her to a more private spot behind some bushes. "Wait, I'll get you the chamber pot." He left and got a bucket at the chuck wagon, and quickly returned.

As he arrived, Geraldine screamed. "Jakob! Help!"

Coming out of the bushes were two large men rushing toward Geraldine. One had a gun raised. Jakob, pushing forward, took his gun from the holster and fired at the one already next to him. He screamed and ran into Jakob, knocking him to the ground.

As quickly as this happened, one, no two, no three of the cowboys, hearing the commotion, were on the scene knocking the other one down. The one Jakob shot in the arm got up and started to pick up his gun when one of the men knocked him back to the ground. Others quickly came with rope and tied up the rustlers.

Jakob got up, somewhat dazed and bloodied, with the gun still in his hand. They quickly checked Jakob to see if he had been shot, but the blood came from the man he had wounded.

Geraldine thought Jakob had been shot, screamed, ran to him, and put her arms around him. Holding him, she sobbed until she realized he hadn't been shot but did have blood on him. The two were tied up and were roughed up by the men until Jakob told them to let them be. The law would take care of them.

He examined the arm of the rustler, which was still bleeding profusely, and saw that the bullet had passed through it. He placed a tight bandage around it and stopped the bleeding.

Looking at Geraldine, George said, "I'm glad we got these bastards. When I didn't see them anymore, I figured they gave up and left. I don't know what they hoped to accomplish by coming back. I'll send Buck and Jim back to the ranch with those two outlaws. They'll know how to handle them. Buck was once a deputy, so they'll take them to the sheriff tomorrow." Then looking at Jakob, he said, "Boy, am I glad you had your gun with you!"

Jakob laughed. "So am I. You know I felt kind of foolish carrying a gun. That was never my thing."

They all started to move back to the chuck wagon, leading the two rustlers who had been securely tied up.

Jakob looked at Geraldine. "I brought the chamber pot. Do you still need to use it?"

She slightly smiled, nodded her head, and carried the bucket behind some bushes. "Stick around and keep the gun handy in case there are more of them out there."

He laughed but thought maybe he should.

As they ate breakfast, Geraldine looked at George. "George, I think I'll ride back to the ranch. I've had enough excitement to last for quite a while. You don't need me to get the herd back. I'm glad I came along, but I never expected what just happened. I'm glad we got those two rustlers. We'll make sure the sheriff gets them. Allen said he'll stay with you."

George smiled. "Lady Geraldine, you are one tough gal. You sure knew what to do in a bad situation. And you, Doc, I'm glad we had you around. You sure knew how to handle that six-shooter. We can get the herd back where they belong without you guys. Sorry you had to go through all of this. You leave whenever you are ready. Buck and Jim will take care of the rustlers." He got on his horse and joined the men. Buck and Jim put the rustlers on their horses and started back.

Geraldine looked at Jakob. "Time for us to pack up and leave too."

The sun was now up, but the wind was bitter cold. There was no trail, but Geraldine knew the way. It wasn't too long before they met up with the two men and their prisoners. They exchanged some words and continued on their way. It was late in the day when they arrived at the ranch. They left the horses hitched in front of the house and climbed the stairs. Prince, the cat, got up and approached them as they opened the door. He slithered inside and rubbed his body on Jakob's boot.

Maria was the first to see them. "Oh, you come back. Is Mr. Allen come too?"

Geraldine answered, "No, he won't be back until tomorrow. Ask Little Deer to make us some dinner and get us a bath. It's been a long ride." They opened the door to their bedroom, and Geraldine fell back on the bed and closed her eyes. Jakob sat on the bed next to her, then laid back and kissed her.

She opened her eyes and smiled. "I needed that. I'm tired, and I still can't get over seeing you on the ground with blood on your shirt from that brute. I thought you had been shot. Oh, Jakob!" She started to cry. "I thought I would lose you. I couldn't lose you; I couldn't live without you."

"Well, you haven't lost me. I'm here." He held her tightly and softly kissed her.

There was a knock on the door. It was Maria, who had come to get Geraldine's bath prepared.

They laid in each other's arms until Maria said the bath was ready.

"You want help, Lady Geraldine? I stay."

"No, you may go. I'll be all right."

She left, and Geraldine started to disrobe. Jakob watched as he saw his beautiful wife stand before him naked. "Are you sure you want to take that bath?"

She smiled. "You mean you would make love with a dusty and sweaty lady?"

Jakob laughed. "Sure. Why not? But I can wait."

He helped her into the tub and washed her back. "I'll let you finish," he said, and then he left. Jakob found Little Deer and told her to just make a snack for now, and they would have dinner later. He also told Eleanor about the past days' events and that Allen would be back the next day. She was astonished by their exploits.

Enter Geraldine, now fresh and in the Kafka she wore that first day they made love. Jakob smiled and remarked he liked her attire. She coyly smiled.

Eleanor said, "I like it too. I've never seen you wear it before. Is it something new? Jakob has been telling me about your escapade. Geraldine, you are something else."

"Well, you ladies can talk. I better wash off some of the trail dust I've acquired. I'll see you later." Jakob left for his bath and couldn't help dwell on thoughts of his lady. She was everything he had hoped she would be. His love for her was deep, and now she would give him another child. *A boy? Oh, what does it matter? Another little girl like her mother would be just great.* With those thoughts, he was led to thoughts of BethAnn. *We have to get back home. I have had enough of this ranching.*

Walking down the stairs to the great room, he saw the ladies sitting and talking near the fireplace. The month was May, but there was still a chill in the air, and a small fire made the room comfortable.

Geraldine spoke first. "Do you still remember how to make a martini? Eleanor, would you like one too?"

"No martini, but I'll have a glass of Chardonnay."

Jakob was dispatched and soon returned with the libations. Little Deer set the table in style and served them game hens with chokeberry sauce. It was a grand meal, and Jakob mentioned that he hoped they could go back home. Geraldine was in agreement and said they would do so in the next few days.

Eleanor wished they would stay longer but understood their need to return to Sheridan. Allen would be back tomorrow. Jakob felt that Allen was enjoying the ranch, was doing a good job, and had been accepted by the men. Geraldine wanted to wait until the herd was returned. It had been a long day, and she was exhausted. They turned in early. It took a while before Jakob was able to fall asleep. His thoughts were of Geraldine, and he wondered whether she should find a way to dispose of the ranch. The responsibility was significant, especially if she found it necessary to spend so much time there. The new baby would keep her plenty busy.

Geraldine asked Raymond to prepare to take them back to Sheridan, but they would first stop at the Homerdings to see how they were doing after the storm. Two of the men were still working there, and it looked like the place was getting put back together. Finally, Geraldine and Jakob, accompanied by Raymond, were on their way back home.

Chapter 15
Jakob Becomes a Town Hero

The trail to the Homerding place was now cleared of all the debris. Geraldine's men were still working on the barn, and it looked like it was almost finished.

Jeremiah approached the wagon as it arrived. "I sure am glad to see you folks. As you can tell, we have gotten a lot of work done since you left after the storm. We should finish up the barn in a week, and then your men can return. I sure appreciate all the help they gave me. But, I have another problem. Rhonda is in bed. She took a fall the other day, and now she's bleeding. I'm worried about her and the baby. Lady Geraldine, maybe you might know what I can do for her. She says she is afraid she will lose her baby."

Geraldine got down from the wagon. "Oh, I'm sorry to hear that. I'll go in and see her."

She went into the cabin, followed by Jakob. Rhonda was lying in bed and looked pale and weak, and frightened. Geraldine asked her what had happened, and she told her she fell doing some cleaning and shortly after that started to bleed. Her blood loss seemed like just a small amount, but it had not stopped since the day she fell.

"I'm worried about my baby. I don't know what to do."

Geraldine saw she was spotting blood. She turned to Jakob. "Jakob, do you have any ideas as to what she might do? I admit I don't really know. I've heard this can happen if you get injured."

Jakob was somewhat embarrassed. "This is a long way from my specialty. I can only say it isn't normal for this to happen, so she should seek professional help. I think we have to get her to a doctor. We're heading for Sheridan, so why don't we take her with us. Ross or one of the other doctors can look in on her."

"Yes, you're right, we can take her with us. Good idea, Jakob. They will know what to do."

Rhonda seemed a little reluctant to leave and would maybe wait a while. "I don't want to put you folks out. Maybe it will stop, and I'll be all right."

Jakob countered, saying one of the doctors in Sheridan would help her, and they could take her with them. Jeremiah was standing in the back, and he agreed she should go into Sheridan with them.

"If you were my wife Rhonda, there would be no quibbling about this," Jakob smiled. "And, I'll make sure you get taken care of."

"But, where will I stay?"

"With us, of course, like we stayed with you during the storm. Or in the hospital if necessary. Geraldine will help you get dressed, and we'll help you get in the wagon. We have plenty of food with us, and we'll be in Sheridan tonight." Jeremiah added it would be all right, and he would go into Sheridan to bring her back in a couple of days.

Geraldine helped get her ready and took all she might need with them. Rhonda was a little apprehensive, but Geraldine helped her get over it.

They laid her in the back of the wagon with her legs propped up. The day was cold but sunny, and the wagon rolled into Sheridan as it started to get dark. Everyone was on the porch to greet them. BethAnn really missed them and hugged and kissed both of them. Chucha said she would make dinner for them and went to work. Geraldine said Rhonda could stay in BethAnn's room.

When Geraldine sat down, Skippy jumped up next to her and put his head on her lap. He really missed her. At dinner, BethAnn would fill Jakob and Geraldine in on everything that happened since they left. Chucha had a bottle of wine opened and poured glasses for them, although Rhonda declined. Geraldine complemented Chucha on how clean the house was, which made her beam.

"We started getting the garden ready for planting, Daddy. It's warm, so Chucha and I started getting it ready. The weather was nice except for the day you left. That day it really rained hard. Did you get caught up in it?"

Geraldine told her what had happened to them and how they stopped at the Homerding's for the night.

"How was everything at the ranch? Did they have the storm there?"

Jakob related the events. "We went looking for the rustlers who stole some of our cattle. "You should have seen how your mother handled them."

"Jakob, you were the one who shot the rustler." She then proceeded to tell the story of how they captured them.

BethAnn was in awe of their exploits. She questioned both and was really impressed.

"Gosh, Daddy, you could have gotten hurt. Wait till I tell the kids at school what you did. And Mom, you were in the middle of all this. Oh, I'm so glad you didn't get hurt. Wow!"

When the conversation simmered down, BethAnn spoke up. "Oh, by the way, I forgot to tell you I learned another song, and I want to play it for you. Harry says I'm doing very good and gave me some new songs." She then sat at the piano, took out the music, and played the beginning of the *Blue Danube Waltz*. "I'm also working on the rest, which he said he'd help me with. You know Daddy, he's funny, but I like him when he plays his classical music. He becomes so serious. But then he plays silly stuff like he plays at the Lucky Lady."

After BethAnn finished, Geraldine looked at Rhonda. "We need to get you to bed. It's been a long ride, and you need the rest."

"I'll help her too, Mother." Being called Mother really touched Geraldine. She embraced her and kissed her.

"I really missed you, BethAnn. Maybe next time we go to the ranch, you can come along. Tell you what. If time permits, maybe we can take the horses out tomorrow."

"Oh, that would be great. I'll look forward to that after school," said BethAnn.

Finishing up, Chucha came in and told them how happy she was now they were back and said she would be doing some more planting soon. "I go bed now if you have nothing for me to do. Good night."

It now left Geraldine and Jakob, who would soon go to bed.

"It's good to be back home, Jakob. I really missed BethAnn. She is such a sweet child, and she's growing so fast."

"And so is her brother or sister. I'm noticing a little bump there. Are you sure you should be riding so much?"

"Dr. Ross said he thought it would be all right for me to ride. He said horseback riding was good at strengthening my pelvic muscles. I'll take Rhonda to see him tomorrow, and I'll ask him again. I do hope she will be all right. I think she's bleeding more. I hope she doesn't lose the baby. She's been looking forward to having it. I know it would break her heart. I'm praying for her."

Jakob looked at her, smiled, and kissed her. "I love you."

Jakob awoke early. He didn't sleep well. His thoughts about Rhonda and Geraldine were bothering him. And then there was the ranch which he hoped would not be a constant problem for Geraldine. It was the first day back, and he had things he had to do. First of all, he had to meet with the sheriff and make sure the rustlers were properly charged. He would also stop by the office and leave a notice he would be in and seeing patients. He could hear Chucha in the kitchen, so he decided to get up.

She had already left Skippy out. "Good morning, Pan. You sleep good?" She handed him his coffee, then opened the door to let Skippy in. The dog immediately jumped up on Jakob, greeting him.

"Okay, Skippy, down now. I missed you too. Good morning Chucha. It looks like it will be a nice day. The sun is up, so I guess we won't be getting any rain."

She was putting his breakfast on the table when BethAnn came in.

"Good morning, Daddy. I'm so glad you're home. I can't believe you shot that rustler. Honest, Daddy, you are something else. But it sure was quiet around here without you. We all missed you."

"I know, and I missed you too. But I'm back. I'll be leaving for the office today, and I'll drop you off at school, so you better get dressed. Is Rhonda still asleep up there?"

"I was real quiet, but I think she may be awake. She didn't make hardly any noise, so I think she slept well."

Geraldine soon arrived, and they were all eating their breakfast. "I better go up and check on Rhonda," said Geraldine. "I'll take her to see Dr. Ross. I hope he can see her this morning. I'm worried about her. She's such a nice person and was so good to us."

When they finished breakfast, Geraldine and BethAnn went to her room. Rhonda was awake and sitting on the edge of the bed. Geraldine went to her and hugged her. "How are you feeling today? Did you sleep well?"

She indicated she was feeling well but still spotting blood. "Well, let's help you dress and get you some breakfast. I'll take you to see Dr. Ross so he can check you out. I like him, and he is very kind and considerate."

Jakob left BethAnn at school and went to see the sheriff.

"Good to see you, Doc. I heard you had some trouble out at the ranch. I'm glad you were able to handle it without getting yourself hurt. I was surprised you were able to get the best of them. Those hombres are not to be reckoned with. I hear you know how to handle a six-gun. You aren't related to Doc Holiday, are you?" He laughed.

Jakob answered. "Sheriff, honestly, I hope I never face the situation again."

"These two guys are really bad apples. They are wanted over in Johnson County and as far as Sundance. I'm glad you got them. We'll charge them with rustling and resisting arrest. I'll see if we should put them on trial here or at one of the other places. Judge Harry Johnson will be holding court here on the fifteenth of June. But they may want them over in Sundance on the charge of manslaughter and a bunch of other things. I'll check with the sheriff over there. If so, it will save our county some money and not have to put up with their incarceration awaiting the trial. These guys are really bad desperados. You're just lucky you got the gun on them first." Jakob gave all the information to the sheriff and filled out the forms.

"Do you want to take another look at them? I got them in the cell in the back."

"Heck no, I don't ever want to see them again; unless I'm needed at their trial."

"I don't blame you, Doc. You shouldn't have to deal with bums like that, but don't worry, I'll take care of them. If there's anything else I can do for you, just give me a holler."

Jakob left but was a little shook up when he realized just what he had been up against. Thank God he had the gun with him. He thought he'd stop by and see Kelly before he went to work.

Kelly was outside of his office talking to a couple of his cronies. As he approached him, Kelly said, "Well, look whose here! Six-Gun Miller." He had the guys laughing. "Don't pull a gun on me, Jake. I ain't armed."

"Kelly, you son of a gun, don't pull that stuff on me. How did you find out about those rustlers?"

"Hey Jake, good news gets around fast. I didn't know you were so good with a pistol. Sheriff ought to deputize you when he needs help. That was pretty good, Kid. Better watch out, though. One of the hotheads who come to town could ask you to draw."

A crowd developed, and there was a lot of laughing. Jakob realized he was getting a real joshing from the bunch. They made him relate the details of what happened, and those there were really impressed at his spunk.

One of the guys, Herby Smith, said, "What does your wife have to say about your use of the gun?"

Jakob laughed. "Next time you see her, why don't you ask her?"

Kelly looked serious. "You know Jake, I got to hand it to you. A big-city boy comes to Sheridan back in '95 and ends up being one tough hombre. Hey, 'fore I forget, I got a guy I'm taking care of that needs a good dentist. Has a real problem; I want you to look in on him. Are you going to your office today? I'll send him over."

The crowd dispersed, and Jakob left for his office. As he approached, he noticed an older man waiting for him. His eye was closed by swelling on the right side of his face, and Jakob's day was just beginning.

At noon Andy Meeks stopped by. He heard Jakob was back and came over to have lunch with him. He wanted to listen to the story of Jakob's thing with the rustlers. Funny how the story got changed to where he pinned down six of them.

They went over to Grandma's Café, where Jakob had to repeat his story about the rustlers to the folks there. He didn't realize it, but he had become the town hero for nabbing those guys. After finishing up at the office, he stopped over at the Lucky Lady. The guys there gave him a real reception. Mayor Burns asked him if he'd like to take over the sheriff's job. Jakob just laughed and told him he had plenty to do as a dentist.

"Glad you're back. We're going to be having a meeting for the county fair in a couple of weeks. I got you down for judging the races. Got some new things we're going to do, so I want your input. I suppose your wife will have some horses down. She sure does have some fine animals, and I suppose you'll all be in the parade. I'm counting on you."

"Not to worry, Mayor. We'll be there. Well, I better get back home. I got some things I have to do. Being away, things pile up."

Jakob left and pulled into the yard. Geraldine and BethAnn were practicing some of the things she had to know for the equestrian competition. BethAnn looked so cute sitting straight as she went through the various events with Geraldine giving the orders. Both rode up to Jakob and greeted him.

"Jakob, I want to get that piece of property over on Badger Street. We can make it into a dressage arena. You know dressage is the fancy name for what the equestrian events are called. It will be bigger than the yard, and she can practice jumping, which she now needs to do. The regulation size of such an arena is 66 ft by 197 ft. We can build obstacles for jumping. That takes a lot of practice, but she can learn. Nelly is really a smart animal and has learned everything well so far, and BethAnn has learned how to lead her."

BethAnn was beaming as Geraldine talked about the horsemanship BethAnn was learning.

"Let's go in now, and I'll tell you about Rhonda," said Geraldine. First, they put the horses in the barn and watered and fed them. Little

Henry would be over later to get them ready for the night. Chucha had dinner on the table, and all sat down.

"I know you all wonder why Rhonda is not here. I took her to Doctor Ross's office, and he did an examination of her and called me in. He believed she was *not* having a miscarriage, and he didn't really know why she had the bleeding. It had evidently stopped, but he thought she should have complete bed rest for a few days, so he asked me to take her to the hospital. He promised he would look in on her. He also said that her pregnancy was almost to term, and she should have the baby in a matter of days or, at most, a week. She evidently miscalculated her pregnancy. That was another reason he wanted her close by. She is in good spirits and happy she will be having the baby soon."

"Well, that's good news," said Jakob. "Jeremiah will be out in a couple of days to look in on her." Then he went on to tell them about the rustlers and what the sheriff said.

"I wondered. Several people asked me about what had happened. They seemed to know more than I did. And you! They had an inflated image of what you had done. They gave me the idea you were a real straight shooter." She laughed at how they viewed the incident. "Honey, you aren't really a gunslinger, are you?"

They all laughed.

"Daddy, someone said you should join Colonel Cody's show."

The laughter continued, and Jakob continued to draw an exaggerated scenario of the event.

"Well, enough of that," said Geraldine. "I'm sure BethAnn has homework to do, and we can talk about some other things. I also found the owner of the property I'm interested in, and it's available. I think we may be able to negotiate a sale. BethAnn will have the dressage arena she can work out in."

BethAnn had gone to her room, and Chucha was cleaning up.

"Jakob, I also had an exam by Dr. Ross, and he said that I was doing fine, and he heard a heartbeat."

"Really? Wow!"

"He also said he felt my riding was not objectionable. He said the riding I have been doing was actually good for me. It had strengthened my pelvic muscles. But he cautioned me not to overdo it, so I do not endanger myself."

This all sounded good to Jakob because he was concerned for Geraldine.

Chapter 16
Jakob and Medicine Crow

Rhonda left the hospital after Doctor Ross told her he felt she was doing well. They made arrangements with one of the midwives to deliver the baby when she was ready. Jeremiah came for her, and they left for their ranch feeling relieved she would not lose her baby.

Geraldine finally bought the property she was interested in for the dressage ring. It was much bigger than she needed, but it was also to be an investment. They started getting it ready to use.

BethAnn was now practicing jumping and getting proficient in her horsemanship. She was excited about being able to do what she had learned. Geraldine loved working with her. For her age, she had become quite a proficient horse-lady.

Jakob was now back in the office and very busy. He enjoyed his ranching experience with Geraldine, but dentistry was his profession, and he was glad to be back with his patients. His fame as a gunslinger spread. The sheriff stopped by the office and informed Jakob he had given up the two rustlers to the sheriff of Sundance to prosecute on their manslaughter charge. Jakob would not have to testify at the trial, making Jakob very happy as he didn't want to see them. They were big, ugly men with very bad dispositions. The one who faced a manslaughter charge had told Jakob he would get even with him. This made Jakob shudder at the thought. Hopefully, the man would be hanged or get a long prison term.

Jakob was now preparing for the coming county fair. He had already met with the mayor and his committee. He agreed to be in charge of the horse races and would be judging some of them. It wasn't a hard job for him because he had other people helping him. Jakob enjoyed the fair even though he was busy with his dental practice. His patients in the surrounding communities often came in for the fair and tried to have their dental work done while in town. The fair was a fun time with the people in Sheridan. Many had relatives and friends come to visit them and take in the fair. The Sheridan rodeo was always a big event.

Geraldine was busy with her Sheridan home, making it a bit of England in the West. She was now active with the Women's Club and fitted in with the ladies who were impressed with her business acumen and talents. Her English manner set her apart from the local ladies, and they liked her native traditions. Sheridan women were a special breed. They were used to the outdoors and rugged outdoor activities, while some were into more intellectual pursuits. There was a group of members who were into helping the needy. These women were from pioneer stock of the early Sheridan days. Some of the riding groups could one day enter into dressage activities Geraldine would be promoting.

The Women's Club was looking for a way to make some money for their current project—a new library in Sheridan. Sheridan had received $15,000.00 from the Andrew Carnegie Foundation. The city had to provide the property, which was located at Loucks and Brooks Streets, and the Women's Club was going to provide funds for the financial support for the library.

Geraldine brought up the idea that they put on an English High Tea which she would organize. It was different from former fundraising. The women were excited to do it in conjunction with the county fair because it would bring in people from all over Wyoming. The event would take place in the Sheridan Inn. Tickets would be sold for three different days. Lucas, the cook at the Sheridan Inn, agreed to help Geraldine. She promised it would be English style in every way. The idea created excitement with the ladies in the club. They wanted to do something different and be recognized for their efforts. The splendor of High Tea was to be held in the Sheridan Inn dining room, decorated with English artwork. Some of the ladies agreed to put on white waitress aprons over black dresses to do the serving. A few even got their husbands to reluctantly act as footmen. Geraldine did the training. She even managed to put together an ensemble to play music. Authentic English items were raffled off—Geraldine had sent for the trinkets from England. The High Tea Event was the talk of Sheridan and turned out to be a grand success financially. Attendees purchased tickets and filled the Sheridan Inn's dining room.

The county fair always engendered a great deal of excitement to Sheridan. It brought in the local tribes of Indians and other tribes who came from great distances. The Crow and Cheyenne always came. They had their pow-wows, and the squaws always brought and sold their wares at the fair. Some of the Indians would even take part in the races. This year they added several more bareback races. The Indians were especially good at riding bareback. Sheridan had the biggest fair in that part of the state, and the gathering brought in people from all over the area and beyond.

Opening day would always start with a big parade and included participants from all the different organizations in town. The U.S. Army would have a detachment and a band, and the Civil War vets loaded on buckboards, waved flags. BethAnn's school had a marching band, as did some of the fraternal organizations like the Elks. Jakob, Geraldine, and BethAnn would be on horseback, and some other families and ranchers joined in as well.

Geraldine rode side-saddle on her white stallion, Sir Richard. She wore her English-style riding garb to help bring attention to the Women's Club High Tea. BethAnn rode Nelly and showed off some of the techniques she had learned. She had a white, large brimmed hat with her hair in a red bowed ponytail; the fancy riding boots she got for Christmas, jeans, and a white blouse. The procession went through town and ended at the fairgrounds.

Everyone had a good time as they rode up and down the streets of downtown Sheridan. This year Colonel Cody was in town, and of course, he was at the front of the parade with some of his troupe. At the very end was a string of automobiles. There were now some automobile owners in Sheridan who would participate. They were kept to the rear of the parade so as not to spook the horses.

Geraldine would have Eleanor bring out some horses from the Oliver Henry, as did other ranches who brought fine animals to show and compete for prizes. There were various contests of home items, cakes, preserves, and talents of dressmaking and furniture crafting for the ladies.

Last year BethAnn had submitted her bunnies in the small animals competition. This year, she would submit pictures of horses she had drawn and the other students' projects in her school. The kids from the various schools had raised animals that were judged. There were rodeos with bronco busting and bull riding. Doc Kelly and the other doctors in town would see some of the riders in the hospital with bruises and broken bones.

Toward the end of the county fair Jakob was in his office with several patients. Waiting for him were several Indians in full regalia. One of them stood by the door to his examining room. A lady nervously knocked on his door. Jakob appeared and recognized Medicine Crow, one of the Indian chiefs. Medicine Crow was a fine specimen of Indian; tall, lean and handsome. He spoke and understood some English.

"Pow-wow, you come. Bring your woman and girl." He nodded to Jakob and smiled. "You come, yes?"

Jakob greeted him and asked, "Tonight?"

The Indian nodded and promptly turned away, leaving the office. Jakob, smiling, watched as the door closed.

The lady who was waiting for him looked horrified. "Doc, are you going to the pow-wow? Is it safe?"

Jakob laughed. "Of course it's safe. Medicine Crow is an old friend of mine."

The lady's eyes opened wide, and she shook her head as Jakob closed the door to his treatment room. He finished his day in the office and left for home. BethAnn and Geraldine were waiting for him on the porch. Both relayed their experiences at the fair.

"We have an invitation tonight," said Jakob.

"What is it, Daddy?"

"Yes, Jakob. What is it?" asked Geraldine.

"Well, it's really special. Medicine Crow stopped by the office and wants us to go to the pow-wow tonight."

"That would be fun, Daddy!" BethAnn was excited; Geraldine was not.

"Does he want us to come too? Or are you just saying so? "

"No, he definitely said you and BethAnn should come. You'll like it. It'll be an interesting experience for you. You'll be glad you did. Tell you what. You can wear that Indian dress they gave me the time I took care of the little girl. Remember?"

"I'll wear mine, Daddy. The dress with the deer on it."

They all dressed in proper attire for the pow-wow. As they approached the Indian encampment, the dogs came out barking, so some of the young men came out and scattered them. Jakob stopped in front of the chief's teepee. Medicine Crow was waiting for Jakob. The tribe gathered by fires in the meeting ground, and their leader looked disturbed.

"Woman, she no look good. She sick."

"What's the matter, Chief?" Medicine Crow moved to the teepee and opened the flap. Jakob looked inside and saw a woman lying on a blanket. Her eyes were closed, and she was breathing heavily. A foul odor was in the tent. The Indian Medicine Man held a bunch of feathers and fanned her with them. He chanted something in his own language and proceeded to sing and dance and drop something on the ground next to her. He held a container with liquid in it and dropped it on her lips as he mumbled foreign words. She laid there, moved her body, and moaned. Jakob noted her lips were encrusted with blood.

He moved the medicine man aside and knelt next to her. The foul odor was oppressive. He felt her forehead wet with perspiration, and it was obvious she had a high fever. He opened her mouth to see her red gums with pus between some of her teeth. Her breath was foul.

Oh, my God, those gums. What a case of ulcerative gingivitis! He had never seen such a case. He went back to the buggy to get his bag of instruments which he always carried with him.

"I need cold water and lots of it," he told the chief. He lifted her head and propped her up with blankets. He gave her some water to drink and two white pills. He now had aspirin to use for pain and inflammation. He noted that some of the teeth were loose, and he held them gently as he took sharp instruments and started scaling. In the background, he could hear the Indian drums and chanting. He showed them how to wipe the perspiration off her forehead with a cold cloth, which would eventually help bring down her temperature. She stopped moaning. The gauze he carried was sopping up the blood and other fluids.

Time stood still as he carefully cleaned her teeth, stopping only to give her a chance to expectorate the blood-stained saliva. She had to be held up because she was weak. When he was finished, he opened up a bottle of hydrogen peroxide and carefully swabbed the open wounds. Clotting was starting to take place.

Jakob sat back. His back was killing him from working in that position for almost an hour. The chief came in to see his woman, who seemed to be better now. The other woman kept mopping her brow.

"You come pow-wow now," he said to Jakob. Jakob instructed another woman to keep up the cold compresses and left. He sat next to the chief and was passed the pipe. He coughed as he inhaled the smoke. He wasn't sure it was tobacco, but it was strong.

He hadn't seen Geraldine or BethAnn near him but was sure they were all right. Food was passed, which he tasted, although he wasn't sure what it was. Several different items were given to him. He recognized the buffalo but was unsure of the chicken-like meat. The fires burned bright, and the dancing and chanting had no end. Jakob was starting to feel tired. He noted the time, and it was now past ten.

"Chief, it is time for me to go to my home."

"You stay here.."

"No, Chief, I must go back. I have patients to take care of tomorrow. Your wife will be all right, but I want you to bring her to my office tomorrow morning so that I can continue her treatment in my office. Where are my wife and daughter?"

The chief raised his arm, and a young man came up. He spoke with him and sent him away. He looked at Jakob and put his strong arm on his shoulder.

"I want you be my brother. Come back for pow-wow."

Jakob was at a loss for words and just nodded. He could see Geraldine and BethAnn coming.

"Hi, Daddy. I had a great time."

Geraldine smiled, and they started off for their buggy. He stopped at the chief's teepee to see his wife resting. Her temperature was down. He gave her caretaker another aspirin to give to her when she awakened. They drove off into the night with BethAnn jabbering and Geraldine just sitting close to Jakob with her head against his shoulder. Everyone was tired, and it was off to bed.

Jakob was up early while the others slept. Chucha had coffee and breakfast for Jakob and queried him about the pow-wow. BethAnn joined Jakob and was still excited about her time at the pow-wow. She enjoyed the children, and she was able to communicate with them somewhat. She learned something about their life she didn't know.

Jakob became concerned that Geraldine hadn't gotten up for breakfast and went into the bedroom. She was awake but complained she was still tired.

"Maybe you should just sleep on for a while. You've been working a lot lately. You've forgotten you're going to have a baby and should be getting more rest. The High Tea has taken a lot of effort, as have the other things you have been doing. Just lie around and get some rest today, and you can catch up. You don't have to do anything in the house, and the fair is just about over."

Geraldine nodded approval.

"I'll be going to the office and will be back for lunch in all likelihood." He told BethAnn and Chucha to make sure Geraldine rested, and he then left.

Jakob had a few people waiting for him at the office and started his day. Medicine Crow and his wife, along with an entourage of Indians, arrived. His wife was definitely better but needed more treatment. He removed more incrustations from her teeth and painted the gums with a solution for serious gum infections. It had iodine in it and stained the gums. He told Medicine Crow she should eat soft foods for a few days. He was concerned with some teeth which appeared loose. He remembered the English sailors of old carried citrus fruits on long voyages to prevent scurvy, and her problem was quite similar. He prescribed some dried citrus fruit Elmer Findlay had in his store. Finally, he had Medicine Crow take her to Kelly's office to examine her. He gave him a note and hoped Kelly would see her. Kelly was not too anxious to take care of Indians. He'd already passed lunch but decided to stop over at the Lucky Lady. Maybe he and his friend Andy Meeks could have some lunch together.

Chapter 17
Welcome, Randolph Jakob

Geraldine had put in a lot of her time and effort with the Women's Club, and the High Tea fundraiser was a financial success. The Sheridan library was well on its way to filling the bookshelves. The past weeks were very busy for Geraldine, and Jakob noticed she appeared tired and stressed. Her day for the baby's delivery was approaching, and he was concerned she might be overdoing her workload and responsibilities.

"You've been pushing yourself hard with all you've been doing. Why don't you lay off with some of your projects so you can rest more? The Women's Club can do without your expertise," said Jakob.

"I know I may have overdoing things, but I feel the library is so important, and I want it to be something special for Sheridan, but you may be right. I've noticed I'm starting to tire, and I'm starting to get some pains, but I think it's normal. Maybe I'll stop by and see Doctor Ross today."

It was later in the day when Geraldine did stop at his office. Doctor Ross examined her and looked at her with a surprised expression. "Mrs. Miller, I think we must have made an error in our calculations for your baby's delivery. In fact, it looks like we're off by almost a month. I can't believe this. Actually, as I see, you are almost ready to deliver. If she is to do your delivery, you better get ahold of Henrietta O'Donnell and let her know. I believe it's just a matter of days for you. I would stick around the house if I were you and stay away from your horseback riding."

Geraldine was shaken up. "Are you really sure?" she asked.

"Definitely!"

Geraldine left his office in a hurry and carefully got into the buggy. She started off to see Henrietta, who lived just out of town. She had not thought much about the delivery; other than she would have to go through it. Henrietta had told her what to do to prepare, but she was so busy with her Women's Club and the Sheridan Fair she had put it out of her mind. But now, the anticipation of the delivery made her apprehensive. She pressed the horse to hurry along.

Henrietta O'Donnell lived alone and was a busy midwife. She had a good reputation with the doctors and was considered the best in Sheridan. The doctors in town didn't care to do baby deliveries. They had plenty of other work, and babies came at all hours of the day and night, interfering with the rest of their medical practice.

Geraldine stopped in front of a neat, shuttered little house with a front yard still covered with flowers. She carefully climbed the three stairs to the front door and knocked to announce her arrival, but there was no answer. After several tries, she started to feel panicky. *Where is she? I have to tell her about my situation.* Then she thought about looking at the back of the house.

Sure enough, Henrietta, who was working in her garden, looked up, startled. "Hi, Geraldine. What are you doing here?"

"I was just in to see Doctor Ross, and he thinks I'm almost ready to deliver."

"Well, now, maybe we better check you over. Let's go into the house, and I'll take a look-see."

Geraldine followed her into the house and into her examining room.

"We miscalculated your delivery, huh?" Henrietta was in her fifties, unmarried and rather plain, although somewhat attractive and definitely caring. Her job was bringing babies into the world, and she was serious about it. Actually, she had delivered many. She took off her garden apron and gloves, carefully washed her hands, put on a clean gown, and slipped on gloves. The room had a plain examining table with a white cloth cover.

"Hop up here." She patted the table, and once Geraldine was in place, she did a pelvic exam and smiled. "Well, Honey, I hate to admit it, but I guess he's right. It could be any time now. You better stick around your house now that I know you're almost ready, and I'll be in touch. Be sure to have everything ready for me. I gave you that list. Don't worry a bit because there's nothing to worry about. I've done lots of babies, and yours is not going to be any different."

Geraldine left feeling a little relieved and happy, but yet she was apprehensive. She came home with the news but was disappointed Jakob was not there yet. Chucha and Wanda greeted her as they went about doing their chores. BethAnn was home from school and was at the piano, so she sat and listened as she played. Skippy immediately came up to her and placed his head on her lap for her to pet it. She sat thinking about what might be her plight in the days to come. Skippy was not satisfied with merely placing his head on her lap. He got up on the couch next to her. He had become quite attached to Geraldine for the attention she gave to him.

BethAnn finished with her piano and sat next to Geraldine. She hugged and kissed her and said, "You just missed Harry. He was here and left a while ago. Harry gave me a lesson and a new song to learn. You know, he is so funny the way he talks, and today he taught me something new that will help me with my new piece. Mother, Daddy said he was worried about you this morning because you have been so tired. He said you should rest more. You should listen to him because he knows. When will my sister come? I'm so excited waiting for her. I learned a song just for her. I'll play it for you and Daddy after supper. Will she be coming to stay with us soon?"

Geraldine smiled. "BethAnn, I'll be all right. I am going to rest more. To answer your question, we don't know for sure it will be a sister. It could be a brother, you know. How about that? You'd like that, wouldn't you?"

"Oh yes. My friend Anna has a brother, and she adores him. So I guess I'll like a brother if you have one."

Geraldine smiled and hugged her. Skippy abruptly left when he heard Jakob arrive and was off to greet him. It was just a short while before the door opened, and Jakob came in with Skippy bouncing behind him. "Hi Honey, sorry I'm late, but I had a problem at the office. There was a big fight over at the Commercial Hotel bar. One of those tough train employees lost most of his front teeth. A real mess, but I got him fixed up. How are you doing? Did you go see Doctor Ross today?"

"Daddy, Mom said she would rest more. I told her that you were worried about her."

Geraldine, a little exasperated with BethAnn, just smiled. "You guys worry too much, but I do have some news for you. BethAnn wanted to know when we would have the baby. Well, it may not be too long. In fact, it might be very soon."

"What?" Jacob let out a yelp.

"I saw Doctor Ross, and he thinks it could be within a few days. We miscalculated the time. I went over to see Henrietta O'Donnell, and she agreed and is alert. In fact, she will be looking in on me. Now, I'm really excited."

They both closed in on Geraldine and hugged and kissed her.

Geraldine smiled. "I thought something was beginning but didn't realize it would be so soon."

While all this was happening, Chucha and Wanda were listening and joined the hugging. The dinner table was quickly set, and they all sat down to have their dinner. It was all baby talk as they had Chucha's chicken and dumplings for dinner. Geraldine said she wasn't hungry and didn't eat much.

BethAnn chattered about school and her piano lesson. She couldn't wait and was up at her piano. She had the music in front of her and slowly played Brahm's *Lullaby*. She sang the words as she played, "Lullaby and good night."

Geraldine and Jakob sat with her by the piano. Tears of joy appeared on their cheeks.

The next days were tense as they all waited for the baby to arrive. Geraldine was having more pains, and finally, the water broke. Henrietta was waiting, and when things were starting to move, she told Jakob to take a walk or a ride. "We need to be alone," she advised him.

Geraldine's pains were coming fast, and she was most uncomfortable.

"Take your daughter with you. You're not needed here. I can handle this."

"But I want to stay," said Jakob. I won't be in the way. Maybe I can help."

"Look, Doctor, I don't need you, and I know what I'm doing. I'm in charge. I don't need your help, so leave, get out, get out! You can come back in a few hours when things settle down. Better make it at least a couple of hours. In fact, better make it three. Okay?"

Geraldine was now really starting to moan, so Jakob went up and got BethAnn. Wanda handed Jakob his coat, and Chucha opened the door. Jakob went out, mumbling that Henrietta was a very difficult woman and that he should stay with Geraldine.

BethAnn was concerned for her mother and questioned Jakob, but he just told her they would take the horses for a ride. There was a brisk wind, and the foliage was starting to change color. He kept up a conversation with BethAnn as they rode out of town. Time seemed to drag as he checked his watch from time to time. They stopped at Goose Creek to watch the birds.

BethAnn looked up at Jakob. "Daddy, do you think we should go back now? She said a couple of hours."

"You're right; it's almost three. let's go back." They picked up the pace and got to the house, and tied the horses to the hitch. Then Jakob and BethAnn ran up the stairs and opened the door to the house. A shrill sound of a little baby crying greeted their ears. The bedroom door was open. Wanda and Chucha, with grins on their faces, watched as they entered the bedroom.

Henrietta stood next to the bed with a smile on her face. "Well, you came back just in time to meet your son."

Geraldine held her baby close to her bosom. She had a big smile on her face. "Jakob, look! I brought you a son, and he's beautiful."

Jakob placed a kiss on Geraldine's forehead and lips and tenderly kissed his son. BethAnn sat on the bed and gazed at her brother.

"Oh, Honey, I'm so happy for us," Jakob said.

With eyes wide open, BethAnn blurted out, "Me too, Mom. I'm so happy to have a brother."

"Can I hold him?" chimed in Jakob as he reached for the baby and took him into his arms. He looked him over carefully and kissed him.

"Okay, Dad, that's enough. Let me have him now," said Henrietta.

"I just got here, and you're chasing me out, already," said Jakob

"Yes, because we're going to have to let this new mother rest after our guest of honor gets his first meal. It's been a tough job these last hours, and we're going to have her get some rest. Say your goodbyes and leave."

Chucha and Wanda silently left, followed by BethAnn and Jakob.

"You too, dog. Out!" said Henrietta, and Skippy slithered out of the room. "The lady needs to rest." She handed the baby to Geraldine, who proceeded to nurse him. The door closed.

BethAnn put her arms around Jakob and kissed him. "Daddy, he is so cute. I can't wait till I can hold him in my arms."

Chucha invited Jakob to the table. She handed him a wine glass and filled one for herself and Wanda.

Toasting, she said, "Nas Drova."(to your health)

They sat down to eat, but the excitement of the moment quenched their appetite as they mostly talked about the newborn.

Jozef, Wanda's husband, came for his wife and congratulated Jakob as they left. BethAnn, who was up past her bedtime, left for her room, leaving Chucha to cleanup. Jakob sat in his chair by the fireplace with Skippy by his feet. Henrietta finally came out and told Jakob she was going. She gave him some instructions and told him she would return in the morning.

He went up to BethAnn, tucked her in, went to his bedroom, and sat in the rocker. Mother and son were slumbering, and soon he was too. Some hours passed, and the baby started to whimper. Geraldine began to stir.

Jakob quietly said, "I'll take care of him," and she dozed off. This happened several more times. Geraldine quietly said, "Honey...come sleep next to me. It's all right. I won't bother you." and she giggled as he laid next to her warm body.

Barely asleep, he could hear Skippy scratching on the door. *Oh no! He wants to go out.* Then he heard Chucha stirring in the kitchen. The door opened, and he quickly fell back asleep, but not for long. The little prince wanted to be tended to, and Jakob got up to change his trousers. However, that didn't satisfy him, and only his mother could do that. He gently placed him next to his mother's breast. By this time, Jakob was completely awake. Putting on his robe, he stumbled out of the bedroom. The fragrance of the boiling coffee took him to the kitchen.

"Good morning, Pan. I have coffee for you. Poor Ta-Ta. You not get much sleep. Little one keep you awake."

Jakob smiled. "You're right, Chucha. It's been a long time since we had a baby in the house." He sipped his coffee as Chucha cut him a slice of sweet bread.

"Can I join you.?" Turning around, they saw Geraldine wrapped in a gown and slightly disheveled, standing in the doorway.

"Honey, you didn't have to get up," Jakob told her.

Chucha moved a chair out for her to sit down. "Panne, you sit down. I get you coffee."

"Oh, thank you. I need some of your magic brew." She blew on the coffee to cool it and sipped it. "Hmm, that tastes so good."

Jakob got up and went to her. Placing his hands on her face, he kissed her.

"How are you doing today after that big night of labor?"

"Well, not too bad, except I feel like I got kicked in the stomach by my horse. It hurts."

Jakob looked at her with empathy. "Wish I could have helped you."

"There was a time when I wish you could have." And she laughed. "Oh, Oh, I hear someone calling me. I better get Lord Randolph his breakfast. Oh, I didn't tell you. If you don't mind, I'd like our son to be named after his great grandfather and you—Randolph Jakob. We can talk about it. Randolph Landry was a great man, and so is his father, Jakob." She left for the bedroom to tend to her son.

Jakob sat back in his chair, somewhat startled. He had not thought about a name for his son. *Randolph Jakob, maybe.* It was funny that Geraldine had not talked that much about her family history. BethAnn joined in, and Chucha had her milk and juice ready for her.

"Oh Daddy, I'm so excited. I now have a brother! I'll tell the teacher and all the kids I have a brother. Most of the kids in my class have a brother or sister. Do you think Mother will let me take care of him some time?"

"Of course. That's what sisters are for."

"I didn't have a sister take care of me," she said.

"Well, of course. You were the first one. Some day when he grows up. He may take care of you. Brothers often do that. That's what it means to have a family. We all take care of each other."

BethAnn listened to Jakob as he extolled about a family.

"Gosh, Daddy, I never thought about that. I better get dressed and get to school."

Geraldine came out of the bedroom carrying her bundle of joy. "That should take care of him for a while, but he is a slow eater. I thought he'd never get through."

"I don't blame him. Those are really nice milk bottles that you got."

"Jakob!"

Chucha came to Geraldine. "I hold baby for you so you can eat breakfast. Not to worry, I know how to hold babies." She smiled and put her arms out.

"Of course you can. I'm just a novice, and you're the expert. You can teach me a lot."

Chucha nodded in agreement.

As they finished their breakfast, Wanda came in and took notice of Chucha with the baby. "I know how to take care of babies, too. I had three sisters and two brothers that I cared for."

Geraldine laughed and looked at them. "I guess we will have plenty of experts looking after our son."

With that comment, the door opened, and Henrietta walked in. "Well, looks like everybody is up and at it in this house, and our baby looks content. I guess you must have fed him. He looks pretty good for a seven-and-a-half-pounder. What did you say his name was?"

"Oh, his name will be Randolph Jakob if his father will accept that."

"Wow, that's a pretty fancy name for the little tyke."

We can call him Randy for short. Randolph was his great-grandfather's name. He was a great seaman and sailed with Admiral Nelson."

"Sounds like he has a lot to live up to. A great grandfather who sailed with Admiral Nelson. and a father who is a dental surgeon."

"Actually, Sir Randolph was captain of an English galleon and was decorated for bravery."

Henrietta picked up the baby and held him up. "Randy, you got a tough act to follow." Her comment brought chuckles and laughter and a dribble from the side of the baby's mouth.

Jakob looked at his watch. "Well, it's about time for me to get to my office. I'll drop off BethAnn at school. Looks like everything is being taken care of here, and I'm not needed."

"Incidentally, Doctor, last night, I didn't mean to hurt your feelings. I just don't like someone looking over my shoulder when I'm working."

Jakob laughed, "I wouldn't let that worry you. I figured you knew what you were doing."

After taking BethAnn to school, he stopped at Findley's General Store.

"Doc, haven't seen you for a long time. Your housekeeper does all the buying now. Glad to see you. What can I do for you?"

"How about a box of cigars?"

"You don't smoke cigars, Doc. Oh my gosh! Your wife had a baby!"

"You bet, and it's a boy—seven and a half pounds. Named Randolph Jakob."

"Son of a gun. You got yourself a boy. That calls for a box of Manual Primos. Congratulations. Wait till I tell the missus. Come to think of it, not too long ago, she was asking about her. She remembered her when she was riding that big white stallion in the parade. Is she doing okay?"

"She's doing just fine. Thanks for asking. Here, you get to take the first one. Well, I better get moving. I have a lot of guys to see."

"You know, Doc, some of the guys were wondering if you'd have another kid. Your wife is one good-looking gal and smart too."

Jakob left with his box of cigars and headed for his office.

Waiting in front was Harley, the barber, with his wife. "Doc, I brought my wife with me. I think she needs those store-bought teeth."

"Come on in, and we'll take a look at her."

Harley's wife, Norma, was sitting in Jakob's dental chair, and Jakob was examining her dentition. "Harley, why do you think that she needs dentures?"

"Well, Doc, she has some teeth that hurt, and she has lost a bunch of others. No sense fixing them. Her ma and pa had them store-bought teeth. So did her aunts and uncles. Runs in the family, you know."

"Harley, that doesn't mean she has to have them too. We can fix her up, and she'll have a pretty smile and be able to chew her food. You should be aware that dentures are a poor substitute for your natural teeth. They are to be made for people who have lost most or all of their teeth. Norma has teeth that can still be fixed, and we can make her some bridges to take the place of her lost teeth. Don't let anyone take out those good teeth when they can be fixed and saved!"

"But Doc, it'll cost a bunch of money."

"Not that much, and you can afford it, Harley. Not to worry about the cost. I know you're good for it."

"Well, Doc, maybe. If you think so, I'll go for it for ma wife."

They made arraignments for his wife to come back, and in the meantime, several patients came in for their dental care. It was noon before he was finished, and Jakob went over to the Lucky Lady to see some of his friends there.

Andy Meeks was behind the bar. "Hey Doc, I see you got a box of cigars under your arm there. Does that mean your lady had her baby?"

Jakob smiled.

"Well, let me have one. Congratulations. Okay, now how about you and me have a drink to celebrate?"

"Nope, Andy. I got to work this afternoon, but I'll take one some other time."

"Your call, Doc, but hey, it's lunchtime. How bout I buy you lunch?"

In the meantime, several other friends received cigars.

Doc Kelly walked in. "Okay, Kid, don't forget me. I get a cigar. Remember, I put you on to that Henrietta O'Donnell. Did she do you a good job?"

"Yes, she did a good job. But you know what, she wouldn't let me stick around and see the delivery."

"Why should she? You may be able to pull teeth, but what makes you think you could help her take the baby out?"

"Kelly, I should have known you'd give me such an answer. Anyhow, Geraldine came through the delivery fine. Here, have your cigar."

Jakob's friends really knew how to josh him. Later, some of them stopped by the office when they heard about Geraldine's baby, and he received their congratulations. Some of the ladies brought in cookies and cakes to take home. He finished his day early and left for home with just a few cigars left. When he got there, at least a half dozen buggies blocked his entrance. Seemed like half the Women's Club came to see Geraldine and little Randolph Jakob.

The house was filled with flowers and gifts of all sorts. When Jakob walked in, they crowded around him, all talking. Geraldine was propped in her high back chair like the queen of Sheba. Chucha and Wanda had baked crumpets and served them with tea. One by one, they left, and Jakob was finally alone with his wife and family.

"Honey, I'm tired," Geraldine admitted. "Those ladies sure can talk, but I love them. Did you see all the gifts they brought for me? They just loved our little Randy, and he behaved so well. He's in the bedroom now. Why don't you bring him out so I can hold him? He must be hungry."

Jakob went into the bedroom and lifted the baby from the crib. He was awake and stirring around.

BethAnn watched as Jakob kissed his forehead. "Can I take him to Mother? I'll be real careful. He's so cute." BethAnn carefully took her brother, kissed him, and carried him to her mother. "I love him so much, Mother. I'm happy I have a brother," she said as she passed the baby to Geraldine, who proceeded to nurse the baby.

Wanda quickly went about straightening up the house while Chucha finished dinner. Geraldine nodded off while holding the suckling baby, who had his fill. Jakob removed the baby from her arms, took him to his chair, and sat with him in his arms. Emotionally overcome, tears flowed down his cheek as he gazed at his son.

It was now generally known in Sheridan that Geraldine had the baby. Jakob had called his parents, who were thrilled to know they had a grandson. Margaret wanted to know when the baby would be baptized as they wanted to come out and be there for the event. Jakob had not talked to his friend Father John Binotti yet.

Geraldine had now pretty much recovered from the delivery and was ready to take on her usual lifestyle. She went riding with BethAnn and attended the Women's Club meeting.

After dinner, BethAnn was at her homework, and Chucha was finishing her work. Jakob and Geraldine decided to do some planning. He asked Geraldine when she wanted to have the baptism. They decided to have it on the second Sunday of November if Father John could do it. The new church, St. Ignatius, was completed, so they would have it there. Afterward, they could have an open house for their friends. Jakob was really excited because he now had a son. He spoke to the priest, and they agreed that the second Sunday in November would be the day.

His parents arrived a week early and would be staying at the Sheridan Inn. They couldn't spend enough time with their grandson. Bob was already making plans for him. They brought many gifts for the baby, and the house on Loucks was starting to get filled up. Jakob's library was made into a nursery for Randy. His office would now be on the second floor, along with Geraldine's.

Jakob had not seen his parents since the wedding. They looked older and somewhat frail, but the baby brought sparkle to their lives. Both had graying hair but seemed quite active. He talked about retiring from his dental practice. Jakob suggested that they move to Sheridan to be nearer to him and their grandchildren. However, Margaret was adamant that Milwaukee was their home. Still, she was excited to hold the baby, who started to react and even smile. She was the perfect grandmother and gave BethAnn a great deal of her attention. She asked Chucha if she and BethAnn could make breakfast for the family. Chucha laughed and said she could make dinner too.

The day of the baptism arrived. They chose Doctor William Ross and Geraldine's sister Eleanor to be the godparents. Saint Ignatius church was filled, and Randolph Jakob was introduced to the congregation.

The ceremony was simple and included the godparents, who would take over should the parents ever become incapacitated or die. Prayers were said, and sins were washed away. Holy oils anointed him, and a white baptismal dress was put on him. He was now a Christian. He didn't much like water being poured on him, but they dried him off quickly.

Jakob decided to change the location of the open house. There would be too many people for his home, so he decided to invite them all to the Sheridan Inn. Lucas put out a table of food and treats. Harry brought his concertina. Jozef accompanied Harry with his violin, and the two of them serenaded everyone. Later, Artie Wulf brought his guitar and Willie Stover his saxophone and clarinet. Some folks even danced, and Randy had his first party, which lasted into the night.

Little Randy had a full day, as did his family, who would later sit around the dining room table at the Loukes Street home. The grandparents took turns holding the baby. It was a long day of festivities, leaving everyone tired, so Robert and Margaret left for the hotel. The rest of the family found their beds too.

Chapter 18
Jakob Faces a Possible Danger

The Millers' visit to Jakob's family was coming to an end. They got to know their grandson and take part in his baptism. Geraldine invited them to come over for breakfast at the house. After their enjoyable visit, they would be leaving for Milwaukee on the twelve o'clock train.

It had been a different experience for the elder Millers, visiting with the people in the west. The special comradery they discovered was something they didn't experience in Milwaukee. They promised they would be back for a visit in the summer and stay at the ranch for a special treat. Margaret was somewhat reluctant, but Bob was all for it. Jakob missed seeing his parents and thought it would be a good idea.

After Chucha's sumptuous breakfast, Jakob took them to the train station to see them off. BethAnn, who now had a special bonding with her grandmother, came along. For her, it was a tearful goodbye.

Jakob then went to his office, where he found a patient waiting for him.

As he was leaving, the sheriff came in. "Doc, I have some news you're not going to like. I got a telegram from the sheriff in Sundance. Remember the rustlers you turned over to me? The ones you caught over on your wife's ranch? I turned them over to the sheriff in Sundance to be prosecuted. One of them was convicted on the manslaughter charge and sent to prison in Fargo for twenty-five years. Well, he busted out, killed a guard, and escaped. He's dangerous. I remember how he said he would get even with you. There's probably nothing to worry about because Fargo is a long distance away and they're out looking for him all over the state. But it might not be a bad idea for you to arm yourself. Not to worry, Doc, but there's no use taking chances cuz he could come back here."

Jakob was flabbergasted—short on words. He just stared at the sheriff for a moment, then remembered the despicable man who threatened him and his wife. Jakob put a bullet through his arm when he attacked them. He made the threat when Jakob turned him over to the sheriff.

Finally, Jakob spoke. "Why would he come here, sheriff? What would he gain by coming here.?"

"I dunno, but this guy is a plain wacko. You can never figure out what he will do. He's already proven that. I can't see why he would come back down here, but it pays to be aware of the possibility. I sort of wondered whether or not I should have warned you, but I felt you should know."

"My God! Do I have to carry a gun with me? I'm a dentist. I work to help people with dental problems. I try to help my community to make Sheridan a better place to live. I have a family; children and a wife. I'm not a gunslinger." Jakob became frightened with the realization of what could happen if this murderer did come after him.

"Doc, my deputies are aware of the problem, and the police chief has his men alerted. If he should dare to show up here, we could take care of the matter, but it would be a good idea for you to protect yourself, just in case. Lodge, the gunsmith, can fix you up with something you can conceal. Stop by my place if you need any help. Just thought I'd come by, but now I got to get back. I don't mean to worry you, but I want you to know what's going on." The sheriff left a terrified Jakob.

He sat down in the chair next to his desk. Thoughts passed through his mind. *What should I tell Geraldine? I don't want to frighten her. I hate the idea of carrying a gun, even if many do carry one around here.*

The door opened, and Kelly walked in.

"Good party you had yesterday. Looks like you have yourself a nice kid. Let's go over to the Lady, and I'll buy you a drink."

"Kelly, I got a problem." Jakob went on to tell him about what the sheriff said about the murderer escaping. "Kelly, you've been here a long time. A lot longer than me. Did anything like this happen to you?"

"Yes, I had a few things happen to me when I first came to town. Had a guy try to kill me because his wife died. He said it was my fault. He came after me when I was playing cards. Lucky the sheriff was there. I did carry a gun after that. There were a few other times, and I had to use it one time. Then I had to take out the bullet for the bastard. This was one rough town in those days. Mostly hard drinking, women, and gambling were the causes. But your guy doesn't sound like he'd come here if he was up in Fargo. Get yourself a gun and keep it concealed. I wouldn't worry if I were you."

"Easy for you to say, Kelly. You don't have a family."

"I know. I know. You're smart. But I don't think that guy would come back where he's known. The sheriff and police are pretty good here. You know that. Worrying won't help but get yourself a piece you can keep concealed, okay?"

They entered the Lucky Lady, which was already filled with people. Jakob remembered how Liz didn't like it, but it wasn't a bad place. Lots of friends used to stop by and talk.

Businessmen and even the mayor were the regulars. It was not a rundown mill of drunks, loose women, and toughs. The Lucky Lady was a clean place where you could have a card game without a gunfight.

"Hi, gents. What'll you have?" Andy said as he sat a bottle and glasses in front of them. "Doc, Harry tells me you had a great party over in the Inn. Lots of people showed up to see your son. He said he had a great time playing the concertina for your friends. Sorry I couldn't make it."

Kelly couldn't wait to get his two cents in. "It's his wife that knows how to throw the party."

Everyone laughed as Jakob gave his views. "Kelly, you old dog; you always cut me down. When are you going to throw a party for all of us?"

They all chimed in as Doc Kelly made his excuses.

It was getting close to dinner, and Jakob excused himself, but Kelley had to have the last word. "Too bad you have to go home, Jake. I can stay here as long as I want. I don't have to go back and see the missus. I'm free as a bird."

Jakob laughed. "Kelly, you're right. Nobody wants an old buzzard like you."

With everybody laughing, Jakob left for home.

The sojourn at the Lady got him over the initial fright he had faced, and he looked forward to seeing the baby and Geraldine and BethAnn. What a lucky guy he was to have them. He put the horse in the barn. Little Henry would take care of him for the night.

As Jakob opened the door to the house, the first to greet him was Skippy, who immediately jumped up. The rest of the family followed with their greetings. Geraldine was nursing the baby as he sat next to her.

After she finished, she handed the baby to Jakob and left for the bedroom with Wanda. BethAnn sat with Jakob and told him about her day while they waited for Geraldine to come back. When she did, she had changed her clothes, and her hair was set by Wanda. She looked great.

Chucha had glasses of wine on the table for dinner. They sat down, and Jakob got a full report on the baby's day.

BethAnn had an observation that she shared with them. "Daddy said someday Randy might take care of me. I think it might be a long time from now."

That made them all laugh.

After their dinner, the family sat by the fireplace talking about Randy's gifts and the party. BethAnn left, and Jakob was alone with Geraldine.

The talk Jakob had with the sheriff clouded his thoughts. He decided not to bring it up before they went to sleep. But he reached into his nightstand and pulled out his gun. Skippy would make plenty of noise if anyone tried to break in, and Jakob would be ready.

Geraldine saw it. "Why do you have your gun out?" she asked.

"Oh, I was just looking at it," he said as he cuddled up to her. "Good night."

Jakob continued to think about what the sheriff said. He tried to fix his thoughts on the idea that there was nothing to worry about and that the murderer would not return to Sheridan. It took a while before sleep came.

He was up when the baby cried and changed his diaper. He awakened again when Geraldine nursed the baby but quickly fell back asleep. It was a tough night when Skippy awakened him at daybreak. The next months would be the same.

Jakob stopped by to see the gunsmith. He settled on a revolver he could wear under his dental coat. He still hadn't told Geraldine about what the sheriff had told him because he didn't want to frighten her but realized he needed to do so. She would eventually discover him wearing the gun.

After dinner, they talked about their futures. Geraldine said she had called her mother. There was now the underwater telephone cable from the United States to England. She told her about the baby and the baptism. Her mother knew she was pregnant, but the mails were slow, so she made the cable call.

Lady Mary was thrilled to learn about her grandson. He was the first grandchild. She said she hoped she might visit the United States and see him. Sir Gerald had passed away, and she lived the life of a widow. Randy, her son, was now the Baron of Landry Manor and managed the manor quite well. He was married but without children. His sister was also married and living in London. Her husband had been divorced. That fact provided a breach in the family because such a thing was looked at as wrong. Lady Mary said she spent much of her time with the Child Welfare organization and was quite enthusiastic about it. She remembered how Jakob encouraged her efforts and told Geraldine to give him a kiss and hug for his kindness. She said the organization and its goals gave her a reason for living.

"Jakob, I miss my mama," Geraldine said. "I wish I could see her. My papa passed away, and I was unable to go to his services. Mama said she would like to visit us, but I wonder if she would be able to make the trip. She is quite old now. Maybe when Randy gets a little older, we can make the trip to my home. I would like BethAnn to see her too. Mama would be thrilled to see her grandchildren."

Jakob nodded in agreement. "That would be nice, and it would be a great experience for BethAnn." They talked in terms of the future when Randy could travel.

Jakob still had difficulty bringing up the rustler but decided he must do so. "Geraldine, something has come up that you must be aware of." He told her about the meeting with the sheriff, who advised him to carry a gun for protection.

"I wondered why you brought it out of your nightstand. I'm aware most of the men in Sheridan carry a gun. If you're concerned, then you should do so. I vividly remember that brute. Hopefully, he will be apprehended. Maybe I should go out with you and do some target practice too. You know, I did hunt birds with my papa, and I was a pretty good shot. Papa wanted a boy, and sometimes he forgot I was a girl."

"That's right. I guess I know you did hunt birds, and you even did some trap shooting. Well, sure, we can go out and practice, but you will have to learn how to handle a six-gun." He was surprised that she took to the idea of weaponry as well as she did.

Jakob took Geraldine out on the prairie, and they did some target shooting. It took her a while to get a handle on shooting the pistol. He wondered if he should buy her a gun but decided against it. He thought about her friends in the Women's Club; and how they might react if she were to carry a weapon. Then one day, he talked with one of the old timers in the Lucky Lady, who told him about how his wife took on a couple of thieves who tried to steal her purse.

"Hope, she don't get mad at me cuz she can shoot straighter than me."

Jakob related the story to Geraldine, and she laughed.

"What's so funny?" asked Jakob.

She continued to laugh. "You don't know Betsy Franks. She is about eighty and weighs about the same. She's the sweetest thing you ever saw.

I can't believe she could gun down a couple of toughs."

Jakob continued to carry a gun when he left the house. It was concealed, and most never knew it. He became used to the idea and soon forgot about it. He might have to face the murderer and would be prepared. He saw the sheriff on a couple of occasions and learned the murderer was still free.

Baby Randy was starting to recognize those around him. He was making noises and using his arms and legs coordinated. BethAnn came home from school and usually went straight to the nursery. She talked and played with him. Each day it was something new, and Jakob got a report on his progress.

Winter arrived in Sheridan. That meant cold with wind and snow. It also meant social season, and Jakob's practice would slow down. It didn't bother him because he had more time to spend with his family. The social season also spurred dinners and parties. The excitement of Christmas brought exchanges of gifts and the big Findlay Party on Christmas Day with many of their friends.

It was Christmas Eve, with temperatures in the teens and blowing snow. Jakob had taken care of an emergency patient with a toothache. He was leaving for home when Kelly and an old man pushed into his office.

"Boy, am I glad I caught you. I just came from the hospital. This is Captain Abraham Howard, and he has a problem only you can take care of."

Jakob saw a very old man whose stature was short and bent. His face was wrinkled—what you could see of his face—because he had a large mustache and beard. The right side of his face was swollen and red, and his eye was almost closed. An old blue military cap was pulled over his head. His hair stuck out from under it, and his ears protruded. He wore a tattered blue military coat that covered his hunched body.

"Captain Howard is a Civil War army veteran, Jakob. In the war, he was shot up bad, and I came on him bleeding and moaning. It was in the battle of Little Big Top. That's where I first saw him in a tent with fifteen, no at least twenty-five others. He was covered with mud and blood. They thought he was dead. The orderly with me started to clean him up and looked for his identification so that he could be buried when he started to moan. I started putting him back together again. I had to take his hand off because the bones were crushed. The orderly bandaged him while I took care of a dozen more men—or maybe it was thirty. I don't remember how many. When I came back to him twenty or thirty hours later, he was still alive. Others weren't. I followed his recovery some days later and found him sitting on the bed. He thanked me for saving his life. He now had pneumonia, and I didn't think he'd make it. This guy had two miracles in his life. Some years ago, I found him working on the railroad. His leg got smashed, and I had to take it off. They put a wooden peg on it. Jake, we have to keep him alive. Look in his mouth. It's no wonder he's emaciated."

Jakob looked into his mouth. He had a large abscess on the right side and a bunch of rotted teeth. "Kelly, I'll open the abscess for now so it can be drained, and I'll take the tooth out in a couple of days. And then, we'll go from there."

"Okay, he's yours. He's got no money. I'll take him back to the hospital. I don't know where he's living. Poor guy is old and a vet. I take care of the Civil War vets every now and then. You know, we have some here in Sheridan."

Jakob took care of the abscess.

Kelly, talking loudly in his ear, explained what was happening. He then put on his coat. "Jake, you want me to bring him back, or will you see him in the hospital?"

"No problem, I'll see him in the hospital. Just have them put on some cold packs for the swelling. And feed the poor guy with a soft diet. He sure can't chew his food."

Kelly left with the vet.

Jakob cleaned up and sterilized his instruments. As he opened the door, the cold wind blasted his face and blew snow around. His horse moved slowly as they headed home. He couldn't help but think about the old soldier he had treated and Kelly, who took him under his wing. Few people knew the good things he had done for people in Sheridan. He seldom talked about his battlefield experiences. It must have been terrible. *A body covered with mud, bleeding; a hand shattered.*

He opened the door to the barn and led the shivering horse in, dried him, fed and watered, placed fresh straw, and blanketed the horse. Leaving the barn, he trudged through the wind-fed snow to the house. He could hear Skippy barking as he opened the door to the warmth. Geraldine and BethAnn greeted him and helped him take off his heavy coat.

"Honey, where have you been? We've been so worried about you. You said you had a patient to take care of, but I didn't think it would take so long." She hugged and kissed him and held his body tight. Her warm body felt good.

Chucha gave him a hot cup of coffee after he sat down to remove his boots. They moved to the fireplace and sat with him. BethAnn sat on the floor, Skippy next to her.

"After I finished with my patient, Kelly came in with one of the old Civil War vets." He described the man and the empathy he had for him. "I thought about myself and all I have, and I just couldn't help doing all I could for the poor soul.

"Then Kelly finally took him back to the hospital. He handled him like he was his father. I always knew Kelly was a good person. We josh each other, but today I saw something that I just can't get over. Today is Christmas Eve. I hope Kelly won't be alone. Maybe he'll spend it with his lady friend. He doesn't talk much about her. I know he can't have the happiness we have, but I hope he is with someone who loves him."

Chucha came in holding two toddies. "I have something to warm you." Handing each of the parents one, she looked at BethAnn. "You come to kitchen. I have one for you too, BethAnn. Later we start *Wegilia*, like my family in Acme. You my family too." Chucha smiled

Randy, who wasn't present, let it be known that he wished to be a part of the group, and BethAnn went in to get him.

Chapter 19
Helping Civil War Veterans

Jakob stopped at the hospital to see the Civil War veteran Kelly referred to him. He found him sitting up in a chair and looked much better than when he had seen him on Christmas Eve. The swelling was down, and he seemed more alert.

"Good morning, Captain. How are you feeling today?"

"Pretty good, Doc. You don't have to call me captain. Gosh, that was lots of years ago! You know, my mind sometimes plays tricks on me, but this I remember. I didn't think I'd make it through that day, and what's more, I didn't even care if I did. I was behind a bunker with my company. I had thirty men with me. The Rebs were shelling us, and one hit our bunker. All I could feel was the pain over my whole body. I could hear my men screaming and, one by one, the screaming stopped, and then it was all quiet, except for the shelling nearby and far. I hurt so much, but all I could do was moan. I heard voices come toward me and then go away.

"One said, 'Oh, they're all dead.' I wanted to say, 'I'm not dead, I'm not dead,' but I couldn't speak. And they went away, and I couldn't hear the voices anymore. But then I heard more voices, but they were far away. Then, then I heard voices real close, and I tried to scream but I couldn't. Then I heard a voice say, 'Did he move? That one over there.' 'Look,' another voice said, 'Check him out. No, he's still now.' The first voice said, 'Check him out anyway.'

"I felt a hand on my shoulder which turned me over, and I could see him look at me, and he brushed the mud off my face, and he put his hand on my neck. I tried to talk, but all I could do was moan. Then I heard him yell. 'This one's still alive!' and another came to me. I still can remember his face. He was called Kelly. That's what they called him, 'Kelly.'

"Then two guys picked me up and put me on a litter. I don't remember; must have passed out because the next thing I know is I was in a big tent, and I was hurtin' real bad. There was a lot of screaming, loud talking, and I guess I did some too and, and I must have passed out because when I woke up, Kelly was there.

"He said to me, 'Sorry, Captain. I had to take your hand off, but you're going to be all right. Just listen and do what the orderlies tell you.' He left, and I didn't see him till the day I was leaving the hospital. 'Going home Captain Howard?' he asked me.

"I nodded and thanked him for saving my life. Kelly shook my hand, my good hand. He smiled and wished me luck. Asked me if I had a wife to go home to. Then he moved on to another soldier. I didn't have a chance to tell him my wife was killed when the Rebs shelled our village.

"I started walking home. When I finally got there, there was no home. I still don't know how I got there or how long it took me. I'm talking too much."

Jakob really didn't know much about the Civil War, and the impact of the captain got to him. This old soldier's words were like an electric shock. "No, go ahead. Go ahead. I've got time."

The old man talked softly. Nurses had quietly walked into the room and listened as he described his life following the war.

"My wife, my baby, my home—all gone. My neighbors, my friends—all gone. I stayed in a barn which was barely standing. I dug up turnips and other roots and found mustard greens. I ate. I survived. Then I found a few of my neighbors. It must have been two weeks, no, a month. Oh, I don't know how long. We survived."

He stopped talking for a moment, then he broke the silence. "Go ahead, Doc. You got something you need to do."

Jakob took a mirror, opened his mouth, and filled out an examination form. One of the nurses who he had trained to assist had his instruments ready.

Kelly had come into the room as the old man talked and just silently listened. "What are you going to do, Jake?"

"Oh, Kelly, you're here."

Then to his patient, Jakob said, "Captain, we're going to fix you up. Today I'm going to take out the abscessed tooth that was hurting you so much. We will get you back later and take out the rest of the rotted roots and snags. There's nothing there I can save. I'm sorry. They're all infected, but I'm going to make a set of dentures for you so that you can eat, chew again, and you'll be able to smile at the ladies with teeth and be your old handsome best again. This won't hurt you because I will inject an anesthetic that will prevent it from hurting. Don't worry."

The nurse was preparing for the injection.

"You go ahead, Doc. I'm ready for you."

Jakob removed the offending tooth and instructed the nurse on how to take care of the patient.

"Kelly, will this gentleman be staying here so I can see him next week?"

"He'll be here for a couple of days, and then I got a place for him to stay after that with Mary Daniels until we can find him a regular place." They walked to the doctors' room. Several doctors were talking. One of them looked at Kelly.

"What are you guys doing here today?" asked one of them.

Kelly answered. "Jake, here, is taking care of that old vet they brought in on Christmas Eve. He was in a lot of pain. You know we got a lot of those guys in town. Most are in tough shape. We have to do something for them."

"What do you want us to do? They're old and won't last long," said one of the doctors.

Kelly just looked at him sternly. "You've never been on a battlefield with body parts, guts, and blood everywhere. Men screaming and dying in front of you, and you can't do anything for them or save them."

"I'm sorry, Kelly. No, I haven't. I know you did, and I got to give you credit for what you done. It must have been terrible. These guys that are left should be helped by our government, but they're not being helped. There's really not that many around."

"Maybe we can help them somehow," said another. "I'll bring it up at a staff meeting. Okay? Maybe we can help those that are left."

One by one, they left the room, and Kelly and Jakob did likewise.

"I'm going to stop by my office," said Jakob as he got on his horse. "See you later."

He stopped at his office. The door was snowed in, and he had to clear it away before he went in. It was too cold to stay around, and he had no other patients scheduled, so he left for home.

Walking into a warm kitchen, he found Chucha making soup. "I have cabbage soup with sausage ready for lunch. Lady, she with baby."

"Jakob, you're home early. Did you take care of the patient in the hospital?" said Geraldine.

He went on to tell her about his patient and the discussion they had with the other doctors.

"I hope they meant what they said and can come up with some kind of program to take care of those poor old men. I guess I never realized they were in such poor health."

"Most of them don't have anyone to help them. There aren't so many here, and we could do it if all the doctors would cooperate. They usually meet at the Grand Army of the Republic building once a month. They still remember and talk about the war and then end up playing cards. There's not much more they can do. Every year there are fewer marching in the Sheridan Parade or someone pushing them in wheelchairs. I never thought much about them until Kelly brought the captain in to see me. I'm sure Kelly will bring it up at the staff meeting. There's enough of us around, so each one would just have to take care of a few of them."

"Jakob, it would be a good idea. Money could also be raised for their needs if people were aware they're here. That Civil War must have been terrible. Some of the ladies in our Women's Club have fathers or grandfathers who were in it and are terribly disabled and sick. Maybe we can get the Women's Club involved."

"Geraldine, you know you're starting to talk like a Lady Mary I know," said Jakob, and he laughed.

"Yes, my mama would help us. But, she has her own thing to work on."

Jakob's patient did well, and he ended up removing the other diseased teeth. He would start making his dentures after the mouth was healed. The doctors met, and there was a general agreement they could take care of the veterans, and a program was being put together.

The cold Wyoming winter kept most people indoors. Geraldine and Jakob enjoyed watching Randy grow. Each day it was something new that he could do or showed a personality he was developing. Chucha was starting to make him special baby foods that he enjoyed. BethAnn would bring some of her friends in to see him, and she had special time she would dedicate to him. She was already talking about taking him outdoors in a buggy as soon as the weather got warm enough.

Geraldine was back with her Women's group. They talked about having a special dinner for the veterans on certain holidays. "We have to show them how much we appreciate what they have done for their country and that we haven't forgotten them," said Geraldine.

Jakob was in the Lucky Lady when the mayor came up to him. "Doc, that was a nice thing you did for that Civil War veteran. I heard about it from a couple different people. I'm always glad to hear about the good things that are done in town. Seems like all we ever hear about are the bad things that happen. Sheridan is a fine place to live. We are a family city. We have more churches here than cities bigger than we are. I plan on having a prayer breakfast and invite the business community to come to it along with the preachers. Be good for Sheridan. Church people are what gives our town strength. They are good citizens and build good communities. I'd like to do that in the summer.

"We've gotten bigger, and I see some bad elements in town. Most people got jobs, but we're getting some coming out from the east, and there are always some that don't do any good for our city. With all the trains coming through, there's an element that hitches rides. They end up camping out of town, drinking, fighting, and doping. I worry about the young people getting caught up with some of them."

"I'm with you, Mr. Mayor. We have to watch out that the young boys don't get involved with those hoboes. One of the things I was hoping to do is get our boys more involved in sports. It would be nice if we could have more baseball teams. When I was in high school, I used to play. It's a good sport, and I was thinking I could get the Elks Club to sponsor a league for the boys and maybe even help them. The city might have to build a ballpark. Be good, especially in the summer. What do you think?"

"That's the kind of thing I'd like to see done. I can take it up with the council at our next meeting."

"I'll bring it up with the Elks' secretary," said Jakob. "I would think they would jump on this. They're all for making the community better, and helping the kids is one way we can do it."

"Always good to talk to you, Doc. We're a growing city, and we have to be prepared for the growth. I see Kelly playing cards. I may just join them. We'll meet later."

Jakob decided to leave for home. It had been an easy day for him in the office. It would still be light for some time, and Geraldine asked Jakob to go riding with her. BethAnn was recruited to take care of her brother, which really excited her. The horses were saddled, and they went riding off toward Big Goose Creek. It was cold, but the ride was exhilarating. They stopped at the creek, which was mostly unfrozen. The trees were bare, and the hills still had traces of snow. The Bighorns in the background were covered with snow, but the foothills showed bare patches.

"Jakob, I guess winter is still here. I can't wait until spring really arrives. I feel I really need to get back to the ranch. It's been so long since we left. Eleanor sent me a letter with George when he came into town last week. She said all was well, but she does miss us. I'd like to take Randy with us when we do go and maybe BethAnn too. I can't wait for Randy to grow up. The ranch will be great for a little boy to see."

"It would also be nice for us to get back for a visit, but it may be a while for this landscape to warm up sufficiently. However, look at the sun now going behind the mountains. It paints a beautiful picture, but it also means that it's starting to go down, and maybe we should get along. Your little boy may be looking for some of his mother's milk, and I am feeling a nip on my nose."

They left Big Goose Creek, got home before the sun got fully behind the Bighorns, and entered their warm kitchen.

Chapter 20
A Tragedy in BethAnn's Life

Spring came early in 1910. The property Geraldine bought was readied so BethAnn could practice her horsemanship. There were a variety of jumps available. She was able to take the various jumps with her horse Jenny showing real skill. Geraldine was planning to have a dressage at the Sheridan Fair. She contacted several riding groups in the communities like Buffalo, Cody, Dayton, and even some as far away as Billings. She felt it would be good training for the young people whose skills were sharpened by the experiences. It was also good for Geraldine, who enjoyed working with young people.

Randy was growing and was a joy for the family. Wanda acted as a nanny for him when Geraldine was not around.

Jakob was busy with his practice, and many new things were happening around Sheridan. The city was growing and becoming more modern than the frontier town Jakob came to. Electric streetcars would soon be traversing the streets of Sheridan and even going to Buffalo and as far as the mining towns like Acme. It was expected they would go even further in the Goose Creek Valley. Streets were being paved, and so automobiles were becoming more popular. This presented some problems to those still using horses and buggies. Still, as time went on, most of the streets improved, and more and more automobiles came into existence in Sheridan. Geraldine and Jakob discussed the idea of buying a car. The paved roads helped traveling in the automobile and, of course, faster and more comfortable. It would make travel to the ranch much faster, although many of the roads still needed development. Jakob's involvement in local politics was becoming more prevalent. The mayor called on him frequently to support his agenda.

BethAnn had arrived from school and as usual went to Randy's room. He was awake and happy to see BethAnn. She took him out of his crib and put him on the floor to play with. He laughed and chattered and quickly turned over on to his fours. He was beginning to crawl and loved to see Skippy who was always nearby. He would reach for Skippy who would step back: then come up to him and lick him. This would make Randy laugh.

Skippy indicated he had need to go out so BethAnn took him to the kitchen door and left him out in the yard. Chucha had made a snack for BethAnn and brought it for her so while she played with Randy, she nibbled on her cookie. Randy was giggling and scurrying around. They were both having a great time. Geraldine was in her office doing her ranch work so when she heard BethAnn and Randy she came down to join them and added to the fun with Randy.

BethAnn could hear Skippy barking up a storm in the yard for some time. She got up and went to the back door to let him in.

"Why is he barking so much, BethAnn?" said Chucha.

"I don't know, but he's probably chasing a squirrel," said BethAnn, and she opened the door. Horrified, she saw her dog lying on the ground under the maple tree. He was not barking but thrashing and moaning in pain. She ran out the door, got to Skippy, and saw a large rattle snake slithering away. Poor Skippy was in terrible pain, looking at her as he moaned. She went to him and got on her knees and hugged and petted him. "What happened? Please, I love you." The snake was now gone. There was some blood on the dog's fur. Frightened, not knowing what to do, BethAnn left him and ran back to Geraldine and told her what had happened. When they got back to Skippy, he laid motionless, whimpering.

"What can we do?" screamed BethAnn.

Geraldine shrugged. "I don't know. He must have been bitten by the snake. I don't know what we can do to help the poor thing. See if Mr. Greeenway is home, and maybe he can help."

BethAnn went to their neighbor and told him what had happened. He came, but Skippy was not breathing. Mr. Greenway felt he was dead. BethAnn was frantically crying. Geraldine went back to the house and called Jakob at his office. He said he would come home but felt it was too late to help Skippy.

Both Geraldine and BethAnn were frantic. BethAnn's eyes were red with tears, and she sobbed when Jakob arrived. Poor Skippy had no pulse. Jakob took BethAnn in his arms and held her. He tried to abate her sorrow, but she continued to sob uncontrollably. They left Skippy lying on the ground and went into the house, all of them in different degrees of grief.

When they told Chucha, tears came to her eyes. Jakob held his daughter, who just lost her dear friend until she was exhausted and fell asleep in his arms. Skippy had been her dog. She cared for him and loved him. He followed her wherever she went and sat by her as she played the piano. He would follow her when she left the barn with Nelly. But Skippy was also everyone's dog, including Randy's, who he watched with loving eyes.

Jakob remembered Skippy as the ball of fur the Indians had given him. He wasn't sure he wanted to keep him but gave him to Liz, who fell in love with him and cared for him during her lifetime. When she died, Skippy mourned her with the rest.

Jakob had Mr. Smith, the casket maker, do a casket for Skippy, and they tenderly placed him in it and buried him beneath the maple tree where he had died. Flowers were placed on his grave, and Jakob made a plaque with his name. BethAnn wrote a eulogy which she read.

Poor BethAnn was so forlorn for her Skippy. She couldn't say his name without crying. At first, she didn't want to play the piano or even go to school. She stayed in the barn with Nelly, telling her how she missed Skippy. She and Geraldine would sometimes ride down by Goose Creek and watch the birds and talk.

"Jakob, I've been thinking, maybe we should go out to the ranch for a few weeks. Maybe that would help with healing her sorrow. Poor child, she has a hard time accepting his loss. I'm sure she's too young to understand." They both agreed, and they made plans for the trek.

Father John Binotti came by one day to see BethAnn. He told her, "Skippy was a gift from God to you, but gifts aren't necessarily forever. Nothing is forever, BethAnn, and you knew he would have to leave you someday. We didn't know when. You have learned to love one of God's creatures, and that was good. Your life will be better having that love. Skippy knew you loved him, so you made him happy. Now, we all have to go on living without him. And, the day will come when maybe another Skippy will come into your life."

Time did heal her wounds, and she talked of maybe getting another dog in her life. Maybe even a cat like the one Geraldine had at the ranch.

They planned on going to the ranch when school was out. Jakob was very busy with his practice, and the mayor was leaning on him as much was happening in Sheridan. And then there was the fair coming up in July.

He was finishing his day and getting ready to leave when Ralph Hofer came in. He hadn't seen Ralph for several years. Ralph was one of the sheep herders—tall, muscular, and handsome. Long graying hair and a booming voice were characteristic of Ralph. A beautiful large Australian shepherd always accompanied him.

"We haven't been together for a long time, Doc. I guess I've been neglecting my teeth, but we sheep headers aren't treated too nice here. In fact, the last time I was here, one of your cow men told me he would have me hung if I came back. I don't know if he really meant it, but it wasn't very nice of him. There's enough room for the both of us, but the cow men don't think so. Hope you don't mind me coming to see you, but I need to see you and like dealing with you. We sheep herders have been doing well in spite of the hardnosed bastards in the cowmen's organization. So can I sit in your chair? I need your help."

"Sure, Ralph. Of course I'll take care of you. Sit down." Jakob looked in his mouth and checked his dentition. "Well, you don't look as bad as I thought you might. I can fix you up in a couple of visits. Where are you staying? Close by? Or do you have to travel a ways?"

"No, my wife's uncle has a place not too far out of town. So I can stay with him while you do your work. I won't show myself around town much. Say, how's your family doing? Last time I saw you, I heard you were waiting for your English lady to come back so you could marry her. I assume she got back, and you married her. Right, Doc?"

"Yes, she got back, and we're married, and I now have a son. She has a ranch northwest of here and raises special horses and some cattle. We're not part of the big cattle organization. We live in town, and her sister and husband pretty much run the ranch. We'll be going back in a couple of weeks for a short stay, so we'll have to get on your problem right away. You remember my daughter BethAnn, don't you.?"

"Sure, Doc, sweet kid. Real cute."

"Well, she's really grown and rides horses and plays the piano. Anyway, we had a tragedy. A dog she just loved and cared for was bitten by a rattler and died. The loss of the dog broke her heart. We didn't know what to do, so we thought we'd take her to the ranch and get her mind off the unfortunate incident."

"That's too bad. Hard for a kid to take something like that. Why don't you get her another dog? That would get her mind off the dead dog," said Ralph.

"We thought of that and will probably do so once I find one for her."

"Hey Doc, I got a deal for you. Duke here was a stud for a beautiful bitch that I have. She gave me six pups that'll make beautiful dogs—Aussie shepherd—three boys and three girls. One of them would make a good dog for your daughter. They're smart and loyal and tough. Make good work dogs. No snake could take one of them. They'll be ready to leave the mother in about a month. We can fix a female for you not to have pups. Got one that's black with some white. I'm not selling, Doc. It would be a present from me for your daughter. Be ready for you in about a month."

"Gosh, Ralph, that would be great. I'll take you up on that."

"The female won't be anywhere near as big old Duke here. He's the daddy."

Jakob left for home excited with his patient's offer of a dog for BethAnn. This will be perfect for her. And it's a good dog for her to raise, but I better wait before telling her. He said the dog wouldn't be weaned for a month. If I tell her now, she will be excited and anxious to get it, and a month is a long time for a kid.

Chapter 21
BethAnn Meets Princess

Arriving home, Jakob was greeted by the family. BethAnn, though resigned to Skippy's loss, was not her enthusiastic self. All tried to be as positive as they could, but she just moped along.

"Did Harry come by for your piano lesson today?" Jakob asked.

"He was here, and we worked on a new piece, but I don't like it."

"Why don't you like it? You've never said you didn't like a piece before."

"I don't know. It's just... I don't know. It's not that nice a melody."

"Maybe you'll get to like it better when you learn it well," said Jakob. He recognized that BethAnn had lost her zest, so he talked about his day's experiences.

"I don't know if you remember, but I had an interesting sheepherder for a patient some time ago. He left the area, and I hadn't seen him for a long time. He came in to see me today. Ralph has some dental problems, and he asked me to take care of him. He said he hadn't been around because of problems he had with some of the cattlemen here. I wish the cattlemen could resolve their differences with the sheepherders. There's enough room for both."

The conversation was not too lively. After dinner ended, Chucha asked BethAnn to help her with the dishes before she went up to do her homework. She agreed, and Jakob and Geraldine left the table.

"I think we have to just let her cry herself out," said Geraldine. "I'm sure she will get over it. Let's go out to the ranch, and she'll have time to get over her grief."

"I agree," said Jakob. He went on to tell her about the dog Ralph Hofer would have for her. "It is from a very good breed—Australian Shepherd."

"Oh, that would be perfect! She could help it grow up. Taking care of a puppy can be a full-time job. And, it's an Australian shepherd, which is a fine breed. That will be great for her. She will really mother the pup. I can't wait till she gets it, but I don't think we should tell her just yet because she'll fret just waiting. Do you think we can leave next week? BethAnn will be out of school."

"That would be fine. By the way, where's Randy? I haven't seen him. We forgot all about him."

"Oh, he was cranky today," said Geraldine. "I wonder if he's starting to get some teeth. I hope he's not coming down with something, but he wasn't himself, so I fed him and put him down, and he's been asleep for a couple of hours. Should we wake him? A little noise will wake him up. You know, I think he misses Skippy, too," said Geraldine.

Just about then, Randy did wake up and settle the issue. Geraldine picked him up and brought him out to Jakob, whom he relished being with, and it started playtime for him. Jakob opened his little mouth and discovered he had several teeth that were erupting.

"That could be the problem," Jakob said. "The erupting of teeth cause inflammation, and that makes a kid cranky. Oops! He didn't like me putting my fingers in his mouth, even after I told him I was a dentist, but I guess it didn't impress him."

Chucha came out with a cookie and gave it to him to suck on. She laughed. "See, Pon Doc. Randy. He liked that."

"Wanda has been taking care of him most of the day, and he has become quite attached to her," Geraldine added.

Jakob wasn't sure he liked it, but using a nanny was the English way of raising children. Geraldine felt that it was acceptable, and she had her Women's Club, which she was now active in. She was especially fond of the library, which was now in use. The Women's Club was also planning a dinner for the Civil War vets at the G.A.R. Hall. The Women's Club took on the veterans as a special project.

"One of our ladies had a father who was a veteran of that war, and she is spearheading the project," said Geraldine. "Oh, before I forget to tell you, Raymond will be coming in this weekend. If it works out with you, we can go back with him to the ranch. However, we do have to bring a bed with us for Randy. He's too spunky if we don't have a bed for him to sleep in. We can take the one you made for him. That will keep him confined and safe."

Early on Monday, the wagon was filled to capacity with the Millers and the supplies Raymond picked up. They left at daybreak on what would be a clear sunny day. The thought of stopping at the Homerdings was brought up, but then they thought not. Randy wasn't taking the trip too well. There wasn't any room for him to move around, so he fussed.

They thought it better to get to their destination as soon as possible.

After a long day's travel, it was good to see the ranch coming up over the last hill. BethAnn seemed anxious to get there. Geraldine told her she would be riding one of the bigger horses now. She had asked to take Nelly, but when Geraldine mentioned a bigger mare, that was enough to get BethAnn excited.

They arrived with a lot of fanfare. Everyone was happy to see them, and there were a lot of shouts and waves. In the corral, the men were branding calves which interested BethAnn, and she immediately left to join them.

"Jakob, we should have done this sooner. BethAnn is really excited with the goings-on."

Allen and Eleanor were especially happy to see them. It had been a long time since Geraldine's last visit. After Randy was born, she refused to leave him until she could take him with them.

Little Deer made them tea and crumpets, and they settled down in the house. Randy had a lot of room to explore as he walked, stumbled, and crawled from one end of the dining room to the other.

"Where's BethAnn?" asked Eleanor.

"Oh, she went over to the corral to watch them brand calves. I guess she's excited to be here." Geraldine told her about the loss of Skippy and how she mourned for the dog. "I believe this may be the anecdote for her grieving."

In the meantime, Randy found Prince, who wasn't quite sure what to think. Prince had never seen a toddler before, and Randy had not seen a cat.

There was small talk and some news Eleanor had gotten from England. Allen seemed to fit into ranching and gave Geraldine some of the information and happenings.

"I'm going out to find BethAnn," said Jakob. "She's been gone a long time." From the porch, Jakob could see the corral with BethAnn seated on the top rung of the fence. Several of the hands were talking with her, and a dog was sitting next to her.

"BethAnn, I've been looking for you," he said as he approached.

"Oh Daddy, I've been watching them rope the calves and then brand them. Slim, here, is going to teach me how to rope, aren't you, Slim? Slim, this is my Daddy."

"Howdy Doc, if it's all right with you, I'll teach your daughter how to rope. My name is Slim. We met before. Remember?"

"Of course I remember, and I think it's a good idea."

Slim grinned a smile with a missing front tooth. He was one of the cowboys, thin, tanned, muscular, and taller than Jakob's six-two. Jakob could see the excitement in BethAnn, which made him happy.

"Daddy, did you see his dog? This is Rover. He's his friend."

Jakob saw a rather non-descript pooch about knee-high, brown with a patch of white on his chest and a tail that wagged constantly. The dog looked up at him, and Jakob said, "I'm pleased to meet you, Rover."

The dog startled Jakob when he barked a big woof, and Jakob laughed. "Why don't you come back to the house now, BethAnn? You haven't even come inside to say hello, and you can get together with your new friends tomorrow."

BethAnn smiled at Slim, told him she would see him tomorrow and left with her daddy. In the ranch house, there was much activity. Randy was still trying to catch Prince, who managed to stay ahead of him.

"BethAnn, you can stay in the bedroom you used before. That's your room," said Geraldine.

Little Deer and Maria worked in the kitchen. Jakob picked up Randy, and they went into their room. Geraldine sat on their bed, and Jakob sat next to her. They laid back on the bed, kissing and petting until Randy made it known he wanted some attention. When they ignored him, he punctuated it by crying a real protest.

"Oh, Jakob, he wants more than attention. He wants his mommy's milk. Please get him and hand him to me," she asked as she started to expose her breast. "He's hungry after that long ride."

Soon, Randy was satiated after his long drink and fell asleep.

"No nap for us until I get his bed put together," said Jakob. He finished putting the crib together and dozed off for a bit. He awoke to a tap tap tap on the bedroom door.

"It's me, Daddy. Can I come in.?"

"Sure, come in."

BethAnn had already dressed for dinner.

Geraldine laughed. "You must be hungry, and we just awakened from our nap. Oh, and you wore that dress for dinner. I like it. Take Randy with you and go down. We'll be down shortly. Oh, and check Randy: he may need to be changed."

Jakob got dressed and left Geraldine to finish up.

A late afternoon breeze blew the curtains in. It was comfortable, and the sun started heading down. Eleanor and Allen were sitting in the living room with its fireplace across one wall. They had their cocktails and were chatting when Jakob walked in. BethAnn sat near the fireplace on the rug with Randy. Prince sat nearby, watching them. BethAnn talked to him, but he remained aloof and just watched them, even though BethAnn tried to coax him over.

"Jakob it's so nice to see you folks here. Can I make you a martini?" asked Allen. "I know you like them, and I copied your formula. We've been anxiously awaiting your arrival. It's been so long since we've seen you."

"I know we've wanted to get here some time ago, but with Randy now, we had to wait for him to grow a little before we could take him. A little baby is so fragile. And don't bother. I'll make the martinis." As Jakob finished the cocktails, Geraldine arrived.

"Geraldine, your Randy is such a delight. We're trying to figure out who he looks like. I guess it's both of you. Allen and I now realize what we are missing. You're very fortunate," said Eleanor. "Incidentally, George said he will be meeting with you tomorrow morning. Everything has been doing well. Just the everyday problems, and the men have been doing quite well too. There are some things, but George will take them up with you."

"Mother, I don't think Prince likes Randy. He won't come near him," said BethAnn.

"Oh, he'll like him after he gets used to him."

The rest of the evening went well. Little Deer made a special dinner of steak, baked potatoes, and root vegetables. Allen and Eleanor were happy to have Geraldine's family here. BethAnn talked about all the things she wanted to do. She was now anxious to learn how to rope calves. It wasn't much later, and they turned in after a long day.

Randy dictated when they should get up. He got up when old Barney, the rooster, made his appearance. Geraldine wasn't ready to serve him his breakfast, but Randy was hungry. So he was satisfied after she provided him with it. He was still being nursed but had other side dishes when she wasn't around. They still weren't ready to get up, but Randy also wanted to be entertained.

"Jakob, do you think Randy will ever fit into our schedule?"

Jakob laughed. "Why don't you ask him?"

"I should have known I'd get that kind of answer." And then she rolled over and kissed him. "It's nice being here. I've missed the ranch. I like being in town, but the ranch is something special. I can't wait till I get out with BethAnn and the mare I have in mind for her. She was so excited when I told her what I wanted to do. Now that she's bigger, she should be able to handle a horse that's bigger than Nelly. She's fifteen going on sixteen now."

"Yes, I know, and I don't like the way the Schroder boy looks at her."

"Oh Jakob, she's not interested in boys yet. She just loves horses. That will keep her mind occupied and keep her busy. I wasn't interested in boys till I went away to school, and even then, I had other things to keep me occupied. I liked to tag along with my papa, and sometimes I think he didn't even know or care if I was there."

"Poor girl."

"No, I really mean it. You should have seen some of the goofs who came by. My parents were concerned, but I rejected some of the ones who came from prominent families. I was the oldest of three sisters, and my parents were afraid I would become an old maid. Then they would have to take care of me for the rest of my life. Then James came along, and he did have some substance and was handsome. He was considerably older than me but very kind. I think I loved him, but our romance melted away, and our marriage just existed until he passed away. I decided to make the ranch my life. Papa wanted me to come back to Landry Manor. Then we met at the Sheridan Inn that day, and you came into my life. Oh, Jakob, I love you so."

Jakob held her close to him and kissed her. "I love you too, and we were made for each other. You've made my life take on a new meaning."

The tender moment of Jakob and Geraldine ended with a rousing sign of indignation by Randy.

Geraldine got up and went to Randy and picked him up. "Randy, how could you do this to us? I love your daddy, and you prevented me from kissing and hugging him."

Randy giggled and laughed.

"You don't really care, do you?"

There was a knock on the door. "Are you up yet? Can I come in?"

Jakob laughed. "Sure, why not join your family?"

BethAnn came in. She was already dressed in jeans and a red blouse with a blue bandana around her neck. Her hair was in a ponytail. "I just wanted to know if you were up. I'll go down and see you at breakfast. Slim is going to teach me how to rope today; remember. Bye." She skipped off.

"Well, that was fast. I've never seen her get up this early in Sheridan," said Geraldine.

"No, and isn't she a delight? I'm glad we brought her here. It's gotten her mind off the loss of Skippy. When we get back, she'll get the pup, and she'll be able to take up where she left off. I guess we better get up. Do you want me to take your son, or will you do that? He seems to be happy with you right now."

Little Deer had a ranch breakfast for the group, and it wasn't too much later when George, the foreman, came in to confer with the boss. BethAnn then went out to learn how to rope calves.

Jakob and Allen took their coffee on the porch to talk. Allen had pretty much taken over the operation of the ranch and liked it. He felt comfortable working with the hands. This made Jakob happy because it would take a great deal of the responsibility off the shoulders of Geraldine.

They chatted, and then there was a ruckus from the area of the corrals. Soon they saw a steer running freely up toward the ranch house and several men chasing it. Slim was at the head of the bunch with his rope twirling in the air and landing over the steer. His heels dug in, with the steer pulling till it slowed to a stop. Slim laid back at a 45-degree angle, puffing and holding the steer until two others put ropes on the animal. And then, there was BethAnn running up and swinging a lariat. Jakob and Allen roared with laughter at BethAnn, who ran from the corral, lasso in hand, toward the steer, who was moving its head back and forth and bellowing. The men started leading the steer back.

"BethAnn, were you going to try to rope that steer?" asked Jakob.

"Oh, no, Daddy. I knew Slim would get him. I don't think I could hold him, but you should see me work on the dummy calf. Slim has taught me how to approach and throw the rope. I missed lots of times but got it twice."

Slim, still puffing, said, "She sure is a good learner. A little more practice, and we may be able to hire her on as a hand."

BethAnn looked at Slim, smiling. "Slim, you must be kidding me."

"No, Ma'am. I don't kid. I mean it." Looking at Jakob he winked. Allen looked on and grinned as they started to walk back to the ranch.

"Why don't you come back to the ranch now?" Jakob said to BethAnn. "Your mother must be through with George and may be looking for you."

Geraldine had finished the meeting with George, who brought her up to date on the ranch. He felt that they had not lost any steers to theft. Since the thieves were caught, they experienced no more losses. Several steers didn't make it through the winter. He talked about the horses they obtained from a crew that brought them from Idaho. They were in the pasture, and they would be brought in as needed. The number of sales had slowed down. They were still waiting for a buyer from England.

Lunch was served on the veranda, and BethAnn talked about her lesson in roping with Slim. She enjoyed it and said she would practice until she was skillful. She never realized how hard it would be, but she felt she could learn it.

"BethAnn, let's go down to the horse stalls, and you can get acquainted with your mare," Geraldine suggested. "She has been named Princess. Her father was Sir Richard. She's a beautiful animal, and I think you'll love her, but you will have to get acquainted with her first. Let's go see her."

BethAnn was ready. She had her new riding boots on and was dressed to meet the Princess. She and Geraldine walked to the main stables, which had twenty stalls. One of the men brought up the horses. When they entered, the horses became aware they were there and neighed and stomped.

Geraldine stopped in the middle of the stable, and one came to the door. "BethAnn, this is Princess. Isn't she pretty?"

BethAnn put her hand up to touch her, and she reared back. Geraldine gave BethAnn an apple which she offered the horse. She slowly came forward and gently took it. BethAnn then touched her forehead, and she petted Princess as she munched on the apple. She softly talked to her and continued the petting. When she stopped, the mare continued forward and put its head out the door.

Geraldine joined in. Finally, she said, "Let's go in," and opened the door.

The horse stepped back as they entered the stall. Mother and daughter petted the horse as BethAnn did most of the talking. She was grinning as Princess responded to her. Geraldine attached the bridle and gave it to BethAnn.

"Let's take her outside," she said as BethAnn led Princess out of the stable. She led her some distance and turned around to go back. Princess behaved and was cooperative.

"We'll go back to the stable, and that will be all for today. I've got another apple you can give her."

BethAnn gave the apple to the mare, and as she munched it, petted her and said goodbye. The horse followed her to the door as she closed it. She put her head down to let BethAnn hug it.

"Well, BethAnn, that was your introduction to Princess. I think she likes you and was attracted to you. I bet next time you can get on her.

She has been ridden by several of the men, and they tell me she is very cooperative. We'll see tomorrow."

After dinner, several of the men came over and serenaded the boss lady. They all sat on the porch as the men played their instruments—a guitar, fiddle, harmonica, and concertina. They played, sang, and talked to Geraldine and the others.

As they left, Geraldine said, "That was very nice of you to come by. We enjoyed it. Maybe you can do this another time. I do appreciate the kindness."

Maria brought BethAnn a biscuit and milk before she went to bed. They then all turned in.

Barney performed as the alarm clock again, and Randy was demanding his right to breakfast with his mother. Jakob tried to keep the sounds of the suckling from disturbing him, but Randy didn't care.

"Do you want to change your son's diaper, Father? I did my end of the bargain. His tummy is filled for now." Jakob was quietly snoring. "You heard me. Don't ignore the inevitable."

Jakob put his head up, grinning. "Looks like you win. Hand him over to me." Changing him, he put Randy back in his bed and hoped to get a little more sleep. As he laid down, Geraldine rolled over, cuddled next to him, and they fell asleep.

Tap tap tap… tap tap tap. Jakob's eyes opened, and he realized someone was at the door. BethAnn.

"Daddy, are you up yet? Can I come in?"

"Yes, we are up now, and you may come in," said Jakob.

Geraldine has also awakened and was irritated. "BethAnn, you really shouldn't check on us to see if we are up."

"Oh, okay. I didn't mean to bother you. If Randy is up, I can take him down and play with him until you come down." She picked up Randy and left.

By now, there was no going back to sleep, and so they appeared for breakfast. Geraldine would meet with George again and told BethAnn they would visit the horse again later in the morning.

BethAnn took her lariat with her to the corral to practice her roping, and Jakob and Allen sat on the porch having their coffee. Allen talked more about his experiences with the ranch and brought up the subject of whether they should become a dude ranch. They saw it could be a new form of revenue, but it would mean a complete change of operation, and he wasn't sure they should do that. They could take on a few customers because there was a guest house, but adding to that meant they had to build more homes and hire more people to take care of the guests. Getting the right staff would be important. He felt the idea would have to be approached very carefully. Jakob was impressed with Allen's thinking. He could see a drastic change in him since they last met.

BethAnn returned, frustrated with her roping. "I just don't know what I'm doing wrong."

Geraldine returned from her meeting with George and turned to BethAnn.

"Shall we go and see how Princess is doing?"

BethAnn's frustration immediately disappeared, and she hugged Geraldine.

"I'm ready when you are. Wait, Geraldine! I should get an apple for her, shouldn't I?"

"That might be a good idea. Go get one from Little Deer."

She ran back and returned with an apple for Princess. As they walked into the stable, the horses reacted to their presence, and they saw Princess at the door. She put her head down to let BethAnn pet it, and then the girl gave the apple to her. BethAnn stroked the neck and top of the head. They opened the gate and took the reins, and she led the mare out of the barn. They walked her a short distance and came back. One of the men came out and put a blanket and saddle on her and gave the reins to BethAnn. BethAnn looked at Geraldine, who nodded a go-ahead. She petted the neck and over the foreleg. Holding the reins, she grasped the saddle horn and put a foot in the stirrup. The horse moved, and she moved with it. Then she hoisted herself on the horse, who again moved, but BethAnn was up and straight in the saddle holding the reins tightly. She looked at Geraldine, who smiled and motioned for her to go ahead and walk her. She walked her to the ranch and then turned around and came back.

Geraldine looked proudly at her and said, "Wait. I'll get a horse, and we'll go for a ride."

One of the men saw what was going on and brought out a horse saddled for Geraldine, and off they rode. She followed Geraldine as they went off on a trail. As it neared lunchtime, they came back. BethAnn got off, petted the horse's neck, and talked to her as one of the men took her into the stall and fed and watered her.

At lunch, Geraldine gave BethAnn accolades. She felt she had handled the horse as well as if she had ridden her a long time. She was really proud of her.

"Jakob, we are going to be riding this afternoon. Why don't you come along? Then we can see the horses we bought. It will be a nice ride for us."

Jakob agreed to go along. The horses were readied and brought to the house. BethAnn was up and ready first. The horse responded to her quickly. They followed a trail that took them north and west of the ranch.

There were trees and foliage all the way. They came onto a beautiful valley with a small stream running through it. At the far end, they could see the horses. There were supposed to be a hundred. When they were aware of their presence, they started moving. Some left the main group and started running. Some just went on grazing. They watched them for some time.

"What are we going to do with them.?" asked Jakob.

"The men will come and get some soon. They will break them, and they can be used or sold off."

They were satisfied with what they had come to see and left, stopping at the stream for the horses to get a drink.

BethAnn was thrilled with Princess. She seemed smart but spirited. BethAnn said that she would like to train her for dressage. Geraldine said that they would not be taking her back to Sheridan just yet. She was disappointed but agreed that they would come back another time.

The time spent on the ranch was necessary for Geraldine. She was now current with the workings and satisfied with the management. It was time to go back to Sheridan. BethAnn had her fill of riding, and Jakob had a rest from his practice. Raymond took them back.

Chapter 22
BethAnn Receives a Puppy

After returning from their vacation, Jakob was anxious to get to work. The first day back, his office was usually filled with emergencies, and some people just came by to say hello and welcome back. However, his day was lighter than usual, so he decided to see his friends at the Lucky Lady. Andy Meeks questioned him about the ranch.

"Doc, have you ever considered making it a dude ranch? There's a number of them starting up around here. Could make a good business."

"Andy, first of all, it's not mine. It belongs to my wife, so I don't make those kinds of decisions. It pays for itself and makes a good profit. We've thought of that, but it would take good management to be a success. Right now, we don't need that sort of headache. I want my wife here in Sheridan, managing the children and me. We like going up there once in a while to enjoy it. Her sister and husband are doing a good job selling horses to England as well as other buyers.

"This time, our BethAnn got a new horse. She really had a good time riding a fine quality animal. It's a good activity for her, and she's learned a lot. You should see how well she handles a horse. She's growing up fast and needs our attention. My Geraldine is doing a good job at being her mother. They have bonded, and there is love between them."

"I bet there's plenty of boys looking at her. She's cute, so I wouldn't doubt it," said Andy.

"Precisely, but she has a lot of talent, and I want her to make use of it. The boys? I think she can handle that."

About that time, Mayor Burns walked in and greeted Jakob. "Glad to see you back. Had a good vacation? We'll have a meeting on the fair next week. I want you to do your job of horse events."

"I'll be there, Mayor. No problem. My wife wants to do a dressage."

The mayor, not understanding what that was, said, "What's dressage?"

"Oh, that's a special kind of competitive horse event. I'll let my wife tell you about it herself. It will be a nice addition to the fair. Something new."

The mayor agreed, and Jakob then left for home.

Everyone was busy, and Chucha had a nice dinner waiting. Sitting down, they began talking about their day. BethAnn said she had done some practicing and liked the last song Harry gave her. The ranch trip and the goings-on really changed her attitude, and Jakob was glad to see her interest aroused with her piano because she was doing so well.

Geraldine talked about the Women's Club and said they were preparing to make the dinner for the veterans of the Civil War, and she would be helping. Wanda had already left, and Randy was in his new high chair. The conversation varied, and BethAnn talked excitedly about her new horse, Princess.

Jakob then informed Geraldine she should talk to the mayor if she wanted to do a dressage at the Sheridan Fair. He told her he had mentioned it to him, and he seemed interested.

Just then, there was a knock on the front door. Chucha left to answer it, then returned to tell Jakob a man named Ralph wanted to talk to him. At first, Jakob was puzzled but then remembered the sheepherder and left the table.

"Ralph, come in, come in. Good to see you. Is everything all right?"

"Everything is fine, Doc. Remember we talked about the pup I had for your daughter? Well, I'm here with it. Where's your daughter?"

"Oh, you brought it with you. That's great! I'll call her. BethAnn, will you come here?"

BethAnn came and stood next to Jakob. "BethAnn, this is Mr. Hoffer, a patient of mine, and he has brought something special for you."

BethAnn acknowledged Ralph and curtseyed. "Hi, I'm pleased to know you."

"Well, BethAnn, I brought something for you, and I hope you will like it." He had a basket concealed behind him and brought it out. Inside was a small ball of black and white fur. BethAnn's eyes opened wide. He took it out and handed it to her.

She squealed, "A puppy for me! Oh, my gosh." She took it in her arms: looking at it "Oh my gosh! Oh, thank you." and then she hugged the man. "Mother, Mother, come here and see my puppy!"

Geraldine was there already. BethAnn held the pup, looking at it.

"Oh, it is so cute!" she said and hugged it. "Mr. Hoffer, did you really bring this for me? Oh, thank you, thank you. I love it. My poor Skippy died, and I miss him so much, and now I have this cute puppy. What's its name?"

"Well, now, she doesn't have a name yet, and you will have to give her one. I sure am glad you like her. She will grow to be a beautiful dog, and I'm glad to give her to you because I know you will take care of her."

She held her to her face and smiled as the pup licked it. "Isn't she beautiful? Look, Mother, I love her, I love her."

"BethAnn, I'm so happy for you," said Mr. Hoffer.

"How nice of you to bring it to her, Ralph. I know she'll take care of it," said Jakob.

"Well, that's exactly why I gave it to her." Looking at BethAnn, Ralph said, "Doc told me about you. I love my dogs. They help me with my work. These dogs are especially smart, strong, and loyal. I had her mother bred by a special dog. She has three brothers and two sisters. I'll keep them or give them to special people. I'm really glad to give her to you."

Jakob looked at him and said, "BethAnn will really take good care of her. I didn't tell you, but she also has a horse she cares for. She's a good horsewoman and is responsible. You made a good choice."

"Well, that's fine. I'll stop by sometime when I'm coming through to see Doc. Now, BethAnn, she's a pup, so don't overfeed her. You can use a saucer or baby bottle for about a month. Remember, she's still a baby. You folks have a good evening, and I'll be going back."

BethAnn hugged the man and thanked him again.

BethAnn put the ball of fur up to her face and smiled. "Aren't I lucky to have this puppy? I'm so happy." She put her on the floor, and the pup waddled across the room. Randy wanted to go after her, but Geraldine stopped him.

"Randy, you can play with her when she grows up, but now she's too little. She's a baby."

The Miller household just grew by one puppy who would change things here fast.

"Can I take her in my bedroom for the night in case she needs me?" said BethAnn.

"I don't think it would be wise. It may keep you up, and you wouldn't get your rest. They do whimper through the night. It doesn't have its mother. Why don't we get a box and put in an old blanket for it to lay on? There's a place in the kitchen for it. She will be all right."

BethAnn was reluctant but agreed, and Jakob found a baby basket and an old pillow that fit just perfect. They gave the little dog some milk and put it to sleep. Chucha was thrilled for BethAnn to have it. They all left for bed with a new stranger in the house.

The next morning Chucha came down and found BethAnn sleeping on the floor next to the basket and the pup lying next to her.

She woke up when Chucha came into the kitchen. "Oh my! Chucha, please don't tell Daddy that you found me in the kitchen. I came to check on her and then fell asleep. I'm going up to my bed."

Chucha smiled and nodded her head in approval. The pup was up and making noises, but Chucha left it alone. It tried to get out of the basket but to no avail.

Jakob came down to have his coffee.

"Good Morning Chucha, I see our new baby is awake. It's going to have to wait for BethAnn to take care of it."

When Geraldine came down, it was frisking around the basket. "How's our puppy doing?" She reached down and picked it up. "Oh, it's wet!" She put it back. "Where's BethAnn? I would have thought she would have been down by now. Well, puppy, BethAnn will be down to take care of you."

They had their breakfast, and BethAnn had not come down yet.

Geraldine went to the stairway and called, "BethAnn, your puppy is up and waiting for you."

BethAnn came slowly down the stairs yawning and rubbing her eyes. "I guess I overslept." She reached down and picked up the happy little dog, who was yipping and wagging its tail. "Ugh, she's wet."

They all laughed.

"Puppies are babies, and they wet. Why don't you feed her a bottle and then clean her up?" said Geraldine. "I'll help you get started with her. Why are you so tired? You went to bed when we all did."

BethAnn just shrugged and got the pup a saucer of milk which she started lapping up. BethAnn had her breakfast and started cleaning up her puppy. In the meantime, Randy entered the picture. He was having his cereal and milk and was very interested in the pup.

BethAnn realized that caring for her new pet was more than playing, and she developed a routine. Her pup was with her when she played piano, and she took him to the barn when she visited Nelly. When she played with Randy, it was close by. Since it was up and moving around, they could all see that the pup was largely black with a white nose and face, white breast, and white front paws.

Jakob was very busy at his office, and the mayor had a meeting about the fair. Geraldine also met with the mayor, and he decided to let her have her dressage. She had already gotten several letters of interest from other cities and thought she should do it.

It was several weeks since BethAnn got her puppy, and her routine of caring was doing well.

At dinner, Jakob asked, "BethAnn, have you decided on a name for your ball of fur? I thought you would have had one by now."

"Daddy, I have been thinking about it since I got her but have not come up with one as yet. I want her to have the right name. She is so cute, and I love her, but she will grow up. She will be bigger, and sheepdogs are strong and fast. They will protect the sheep and are loyal to their owner. I read books with dogs in them, but somehow they will not fit my dog. I read a book about African animals, and I did find one I thought might in a way fit. The Africans call the lion Simba. The lion is the king of the jungle. They are smart, strong, and fast. That's how my dog will be. What do you think if I call her Simba?"

"Simba? That sounds interesting. I kind of like that." said Geraldine.

Jakob pondered and stroked his chin. "You're right. That does sound interesting and different. I bet there isn't a dog in the world with that name. I think it sounds good."

"At first, I thought I'd call her Skippy, but she isn't a boy." They all laughed.

"So, why don't you name her Simba?" said Jakob.

It was generally agreed that it would be Simba.

"Gosh, I thought you might think the name was silly, but I liked it," said BethAnn. She picked up her puppy and hugged it.

"She is so cute, and she knows me now. She does mess, but I don't mind. Someday she'll learn to use the toilet. Well, I mean, she will be trained not to mess."

Randy was enthralled with the dog and wanted to touch it, so BethAnn put it against his face, and he really laughed.

As time went by, Jakob had to find ways to contain Simba. She outgrew her basket, and when left to go free, she could cover the house in her travels. BethAnn devised means to keep her from messing her territory.

BethAnn was now preparing for the dressage, which would be held at the Sheridan Fair. She was well prepared. There would be four contestants, and they would compete for prizes.

Sheridan was filling up with outsiders. The hotels were filled, and there was excitement in the air.

Jakob was invited to a Pow-Wow of the Crow Nation. He would become a blood brother of Medicine Crow. The chief had many reasons why he chose this honor for Jakob. He had taken care of the people and was instrumental in keeping peace and tranquility with the tribe on several occasions. BethAnn and Geraldine were present for the event that consisted of making cuts and mingling of blood. They dressed in their Indian ware and sat with Jakob on the campground while the Indians danced to the drums. They put a headdress of feathers on Jakob. It was an impressive ceremony.

The next day was the big Sheridan parade, which was well attended. Sheridan Main Street was decorated with flags and bunting. The parade consisted of many different groups. The Fort McKenzie detachment marched with its band. The Sheridan High School band and the cheerleaders participated. Some of the Civil War Veterans walked, and some rode. Spanish War Veterans, Elks, other fraternal groups, the Elks' baseball league, and many other organizations were represented. Bill Cody wasn't present because he was in Europe. Jakob, Geraldine, and BethAnn, plus many other riders, made it a rousing parade. The automobiles came last, decorated and just as noisy. The parade always ended at the fairgrounds. This year the governor would be there to review it. Later, there would be a big shindig for the politicians at the Sheridan Inn.

Geraldine's dressage would be held on the third day in front of the main grandstand. BethAnn was getting nervous. Even though she had trained, she was apprehensive. She was taking on a big thing. There would be judges for the event. The other participants were older than her.

The dressage was an event of skilled horsemanship. The participant had to teach his mount to perform certain behaviors when commanded to do so. The horse had to be trained to be manageable and must be properly groomed. The rider gave cues to the horse and communicated what they wanted it to do, showing they were in harmony with each other. There were a series of tests to be performed in the competition, some at a trot and others at a canter.

BethAnn had learned the skills, but so had her competitors. BethAnn got up nervous, but they kept her on a light note. Her horse, Nelly, was groomed and fancied up, and BethAnn wore her English riding garb. She looked cute and didn't show her nervousness when she met the other contestants. She would be third performing. They all had to ride in front of the grandstand. She didn't know, but the grandstand was filled with her friends and Sheridan people to cheer for her. Her name was announced, and they cheered when she rode by. She waved as she and Nelly moved in front of the stands.

Helen Smith was the first up. She looked like she might be twenty. Helen was pretty and blond and sat up straight in the saddle. She performed flawlessly and was given great applause. The next one was Mary Fletcher, who came from Cody, Wyoming. Mary was smaller and dark-haired with a white pony. She did very well but lacked one skill.

BethAnn rode up confidently and sat ramrod straight. Her performance seemed perfect, and the crowd gave her the biggest applause. The fourth performer was Betty Williams, who did well but was probably the weakest. They gave her a good hand. It seemed like forever before the judges gave their decisions.

Then came the results. Betty, who was from Buffalo, got fourth place. Mary, from Cody, earned third place. That left Helen from Cheyenne and BethAnn from Sheridan. Geraldine and Jakob stood next to their daughter, and it looked like Helen's father stood next to her. The judges gave second place to BethAnn. She put her arms up and screamed. When the crowd quieted, Helen Smith won first place. She hugged BethAnn, as did the others. Naturally, the public thought that BethAnn should have won. The judges didn't indicate why they picked Helen. All the girls received trophies and cash. Second place received one hundred dollars.

After the congratulations from friends and acquaintances, Jakob wanted to celebrate the event and go to the Sheridan Inn for dinner. Jakob invited the other girls, which they graciously accepted.

The inn was crowded because of the fair, but they found a table big enough for the girls. Annabelle was excited for BethAnn, and many people came to congratulate her. BethAnn would always introduce the other girls. At the finish of the evening, the girls hugged each other and left as good friends.

Coming home, BethAnn was still on a high. She thanked and hugged Geraldine for all the help she got from her.

"BethAnn, you just made me so proud of you," said Geraldine.

Jakob told her she had made him proud too.

They all left for bed on what was a great day for the Millers.

BethAnn was up early with Simba, who was very frisky. She liked to romp through the house. BethAnn, with Geraldine's help, was training the pup as best as pups can be trained. She now wore a red collar, and BethAnn could walk her.

Jakob had to go to the hospital to take care of a bull rider who was thrown and lost his front teeth. Kelly fixed the rider's broken arm and ribs, and Jakob removed what was left of the damaged teeth. They met in the doctors' lounge with some of the other doctors.

"Jake, I saw your daughter perform yesterday. That was really some show those girls put on. Where did she learn all that?" said Ross.

"She's been training for a couple of years. Geraldine is the horsewoman. They worked on that together. She loves horses."

"Well, she really did well. In fact, all of them did well. Nice to see kids do things like that. My oldest daughter should be ready to try soon," said Ross.

The other doctors were very complimentary, and Jakob thanked them all.

Chapter 23
Jakob Meets President Taft

The best newspaper in Sheridan was not a newspaper but the Lucky Lady. Standing at the bar, the news was exchanged and passed on. Jakob was there talking with Andy Meeks and filling him in on various aspects of the fair. The Sheridan County Fair was now history. It was a success, and most agreed it was the best ever.

Mayor Burns came in and stood next to Jakob. "Well, Doc, you did a good job, as you usually do. Having that horse show or whatever you call it—dressage—was definitely a good thing. Those kids really did a good job of horsemanship. I enjoyed watching them."

"That wasn't my thing, Mayor. My wife handled that. She's the horsewoman in the family. But you're right. It was a nice display of horse handling done by the young people."

"I agree, Doc, and I am pleased with our success. But there's something I want to discuss with you now. Let's go sit over in the corner. It's quieter there, and we can hear each other better." They moved to the table and sat down.

"Can I buy you another drink? You know, while we talk."

Jakob was a little taken aback by the mayor's show. *What's the mayor got for me now?* "No, Mayor, I'll be heading home in a little while. I've had one already. What you got on your mind?"

"Well, it goes like this. At the last meeting we had at the city hall, you learned the President of the United States will be coming to visit us in October. Yes, that's definite. Congressman Duffy made the arrangements back in May. Our Fort Mackenzie was built back some years ago when there was a problem with the Indians. Actually, it wasn't really that significant a problem. However, building the fort was a good way to get Washington to spend some of our tax dollars here. It would bring in a barracks full of men, which would be good for Sheridan's economy. Soldiers go to dances and parties with the young ladies and spend money. All in all, it was good for Sheridan, and the men stationed here could be just as available here as somewhere like Cheyenne or

Billings. It was a good deal for us. Remember how they helped in the flood of '98?"

"Okay, Mr. Mayor. So what's this all about?"

"Well, Doc. Here's the problem. We got to set this up. It's a big deal to entertain the president while he's here. It will cost the city some money, but we'll make some money with people coming to Sheridan to see him and that sort of thing. The main part of this is, one of the big shots in Washington wants to shut down our fort and take out the men. They say they want to save the money spent on the fort and spend it somewhere else. You know how it goes in Washington. Our job is to impress on the president the need to keep the fort going and keep it here in Sheridan.

"President Taft will come here by train, and we will meet him at the train station. He'll have the presidential train car to stay in while he's here, but then there's the parade to organize and take him around town. Show him Sheridan and how great it is. Then we'll have a big rally for him and invite everybody who should be there—businessmen and professionals and some people off the street. Doc, I want you to be his escort and show him what a great city Sheridan is. You know Sheridan and have been important in its development since you came here. You're not a cowpoke or a sodbuster. You're class—a doctor."

"Whoa! Why me? You got your Washington bigwigs to do that."

"Now Doc, you're Mister Sheridan here. The guy who gives his all to the community. You're the guy who represents our city spirit."

"Mr. Mayor, I'm just a dentist trying to make a buck and do something worthwhile as I do it. You flatter me, but—hmm—maybe you're right. Yes, I will. A guy doesn't meet up with the President of the United States every day. Yes, I'll do it, but I got to take it up with my second in command. I'm sure she will go along with the idea. Do you want me to drive him in my car? I just got it, and I'm not that good a driver."

"No, Doc. You are the escort. We can use Frank Wolston as your driver; besides, he's got the biggest car in town. Your job will be to gain the president's confidence and sell him on the idea that our Fort MacKenzie should stay active for Sheridan. We can figure out all the reasons why it should stay here. Good, then you'll do it. I knew you would. And I know you're the best one for the job."

"President Taft, he's a big guy, isn't he? Is he coming up for election? That might play into this thing if he knew that Sheridan will be backing him. Mr. Mayor, you got yourself an escort to the President of the United

States who will show him what a great city we have here. We'll talk more later because I have to leave for dinner."

Jakob left for home, all excited about the job the mayor wanted him to do. Then he thought if he brought this up to the family, it might be somewhat premature, so he better keep it quiet for the time being. He'd just tell Geraldine for now.

Dinner went well, and BethAnn gave her a report on her day in school before going off to her room to do homework.

Jakob could hardly contain himself with the news he would be taking the President of the United States around Sheridan. He saw this as an honor and a really exciting event. Geraldine was thrilled with the idea, and they decided not to let the news out for the time being. They talked about all the things that could be done and made lists of ideas. Jakob had been active with the Sheridan Fair, so he knew lots of people he could call on to help. As the weeks passed, the news Jakob would be Sheridan's escort to the president came out. Everybody was excited for him, and many asked him to introduce them to the president. Handling that situation would be a problem for him because there were others involved in the program. They planned to have a parade like they had for the Sheridan Fair, followed by a big show in the fairgrounds with the army from Fort MacKenzie and those who made up the Sheridan parades.

A banquet for the business people was scheduled for the Sheridan Inn, with Lukas, the chef, providing a special menu. The president was a big man, and it was thought he was a big eater.

The day of President Taft's arrival came. The train station was filled with people, high school band and all. Flags and bunting decorated the station. Main Street was an arch of American flags and bunting. The train came in from Washington with the president, a delegation, and a small army of lesser dignitaries.

Jakob, along with other local officials, boarded the train. The back of the platform was loaded. Mayor Burns would take over after all the introductions and handshaking. Finally, he nudged Jakob to meet the president.

"Mr. President, I want you to meet Doctor Jakob Miller. He will be Sheridan's personal guide for you. He'll show you what we are proud of. We're humbled by your presence here."

Jakob, with a big smile on his face, shook the president's hand. As he looked at President Taft, he saw a big man—not in height because he was shorter than Jakob. But the 5'11" man with a friendly smile and big mustache weighed more than 300 pounds.

"Mr. President, it's my honor to meet you and serve you. We here in Sheridan are honored to have you with us, and I can assure you we'll make this visit enjoyable for you," said Jakob

Taft was impressed and thanked all for their presence. He turned around and faced the crowd of cheering citizens. He put up his hands for them to stop and addressed the crowd. Short and sweet, he accepted the applause and was led down to the waiting car. A brand new spic-and-span machine came out from the freight yard with Frank Wolston driving. The president sat in the back seat with Jakob next to him, and Mayor Burns rode in the front seat with Frank. They drove down Main Street with its array of decorations. One of the Secret Service men told Jakob to keep the car going and avoid stops because the president liked to talk, especially to the children. "We have to keep the car moving," the Secret Service man explained

As they slowly traveled down Main Street, a bunch of kids stood at the corner.

"Driver, I want you to stop by those children so I can talk to them," said President Taft.

Jakob decided he would not tell the President he couldn't stop and talk to those kids. So he tapped the driver to be sure he stopped. The kids were quiet as President Taft spoke to them and asked questions of them, which they shyly answered.

"That was a fine group of youngsters. You should be proud of them," he said to Jakob.

"I agree, Mr. President," Jakob replied. And then he told him how good education was of primary importance in Sheridan. Riding on, the next group looked high school age.

"There's another fine group of young people. Let's stop so I can talk with them." Taft stood up and got out of the car, shook their hands, and gave them words of advice.

"You know, I really never thought about being President of the United States. I graduated from Yale, like my father, and the law was my interest. Shortly after graduation, I became Solicitor General and a circuit judge. Then President McKinley needed a governor in the Philippines, and I accepted the position. It gave me an insight into that part of the world. I want you young people to study hard. Our country needs fine young people to take over. Your world is what you will make it."

The kids were enthralled with the message.

Later, he stopped to shake the hands of some Civil War vets who waved to him. The ride was slow but speeded up as they left for the fairgrounds. They got out of the car and went into the grandstands to view the parade. The commanding officer of Fort MacKenzie and the other dignitaries joined him. All the while, Jakob talked to him about various points of interest. The president was a good listener as well as a generous talker.

With the parade ending, Jakob and Mayor Burns took the president back to his railroad car to rest up before the banquet.

"Well, Jakob, that was a good start. We'll pick him up at six and continue with our Presidential visit."

At six o'clock sharp, Frank drove up to the railroad car. President Taft looked refreshed. There were other cars to take the dignitaries. The Sheridan Inn was just a stone's throw away from the train.

Jakob was dressed in his English dinner wear. The ballroom was filled with people—cattlemen, professionals, and business people of all sorts. Jakob, Geraldine, and BethAnn sat at a table next to the front. When President Taft was seated, Jakob motioned for Geraldine and BethAnn to come forward, and he introduced them. The president gave them his big smile.

"Why, Doctor, what a beautiful family you have. Your daughter is a charmer. Young lady, what will you do with your life when you grow up?"

BethAnn curtsied and gave a coquettish smile. "I really haven't made up my mind yet, but I've thought about following my father as a dentist. Or maybe a nurse or medical doctor. I want to help people like my father does."

"You just follow your dream, and I know you will be successful. And mother, you are English. I can tell by your accent. I would bet your father is a member of the House of Lords. Am I right? I can tell. I wish we could talk more. I know some of those gentlemen. Doctor, you are a lucky man with a fine family. You know, I have four children to be proud of."

A line developed of others who wanted to talk to the president, and Geraldine and BethAnn returned to their table.

Lukas found out what President Taft liked and fed him oysters on the half shell, pheasant, and all the accompaniments. The dinner lasted two hours. Jozef played his violin to serenade the president. There were speeches and accolades to their honored guest. The evening ended at eleven, with everyone filled with food and spirits. Lukas did a great job. Jakob took a happy president back to his rail car. He profusely thanked Jakob for a wonderful evening.

The next day Jakob was at the presidential rail car, ready to take him through Sheridan. He brought a ten-gallon hat, neckerchief, and a warm denim jacket because it would be chilly in the open car. President Taft looked like a typical Wyoming citizen, and he was delighted with the outfit. There were two other cars with dignitaries and, of course, members of the Secret Service.

They made stops at the various schools, the hospital, and important businesses. They drove to Acme to view the mines and the beet factory. A visit to Fort MacKenzie was made with a ceremonial presentation of the colors. The Colonel showed him the fort as the brigade looked on. As they left the fort, Jakob had a heart-to-heart talk with Taft as to why the fort was important to Sheridan.

He listened and agreed it should stay there. "I will look into the matter, and as long as I am President of the United States, Sheridan will have Fort Mackenzie. I can promise that."

Jakob was amazed he got such a response. "Mr. President, Sheridan was a frontier town when I came here. It has grown to be an important city in Wyoming. It has a long way to go."

The president was impressed with Sheridan. He invited a number of the town dignitaries to dinner on the train.

The next morning Lukas came with a couple of his people carrying local fare—venison, buffalo, pheasants, ducks, and trout from the streams. Taft would certainly remember Sheridan as he enjoyed the Sheridan special dinners in Washington, DC. As the train was ready to leave, he stood on the observation platform, waving goodbye. Train wheels began to turn.

Taft turned to Jakob, who was standing below. "Doctor, I will keep my promise. Be sure to visit me in Washington and the White House."

Mayor Burns looked at Jakob in awe. Grinning, he said, "You did it, Doc! By golly, you did it. I just knew you could."

They left the station and went to the Lucky Lady. The Lady was filled with people who drifted in after the train left. Jakob got accolades and pats on the back from the crowd. No one really knew what President Taft's parting remark meant except the mayor, who knew what Jakob had done.

Andy placed a drink in front of Jakob. "This one is on the house. You're the first guy I ever knew who could handle a President of the United States."

Chapter 24
Letter from the President

Chucha had Jakob's coffee ready when he came down for breakfast. He noticed Simba begging to get out from her night enclosure and reached down to pick her up.

"I'll take the dog out for her morning relief," said Jakob, as he put a leash to Simba's collar and took her outside. She sniffed around and seemed to find the right spot and relieved herself.

"Good girl Simba, Good girl Simba," Jakob said, and he gave her a dog biscuit. They went back into the house, and he put her back in her enclosure.

"Pan, you happy. You be with President Taft; big-shot." She laughed.

"No, Chucha, I'm not a big shot, but it was quite an experience. The president was a very nice person to be with. He's just like you and me, Chucha, except he is the president of our country. Chucha, does your country have a president?"

"No, Pan, I have no country. My country was stealed by Russia, Prussia, Austria. They steal my country." Tears came down her cheeks which she wiped away. She soulfully moved her head back and forth. "My country is no more, but someday Polska will be again. I now American. My country be good. I American now."

Jakob was somewhat stunned by her reply. He had not known that historically Poland was partitioned by its neighbors. It was the impetus for so many to leave their homeland and seek freedom in America.

"They take my language. Make me speak German. Teach my children German. We not Russian, Austrian. My people Polska."

Geraldine had come down and listened to the conversation. "Someday, I would like to learn more about your life in Poland."

Shaking her head, Chucha said, "No, No. Not good, Lady Geraldine. Not Good." She turned away and started making the breakfasts.

BethAnn arrived and picked Simba out of her enclosure.

"I took her out, and she did her duty, so you must be doing

something right with her," said Jakob.

BethAnn hugged her dog, who licked her face. Then she put Simba on the floor.

"Daddy, are you still excited about being the guide for our president? Tell us what you thought about him. How did you feel talking to such an important person?"

"Hmm. Well, it really was an experience to be with the leader of our country. At first, I was a little nervous, but the more we talked, the easier it became. Sort of like talking to my father. With respect and confidence so that he respects you. He told me about his family and what they were like. It sounded a little bit like ours. He told me about their vacation to Yellowstone. Can you believe he was right near Sheridan? He liked to talk to young people and was concerned for them and their future."

"Daddy, someday you could come to school and tell the kids about your experience."

"Good idea. He did make it a point to stop and talk to the children. He said he was a lawyer, and yet he was the President of the United States. I guess the president has to know about the laws of the land. He had a big smile. Looked like he had good teeth."

"Daddy, you didn't ask him about his teeth, did you?" Geraldine laughed.

"Of course not, but when he laughed, I could see all his teeth."

Geraldine continued laughing. "Jakob, you never stop being a dentist. Even when you're with the President of the United States."

Then Jakob started laughing. "If I saw he had any problems with his teeth, I would inform him to come to my office, and I would take care of them. This reminds me that I do have to go to my office. We'll talk more at dinner time."

BethAnn got up and went over to Jakob. "Daddy, you sure know how to talk tall tales." Laughing, she kissed him.

Jakob must have become the most talked-about man in Sheridan. All the people he saw wanted to talk about his experience with President Taft. His first patient, Mrs. Goodbe, wanted to know if the president would be seeking reelection before she even sat down in his chair.

"Mrs. Goodbe, I can assure you we didn't talk politics. Now, that molar that I filled last week. Is it comfortable now?"

"Well..."

Some patients were not that easy to dissuade from talking. But he finished his day on time and was closing up when Doc Kelly walked in. "Jake, did the president give you a job in his cabinet? You know, like

Secretary of Dentists; Huh? Or maybe...?"

"Kelly, you old dog. Cut it out. But, I did throw your name in as Chief of Sawbones."

"Okay, Kid. Just as long as you got me a desk job. Let's go over to the Lady and shoot the breeze."

As they walked into the Lucky Lady, the house broke into cheers and whistles for Jakob, as well as slaps on his back as he made his way to the bar.

Mayor Burns was waiting. "I thought you'd be here. How do you feel being the toast of Sheridan?"

"Come on, Mayor, you'll make me blush, and I don't blush."

"Never mind, Doc. You did a good job, and the town appreciates it. We need the fort. Not for protection but as an important part of our history. President Taft is really a fine gentleman, isn't he?"

"Yes, he is, and I'm sure he's doing a good job. I'm sure it isn't easy to try to satisfy the needs of all our states." Jakob looked at his watch. "Speaking of needs, my family needs me," and he left.

Jakob entered his home. Geraldine was holding Randy, who was laughing. When he saw Jakob, he put his arms out so that his daddy would take him, which he did. Randy placed his hands on Jakob's face, laughing. He was bonded to Jakob and loved to be with him, even as he sat in his chair reading his newspaper. BethAnn stood by, asking her brother to come to her, but he refused, so she sat on the floor with him.

Randy was growing so fast and was making all sorts of sounds, but he could also be demanding. He loved everyone. He was especially curious, and Simba drew his attention. He would seek to touch her, but she would withdraw. He was lovable. He was good with Wanda, his nanny, so Geraldine could leave him with her and not worry he missed her. Randy was growing and was a loving part of the family. Though he resented Jakob putting his fingers in his mouth. Jakob said his teeth were arriving on time.

Geraldine brought up the subject of the dressage and how she felt BethAnn had done so well. She also thought Nelly had done well too. "Nelly is a mustang, and they don't always learn. You have trained her to perform well. Next time we go to the ranch, we can work with Princess."

BethAnn liked the kudos but accepted them with humility.

They got around to Jakob's meeting with the president.

"Daddy, in history class today, our teacher said to me he hoped you might give the class a talk about your visit with President Taft. I told him I would ask you, and then he could set up a date."

"Did he make the suggestion, or did you generate the idea?"

"No, Daddy, he brought it up and thought it would be a great idea." Jakob smiled and said he would like to do it.

The evening ended when Randy reminded Geraldine that he was ready for his bedtime snack. BethAnn took Simba for her evening relief.

Daylight was just breaking, and Jakob's eyes opened. Skippy was moaning, and his paw was scratching Jakob's back. *Skippy is dead!* Jakob suddenly rose up and saw Simba's eyes beaming at him. *Oh, no! What the heck is going on?*

In a voice between quiet and a decibel above, he shouted, "Simba get out of here. Get out!" *How did she get out of the enclosure?*"

The dog just looked at him with its tail wagging. "Go, go, Simba."

By this time, Geraldine awoke. "What's going on, Jakob? Why is the dog in our room?"

"I don't know, and she won't leave. Get out of here, Simba." But, the dog just moaned and whimpered. "I guess she wants to go out. If dogs could just talk."

Jakob put his legs out of bed and on the floor, and Simba moved to the doorway. Jakob got out of bed, and Simba moved to the kitchen door, waiting for him to open it. He stood on the porch, watching the dog find the right spot. Happily, she came back as Jakob opened the door.

Chucha had just come down. "Pan, you take dog out?"

"No, Chucha, the dog took me out," he said and went back to the bedroom, only to find Geraldine putting on her robe to go out.

"Might as well stay up," she said. "I think the dog wants company." They had their coffee before BethAnn came down.

"BethAnn, we have a problem. Your dog got out of her pen and woke me up."

"Did you scold her, Daddy? That wasn't nice of her."

Jakob laughed and said, "We'll have to find a way to keep her confined at night."

Jakob's first stop before going to the office was the Post Office. Freddy Walt was the postmaster.

"Hi, Doc. Coming to pick up your mail, Huh.? There's a pretty important-looking letter in there for you."

Jakob opened his box and took out several pieces of mail. Freddy was watching him as he sifted through the letters and stopped at one. His eyes opened wide.

"I see you found it: White House, Washington, DC. Must be important."

Jakob opened and read it.

Dear Doctor Miller,

I just wanted to send you a short letter of thanks for the fine time you showed me when I visited Sheridan. I greatly appreciated your hospitality and that of Mayor Burns and all the people in Sheridan. I am impressed with your community and all you have achieved. You are no longer a frontier town. You have risen above that. I have spoken with the Secretary of War about Fort Mackenzie, and it is there to stay.

I was pleased to meet your family. Please extend my best wishes.

Your President,

William Howard Taft

The letter was a surprise to Jakob. Postmaster Walt couldn't wait for Jakob to reveal what he had received.

"Interesting letter from the president. Thanked me and the town for our hospitality. Never thought I'd be getting a letter of thanks from the President of the United States."

"I guess he was really impressed by Sheridan," said Freddy.

Jakob left for his office and found several patients waiting for him. He was finishing up when Andy Meeks came in.

"Hey Doc," Andy said. "What say we have lunch together? Haven't talked much lately."

Jakob agreed, and they went to one of their favorite Chinese restaurants. Mee Low. Mrs. Low was Liz's student when she started adult language classes. She recognized Jakob and always talked about how Liz taught her how to speak English.

They had their lunch and talked about happenings in Sheridan.

Jakob showed the letter he got from the president to Andy. "That was quite an experience you had," Andy said. "Nice of the president to do that. Seems like he appreciated our show. Before I forget, I want to tell you something. You know, Doc, the other night Kelly was playing cards, and all of a sudden, he grabbed his chest in pain. Kelly grabbed a little bottle from his pocket, got a pill from it, and put it in his mouth.

Sat back moaning and holding his chest. A couple of minutes later, he seemed all right. The guys wanted to take him to the hospital, but he wouldn't go. Said he was all right and started dealing cards again."

"Oh, another angina attack. I don't know, but he won't change his lifestyle. He should know better, but that's Kelly."

They left the restaurant and went to their respective jobs.

Sitting at the dinner table, BethAnn handed Jakob a letter. The teacher asked him to come to the history class and talk to the children about his meeting with the president.

"He said you should name the day and time, Daddy. The kids will really be interested," said BethAnn.

"Well, in that case, I will bring this letter with me." And he gave the president's letter to BethAnn and all to read.

"Now that's over with, I have real news for all," said Geraldine. "When Jakob came in, I was holding Randy. When he saw Jakob, the baby said, 'DaDa.' How about that for our little boy?"

A moment later, Randy repeated, "DaDa." That brought excitement to the family.

The next week Jakob attended BethAnn's history class, and Mr. Roberts introduced Jakob to the class. Actually, two classes listened and asked questions. Jakob was a success. He enjoyed doing it and brought them a message from President Taft.

Chapter 25
A Tragedy in Acme

Geraldine and Jakob talked about buying an automobile for some time, but Jakob was not really interested. The horse and buggy were all right as far as he was concerned. His father had a Ford and liked it, but Milwaukee had good, paved streets. However, Geraldine thought it would be a good idea. Back in England at Landry Manor, her father bought one of the first available. They found it especially useful for travel between the manor and Ipswich station. It was really special with all its brass trim, but it was not available here in the United States.

There was now a Ford dealer in Sheridan, so Geraldine talked to him about an automobile. The latest model was a 1912 Ford Model T, and he had one available in a touring model. It was not too fancy—no brass, just an all-black automobile that all of Mr. Ford's cars were painted. Geraldine was surprised it was so inexpensive compared to the cost of an automobile in England.

Their wedding anniversary was coming up, and she wanted to get Jakob something special. She thought about it and was excited to surprise him with the gift. It was to be delivered to his office. She talked with the Ford dealer, Jerome Wells, who would stop at the office with it on Tuesday at 11:00 am.

Last year Jakob took her to the Sheridan Inn for dinner and gave her a ruby ring as an anniversary gift. Jozef played violin for them, and they danced. They were deeply in love, and her dreams were fulfilled. He had not mentioned anything about the anniversary this year. *Maybe he forgot. He's been very busy. This year I will buy him a gift from me, and the automobile will be it,*

At eleven o'clock, Jerome Wells went into Jakob's office. He waited until Jakob finished with his patient and announced he had something outside he wanted to show him.

Jakob wondered what it was all about and followed Wells outside.

Geraldine was sitting in the driver's seat of the Model T. Jakob was stunned, and then he realized Geraldine bought it.

"Happy anniversary, Jakob. I remembered our special day when you took me for your wife."

Jakob was completely without words. He looked at the salesman and then at Geraldine. "I can't believe this!" He walked to the driver's side, got on the running board, put his arms around Geraldine, and kissed her. She stepped down from the car, and Jakob put his arms around her again and kissed her passionately.

The salesman smiled and said, "Doctor, would you like to take a ride in your new Ford? I'm sure you don't know how to drive yet, but I'll teach you. See what it feels like to be the owner of a new car."

Jakob opened the door to the back seat for Geraldine and sat next to Wells, who began to explain how to start the automobile and put it into gear. By this time, a crowd gathered around to see Jakob's new car.

One said, "Doc, you're not really going to give up your horse for that contraption, are you?"

Others laughingly made similar remarks.

He smiled and took the teasing in good spirit. Jerome Wells started the automobile. They waved to the crowd as he put it in gear and slowly moved away. It lumbered down Main Street, slowing for a buggy which then moved to the side of the street; continued past an electric streetcar, and turned down Loucks Street to stop at Jakob's home. Before turning into the drive, Jerome said, "What do you think, Doc? We did that in less than fifteen minutes."

Chucha and Wanda, hearing the engine's noise, came outside to see what was going on.

"Pan, what you do?" Chucha asked.

Geraldine answered, "Chucha, this is Jakob's automobile. He will be driving this to work now."

Chucha shook her head. "I dunno if I like."

Wanda laughed. "Chucha is afraid she might have to ride in it, but I would like to."

Jerome Wells started telling Jakob all about the greatness of the Model T Ford and how sales were sweeping the nation. "I'll tell you what, let's drive over to the Sheridan Inn, and I'll buy you and your wife lunch. I'll let you drive it with me next to you. Don't worry, you can learn."

Jakob nervously sat in the driver's seat.

"Okay, Doc, now turn on the ignition switch. That's right."

He started it little by little, and Wells had him put it in reverse to slowly back out the drive. Soon he was driving down Loucks. Some of the neighbors opened their doors to see the automobile going down the street with Jakob driving. Surprised to see him, they waved. Loucks was a rough street, so he drove slowly. He turned down Main Street to Broadway and then the Sheridan Inn. Several horses were tied up and nervously moved, so he gave them plenty of room. He stopped and turned off the ignition switch as he was directed.

"See, Doc, I knew you could do it."

Jakob was proud of himself for driving the car, even though Wells was with him. They went inside, and the desk clerk, Clayton, said, "Hey Doc, I hear you got a Ford. How do you like it?"

News travels fast. "Not sure yet, Clayton, but I'll give it a try. My wife bought it for me."

Annabelle saw them come in and took them to a table. Lukas had a good lunch for them. Wells told Jakob and Geraldine all about the Ford and how he once met Henry Ford in Dearborn, Michigan.

After lunch, Jakob had a chance to drive back to the office. Wells told him he'd be back and help him bring the Ford home after Jakob finished with his patients.

Kelly came into the office, laughing. "Jake, don't tell me you bought that Tin Lizzy out there? I can't believe it. What you got against horses?"

"I'm not against horses. I like horses. My wife bought it for me. If you had a wife, maybe she would buy you one."

"Maybe that's why I'm not married. I never thought I'd see the day you would be riding around in one of those things. Wait till the guys at the Lady hear about this."

Kelly would have continued, but one of Jakob's patients came in, and he left. The rest of his day was spent with patients with whom he either defended his Ford or thanked those who were excited for him.

When Wells came back, he had Jakob drive the Ford. Jakob knew he had to eventually meet the Lucky Lady crowd with his automobile, so he thought he'd go over there with Wells and let him help take the ribbing. They drove to the Lady, but there was no room to park because of all the horses tied up, so he parked in front of the boot store.

They went in, and the crowd started in on Jakob, and he introduced Jerome, who gave a good sales pitch on the Ford. There was a lot of laughter, and Jerome took it in good spirits. Andy asked Jakob how much it would cost to feed the machine.

Jakob answered. "It wouldn't cost any more than to feed my horse, and I wouldn't have to pick up the manure."

A couple of guys in there with cars—including Frank Wolston—knew how to lay it on. Frank had driven President Taft and Jakob around town during the Presidential visit. It was all in good fun, and Jakob left with Wells for home. He felt more confident as he turned on the ignition switch and put it in gear. They drove into his driveway, and he turned off the switch.

"Think you want me to come back tomorrow morning, or do you want to give it a try yourself?" Wells asked. "Don't forget it may be a cold start, so you'll have to give it a little more gas to warm up."

Jakob said he'd give it a try.

BethAnn and the rest of the household had come outside and were standing next to Jakob.

"Daddy, you aren't going to give up your horse, are you? That would be a mistake."

"No, Dear, I won't give up my horse. You and I will still go riding together."

They went into the house, and Jakob asked Chucha to bring up some wine, which she did. He poured them all a glass, and he turned to Geraldine. "I want to toast my wonderful wife Geraldine for buying me the automobile. It was my anniversary present. We will all enjoy riding in it. Thank you, dear." He kissed her.

Geraldine said, "The automobile will be the transportation of the future, but we'll always have horses who will be our companions."

Chucha said that she would try it out but was not sure she would like it.

After dinner, the conversation moved to the drawing-room, as Geraldine now called it. BethAnn took her brother Randy, and they lay down near the fireplace. Simba joined nearby, and Randy tried to catch him. Randy was starting to make attempts to stand and would if you held his arms up. He was a happy baby and loved by all.

The next weeks Jakob would drive his Ford to the office. He had some problems, but Wells would stop by and help him resolve them. Later he would stop by Findley's General Store to buy his gasoline. Elmer was the first in town to put in a gasoline pump.

On Sunday, he would take his family to church in the Ford. Chucha went with them and found out she liked to ride in the automobile. However, she always carried her rosary in her hands. She did complain a little because she didn't like its sound or the smell of the exhaust.

It was getting cold in Sheridan, so the isinglass curtains were installed, which kept the cold wind out. Once in a while, a horse would get spooked by the car being too close to pass, and the driver would give Jakob a dirty look.

Jakob wanted Geraldine to learn to drive. She said she would but was satisfied with Jakob's performance. In England, her father hired Sampson for the task. He wore a uniform and took care of the automobile. Though he wasn't little anymore, Little Henry did wash the car as a side job when he took care of the horses. With all the dust in the air, the black Ford got dirty, especially after a rain. Jakob had a garage built next to the barn to store his Ford.

Jakob and Geraldine had just arrived home from church and were waiting for lunch. BethAnn was playing with Randy and Simba. There was a pounding on the front door, and Chucha answered. Doc Kelly came in very distressed, asking for Jakob.

"What's going on, Kelly?"

"Explosion in a mine at Acme. Lots of injuries and some fatalities. They're bringing some to the hospital. They need us. Let's go!"

Geraldine looked at Jakob.

"I'm going in, Honey. I can't wait for lunch," he told her and immediately left. Jakob drove the Ford. It was a cold, windy November day. They made it to the hospital in twenty minutes. There were buggies and ambulances parked. The emergency room was filled with doctors, nurses, and gurneys with black soot-covered miners moaning and screaming in pain. There were four doctors and Jakob, some scrubbing and some already gowned and working. Jakob started scrubbing along with Kelly while a nurse with sponges was cleaning up a miner. His face was covered with black soot, blood, and pieces of coal, which were embedded in his skin. Jakob cleaned up his face and removed the embedded particles while Kelly attended to the man's mangled arm. He splinted it and went on to another patient with a crushed leg. Jakob filled in wherever he could. The injuries were to all parts of the body. There were twenty brought in, but two already didn't make it.

One had a broken jaw that Jakob started on. He was without any teeth and would have to be wired directly. Jakob did his best to stabilize the mandible parts from moving. They would have to give him general anesthesia and could do it the next day. The nurses cleaned up the bodies as best as they could. Some burns had to be dressed, and fractures had to be set the next day. They worked into the night.

Kelly came up to Jakob. Most had been given some kind of aid and were tended to by the nurses. Some already had surgery.

"Did you take out any teeth?"

Jakob nodded. "Yes, a bunch, and we got a couple of fractures. One has to be wired. He didn't have any teeth. Do you think we can do it tomorrow? It will have to be under general."

"We'll have to put it down in the schedule. There may be some internal injuries that have to be done first. We might as well leave now. We've done as much as we can today. I'm bushed," said Kelly.

Several of the doctors were sitting in the doctors' lounge and softly talking about the day.

"Let's get out of here," said Kelly. "We'll stop at the Lady for one, and maybe Grand Ma's is still open for a sandwich," said Kelly.

They went into the Lucky Lady. It was quiet. They'd all heard about the mine explosion and were just talking about it. Andy looked at Jakob.

"I guess it's pretty bad, huh?"

Nobody felt like talking.

"I hear they brought in twenty," said Andy.

"Yes, and eighteen are still living," said Kelly.

They took down their whiskey, and Kelly said, "Let's get out of here. I'm starved."

They got to Grand Ma's before she closed, and she made them soup and a sandwich. She tried to engage them in conversation, but they were just tired. It was after 9:00 pm when Jakob pulled into his drive. Kelly left in his buggy. Jakob put the Ford in the garage; and climbed the stairs to the kitchen door.

Geraldine was waiting for him with BethAnn. "You look like you had a tough day." She approached him and put her arms around him, and kissed him. "I've got some bad news for you. Chucha left for Acme with Jozef. Her brother-in-law, Walter, was killed in the mine explosion. Poor lady, she's devastated, and she was crying when she left. She didn't want to leave us, but I insisted she go with Jozef. Walter worked in the mines all his adult life. I guess he was like a foreman there. They had eight children, and he was supposed to retire next year. Wanda didn't leave. She said she would stay with us and go to the funeral."

Jakob listened as she told him about Chucha and the close relationship she had with Walter. "I feel for Chucha. The explosion must have been terrible. We had twenty, but two were dead on arrival." Jakob told her about what they had done, and he felt all the others would recover, but some would never be the same with their injuries. He had two that had jaw fractures he would have to repair.

BethAnn silently listened as they talked and then said, "Why did this have to happen?"

Jakob shrugged, "I..., I don't know. Working in the coal mines is dangerous. Gases form, and then a spark ignites them."

They sat mostly silent until Geraldine went into the kitchen and brought out two snifters and poured some brandy in them. They slowly sipped from them.

Geraldine looked at BethAnn. "Why don't you take Simba out? I'll get you milk and one of Chucha's cookies before you go up."

Later, as she was going up to her room, BethAnn turned around. "I feel so bad for Chucha. She's such a sweet lady. She cried so. I wish I could do something for her." And tears showed on her cheek.

Geraldine took her in her arms. "Yes, I know. We all feel bad for her, and we'll do something. But for now, you can say a prayer for her and her family. God will hear it and help them through this terrible time."

BethAnn nodded and went up to her room.

Jakob thought a long moment. "It's tough for a child to face tragedy. She's was too young to remember much of Liz, and she is close to Chucha. She practically raised BethAnn until you came."

Wanda had the coffee made when Jakob got up. She talked freely about Walter Kowolski, who she thought was a fine man. "He had good children. The oldest is in his thirties, and the youngest is in his twenties. He and Helen were inseparable. They had many friends, and Walter belonged to two lodges. The visitation will be in four days. Do you plan on going to the wake?"

"Oh, of course, we will go. Maybe tomorrow, and we can take you with us."

She said she would try to fill in Chucha's place.

"Don't worry. I'm sure you will," said Jakob.

Geraldine came in and hugged Wanda, who already had her coffee ready and was getting breakfast together.

BethAnn came down and took Simba out. "Oh, is it ever so cold out there!" she said. She scolded Simba for jumping and then gave her some table scraps.

"If you get yourself ready, I'll drop you off at school when I leave for the office. I have to take care of a patient in the hospital," said Jakob.

Sheridan High School classes began at 8:00 am, and she was on time. He then stopped at the office. Someone was waiting for him, and he took care of him. He planned on going to the hospital to take care of the jaw fracture, so he got his things together to do that. But several other patients came in, and a five-year-old came in crying.

"I just don't know why she's crying," said the mother. "She keeps saying her tooth hurts. It's just one of those baby teeth."

"Come on, Mary, I'll take care of the tooth. I'll fix it so it won't hurt. Mommy, you wait outside here. Mary will be fine with me."

"But, I can come…"

"Mary will be fine, Mommy," said Jakob as he closed the door. "Here, Mary, you just sit in my big chair. Oh, wait, I have something I can put there that will make you bigger." Jakob put a booster seat on the chair, and Mary was up higher. "Do you go to school, Mary?"

She shook her head.

"Well, I thought you were big enough to go to school. Show me the tooth that hurts."

She opened her mouth, and Jakob looked in. *Oh my God, every tooth in her head has a hole in it! Rampant caries.* He took a cotton swab and moistened it in a solution, then swabbed the area around the tooth. He filled a syringe with anesthetic and waited, talking to Mary about her doll and carefully injected the tooth. "I bet that tooth isn't hurting now, Mary."

She shook her head, and he carefully placed a forceps over the tooth and slowly removed it while talking to Mary about her doll.

"Mary, you were so good a patient that you can go over to my treasure chest and take whatever toy you want. I have to talk to Mommy."

Jakob then told the mother the seriousness of Mary's dental condition and told her what had to be done. Mary left with a trinket, smiling.

It was almost noon when he was finished. He took instruments and what he would use to take care of a broken jaw to the hospital.

Kelly had been there all morning when Jakob came in. "Let's get something to eat before you start," said Kelly. He told him what he had done.

When they returned, Jakob had x-rays of the jaw and fortunately found no broken teeth to remove. He fitted arch bars and wired the upper and lower jaw together. The poor guy could not talk English. He only spoke Italian. His arm was also fractured, and one of the doctors had put a cast on it. One of the nurses spoke Italian, and Jakob gave her instructions on his care, including a liquified diet. The tragedy of the Acme mine was felt in Sheridan by all. Acme was in mourning for those whose lives were lost.

Jakob and his family would leave for Acme the next day. The road there was in good condition, and they arrived in less than an hour. Wanda gave them directions to the Kowolski home. It was in a neighborhood of nicer homes. It was neat and painted white with gray trim and had a porch with a swing. A white picket fence surrounded it with grass and flowers that had died in the fall. There were horses with buggies and wagons parked on the street. Next to the front door was a basket of flowers, and above the door draped grey and black ribbon. The porch had chairs where men sat and stood talking and smoking cigarettes. Most were in their Sunday church dress.

Jakob parked, and Wanda led the way. BethAnn led Randy. They climbed the stairs to the porch. Several of the men recognized Wanda and tipped their hats or smiled at them.

They opened the door to a vestibule and living room. The house was filled with people. As they entered the living room, they saw the wooden casket with a kneeler in front of it. On each side was a toucher containing a burning candle. Men sat next to the bereaved, holding a Rosary.

The casket was closed and had a picture of Walter on it. Behind the coffin was a large wooden crucifix with black and grey ribbon draped over it. The whole wall contained flowers in baskets, as did the different parts of the room. The two people kneeling by the casket left, and Jakob and Geraldine kneeled. The room was hushed, and people could be heard softly speaking. They said their prayers for the deceased and got up.

Mrs. Kowalski was seated behind them and wore a black dress and small hat with a black veil. Next to her was Chucha, also dressed in black, who got up when she saw Jakob and Geraldine. Red-eyed from crying, Chucha put her arms around Jakob and Geraldine and kissed them, thanked them for coming, and introduced them to her sister. Jakob and Geraldine said their condolences to Mrs. Kowalski, who was most gracious. BethAnn hugged and kissed Chucha, who introduced them around to the family.

The house was filled with people. The kitchen table was filled with foods of all sorts and another table with liquors and glasses.

One of the sons introduced himself and offered Jakob a whiskey. He accepted and drank with him. "Naz Drovye," the son said, which is the Polish toast to your health. The son also offered a honey liquor called *kruptnic* to Geraldine and Wanda.

They stayed and talked with the mourners. Each one told them something about Walter Kowolski, who was deeply loved and admired.

Chucha said she would return after the funeral and thanked Jakob for his concern and for coming. Two men with large badges sat next to the casket. They were members of a lodge he belonged to, and they would take turns sitting with the deceased through the day and the night. Later, Fr. John Binotti would come and lead them, the mourners, in prayer.

The next day they moved to their church, Saint Mary's, and then to the cemetery for the burial nearby.

Randy was starting to act up. It seemed neither Wanda, Geraldine, or Chucha could satisfy him, so they decided it was time to leave.

The bereaved wife thanked Jakob and Geraldine for coming, and they left.

Following the coal mine explosion, the company shut down the mine. There was an investigation as to the cause. The deaths and injuries were significant. The families with losses were left without loved ones. Chucha went back with the Millers. She suffered from her loss but carried on.

Chapter 26
Chucha is Replaced by Helen

The new City Hall on Grinnell Avenue was finally finished. There was a need for the new City Hall since Sheridan had grown significantly. Mayor Burns now had a fancy office, but there would be other changes in the future for Sheridan. It would be changing to a commissioner form of government, and the commissioners would be elected. Jakob's position was probably in jeopardy because he had worked as a volunteer with the mayor. He had no desire to run for any political office. However, he liked being able to put forth his views. A big celebration and ribbon cutting for the new City Hall included a performance by the high school band and speeches by some local politicians. Jakob and Geraldine were there for the event.

Afterward, they drove to the Sheridan Inn for lunch. It was just a couple of weeks until Thanksgiving Day, and the inn was decorated for the event. Dr. Ross and his wife Jane were there, and when they saw Jakob and Geraldine, they invited them to sit at their table. Geraldine saw Doctor Ross professionally before she had Randy. He was a good friend of Jakob, but they were not so close socially.

The Ross couple had three children, and they were very impressed with BethAnn's riding at the Sheridan Fair. "Where did she learn to ride like that? She really put on a great performance," said Jean.

"That was through instruction by Geraldine, who said she must have been born on a horse."

They laughed at that.

"BethAnn liked riding, and Geraldine thought this would be a good activity for her. And she really enjoys it," said Jakob.

"I want you to meet our daughter. Her name is Sarah, but we all call her Daisy," said Jane. "She would be a year younger than your BethAnn. Daisy said she knew BethAnn from school. Do you think she could learn to ride like your daughter? She has a horse but doesn't ride much."

Geraldine had an idea. "BethAnn and I always take a ride on Thanksgiving Day. Your daughter could come along with us. It would be for just a few hours, and then she could see whether she would like to go on with her riding. She wouldn't have to train for dressage. That takes dedication."

Jane thought it was a great idea. "Afterward, you could spend Thanksgiving dinner with us. We'd love to have you join us."

The lunch was interrupted by an older lady who wanted to know if Jakob would be in his office today. He told her that he could see her at 2:00 pm.

She left, and Ross remarked, "I thought I was the only one who was always interrupted at mealtime by patients."

Jakob laughed and told him he had experienced it before. "I remember the time an Englishman named James Whitaker interrupted my dinner."

Geraldine looked at him and said, "Tell them the rest of the story Jakob."

He smiled, then continued the story. "I was dining with my first wife, Liz, and an English gentleman came in here and asked for me. He was having a lot of pain and needed a dentist. Annabelle directed him to me. His name was James Whitaker. I took care of him that day, and for several years afterward, he was my patient. Then my wife died during an influenza epidemic. Five years later I came here for lunch with my friends. As I was leaving, I saw someone I knew. She was a beautiful lady; she was the wife of James Whitaker, whom I had not seen for some years. We talked, and I learned James had died. That night I had dinner with her, and two years later, I married her."

Jane looked at him. "What a beautiful story! And that's how you found your wife."

Geraldine smiled, "And that is how I found my husband."

They talked at length and found they had much in common. Jane was wrapped in the lives of her children and didn't do much else. Geraldine invited her to go to the Sheridan Women's Club with her. They would soon become good friends.

Thanksgiving Day came, and Geraldine and BethAnn rode to the Ross house and met Daisy, who would go riding with them. She was a year younger than BethAnn, and they became friends. It was good she had someone her age to ride with.

Michael Ross was considered a good doctor. The other doctors in town elected him chief of staff at the hospital.

Since the loss of her brother-in-law, Chucha showed signs of depression and was withdrawn. It really bothered her. She didn't seem to have the spunk she used to have, and they became concerned for Chucha. She did her work, but it slowed down considerably. Geraldine came in from a Women's Club meeting and found Chucha sitting next to the table, and her head was lying on it. Wanda told Geraldine she was concerned for her. They got her up and helped her to her bed.

Wanda said she would make dinner. Chucha didn't come down for dinner, so Wanda brought her up some food. She didn't eat much, and Jakob became concerned. She complained of being tired. He took her temperature, blood pressure, and pulse and then saw that her ankles were swollen. *I never noticed her ankles being so swollen. That's not good.*

"Tomorrow, we'll get you to the doctor," said Jakob.

The next morning she showed no change. Jakob and Geraldine took her to see Ross. Geraldine stayed with her, and Jakob left for his office. Ross did a physical examination and thought she should be seen by John Hudell. The latter had heart specialty training at Johns Hopkins University. He had been in Sheridan for a short while.

"I believe she has a heart problem called congestive heart disease," said Dr. Hudell once he had examined her. He prescribed several drugs for her and said she should not be working. "Apparently, she has some heart damage."

"I feel better today," she argued. "I take care of my family. Not work. I be all right." She felt she had to work because they needed her.

"Chucha, you need to rest and shouldn't do the work you are doing." said the doctor. "Your heart needs to rest. The medicine I will give you will make you feel better, but you are not a young lady anymore. The Millers will find someone to take your place." She bristled at those words and told the doctor she would be all right.

Geraldine decided to try to help. "Chucha, you don't have to worry about us. Wanda will help us for now. You need to get more rest. Nobody can ever replace you, but we'll get by. Jakob wants you to get well." This was enough to get her to cooperate.

"I rest and take easy. You right, Lady Geraldine."

Geraldine realized she was a sick lady and would not be able to continue working. As long as Wanda was there, they would get by. She had worked for Jakob since BethAnn was born. Wanda could take over, but it would be difficult. Chucha had made herself indispensable. They left the doctor's office and stopped to get her prescriptions filled.

"Looks like your lady has a serious heart problem," said Howard Smith, the pharmacist.

Jakob and Geraldine realized that she had to be replaced, but the question they both had was how they would do it and who they would get.

The next morning Josef stopped at Jakob's office to talk with him. Chucha was his aunt, and he knew she could no longer do the work of the Miller's housekeeper. Jozef had recently been made the vice-president of the bank. It was just a matter of time, and he would be the president. Roland Foster was close to retirement, so Wanda didn't really have to work.

"Wanda likes working for you, but I really want her at home, and we want to start our family. I don't think she should be taking on more. She'll stay with you and help until you get someone to take over Chucha's job. However, I have an idea that might work." said Jozef. "Chucha's sister Helen, whose husband had died in the mine explosion, might be a possibility. She is the youngest of the sisters, and her children are now old enough to take care of themselves. Aunt Helen would be perfect. She is a great cook and housekeeper like Chucha. If we told her that she was helping out Chucha, she might be motivated to do it. Since Walter died in the accident at the mine, she has been depressed and needs to be doing something to get her mind off the loss. Wanda will do well for now. You will like Helen. She speaks pretty good English and loves children. In fact, she had eight of her own."

Jakob felt uncertain about the lady, but she came from the same stock as Chucha. Maybe she would work out. That night he told Geraldine what Jozef had suggested.

"It's been some time since the loss of her husband. This might be good for her, and maybe we could motivate Chucha to feel her leaving would help her sister, and she wouldn't feel like she was abandoning us. I know she feels bad she will no longer take care of us, but she might accept it if she feels she's helping her sister. I'm all for trying," said Jakob.

"I'm sure we can get used to her sister," said Geraldine. "I will miss Chucha, and I didn't know Wanda wanted to start a family. One thing at a time. We can talk this over with Jozef, and Chucha can stay at home. I know she's worried that she won't be able to do the job."

Jakob was satisfied they had a solution for their problem. He saw Jozef that afternoon and presented the idea to him.

"I think this will work," Josef agreed. "Aunt Helen will be another Chucha for you. I'll talk with her first and bring her out for you to visit with her. I know you met her at the funeral, but this is different. If she feels she's helping Chucha, I'm sure she will be interested."

Jozef approached his aunt, and she was interested, so he brought her out to meet with the Millers. Jakob told her how much Chucha had pleased them by being their housekeeper all those years, but they worried about her health.

Aunt Helen was the image of a younger Chucha. She was sixty-eight years old and possessed the same spryness Chucha had. She was worried about her sister and didn't want her to work. "Chucha taught me everything I know about cooking, and Wanda will help me get started. I know all about your children, and I will be their Aunt Helen."

Geraldine was thrilled with her and everything she said. It was not a problem to accept her. It was how soon she would be able to start. Now, they had to break the news to Chucha.

The next Sunday, they drove to Acme, taking BethAnn and Randy with them. Chucha was sitting in her house dress and was waiting to see them. Randy immediately went to her and kissed her and sat on her lap until he had enough, and she let him go. BethAnn told her about school and her new friend Daisy. Then it was Jakob and Geraldine's turn.

Jakob told her she looked like she was doing well. He had talked to her doctor and agreed that she should not be working. It was not good for her heart. Nobody could take her place, but he found someone he thought might be almost as good, and she could help Wanda.

"I feel much better now, and I could still help my family," said Chucha.

"No, that wouldn't be right. I wouldn't want you to get sick again. Let me tell you who I found. Your sister, Helen! The job would be perfect for her, and it would help her get over the loss of her Walter."

"Helcha. Helen. I not think of her. Yes, poor Helcha. She miss her Walter bad. Be good if she find work. She be good for you. She cook like me and make *pierogi*. She be good. I tell her how to do everything. Poor Helen, she be so sad without Walter. She take good care of you. She be good housekeeper and cook. I tell her. I not worry for you."

Jakob looked at Geraldine and smiled. "Chucha, you really know how to pick someone to take your place."

She laughed. "Pan, you be good boss."

Helen was anxious to start working. She would stay with the Millers in Chucha's room. Wanda helped her settle in, and Chucha insisted on coming out to tell her what she had to do.

Geraldine got nervous, hoping it wouldn't discourage Helen when she found out. But it didn't, and Helen started off with a bang. The first day she baked the *chleb* and had a fine dinner for them. Wanda said she would stay on until they were able to find someone to take her place. She said that she would be looking too.

Sheridan was having a typical Wyoming winter—cold and plenty of snow. Jakob took the Ford to the office, and when he came out for lunch, he found it snowed in. He swept away the snow, got in and started it with some difficulty, and got a far as the Lucky Lady. He and Andy Meeks were having lunch together at Grand Ma's Diner. They finished and came out to find Jakob's Ford covered with snow once more. He brushed the snow off again and started it up, except it was stuck, and the drive wheel just spun. Andy got behind it and pushed until Jakob started to move, and Andy hopped on. They got as far as the Sheridan Inn, where a drift of snow stopped the car. Andy got out and tried pushing but to no avail. The car was stuck. What to do? Frustrated, Andy went into the inn and gave Wilbur at the livery a call to come and help Jakob.

They both sat in front of the fireplace, thawing out until Wilbur came with a team of horses. "Hey Doc, I see you got a problem. Want me to hitch my team to your car? I can get you and the car to your home. It won't cost you much." He and Andy started laughing at Jakob.

"What's so funny?" asked Jakob.

"Oh, nothing, Doc. I just thought that it's a good thing we still have horses around."

Jakob started to laugh. "Yeah, it's lucky we still have horses. Hitch me up and get me home."

Chapter 27
Jakob Declines Politics

The Wyoming winter lingered on with heavy snows and strong winds, which drove the snow into drifts. Jakob's Ford was now in the garage waiting for spring. Even the horses had difficulty managing the weather. Jakob used the sled, or he just rode horseback to his office. The Millers spent most of their time at home. His practice was slow. Toothaches and emergencies were generally treated, but patients avoided the difficult weather if possible.

Geraldine's Women's Club had few events. They kept the library open with volunteers, and the book club was generally attended. BethAnn kept herself busy and didn't miss school except for during the biggest snowstorms. She practiced her piano, and Simba was always with her. She would usually go to the barn to see Nelly, and weather permitting, even try to ride her to give her some exercise. Simba would always follow along. She was an outdoor dog and liked to romp in the snow.

Simba got a lot of attention from everyone and was trained and obedient for her age. She shed her puppy traits and got used to Randy, who liked to chase her, but his hands and knees were not fast enough to catch her.

It didn't take too long, and Randy was able to stand, holding on to whatever he could, and then he was striking out trying to walk. He was now making sounds like words. DaDa was the first. Wanda, who was good at sewing, made cute outfits for him. Jakob spent a lot of time in his workshop making furniture for Randy's room. He also made him a rocking horse which he liked to be put on and ride.

Jakob was a perpetual student and spent much time with his textbooks and dental journals. He studied the new techniques in dentistry and was in contact with his former teachers. He would sometimes stop at the slaughterhouse and obtain a calf's jaw to practice a surgical procedure. Jaw fractures were not uncommon with fistfights in the saloons, and he was the only one in town who knew how to take care of them. He still had it in his mind to go back to dental school and get more training under Dr. Logan, the surgeon. But he was needed at home, and he kept putting it off.

Wanda was still working as a housemaid and personal maid for Geraldine. But, Helen found someone to take her place. Anna was her name, and she was related to Walter's sister. She was younger but seemed talented and spoke good English.

Helen vouched for Anna, and she would soon be starting. Anna was twenty and was an attractive red-haired young lady. She had completed some high school but left because education for women was not considered important in those days. She had learned her home arts studies of sewing and cooking as well as reading and writing. That was enough for women because it was thought they would marry, become housewives, so schools stressed that in educating girls. However, Anna didn't seem to find a suitable mate to marry. Her family was disappointed. There weren't many jobs in Acme for young women. Those that were available had little opportunity. Anna had a nice personality. Helen said she had a beautiful singing voice. Jakob wondered whether she would like being a housemaid and would take on the job of a personal maid for Geraldine, but he would give her the opportunity. He noted that she had good penmanship and was very neat in appearance. Wanda and Helen taught her the tasks she was to accomplish, and she was a good learner. She turned out to be a great cook. She was every bit as good as Chucha and with more variety.

Jakob and Geraldine went to the Sheridan Inn for dinner. Lukas had a special menu item for them—duck with chokecherry sauce. Annabelle had their martinis ready for them. It had been a least a month since they went out for dinner. This was to be a special date for them. There was music by a local band, and so they danced. They met and talked with friends but ate by themselves.

"Jakob, I got a letter today with some surprising news. You remember the letter we got from my brother Randy at Christmas. He said he and his wife, Jenny Lynn, would be coming to visit us in the spring. Well, they are coming in April and will spend time with Eleanor and us. In fact, I even thought maybe we could go out to the ranch with them and spend more time together. You never met my brother, and I know you'll really like him and his wife, who is a doll. He said he was trying to get reservations on a new ship. It's supposed to be something really special and is the White Star Line's newest and biggest ship.

Remember when we went across the Atlantic? It was on the White Star Line RMS Oceanic. Well, he said this ship is even bigger, and to really make it special, it will be its maiden voyage. It will leave Southampton and stop at Cherbourg, France, and Queenstown, Ireland, before crossing the Atlantic. It really is supposed to be the most luxurious ship ever built. He had trouble getting reservations because some of the wealthiest people in Europe will be on board, and the reservations went fast. It's called the HMS *Titanic*. After they arrive, they can stay with us in the bedroom we just finished decorating. They'll appreciate the English-style furnishings. I can't wait till they come. The spring weather should be here soon."

"Oh, that is great. Yes, it's something to look forward to. You could even have a party here; I'm sure our friends would like to meet them. That might be fun going to the ranch with them. I'll bet they never experienced anything like it."

The next weeks there was a lot of talk about Geraldine's brother and wife. After Sir Gerald died, he became the Baron of Landry and even became a member of the House of Lords, so he knew a lot about England's goings-on.

Jakob went to the Lucky Lady after leaving his office and was talking with Mayor Burns. It was the first day out with the Ford since he garaged it for the winter, and it ran great.

"Jakob, I'm going to retire from this job. You know, I've been mayor of Sheridan a long time. Should have quit long ago, but I like the job, and they kept re-electing me. Time for new blood to take care of Sheridan. Doc Kelly says the stress will kill me if I don't quit. Well, I've been at it a long time, and it hasn't killed me yet, but my Bess also says I should quit. If anything will kill me, it's Bess if I'm around the house too much."

Jakob started laughing.

"No, I mean it, Doc. She'll be following me around with that gall-darned cuspidor. You know how she hates me chewing my chaw."

"Even more than I do? I gave up on you with you chewing tobacco," said Jakob.

"Yes, even you, Doc. Aw, she's a good woman, but she sometimes just gets under my skin with her nagging. You know, I've been thinking about who should take over. Why don't you take over, Doc? You would make a good mayor. You're young and got a lot of good ideas. You'd be great."

"Whoa, no way! I do not want to be mayor."

"Why not? You'd be perfect for the job. A lot of friends. Everybody knows you. That stint with President Taft when he was in town gave you a hell of a lot of exposure, and you proved you could handle big people. We need someone who can talk and negotiate and have Sheridan as a dedication."

"No, Mayor. I like my job. I don't need the kind of stress you want to get away from. I like doing dentistry and taking care of the people here in Sheridan. That's my dedication, but I appreciate your confidence. I liked working with you, but being in politics is not for me. I'll work with anyone who becomes mayor, but the job is not for me," said Jakob.

A couple of the guys heard the conversation and tried to talk to Jakob, but he was adamant about not wanting to get involved in politics.

Kelly walked in and headed straight toward Jakob. "Jake, you're just the guy I wanted to see."

"Now what, Kelly? What are you going to accuse me of?"

"What do you mean? I don't accuse you of anything. You're my friend and the best dentist in town. I wanted you to know I took care of an old patient of yours. A guy who once saved your life." said Kelly.

"Saved my life?" said Jakob.

"Yes."

"Who are you talking about?" said Andy Meeks, who was listening to the conversation.

"You forgot, huh? Zeke, the guy who took you elk hunting and killed the bear who was getting ready to take you. Zeke's in the hospital. He got into a fight over at the Cowboy saloon yesterday, and he really got worked over—busted some bones and even the false teeth you made him. I'm not sure, but his jaw might be broken. Why don't you take a look at him? Poor guy's in bad shape."

"Oh, that's too bad. He has a problem of talking when he should be listening. Feisty guy too. You're right: he did save my life. That bear was almost on top of me. I still have bad dreams about the event. Look, my arm still has the scars of those claws. Poor guy. That's how I got him as a patient. He got into a fight with a guy twice his size, and he busted all his front teeth. Yes, he's a feisty old codger. I'll stop by and see him," said Jakob.

"Is that your Tin Lizzie out there?" Kelly asked. "I thought you gave up on her when you had to call Wilbur to tow you in from the snowbank."

"There are no snowbanks now, and she runs pretty good. You ought to get one, Kelly, and give that old nag of yours a rest. I'm going to stop and see old Zeke. You guys can take it easy."

Jakob left the laughing group and headed for the hospital. He vividly remembered the event of the bear.

Entering the hospital, he found out where to find Zeke. Zeke was sleeping as he entered the room. A nurse nearby recognized Jakob and greeted him. Zeke's dentures, broken into several pieces, were in a container located next to his bed. His left forearm was broken and in a cast. His chest had been taped, so he must have some broken ribs. His face was bruised and swollen with cuts that had been sutured. His left eye was closed, and it looked like the zygomatic—cheekbone—was broken and pushed in. Poor Zeke was in bad shape.

His right eye opened, and he moaned. "Doc, sure glad to see you. I'm hurtin' Doc. That gorilla almost did me in. I think he was trying to kill me. All I did was to call him a son of a bitch. And the next thing I know is I'm here in the hospital with Doc Kelly looking me over."

Jakob carefully put his hands on his lower jaw and felt for a broken bone but found none. He opened his mouth to looked inside and saw lacerations. *They must have come from the broken false teeth.* Fortunately, the lower jaw was not fractured. They could take x-rays to be sure.

"Zeke, it looks like I'm going to have to do some suturing and straighten out that cheekbone. I'll be back tomorrow. They'll take some x-rays too.

"What about my false teeth, Doc? They's broken. I can't go around looking like this."

"I guess I'll have to make you some new ones."

"Okay, Doc. You know what you're doing. When do we start?"

"I'll be back tomorrow, and we'll fix that cheekbone and sew up the inside of your mouth. You just hang in there. They'll get the x-rays and put on some ice packs to get the swellings down. Give you something you can eat."

As Jakob left, he gave the nurse the orders as he wrote them down. The Ford quickly started up, and he headed for his home. The street was cleared of the winter's debris, but Loukes was still not paved, even though it had some of the nicest homes in Sheridan. He parked his Ford and noticed BethAnn was in the stable. "Hi, Honey. What are you doing?"

"Oh, I had Nelly out. We went over to Daisy Ross's home, and the two of us rode to the creek and saw some of the birds. I like riding with her. She's doing well since she started up. It was good exercise for Nelly.

I'm finished up. I fed and watered her, and she's ready for the night. I'll go in with you."

They went into the kitchen, and the aroma of dinner permeated the house. Helen was finishing up, and Anna was setting the table.

Geraldine and Randy were in the living room. Seeing Jakob, Randy worked his way off her lap, laughed with his arms out, and started walking to him. He didn't seem to realize he was walking until he got to Jakob, who picked him up. He put his hands on his face and kissed him.

"Da, da, da."

He and Jakob were really bonded, and he followed him around on his hands and knees, but now he was walking.

"You know, I think he's been waiting for you. I had him on my lap, and he kept looking toward the kitchen. Seems he knows you'll be coming from there," said Geraldine. "He's been so wiggly. Simba has been coming up to him. He puts his hands out to touch her, and she'll lick them. They're fun to watch. So how was your day?"

"It was interesting, to say the least, and busy enough." He told her about the meeting with the mayor.

"You're kidding. Would you really want to do that? It might be interesting. You have a lot of friends."

"And I want to keep my friends. No way would I want to be in politics. This has come up before, but I would not want any part of that.

"I saw Kelly at the Lady, and he told me about a former patient of mine who got into a fight and really got banged up. He was the guy who took me elk hunting, and I almost got eaten by that bear. Well, anyway, I saw him in the hospital, and I'm going to have to take care of him. That's the kind of thing I want to do. I can help him get through his injuries. No, not politics for me."

"I know you're right. I am so proud of you and hear so many fine things you have done," said Geraldine.

BethAnn had been listening and said, "I am too, Daddy. Someday I would like to help people who are sick or maybe be a dentist like you. I think I'd like that."

"That would be fine, honey. I remember you said something like that when the president asked you that question. I would be proud to see you do something like that. I know you could."

Dinner was now on the table, and they continued with the conversation.

"BethAnn, tomorrow is Saturday, and you don't have school. Would you like to come with me to the hospital and watch me work? It would give you an idea of what a dentist does, and you could talk to the nurses, and they could fill you in on their profession."

"Oh, yes, Daddy, I would love that. I thought about doing it sometime, but you're so busy."

"Not so busy that you couldn't come with me and watch. You're far enough in your schooling so that you should be considering a career after high school. Maybe I could teach you to assist me in my office. I could use some help. I could even pay you for helping me, and you could have money to spend or save in your bank account. How does that sound to you?"

"I think that sounds just great. What do you think, Mom? There are some girls in my class that have jobs. Laura Thomas milks cows before she comes to school in the morning."

Geraldine smiled and said, "I think you could fit it into your schedule, and it would give you an idea of what your career in life could be. Good idea, Dad."

The next morning BethAnn came down for breakfast dressed for her visit to the hospital and Jakob's surgery. She took care of Simba and was ready for the trip. She had never been in the hospital and was surprised at how big it was. Jakob introduced her to the nurses and told them she would be watching him work. They were surprised she was there. As he was scrubbing up, they put a white gown on her and a cap on her head.

Zeke was awake, and Jakob introduced her to him.

"I shore like to see them pretty ladies around me," said Zeke.

Jakob had seen the x-rays and decided the jaw was not broken. One of the nurses placed the mask over his mouth, and drops of either wet it, and he was soon asleep. The cheekbone had to be repaired. That didn't take too long, and soon he was suturing a laceration in his mouth. One of the nurses helped Jakob and seemed efficient. Several cuts had to be done, and he finished them. It wasn't too long, and Zeke woke up, and they took him to his bed.

BethAnn followed Jakob out of the surgery. He filled out the chart and left orders for the nurses. Jakob had introduced BethAnn to one of the nurses who would take her around the hospital and answer her questions. They gave BethAnn a good look around and told her about nursing as a career.

He sat in the doctors' lounge and talked with one of the doctors.

When she came back, BethAnn was all smiles. She really thought the day was great. There were many questions she had for Jakob, which he answered. They stopped at his office, and sure enough, there were a couple of patients waiting for him. One was the little boy he had taken care of several months ago. His mother never did bring him back for more care. He had a bad toothache. Jakob sat him in his chair with the mother outside. BethAnn engaged him in conversation. Jakob already had his trust and was able to remove the tooth for him.

When the morning was finished, Jakob took BethAnn to Grand Ma's for lunch. They sat together and ordered. BethAnn was filled with questions about what had taken place. She told him about the visit with the nurses. She was so excited and interested in what she saw; it was a delight to have been with her. Jakob had wondered why he had not done this before. He thoroughly enjoyed the time spent with his daughter and knew he had to do it again.

When they arrived home, she shared what had happened with Geraldine. There were things she had to do, and she went straight to them. He sat down with Geraldine, and they talked about BethAnn.

Jakob looked at Geraldine. "Funny, I guess I never truly realized my daughter was growing up. All of a sudden, she seems to be so mature."

Chapter 28
A Tragedy Hits Home

Jakob was having his lunch with his usual business friends in the Sheridan Inn bar room. He was one of the earliest members of the group, which had regularly met since Jakob's early days in Sheridan. Lunch was served in the far corner of the bar room.

Ray Johnson, the pharmacist, approached Jakob. "Jake, I understand you had a meeting with the mayor the other day, and I heard tell from a good source that he was planning on retiring. Is that true? Did he say anything about who would run for mayor, or doesn't he know yet? I also heard by the grapevine he asked you."

"I don't know what you heard, Ray, but yes, he's planning to retire. Said something about the stress of the job, and he has been mayor for too long. No, I don't think he knows who will be running. Yes, he asked me to run for mayor, and yes, I have no interest in running for mayor, period."

"Is this all for sure? Aren't you interested in running for mayor? I have absolutely no doubt you would be elected," said Harley Jenkins. Harley owned the Mountain Brewery and was a driving force in Sheridan.

"Let me put it to you guys straight. No, I'm not interested in running for mayor. Just because I go to the meetings at city hall doesn't mean I want to be mayor. I go because I plug some of the stuff which I believe needs to be done around town. All you guys should go to the meetings. We need to pave some more streets, we need more street lights, and we need more places for the kids to let off steam—for example, playgrounds. Sheridan is growing fast, and we got to do things around here to make it better. Okay, that's my pitch."

There was plenty of discussion going on about the mayor when Elmer Findley came in.

"Elmer, we haven't seen you for a while," said one of the members. Where you been?"

"Yes, I know, I know. But just when I'm ready to leave to come here, something happens at the store, and I have to straighten it out. Sorry boys, I'll try harder. Hey, did you see the newspaper this morning? The front page has a picture and story about that new super English liner, the HMS *Titanic*. Well, it sunk! Says here it hit an iceberg. Can you imagine that? It was supposed to be unsinkable. Look here in the paper at the headlines. It says 1,500 people lost their lives."

Jakob stood up. "Let me see the paper, Elmer." He viewed the front page. His expression was aghast. "Oh my God! Oh my God!" He slowly sat in his chair. His complexion had turned white.

One of the men looked at him. "What's the matter, Jake?"

"Oh my God! Geraldine's brother and his wife were on that ship. They were coming to visit us. We expected them here in a couple of weeks. My poor wife. He was her younger brother. They were going to stay with us, and then we would be going to the ranch together."

"Oh, that's terrible," said Elmer. Others chimed in on their feelings for Geraldine.

"It says here some of them were saved. Maybe Geraldine's brother and his wife were saved because it said some were saved, and their lifeboats were picked up by another ship," countered Harley.

Others then chimed in, "Yes, some were saved, but it didn't list any names of who was saved. Maybe Geraldine's brother and sister-in-law were saved.."

Jakob was now shaken up. "I better go home and tell my wife what has happened; if she hasn't heard already. She will be really upset when she finds out. Thanks for your concern." Jakob was very upset and worried for Geraldine. He wondered how they would find out whether the brother and wife were saved. As he drove home, thoughts raced through his mind. *If she hasn't heard about the* Titanic, *I'll have to tell her. Oh, how terrible. What can I say?* He entered the house.

Geraldine was eating lunch. "I thought you were having lunch with your friends today. Did you forget?"

"No, Hon..."

"What's the matter? Is something wrong?"

"Yes, I guess you haven't heard. Elmer brought the newspaper with him. The headline said the HMS *Titanic* has sunk. It hit an iceberg. They say 1500 people went down with it."

"Oh, Jakob, Randy and Jenny Lynn were on the Titanic. Oh!" She burst into tears. "Did all the people die?"

Jakob held her and said, "Those who stayed with the ship but some got into lifeboats, and I understand they were saved. The article didn't say how many lived. It mentions a ship not too far away came in time to pick up those in lifeboats. So I guess it's possible that Randy and Jenny Lynn got into one. Maybe they were saved. I don't know where we could find out, but we can start checking."

"Oh, then there's hope. Maybe they did make it. Oh God, I pray Randy and Jenny Lynn are safe."

"This article doesn't really tell too much. Maybe we can call the shipping line in New York." Geraldine was heartened. Some were alive, but no one knew how many survived, which left them under a cloud.

They tried calling the White Star Line but to no avail. All the phones were busy. Next, they tried calling different newspapers in New York but could not get through. All the phones were tied up, no matter how many times they called. Jakob went to the *Sheridan Post* and talked to his old friend Edgar Wright, hoping he might have a direct line to a New York newspaper, but he too was stymied.

All they knew was that some passengers were rescued by a ship called RMS *Carpathia*, which was not too far from the sinking *Titanic*. The news article said the *Titanic* carried 2224 passengers and crew, and 1500 went down with the ship, so it would seem there must have been 724 who lived. Nobody knew who the survivors were. They went to bed, not knowing if Randy and Jenny Lynn were alive. Both tossed and turned and wondered throughout the night.

Jakob woke up hearing BethAnn with Simba, and then she evidently brought down Randy, who had decided to get up.

"I'm sorry if I awakened you, Daddy, but Simba needed to go out, and Randy was also awake, so I brought him down. I'm so sorry about Mom's brother Randy. You can't find anything out, can you? Oh, I hope they're alive."

"I am too, honey. We were so happy and excited they would come here and see us. And now we don't even know if they are alive."

Helen and Anna were getting breakfast ready and sharing concerns for Randy and Jenny Lynn. Geraldine came down deeply concerned for her brother.

"Randy is such a great guy. We would have so much fun together. He was so kind to me when I lost James. I thought about calling Mama, but she would probably not know any more than we do. I'm sure she's frantic if she heard about the sinking."

After breakfast, they started making calls, but it seemed all the lines were busy, and the calls could not get through. Geraldine was terribly distraught but seemed to be holding up. They got the daily newspaper, but it didn't have anything new, except that the rescue ship would be arriving in New York on the eighteenth.

"What should we do, Jakob? Should we go out to New York and meet the ship: hoping Randy and Jenny Lynn were saved? Or, should we just wait and see what happens?"

"I wish we could just contact the White Star offices, but we can't get through," said Jakob. After much effort, they finally talked to a White Star agent who couldn't give them much information other than the ship would arrive on the 18th and probably in the morning. The names list they had available did have Landry on the list of those saved. When they arrived, the survivors would be put up in New York hotels. They didn't know which ones. Some were injured, but none too seriously.

Geraldine and Jakob were heartened by the news that the name Landry was on the list, but two should have been listed. They were in a quandary as to what to do. To meet them, it would take a minimum of three days by train if they were able to get reservations, and they would have to leave tomorrow to get there when the ship arrived.

"Jakob, what should we do? If they come in, they will need help. I hope you can go with me. You know your way around better than me."

"Of course I'll go. Let's go to the depot and see if Henry Smit will help us with the train reservations."

They headed for the train station and told Henry of the problem. He certainly would try to get the tickets, and he did get suitable reservations.

"There is a train leaving at noon tomorrow, which will arrive in Chicago on the 17th before noon. Then the New York Central train will leave at 4:00 and arrive in New York before noon on the 18th," said Henry.

They had tickets, so now they had to get ready to go.

BethAnn and Randy would be all right with Helen and Anna to care for them. Anna was very good with Randy. He was used to her, and BethAnn would help. They quickly packed a minimum of clothes. There was a lot of apprehension, and the trip to New York was not exactly a happy one. They still were not completely sure Randy and Jenny Lynn would be there. There could be another Landry.

Andy Meeks took them to the station, and they boarded the Burlington Missouri. They had a small compartment which they could sleep in, and there was a dinner car. The train made stops at the bigger cities, but there were also stops for coal and water and a change of trains at Burlington, Iowa. The trip then crossed the Mississippi and on to

Chicago. Time seemed to drag. Cornfields were just starting to show green, and then the tall buildings of Chicago came into view. They had their things together when the conductor announced Chicago Union Station. Their baggage was transferred to a taxi, which took them on a frantic drive across Chicago to the New York Central Station on Randolph Street. They checked their luggage for the Twentieth Century Limited, which would take them to New York City.

Jakob looked at his watch. "We made good time, and we haven't had our lunch. Let's take a cab back downtown. I'll take you to one of my favorites, the Black Hawk Restaurant, and if there still is enough time, we'll go to Marshal Fields for a real treat." The cab stopped at the Black Hawk on Wabash Street. They sat in a booth, ordered martinis, and sipped them until their lunch arrived. There was some time left for a short walk to the Marshall Field department store. They bought some special items for BethAnn and Randy, and it was time to take a taxi to the New York Central Station.

They found the platform to what was called the Red Carpet to New York. Going aboard, they located their compartment and readied themselves for the journey to New York. Why didn't White Star give them two names? It wasn't to be an enjoyable or exciting trip. They had a mission in the big city. They still were apprehensive about Randy. They bought the Chicago Tribune newspaper, which had a full-page story on the *Titanic*. The RMS *Carpathia* would be bringing the survivors to New York tomorrow. Nothing too helpful. The dinner car waiter came by announcing dinner was now being served, but they weren't ready to eat, having had a big lunch at the Black Hawk Restaurant just a short while ago.

"They'll be serving late, so we can get dinner later," said Jakob.

They read the newspaper and learned all about the *Titanic* and as much about the iceberg that it hit. They found it hard to understand the *Titanic* was so negligent not to be careful when they knew there were icebergs in the vicinity. Later they heard the porter come by, and Jakob asked for direction to the dining car.

"It be two cars back, Sir."

At 8:00, their hunger pangs were discovered, so they made their way to the dining car. There was someone ahead of them, and they waited just a short while until a table was available.

A white-coated waiter greeted them and placed a menu in front of them. "May I get you a cocktail or a glass of wine?"

Jakob replied, "Does your bartender make a good martini?"

The waiter smiled. "Of course. You name it, and he can make it for you."

Jakob ordered the martinis, and they soon were sipping them and having their appetizer of oysters on the half shell.

"It isn't very often we can get oysters," said Geraldine, and they enjoyed them.

Then, a prime rib dinner was served. The dining car was full, and they enjoyed their meal. They heard people at an adjacent table talking about the *Titanic*. Evidently, they were hoping to see their parents, who were rescued. Jakob tried to speak with them, but they weren't interested in a conversation. When they got back to their compartment, their beds were ready. Looking out into the night, some lights were seen as the train moved quickly by. It wasn't too long, and they chose to sleep.

Light crept through the sides of the shades, and the clickity-clack and sway of the train awakened Jakob. Geraldine still slept. He heard sounds of people passing by their compartment going to the dining car, but he just laid there, and thoughts came to mind. *Because White Star Line just had one name, Landry, it made him wonder if just one survived, but then, no, they just had the family name*

Finally, Geraldine stirred and lifted her head. "Oh, you're awake, Jakob," and she kissed him.

"I've been awake for some time. But I let you sleep. I've been doing some thinking. I hope we can make contact without too much trouble. They should be able to help us at the dock. With over seven hundred twenty survivors, they should be organized and be able to help put us in touch."

"I will recognize Randy, and I do remember Jenny Lynn."

They got dressed for breakfast and were soon drinking their coffee. Bright sunlight entered the dining car, and soon various city buildings were being passed. An occasional rail crossing and switches were felt. New York City was not too far ahead, and tall buildings became visible.

After breakfast, they were ready to leave. Once more, apprehension was gripping them. The porter came by and asked if they needed any help. They just had their carryons. Their luggage would be in the station, ready for them to claim it. Finally, the call came. They had arrived at Grand Central Station. The luggage was located and brought out to a taxi.

"Where you headed, mister?" the cab driver asked.

"Take us to the St. Regis Hotel."

The trip through the city was hectic. Traffic was heavy and moved slowly, but soon they stopped at the St. Regis Hotel. The baggage was taken inside, and Jakob registered.

A bellhop led the way to the room. "Are you folks going to the steamship docks to see the *Carpathia* with the survivors of the *Titanic*? Lots of folks are going there. It should be docked by now. Supposed to get in at 9:30."

Jakob looked at his watch, and it was 11:00, which meant the ship was there already. He thought it would be in later. He tipped the boy and thought they should leave for the docks right away. They freshened up quickly and were in a cab. They had a copy of the New York Times, which said it would be docked at Pier 54.

There, the traffic was almost impossible, and they became very nervous because of delays.

"I wonder how we will find them," said Geraldine.

"I'm sure White Star will have a place where we can make contact."

They stopped near the pier and had to walk to it. It was very large. You could see the *Carpathia*, and people were still going down the gangplank. It became almost impossible to move through the crowd. There must have been thousands of people present. At one side, there was a big sign that read White Star Line. On the other side were smaller ones for the Women's Relief Committee Aid Society. Further down was another sign that said Council of Jewish Women. They went to the White Star office, where there were several lines of people. The lines moved along quickly, and they were soon standing in front of a lady.

Geraldine said, "We're looking for my brother and sister. The names are Randolph Landry and Mrs. Jenny Lynn Landry."

The lady searched several pages.

"Oh, here it is, Mrs. Jenny Lynn Landry. Oh my, there is no Randolph Landry." She looked further and then sorrowfully looked at Geraldine. "Oh, my. Mrs. Landry is here, but her husband evidently didn't make it. I'm so sorry. I guess they must have got separated, and he didn't get in the lifeboat."

They both stood frozen to the ground, and tears started down Geraldine's cheeks. "Oh Jakob, Randy didn't make it."

He held her close.

"Oh no," she softly sobbed.

The lady looked down on her lists; then, looking up, she softly said, "I have Mrs. Landry here." She paused. "I guess she's been checked in and has been referred to the Traveler's Aid Society. They are on the other side. I'm so sorry. This tragedy has been so difficult. I've talked to so many who lost loved ones. I almost feel like I know them. There is no way to explain this." She looked up at Geraldine. "I'm sure she's being taken care of by the aid group. They'll help you find her. Thank you for coming because I'm sure she will need you."

They slowly walked away. Geraldine seemed to regain her composure as they headed to the Traveler's Aid Society. Opening the door, they entered a large room with many chairs, some desks, and separate rooms across one side of the wall. It was filled with people. In the middle was a counter with an information sign, where they stopped.

Geraldine asked the man attending, "I'm looking for my sister-in-law, Mrs. Jenny Lynn Landry."

He looked at his sheet. "She's here and has been checked in. Now we have to find her. She's in room 106. Suzie, will you take these people there?"

Suzie, one of the aid people, led the way. Room 106 was a rather large room furnished with chairs, couches, lamps, and tables with magazines and newspapers. A group of people sat on one sofa talking. On the other side of the room, seated on a couch, a young woman talked to a young man who was standing. There were a couple of packages and paper bags next to her. Her eyes stared past the man. She looked sad and disheveled in her plain black skirt, wrinkled white blouse, and dark unbuttoned sweater. Her hair was a mess, and her face was pale.

"Jakob, I think... there she is. Yes, that's Jenny Lynn." Geraldine half ran and walked to her. "Jenny Lynn Landry."

She looked up at Geraldine, startled. "Yes. I'm Jenny. Oh my. Geraldine, it's you!" She started to cry as Geraldine sat down next to her, put her arms around her, and held her close. Jenny buried her head in Geraldine's bosom, sobbing uncontrollably as Geraldine held her.

Finally, she looked up, still sobbing. "Geraldine, Oh Geraldine, I'm so happy to see you. This has been a nightmare for me. I can't believe you're here. They have been trying to help me get a place to stay and to call home. I just didn't know what I should do. I wished I had stayed with Randy, and we would have died together, but now I have no one. And now you've come. Oh, Geraldine, I'm so unhappy. I lost my Randy." And she began to sob again.

The young man looked bewildered but saw Geraldine was ministering to her. "I'll be at my desk if you need me," he said as he left.

Geraldine softly spoke to her, trying to reassure her that she was safe and that she would take care of her. Others came into the room and left, but Geraldine stayed with Jenny Lynn. She had lost her husband, she was frightened, and she was hurting deep inside. They sat and talked, and Geraldine tried to reassure her everything would be all right. But it couldn't be because she had lost her husband. Her worldly possessions were reduced to the clothes she wore and the few things given to her by people on the *Carpathia* who were very kind to her.

Jakob talked to the young man who worked for the aid society and told him that he would take her to the hotel and care for her as long as needed.

Arrangements were made with White Star and the aid society. White Star assumed the responsibility, and they left for the St. Regis Hotel. Several newspaper reporters tried to get her to tell them about the sinking. Jakob refused to allow the reporters to bother a very emotional Jenny Lynn. They soon had her in a taxi to the St. Regis.

They entered the hotel, and Jakob made arrangements to have adjoining rooms. Jenny Lynn was quiet and didn't talk. She just sobbed off and on.

"Jenny, you must be hungry. We'll get something for you to eat. I'll call room service."

She shook her head. "I'm not hungry. I don't want anything. I'm afraid I'll throw up."

"You must eat something. You need some nourishment. It will be light. Maybe some soup and a sandwich. We'll help you," said Geraldine.

Jenny laid back on the bed, rubbing the tears from her eyes. Geraldine helped get her legs on the bed and covered her. Both Jakob and Geraldine were emotionally distraught. They suffered along with the poor young woman who had been through such a trauma. She fell asleep, and they called room service for their lunch. They felt Jenny needed to rest and could eat when she awakened. The room was almost dark, and she slept. She was evidently emotionally exhausted, but she moaned and cried and waved her arms.

"What are we going to do, Jakob? She has gone through hell. We need to call home and let them know we're with her. We have to tell them about Randy. We can't send her back home. I think we should keep her here with us in Sheridan. Give her a chance to recover from this terrible event. What do you think?"

Jakob thought a moment and nodded his head. "I think you're right. We can't let her go. She could be headed for a nervous breakdown. She needs all the love we can give her. We can afford the time and effort."

They could hear her stirring, and Geraldine looked in on her. She was awake.

"Do you feel better, Jenny? You did get a good sleep."

She nodded her head. "Yes, I think so. Maybe I can have something to eat now."

"We'll have something for you shortly. You can have your lunch, and there is a nice bath in there that will be waiting for you. I can give you some of my things for you to change into. Tomorrow we'll go shopping for your needs. Jakob and I have decided you should stay with us until you recuperate from your ordeal. I'm going to call home and tell them you're going to be fine."

"Geraldine, you don't have to do that. Give me a couple of days, and I'll be able to go back. You have been so kind to me."

"This unfortunate trip was to visit us. Let's use it as a way for you to rest from the ordeal you have been through. Tomorrow we'll go to Macy's and get you the wardrobe you lost. Don't worry, we'll get in touch with home so you can tell them you are with us and will stay until you rest up. You'll be fine with us, and you'll also see Eleanor at the ranch. We love you, and we want this for you," said Geraldine.

She came up to Geraldine and hugged her, and thanked her for her concern, and she would do what she suggested. Her lunch arrived, although it was time for dinner. They decided to place a call early the next day, but they had already sent off a telegram saying that JennyLynn was safe and a call would be coming.

It seemed Jenny Lynn was better. She had her lunch and bath. Geraldine helped her and noted a large bruise on her left side, which hurt when she touched it. Jenny said that she got hurt when the lifeboat hit the water, and a wave smashed it against the ship, causing her to fall. She said many fell when the *Carpathia* caused a big wave as they came alongside. The rest of the evening was small talk and about her stay in Sheridan. Jenny Lynn went to bed and fell asleep early.

"Jakob, she's doing better. I don't look forward to the long train ride, but we can try to keep her comfortable so she can rest."

"I thought we might break it up and see my parents in Milwaukee. But maybe it might not be the best thing to do," said Jakob. "Let's just see how she does."

The day had been stressful for Geraldine and Jakob. Geraldine's loss of her brother left her with a deep emotional feeling. She remembered how they had a relationship during their youth. He was just two years her junior. She talked freely about him with Jakob, who had not met him. They fell asleep, knowing that the next day would be easier.

Jakob left an early wake-up call because they would have to put through a call to England. The time difference made it necessary to call early to get the news to the family in the morning. He and Geraldine were up and ordered coffee and rolls. Jenny still slept. The call was put through, and they had to wait for it to be answered. It was more than an hour before it was finally connected. The butler answered and immediately notified Lady Mary, who picked up the phone.

"Mama, this is Geraldine in New York. Did you get our wire yesterday?"

She had received it and was aware that Randy had perished in the *Titanic* disaster. She was still emotionally upset and could hardly talk. Geraldine told her that Jenny Lynn was saved. They spoke as best they could with her mother sobbing. She gave the telephone to Geraldine's sister, who was more coherent. They talked at length about their plans and asked her to contact Jenny Lynn's parents, the Herberts, and tell them she was doing well under the circumstances.

Geraldine and Jakob had their coffee and made plans for the day while Jenny Lynn slept. After she woke up, they had breakfast. Geraldine took Jenny Lynn to buy her some clothes. Jakob made calls and got train reservations to go back home. It was late in the afternoon when the two women arrived with boxes and bags of clothes for the trip to Sheridan. Jenny dressed for dinner, and she looked beautiful. She didn't talk except to answer their queries.

The trip back to Sheridan was with little conversation. Jenny Lynn had suffered a deep hurt. She carried the *Titanic* tragedy inside and would not talk about it. They arrived in Sheridan, happy to be back, but knowing that the coming days would be a challenge.

Chapter 29
Zeke Gets New Teeth

Jakob was up bright and early. He knew he would be busy as soon as his patients found out he was back in town. Zeke would be ready for his new dentures, and the patient with the broken jaw should be healed by now. He would be anxious to have the wires removed.

Helen was already in the kitchen, and the coffee was ready when he came in. "Doctor, we're glad you came back this soon because little Randy really missed you, as did BethAnn. They were really easy to take care of. Your BethAnn is so grown-up. She was very helpful in taking care of her brother, but the children did miss you and Lady Geraldine. That is so terrible what happened to her brother and his wife. I'm not sure what I should call her. She is also called Lady Jenny, isn't she?"

"I think you can skip the formalities and just refer to her as Jenny Lynn. Right now, she's going through a terrible period, and I might even call it sick. The loss of her husband and the circumstances of that loss have her in a very emotional state. We have to help her get through the tragedy. You just treat her kindly, as you would any one of us. I'm sure you can empathize with her because you lost your husband just a short time ago."

Jakob heard Simba coming down the stairs, and soon she was paws up on Jakob's lap. Jakob gave her a hug and went to the door to let her out. BethAnn was also on her way down and carried Randy, who saw Jakob and held his little hands out to him. Jakob took him and received kisses. He was so happy to see his father. He was a lovable little boy.

"Daddy, we're so glad you came back. We didn't know when to expect you, and we missed you and Mama. Everything was fine here, but Randy fussed a little. I think he just missed you and Mama. Helen is so nice to us. She's just like Chucha. You know, Daddy, I still miss Chucha. Do you think we could go visit her sometime?"

"I think we could. I'm sure she would be happy to see us."

Geraldine walked in, and Randy's attention immediately changed to her. She took him from Jakob, and it was kisses for her. They sat at the table. Helen had baked a breakfast cake and gave Randy some. He was all for the cake.

"I wish he was as excited about eating his carrots as he is for the sweets," said Geraldine. "I see Jenny Lynn hasn't come down yet, has she? We'll just let her sleep a while longer. I hope she's not using sleep as her way out of reality. Coming back on the train, that's almost all she did. Jakob, do you think we should ask Father Binotti to help us? She is a member of the Episcopal Church, so their differences are not significant. Maybe he has run into situations like this, and he is so knowledgeable. I feel so sorry for her, but I really don't know what more we can do that will help her."

"That thought came to my mind too," said Jakob, "We could take her to church this Sunday, and that way, she could meet him. Good thought. I'll be going down to the office this morning. I'll probably stick around there for a while in case I have patients, so I don't know exactly when I'll be back. You'll have some time with Jenny and can get her acquainted with the house. Do you know whether she rides? If she does, that might be a way for her to get some exercise and get her mind off her misery." Jakob then left.

His first stop was at the post office. The postmaster inquired about the New York trip and if Geraldine's brother made it. Jakob relayed the story of the loss. He was touched by the tragic circumstances.

Jakob did get some mail from his alma mater about a homecoming. *I haven't been to one in a long time. Maybe, I should go. Be nice to see my parents too.* There was also a letter from his mother.

He made it to the office and started getting it straightened up when Kelly showed up. Kelly didn't look good. He'd been losing weight, and Jakob was concerned about his friend. He asked about the New York trip, and Jakob told him about what had happened. He had a thought about Jenny's problem.

"It's really no different than the shell shock some men had in combat. I saw a lot of that in the war. It took me a long time to get over it. Get her talking about what happened. Don't let her keep it inside."

They talked until one of Jakob's patients came in, and then Kelly left. There were several more toothaches he took care of, and then it was lunchtime.

He stopped over at the Lucky Lady to catch up on the news and maybe have lunch with Andy Meeks.

"Good to see you, Doc. Sure we can have lunch. Harry, you can take over. I'm going to lunch."

They stopped over at Grand Ma's place. Jakob filled him in on the events in New York.

"Doc, have you seen Kelly lately? He doesn't look too good. He had one of his spells the other night. We didn't know what to do for him until he took one of his pills and got over it. This has happened a few times now. I think he's drinking more too. You know him. Maybe you can talk to him and find out if he's having a problem."

They talked about the mayor and wondered if there was a definite plan for a new mayor yet. There would be an election. Jakob left for the office, and Zeke was waiting for him.

"Doc, I shore hope you can get me fixed with them teeth. I can't chew anythin' since I got that busted jaw."

Jakob noticed Zeke had lost some weight.

"I'm gettin' skinny. Got to wear suspenders to keep my pants up. Think we can make a deal like last time? I'll take you elk huntin', and you make me those teeth."

"I'm not sure I want to go. I still remember last time. My souvenirs of that deal are on the wall out there in the waiting room. That bear almost did me in. Look. See the scars on my arm?"

"Doc, that there's not my fault. I dint know that bear was around. I shot him, dint I? And I got you back so's Doc Kelly could fix you up."

"Yes, I guess you're right. I can't blame you for that bear attack, but I'm not so sure I want to go. I'm pretty busy right now. I got a number of other things I need to do."

"Doc, you once tell me some folk you know out east want to go huntin'. How bout if I take someone else and you? You know a friend. I ain't got the cash to pay for the teeth, an' I ain't been workin' since I got busted up. I need my teeth."

Jakob realized Zeke was not the best-paying prospect, but he had known him since he came to this town. Actually, he was his first patient when he came to Sheridan in '95, so he knew he had to help him out. Then he thought about his father, who mentioned once that he would like to go elk hunting. *I once promised dad I would take him. This might be a good time to do it.*

"Tell you what I can do for you, Zeke. I'll make the dentures for you if you take my dad and me hunting. How's that sound to you? Just like last time, you furnish the guns and gear for us, except no bears. We can do without them. What do you say?"

"Hey, that be great, Doc. When do you want to go? Next week?"

"I can't do it now. I have too many things going on. It would have to be in the fall—October or November."

"Doc! I can't wait that long to get teeth. I needs them now. I can't eat a decent meal without them teeth."

"Okay, okay. I'll do the teeth now, but you got to promise me you'll take us hunting in the fall. No ifs, ands, or buts. You promise to keep your part of the bargain, and I'll start to make the teeth for you now."

"Shore Doc, you can trust me. I'll take you huntin' anytime you want. So can we make the teeth now? "

"All right, Zeke, you sit in the chair, and we'll start." Jakob started getting his impression trays ready.

"Now, Doc, you ain't going to put that white stuff in my mouth like you did last time, are you?."

"Sorry, Zeke, but just like last time. I have to take impressions of your jaws, and Plaster of Paris is the only thing I have that is accurate. Quit your complaining, or I won't make teeth for you. You'll have to do without eating a decent meal and go around looking like an old sod. Ladies won't even want to talk to you because you don't have teeth and can't smile."

"Sorry, Doc. I won't complain."

Jakob took impressions of his jaws and started the procedure of making his dentures.

Zeke left the office, picking bits of plaster from his beard and mumbling that he didn't understand why he had to use that stuff in his mouth.

Jakob started thinking about asking his father to go hunting with him but hadn't come up with a date

The following Sunday, they went to Father John Binotti's church and took Jenny Lynn with them. She seemed to be doing a little better and wanted to go. She had talked with her parents, and they thought they might come out and get her so she could return to England. The Herberts were anxious to bring her home but were agreeable that she stay with Geraldine and Jakob. At church, she met Father Binottti. He made arrangements to visit her that week. His visit proved to be helpful, and he was anxious to spend some more time with her.

Jenny Lynn was starting to enjoy her stay. Little Randy took a liking to her, and she would take him out in his buggy. Father John stopped by to see her again, and the visit was good for her.

Plans were now being made to go to the ranch. BethAnn was anxious to go to see her horse and work on her lassoing. There was a post in the yard that she practiced roping, but she was not too successful. She talked about Slim teaching her.

Jakob had finished the dentures for Zeke. He came in all shined up. He had gotten a bath at the Spokane Bath House, had his hair cut and beard trimmed. Jakob put the dentures in his mouth, and Zeke was a new man. He grinned approval when he saw himself in the looking glass, thanked Jakob, and was anxious to show off for his friends.

Jakob's advice to him after he had adjusted them was, "Zeke, take your teeth out of your mouth before you get into a fight. And don't pick a fight with Big Homer."

"Me and Homer are friends now," said Zeke.

"Remember now, you're going to take my dad and me elk hunting this fall."

"You jess let me know, Doc, when you want to go." He grinned a big smile. "I'll see you later. Got to see ma friends over at the Cowboy Saloon."

Word came back to Jakob that Zeke was really proud of his teeth. He would take them out and show them to anyone he talked with. And, he would tell them who made them for him. Jakob had a rush on patients who wanted false teeth. However, most of them were not able to pay the price, and he wasn't interested in more deer or elk hunting. He already had one date set up.

Chapter 30
Meanwhile, Back at the Ranch

The Millers prepared for the trip to the ranch now that BethAnn's classes were over for the summer. She had passed into the senior year of Sheridan High School. She was starting to think about what she wanted to do after graduation the next year. BethAnn always talked about doing something that would help people. She admired her dad for doing dentistry and had spent some time in his office helping him. When Jakob did some work in the hospital, she came to watch him, which led her to become interested in nursing. BethAnn talked with the nurses there and wondered if that might be a career for her. The nurses really excited her interest.

However, Jakob remembered the time she said she wanted to be a teacher like her mother. Of course, she had no memory of Liz. She was just two when her mother died, but many people told her about Liz and how she was such a great teacher. Her grades were high, but she didn't seem to want to go to college because it meant she had to leave home. BethAnn was a homebody, and there was no college in Sheridan or nearby. Jakob felt she would finally come up with a career that satisfied her interests.

She loved animals and especially horses. BethAnn had become an expert in horsemanship. She was already planning to enter dressage events in the summer, maybe going to Laramie or Cody in addition to Sheridan. She was teaching her friend Daisy Ross to ride, and the two girls would often go out riding together. And, of course, there were boys. She was a beauty. Tall and slim with an infectious smile, she resembled her mother. Jakob could never really forget Liz because of BethAnn. She even had her mother's mannerisms. She had long blond hair, which she wore in a ponytail, and she sat tall in the saddle. It was no wonder the boys would carry her books home from school, although she didn't seem too interested in them.

"Boys act silly," she once said to Geraldine. But there was Mark Ross, Daisy's brother, who was now in medical college. He said he wanted to be a doctor, and BethAnn noted he seemed to be more serious.

BethAnn was anxious to go to the ranch and ride her new horse, the chestnut named Princess. Princess was more spirited than Nelly, and she liked that.

Jakob had mixed emotions when it came to the ranch. He enjoyed it, but he always had one foot back in Sheridan. This time he thought he would drive the Ford instead of going by wagon. They would save a lot of time. There were new roads that went most of the way, and the final trail would be tolerable. Raymond would be coming in for supplies, and he could follow them with the horse and wagon. Should they have a problem with the car, he would be a help. Jakob had learned a lot about the vehicle and could even do some repairs if necessary. He was mechanically inclined, which seemed to be the nature of dentists.

He topped off the gas tank at Findley's. He even carried some spare cans of gas and extra water for the radiator if necessary. They left at sunup with Raymond following. The roads out of town were good, and they were making good time, but then they came to a stretch of road damaged by a recent bad rain storm that cut down their speed considerably. Geraldine let Jakob know they could have taken the wagon and maybe have done just as well. But Jakob thought they would make up any time loss later on. They did hit a good stretch of road and made up for the washed-out bit. At about noon, they turned off onto the trail which would take them to the ranch. Before too long, they hit a bump, and the left front tire blew and went flat.

"Don't worry. We'll be all right. I'll just change it with the spare," said Jakob. They all got out of the car and sat under a nearby tree in the shade, watching while Jakob changed the tire. "It wasn't all bad having the flat tire," he said, "because when the engine stopped, the radiator showed it was overheating." By the time Jakob finished changing the tire, he could add water to the hot radiator and continue the trip to the ranch.

At 2:00 pm, they parked in front of the house. There was a lot of excitement when the ranch hands saw the Ford drive up. Eleanor and Allen came out to see what was making so much noise. The men carefully inspected the car and, smiling, shook their heads. They greeted Geraldine and Jakob but said nothing about the automobile.

Little Deer had a cold drink for them, and they sat on the porch talking about the trip and the few unsavory events. They rested awhile and talked before going up for baths to wash off all the trail dust.

Randy was finally able to get off Geraldine's lap and move around on the porch. The trip and being on his mother's lap all that time were not easy for him. Prince, the cat, caught his fancy, but the cat would not go near him, and he pursued it in vain.

Eleanore greeted Jenny Lynn, and they embraced. She held Jenny tightly, expressing her sorrow for her loss. Her husband was also Eleanor's brother, and she, too, felt the loss. The ladies talked and then left to be together. Eleanor knew Jenny, having met her when the Herberts once visited the Landrys two years ago.

This now left Allen with Jakob. Allen talked excitingly about the ranch and his experiences. He appeared to have changed his feelings. Taking part in the workings of the operation seemed to have made all the difference. He took pride in what he was doing.

BethAnn went to the corral and talked with some of the men she met before, but Slim wasn't there, so she left and decided to go to the stable. She wanted to see her horse. Princess saw her as she walked in and recognized her, making a fuss at the door to her stable. BethAnn patted her head, and the horse showed her fondness for BethAnn. She opened the door and went in to pet her mare and talk to her. She obviously became bonded to BethAnn when she was there before. BethAnn saw one of the stable boys and told him she wanted to walk Princess. They put on a halter, and she led her from her stall out to the yard. She walked the horse to the ranch house where Allen and Jakob were talking. Jakob was concerned the horse might prove to be difficult to manage.

"Don't you think you should have waited for Geraldine before taking Princess out?" he asked.

"No, Daddy. She was real happy to see me, and I'm just taking her for a walk. She needs the exercise. I'll ride her tomorrow. We're just getting acquainted again, and she likes it."

The horse nickered and seemed happy to be led by BethAnn, and they walked back to the stable. BethAnn led her to the stall and put her in. "See you tomorrow, Princess." She petted and hugged the horse and left.

Near the entrance to the stable was a large stall. It was always empty, but this time it was occupied. A mare came to the door as BethAnn passed. She couldn't help herself and went to pet the horse, who liked the attention. BethAnn noticed it was a mare with foal. She talked to her and stroked her neck.

"I'll be back tomorrow and bring you an apple," she said as she left.

Taking in the views of the ranch, she noted one of the corrals with many horses in it but walked back to the house. Jakob and Allen had left, and she met Geraldine inside.

"I understand you walked Princess. Do you think she remembers you?"

"Yes, she did, and I just can't wait till I can ride her tomorrow if it's all right with you. She was really excited I was there. Can we go out tomorrow? I just want to ride her. She is so nice, and I love her. I also noticed there's a horse in the big stall by the stable entrance that is very friendly. She greeted me, and I talked to her. I want to bring her an apple tomorrow."

"Was Gregory with her? She's in that stall because she's going to have a foal soon. Would you like to be with her when she does? You've never seen the birth of a foal. Gregory will let us know when this will happens."

BethAnn's eyes opened wide.

"Oh, would I! Yes, yes. I want to be there. Oh, can I? That would be just perfect. When is this going to happen?"

"I'm not sure when, but it could be tonight or possibly tomorrow morning."

BethAnn was really excited as she went to her room to get ready for dinner.

They all met in the drawing-room for cocktails. It became cool inside, and the fireplace had a small fire in it for the chill in the room.

Randy entertained the group as he went from one person to another. He could stand up but only take a few steps and sit down. Prince avoided him and moved away so he couldn't catch him.

BethAnn came down all cleaned up and excited about the prospect of seeing the foal delivered.

Maria then came in and invited all to dinner. The table was set elegantly with candelabra burning. Little Deer had made a sumptuous dinner of baked chicken. They had a white wine which they toasted with. Jenny seemed to be doing fine. Eleanor made her feel welcome, and she was helping plan her visit.

The talk was about the workings of the ranch, which seemed to be going well. Geraldine would be meeting with George the next day. They had no sooner finished dinner and were going in for the traditional port wine when the stable boy came in to notify Geraldine and BethAnn to go to the stable because the mare was getting ready to deliver.

They entered the stable, and the mare was lying down in position for the delivery. Her water broke, and she sounded nervous. Gregory and one of the stable boys were attending to her. Gregory said most mares foal at night. He thought it could be a filly because she was delivering early.

Geraldine explained to BethAnn the period of gestation of the horse is usually eleven months. If she foals early, it is generally a filly. He asked BethAnn if she would like to feel the foal.

She timidly approached the horse."Oh, my gosh! I can feel the baby horse. It's moving. It's moving. Oh, my gosh."

They could see the delivery had begun. The mare was referred to as a dam, and she was starting to show contractions of labor. Gregory was behind her waiting for the show of the feet. He could feel the foal moving.

"It's coming," said Gregory, but it seemed to stop for a while with just the feet sticking out. He waited, but the movement stopped. He had hold of the feet and started to pull on them. Slowly the foal started to move and finally it came out. It took almost twenty minutes. The mare began to nuzzle and lick the foal to clean it of blood and mucous. "This helps blood circulation as the mother nuzzles and cleans her foal," Gregory explained. "It also creates a bond and enables the mare to distinguish her foal from others later on. Watch now, and the foal will try to stand."

With Gregory's help, the foal stood and shivered and then almost immediately moved to the mare and started to nurse.

BethAnn was wide-eyed the entire time, with Geraldine telling her what was happening. She held Geraldine, hugged her, and thanked her for being there and seeing the birth of the foal. Gregory and the stable boy were tending to the mare. It had been almost two hours since BethAnn arrived to watched the birth of the foal.

Geraldine thought they should go back to the house. "It's getting late, and I think we should leave now and come back tomorrow. This really tops off the day for us."

BethAnn had all kinds of questions for Geraldine. She had her thrill for the day and couldn't stop talking until she went into her bedroom.

BethAnn was up early and in the kitchen with Little Deer and Maria, telling them about her experience. She patiently waited for the rest to come down for breakfast. Prince made himself noticed and rubbed himself on BethAnn's leg until he saw Randy when Geraldine brought him to the kitchen. He immediately left. BethAnn excitingly told all of them about the delivery of the foal. She was ecstatic about the event while they finished their ranch breakfast of flapjacks, sausage, eggs, and berries.

George arrived to talk with Geraldine, and they left. BethAnn was a little exasperated because she wanted to go riding. Geraldine told her she would return, and then they could go for a ride.

Jenny Lynn opened up and seemed more relaxed. She started to talk about her life at Landry Manor and her family. Jenny was looking forward to going back to England but was happy to be there with them. "I'm just anxious to see my family and get on with my life," she said. "But I'm going to go riding with you today. This will be different for me."

They noticed that she seemed more relaxed each day and all of them felt being at the ranch was good for her.

BethAnn went to the corral to watch the men at work. Slim wasn't around, and she couldn't practice her roping, so she went to the stable to see the foal. It was moving around but always close to the mare who seemed protective of it. The mare saw BethAnn and came to the door to greet her. She remembered her from yesterday. BethAnn felt bad; she forgot the apple. Petting the mare, she told her she liked her foal; then, she went to see Princess, who was waiting at the stall door. She spent some time with Princess; then left to go back to the house.

"She's so cute and looks like her mother," she said to Geraldine, who came back from her meeting with George.

"Yes, I stopped by and saw it. It's going to be beautiful. I like its shape and color. I also told the stable boy to get the horses ready after lunch so we can go off on a trail you haven't seen. Jenny Lynn will be going with us."

BethAnn was the first to get to the horses and was in the saddle when Geraldine and Jenny Lynn arrived. They followed Geraldine on the trail toward the foothills of the Big Horns. The path was little-used and was not easy. Jenny Lynn had a hard time keeping up and slowed down Geraldine and BethAnn, but that didn't matter because they were in no hurry to get anywhere. They stopped at a stream to give the horses a rest and a watering. The views of the mountains were spectacular. BethAnn thought she saw a bear in the distance. She found Princess a great horse to ride.

They noticed that Jenny Lynn didn't seem to be well, so they decided to return to the ranch. They were concerned she might be sick. She didn't complain much but seemed to be uncomfortable. Returning back to the house, she left them and went to her room.

BethAnn saw Slim at the corral and asked him to help her with her roping. It took a while, and she now seemed to have the hang of it and was successful. Dinnertime was approaching, and the men were leaving for the bunkhouse, so BethAnn finished her roping.

Slim suggested she practice some more and was doing well. "When we're branding, you could give it a try with the calves."

She continued practicing her roping until Jakob came to get her. She showed him how to rope a calf and seemed to be successful. "You want to try doing it, Daddy?"

Jakob laughed and said he might try sometime later, but dinner would soon be served. He suggested she get ready for it. They left for the house. BethAnn had a full day.

They had their cocktails, but Jenny Lynn didn't come down, so Geraldine went up to see her. She opted not to come down but said she might try having something light for dinner. Little Deer made her some soup. After dinner, she went back to her room, and the rest all met in the drawing-room.

"I think I will try to teach Princess some of the things she will have to do if I take her to a dressage. She is very smart, and I'm sure she will learn," said BethAnn.

Geraldine agreed. "Princess is younger, and I'm sure she will learn quickly."

For the next few days, Jenny Lynn continued to feel sick and wake up vomiting. She felt better during the day but would wake up in distress.

"Jakob, you know what I think? I believe she is going to have a baby. I don't think it's intestinal distress. She has the same symptoms I had when I got pregnant."

"You should go talk to her," Jakob advised.

That evening at dinner time, Jenny Lynn did feel better and ate with them. She then announced to all that she thought she was going to have a baby.

They stayed at the ranch for several weeks. Jakob was anxious to return to Sheridan. Jenny Lynn could see a doctor and confirm her pregnancy. She was thrilled to have Randy's baby and felt the baby was given to her to fill the gap in her life with the loss of her husband.

Chapter 31
Planning a Trip to England

The trip was refreshing, especially after the cold, snowy winter, and Jakob enjoyed it. Country life was considerably different from living in the city. Ranchers had to be more self-sufficient, able to do without, and able to cope with danger. The cowhands were a special breed. Jakob admired Geraldine for being able to live the ranching lifestyle after coming from her English aristocracy life. *I guess she liked the challenge.* He was glad to get back to Sheridan. His practice was his life, and he enjoyed being around the people in Sheridan. Using his Ford for the trip, he made it back to Sheridan in record time. No all-day wagon ride. The Ford gave him no problems other than the engine did overheat when he pulled into his drive on Loukes street, but he was home now.

He was also glad to get back so Jenny Lynn could see a doctor and be sure she was pregnant and not have something else. She continued feeling sick, and he was concerned about her. She had been through a lot of stress and hardship with the loss of her husband. Geraldine said she would take her to see Doctor Ross.

The home staff was glad to see them come back, and they had the house immaculate. While they were gone, they did a thorough housecleaning. Like Chucha, Helen loved gardening, and she even planted some vegetables.

Simba really greeted them. She missed them and especially Randy. She was all over him, and he loved it. Randy had learned to play with her, and she followed him around wherever he went. If a stranger came into the house, she would seem protective of Randy.

BethAnn wanted to take Princess back with them. Geraldine said Raymond would bring her when they brought horses to be displayed at the Sheridan Rodeo and Fair in July. BethAnn almost immediately went back to the stable to see Nelly. She nickered and snorted when the girl walked in and opened her stall. She accepted the apple BethAnn gave her and followed her out into the yard. Beth Ann hugged and petted her and told her all about her experiences at the ranch. Nelly liked the attention, and as BethAnn walked, she followed her. BethAnn mounted her bareback, and they moved about the yard.

Jakob took Randy out to see the yard and was followed by Simba, who immediately saw a squirrel, barked, and chased it up a tree. Randy was quite sure of himself and followed Simba to the tree. He saw the squirrel and went to the tree, hugging it while the squirrel turned around and chattered at them.

Helen put together a special dinner for them, and they celebrated being home again. It felt good to be back. They each talked about the ranch and their plans now that they were back. Jakob asked BethAnn to come with him to the office in the morning to help clean it before seeing his patients. She agreed to help him, and then she went to her piano to play something. She said she missed the piano while they were away. Exhausted from the trip, they all turned in early.

The next day greeted them bright and sunny. Helen had made her cinnamon rolls for breakfast, and they were warm. Jakob decided to drive the Ford to the office. It overheated when they arrived, so he filled the radiator with water, and it started right up. He parked in front of the office and was surprised to see a patient waiting for him.

"Heard you were out of town, Doc, but thought I'd stop by just in case you would be back."

"Well, I'm back, Frank. What's the problem?"

His day began with a patient in need, so BethAnn went right to work cleaning up his waiting room. Seeing a stack of magazines, she started removing some old Colliers which had been tattered and torn. Other people walked in, and a lady engaged BethAnn in conversation. She recognized her from her exhibition of horsemanship at the fair last year and talked with her about her riding.

"Will you be in the rodeo this year?" she asked.

"Yes, I plan on doing some jumping. There is an event planned that has different obstacles that have to be jumped on a measured course. We will be judged on our skill and time to complete the course. Will you be going to the rodeo?"

"Oh yes, we always go to the fair. I brought my Lola in because she has been crying with a toothache. I hope Doctor Jakob can see her. He took care of her once before. She's so afraid, but they're just her baby teeth."

"Oh, my daddy will take care of her. But, Mrs. Ryan, you shouldn't wait so long to have her teeth fixed. If you have him fix the tooth when it has just a little hole in it, the tooth won't hurt, and he won't have to take it out." BethAnn looked at the little girl and hugged her. "Don't worry, Lola, my daddy will stop the tooth from hurting. Tell you what. I'll go in with you and hold your hand. You'll be all right."

Lola had been crying, and BethAnn took her and sat next to her, holding her hand. That seemed to allay her apprehensions, and she talked to BethAnn while they waited.

When Jakob was ready for Lola, BethAnn went in with her and held her hand. Jakob was especially good with children. He liked taking care of them and gained their confidence. He removed her tooth with no tears. She even hugged him after getting her trinket from his treasure chest of toys. Lola knew that children could choose one for being a good patient.

As they were leaving, BethAnn said to Mrs. Ryan, "Don't forget to bring Lola back so my daddy can fix her teeth. We don't want her to have another toothache."

Mrs. Ryan just smiled and thanked Jakob as she left the office.

Jakob was amazed by BethAnn's approach to Mrs. Ryan. "Honey, I should keep you here to help me with my patients. Some come in with fear, and all it takes is a little kind talk to put them at ease, and you have done that."

BethAnn had learned how to sterilize his instruments and clean up after he took care of someone, so Jakob could talk with his patient while she got his chair ready for the next one. BethAnn liked working with her father, and of course, he always paid her for her help. It was money she always had for special things she wanted to buy.

At lunchtime, he took her to Grand Ma's. It was his time to spend with his daughter. BethAnn was quite mature, and they had good conversations. His day wasn't too busy, and they got the office cleaned and ready for the next day.

They stopped by the post office to get his mail. Jim Rogers, the postmaster, was there to greet him.

"Got a lot of mail for you, Doc. And got some mail for your English guest, Lady Jenny Lynn Landry. How long is she going to be around here, Doc? One of them letters looks like it's important. Comes all the way from London. It's thick. Glad to see you back, Doc."

Jakob laughed. "Old Jim likes to look over the mail that he hands out. Actually, there are several letters for Jenny Lynn."

Everyone was busy when they walked into the house, but BethAnn broke the ice when she told Geraldine about her day at the office.

"You know, Jakob, I think it's a good idea for BethAnn to work with you. She will soon be choosing her career in life. Her experience in your office will help her see what it's like to be a dentist or even a nurse. But, I still think she should go to college first."

"I do too, but we'll see what she wants to do," said Jakob. "Did you take Jenny Lynn to see Ross?"

"Yes, I did, and he did give her a good exam. We were right. She is pregnant. He gave her a good once over. Said she was in good shape, and the baby would probably be due in November. You know, I believe this is good for her, and she is happy about the whole thing. She said that, with the baby, she will still have Randy with her. I think she's coming out of her distress."

"I got some mail for her," said Jakob.

"She'll be down. We had a busy day for her. I took her shopping."

Randy was already sitting in Jakob's lap. Simba sat in front of them with a ball in her mouth. She was ready to play ball with Jakob as Jenny Lynn came down with a new dress they had bought on their shopping spree.

"I like the dress. You have good taste," said Jakob.

They talked, and Jakob gave her the mail. She moved away and started opening it. Reading it, she became very quiet.

"Jakob...,"

He looked up at her and noticed tears coming down her cheeks. "What's the matter?" he asked.

"I don't understand. Will you read this?"

Jakob took the letter and started to read it. "Oh my gosh! It says they found Randy's body. It was afloat near where the *Titanic* sunk. It says the White Star Lines commissioned a cable repair ship, CS Macky-Bennett, which was in Halifax, Nova Scotia, to search the waters. It says here that after getting the ship ready, they immediately started the voyage for recovery on April 17th. They found 328 bodies. Some of them were buried at sea, and 190 were returned to Nova Scotia. It took some time to identify them. Baron Randolph Landry was finally identified with the help of the Army records in London. He will be sent back to England for burial." Stunned, Jakob stood silent. "It says you will get more information later."

Jenny Lynn recovered from the initial shock and said she was grateful they found Randy so now he could have a proper burial near home. She thought she should make preparations to go back to Landry Manor and make ready to receive him. "I'm going to call my parents to let them know I'm coming back because they had indicated they might be coming here for me. Also, I want to inform Lady Mary about the turn of events. She has to know that Randy has been found. I know she will feel better knowing his presence would be near his home. We can have a nice service and Christian burial for him."

The next day Jakob went to his office. He had a busy day of patients that had waited for him to return from his vacation.

When he arrived from the office that evening, Geraldine was anxious to talk with him. "Jakob, I got a phone call from my mother today. We talked about Randy and his being found. A service and burial next to the Trinity Church where my daddy is laid to rest have been arranged. She asked if we could come to Landry Manor and take part. Her wish was that we would come. She feels she is getting too old to come here to visit us and would like to see her grandchildren, who she has never seen. She felt this would be a good time for us to make the visit and be a part of Randy's burial service. Jakob, I would like to do that. What do you think?"

Jakob listened as Geraldine made her plea. His mind mulled over as she spoke. He was silent as he continued to digest the words. "I never thought of it, Hon. I guess it would be nice for us to attend the services. It's not exactly the best time for us to go. The Sheridan Fair is coming up, and if we were to go, we would have to miss it. I'm sure they can do without us. I've thought about us visiting your mother. I'm sure she would like to see her grandchildren. I kept thinking she might visit us, but maybe the trip would be too difficult for her. It would be good for us to make the trip, but it won't be easy for us with the children. What are your feelings? I know you said you would like to go."

"Oh yes, Jakob, I think we should go. I do miss my Mama. It would be good for the children, and I would like to be at my brother's burial service. I missed my Papa's, but we couldn't go to it. Then it's settled; we will go to England. Maybe we can leave with Jenny Lynn. It would be a help to her. We can plan on being away for a month."

Nothing more was said that evening as Jakob and Geraldine mulled over their plans.

The next morning at breakfast Jenny Lynn brought up the need to make reservations to return to England.

Geraldine answered. "Jenny Lynn, Jakob, and I have been talking about going back with you. Mama called me yesterday and asked that we come. We would attend the service and visit Mama."

BethAnn looked at her mother. "What about us—Randy and me?

Can we go too?" She said it with tears in her eyes.

Jakob smiled, "Of course you will go with us. We wouldn't leave you behind."

BethAnn and went to Jakob and hugged and kissed him.

"We want you to see your grandmother Landry. Randy will go too. This will be a family trip. We'll all go together. We'll make our reservations on the White Star Line. I'm sure they will give us priority."

"Yes, they will," said Jenny Lynn. "I also received a letter from them, and they said I should contact them for reservations to return to England. They mentioned the HMS Celtic would be leaving on the 20th for Southampton."

"That won't leave us too much time to prepare for the trip," said Jakob.

The next days were ones of planning for the trip to England. Jenny Lynn was starting to feel better and was eager to get back home.

White Star was anxious to accommodate Jenny Lynn and made arrangements for Jakob's family.

Jakob had a lot of scheduling changes to make. Most had to do with the fair, but he also had to have someone care for his patients in emergencies.

Chapter 32
New York To Southampton

Andy Meeks drove the Millers and Jenny Lynn to the train station. Some of Jakob's and Geraldine's friends, including Eleanor and Allen, also came to see them off. They all had lunch together at the Sheridan Inn, a short walk away from the train station. It was a happy group who bid them farewell. The Chicago Burlington and Missouri Railroad would take them to the Mississippi River, where they changed trains. It was then the Chicago Burlington and Quincey to Chicago. The rail cars were newer and definitely an improvement from the ones they had traveled before. They had compartments and even a dining car, but it still wasn't easy for rambunctious Randy to be confined. Looking out at the landscape eventually lost its attraction for him.

The trip across the Mississippi River did catch his interest. He had never seen such a large body of water and the sight of boats and barges on it. But then those flat green fields of Illinois didn't excite him until they approached Chicago. The view of the skyscrapers got his attention, with each one bigger than the last. The railroad trains passed one another, jerking the train from one track to another until it slowed to a stop, and the conductor came by shouting, "Chicago! Chicago! Chicago! End of the line! Union Station." People scurried around and pushed one another to get off the train. Union Station, with its high ceiling and so many people, was an exciting place to be.

Their luggage was located and was taken to cabs, then loaded. Jakob directed the driver to take them to the Congress Hotel on Michigan Avenue. It was a slow ride in the heavy Chicago traffic. Confusion was the order of the day, amplified by loud horns and bells; streetcars, automobiles, and horses pulling wagons. BethAnn was thrilled to see the tall buildings and watched bridges rise to let boats on the Chicago River pass through. Vendors shouted and touted their wares on the street corners.

They finally arrived at the Congress Hotel, which was a large white ornate building on Michigan Avenue. Across from the hotel was a large park with huge statues of horses and their riders. The fancy-dressed doorman opened the doors to the cab as young uniformed men began removing the luggage from it. The luggage was put on carts and whisked inside. The Millers then climbed the stairs to the hotel's main entrance. Big doors with lots of shining brass were opened for them and they entered the hotel lobby.

BethAnn held Randy's hand as they stepped inside. The room was huge, with carts loaded with luggage being pushed around and people milling about. Jakob stopped at the front desk to register for their stay, which would be just one night. Large pillars and mirrors formed a wall, and a high ceiling had large crystal chandeliers shining brightly. All this was new and interesting to the children.

People turned around to look at them as they passed by, dressed in western style and wearing their big-brimmed hats and boots. Why not? After all, they did come from Sheridan, Wyoming. Some people would just smile at them and issue a warm greeting. The boys would give their best smile to BethAnn, who was really a show stopper. She was tall, with her blond ponytail tied with a red ribbon and wearing her white Stetson. Some girls stopped her to ask where she was from and wanted to continue talking, but the bellman was ready to take them to their rooms.

The elevator stopped on the sixth floor, a suite on the east side of the hotel facing Grant Park. The sitting room had flowers and was furnished with Queen Ann chairs and a couch. A small lavatory with glasses, dishes, and a pitcher of cold water occupied one corner of the room.

Jakob remarked, "White Star really pulled out the stops when they made these reservations for us. This has to be the most expensive suite in the hotel," said Jakob.

Jenny Lynn came out of her bedroom. "I'm so glad you have come with me on this trip back home. I would have been so confused and lonely being alone. I still can't stop thinking about my loss of Randy." Tears came to her eyes. "You have been so kind to me."

Geraldine held her tightly. "We're here because we love you and know what a difficult time you've had. When you get home, you will be more comfortable and have others who will look after you. You must be tired from the trip. Why don't you take a nap? We all need one after this hectic day. Afterward, we can do something in this big city."

"I know what we can do," said Jakob. "We can go to one of the beaches—Chicago has lots of them—and go for a swim. But first, we will need to get swimsuits, and then we'll get a cab to take us there."

That really got the children's attention. "I'm not tired," said Randy. I want go beach."

Geraldine laughed. "You'll feel better after a nap, and so will I. So let's rest first and then the beach."

Reluctantly, BethAnn went to her room. Geraldine decided she would sleep with Randy at her side to be sure he napped.

The sleep time was not too long, but Jakob and Geraldine were refreshed. Randy and BethAnn patiently waited to go to the beach. Jakob took them to a hotel store, where they got the latest in bathing wear. Jenny Lynn decided against going. They all put on their bathing suits under their clothes, and Jakob got a cab to take them to Oak Street Beach.

They faced even more traffic on Lake Shore Drive, but the cab finally stopped next to the beach area. The yellow sandy area extended several hundred yards from the street. Thousands of people crowded on it with their umbrellas and blankets. Before you could even see the water, it looked like it extended a mile past where they stood. Jakob made arrangements with the driver to come back later and pick them up.

They made their way over the crowded beach and moved closer to the water. Sitting in a chair high above the sand was a sunburned lifeguard who gave BethAnn a stare when he saw her. They finally found a small open area to take off their clothes and sit in their bathing suits. They were near the water, and BethAnn took Randy's hand as they tiptoed into the lake.

She quickly withdrew. "Oh!, oh! It's cold! It's really cold!"

Jakob stood in the water laughing at the children. Randy wasn't sure what to do but finally went in with Jakob and laughed too.

"Lake Michigan is always cold, but you'll get used to it. It's not like The Plunge in Sheridan, where they heat the water. You should remember Little Goose Creek. It's really cold, and you swam in that." He splashed BethAnn and went into deeper water, carrying Randy. BethAnn followed, and they spent enough time splashing and diving to get somewhat used to the cold. It was refreshing. After they got their fill, they walked back to the shore. They had enough, so they got out and warmed up by sitting on the sand. BethAnn started to build castles with Randy while Geraldine and Jakob laid on the warm beach and sunned themselves until the cab came for them to take them back to the hotel.

They dressed for the evening. All showed signs of sunburn. They loved the beach and asked if they could go back the next day.

They dressed for dinner and would take a cab to the Blackhawk

Restaurant for dinner. This was one of Jakob's favorite places. The taxi stopped at the Wabash Street location.

"Look up! Do you see the train tracks? See the train? They call that the El."

The children saw train tracks above the street and an elevated train riding on it. This was a first for all of them.

For Jakob, Chicago was his second city, and he knew it well. He got his dental education here, so nothing was new for him. They enjoyed the waiter making a special Caesar salad for them. He had a big wooden bowel that he spun around as he added the various ingredients.

"This is my singing bowel," he said to Randy as he spun it around.

As they ate, a small group of musicians played in the background.

The next morning after breakfast, they took a buggy ride around the area and even stopped at the Marshal Field store to buy a special gift for Lady Mary.

BethAnn was amazed at the way the people who waited on customers treated them. "They are dressed impeccably and speak so politely to the customers," said BethAnn.

The Chicago visit ended with lunch at the hotel. No time for another swim. It was time to check out of the hotel and go to the Randolph Street Station to catch the New York Central train. New York Central billed it as the red carpet treatment. As they left the station, they walked on a red carpet all the way until they boarded the train. It was an overnight ride to New York City, with very special onboard treatment.

All the luggage—and there was a lot—was placed in the cab which took them to the New York Passenger Ship Terminal. Much like Chicago but even more, New York was congested. The HMS *Celtic* loomed ahead high and sitting next to the Chelsea pier. The size of the ship was incredible.

Randy was so excited to see this big boat. "Mama, are we going on that boat?"

BethAnn was extremely impressed with its size. The *Celtic* carried 2,857 passengers, of which 300 were first class. It was not the fastest liner, as she was rated at 16 knots, but she was a large 701 feet long. A long boom could be seen swinging over the side, loading boxes and crates of all sizes. Two high smokestacks were impressive. There were some people in a line waiting to get on.

They found the White Star Line office and were graciously accepted. They would be boarding the HMS *Celtic* shortly, the agent told them.

"This is one of White Star's finest liners. We will be crossing from here to Southampton. Normally, the *Celtic*'s home port was Liverpool, but since the loss of the *Titanic,* there were changes made, and it will dock at Southampton."

They were welcomed and given early boarding. A cabin boy led them to their staterooms on the promenade deck. They would be in what was called the owner's suite, which had just about everything you could imagine in a ship's stateroom. Everything was lavish.

Jenny Lynn was treated as best as they could, but she was not enjoying her return voyage. Memories of her *Titanic* experience made her nervous about the journey. It seemed like everywhere she turned, she felt she was on the *Titanic.* The cabin boy suggested personal valet services for Jakob, which he refused to accept but said he could take care of his clothes. The ladies requested personal maids.

The *Celtic* left the New York dock with all the fanfare of a luxury voyage and passed from New York harbor into the Atlantic ocean. This was summer now, and the seas would be more comfortable. They got themselves situated in their rooms and then went on deck to watch the New York skyline until it was hardly visible anymore.

Their first seating for dinner was announced, and they were dressed and waiting. Jakob and Geraldine wore English dinner attire. Because she was in mourning, Jenny Lynn wore a calf-length black dress. BethAnn was a beautiful, attractive young lady appropriately dressed in a light blue gown. Randy wore a blue nautical suit that Geraldine bought for him in the hotel store.

The maitre d' seated them at a preferred table with all the luxury and comfort White Star Line could provide. A band played, and people were on the dance floor. The wine steward provided them with a menu of the various wines available. He described each suggested wine and its history. When he finished, the waiter gave them dinner menus and then proceeded to tell them about special items. They made their choices and ordered.

Jakob asked Geraldine to dance, and they moved to the floor. Geraldine's beauty always drew glances from admirers. They danced until they noticed the wine steward.

Wine was poured with each course as the dinner was served. The lavish dessert was enjoyed by all.

After dinner, the music continued, and this time Jakob took BethAnn to the floor. Jakob had danced with BethAnn at father-daughter events at her high school, so they did quite well together. He was very proud of his beautiful daughter. Geraldine had a hair attendant set BethAnn's long blond hair. They returned to the table, and a young man came up to Jakob and asked if he could dance with BethAnn. Startled, Jakob laughed and approved.

"BethAnn, this young man would like to dance with you."

She smiled. "Of course, Daddy. I would like that too." She put out her arm. He took it, and they went to the dance floor. Jakob smiled.

"Well, I guess I lost my partner. This is the first time I ever saw my daughter leave to dance with a handsome young man."

Jakob watched as the young couple, both formally attired, moved expertly to the music.

Geraldine smiled. "You still have me to dance with."

After two songs, the young man brought BethAnn back to the table. "I want to thank you for allowing me to dance with your daughter," he said. "May I introduce myself? I am Roger Mane. I live in Lancaster, just out of London. I'm here with my parents, May and Frances Mane. Perhaps I may have the pleasure of a dance with BethAnn another time."

Jakob was impressed with the manners of Roger Mane and gave a positive reply. Roger was introduced to all at the table, and the young man graciously excused himself and left.

Jakob spoke to BethAnn. "Did you enjoy the dance with that fellow?"

She blushed a little and smiled. "Yes, it was very nice. He didn't talk much, but he told me he and his parents were returning from a vacation to New York and asked if we could dance again. He really had a strong English accent. He said he would like to introduce me to some of his friends."

Geraldine smiled. "Well, that was nice. Maybe you'll meet some nice friends on the trip and really have a good time."

They sat and talked until the music stopped. They left for their stateroom but first decided to go out on the deck. Jenny Lynn decided to go back to the room. There was a three-quarter moon with scattered stars and clouds high over a dark sea. Waves with painted crests approached the ship. They walked slowly along the rail. A cool but light wind met them. Other passengers were taking in the nocturnal delight. Jakob put his arm around Geraldine, drew her close, and kissed her. BethAnn caught a glimpse of her mother and father and smiled. Randy was too busy watching the waves.

They had enough of the night and sea and went back in. Entering the suite, they found it prepared for sleep. The beds were turned back and had a chocolate by the pillow. They sat in the parlor area of the suite.

There was a tea service and cookies on a table. Randy immediately found them and was munching on them. Geraldine, smiling at Randy, said, "Randy, it's time for bed. We've had a long day. Finish your milk, and don't forget to brush your teeth. I'll be in and tuck you in."

Reluctantly Randy went into his bedroom and later was followed by Geraldine. Jakob stood before the window, looking out at the moon and sea.

"How about you? Are you ready for sleep? I've had a long day," said Geraldine upon her return.

Jakob put his arm around Geraldine, and they kissed and went into their room. Laying in bed, Jakob said, "This trip is quite a lot different than the last one we made."

"Yes, a different set of circumstances. We were so in love."

"We still are, aren't we?" Jakob asked.

"Of course." She turned to him, and they kissed.

A melodious sound and a voice in the companionway announced breakfast was to be served. Jakob's eyes opened. The room was still dark until someone came in and pulled back the drapes. It was the cabin boy. He asked if they would have breakfast in bed or in the dining room.

"We'll have it in the dining room, but you may bring in some coffee before we dress," Jakob replied.

The cabin boy said he would bring them coffee and juice. The others were up and talking as the cabin boy came back. Randy was looking out the window at the sparkling sea. Everybody was awake and excited.

There was a white envelope addressed to Jakob on the desk. He opened it and announced that they were invited to have dinner at the captain's table the next day. "That's something to look forward to," said Jakob. "Now, let's get dressed and ready for breakfast."

They spent the day getting acquainted with the ship. Roger found BethAnn, and she went with him and his friends to play shuffleboard. Jenny Lynn stayed pretty much to herself. She sat on a deck chair while Jakob and Geraldine met and talked with other passengers. After lunch, Jakob decided to go to the bridge of the ship. The captain was talking with two of his officers as another approached Jakob.

"I am Lieutenant Bernhardt. How may I assist you?" Jakob introduced himself as Doctor Miller, one of the passengers, and he would like to make arrangements to see the workings of the bridge.

"I've sailed on the HMS *Olympic* and visited its bridge. I would like to see the bridge of the *Celtic*. I'm especially interested in the navigation of the ship. I can come back any time you have available."

"We would be happy to show you the bridge. Our captain is Commodore Edward Bertram, and he is proud of the *Celtic*. He is happy for interested visitors to see the bridge. But if you are especially interested in navigation, come at 1100 tomorrow, and I'll show you how we do navigation. I will be doing the LAN—local apparent noon—at that time. I am the ship's navigation officer. I will be doing that observation, and I'll explain it to you. And, maybe I can help you do it with a sextant."

Jakob thanked the officer and said he would be back the next day. He was excited to learn something about the navigation of the ship.

The rest of the day was spent seeing the ship and talking with various passengers. Geraldine met several passengers who were living near Ipswich, the town near Landry Manor.

"It's been a long time since I've been home," Geraldine said to Jakob. "I miss my mama, and I know she misses me. I've talked to her on the phone, but that isn't like seeing and being with her. She's getting older, and I fear for her loss. My papa is gone. I miss him so. I wish you could have known him. I'm sure you would have found common ground with him. I know he loved me, and we did much together. No, not like you and BethAnn, but his way was different. I want Mama to see our children. And, they should meet her. I know she will love them. She always questions me about them. She was always hoping Randy and Jenny Lynn would bring her grandchildren. I also want to introduce the children to England. It's part of their heritage too."

Little Randy was excited with everything he saw. The day was bright and warm, and the seas had light action. Occasionally they would see flying fish, which really interested Randy.

"What is that, Daddy? Can fish fly?" He couldn't understand how fish could fly.

Jakob tried to explain that they didn't fly like the birds, but he wasn't sure Randy understood.

Cocktails were served in the pub. Jakob and Geraldine treated themselves to martinis. There were games for Randy and BethAnn, who developed friends with the young people, so the parents snuck away for one. They reminisced about their first voyage to England but were also satisfied with this one.

The young people were interested in BethAnn's life in Wyoming. They were amazed she had become so proficient with horseback riding. Some did ride horses, but her being from Wyoming really impressed them. One asked BethAnn if she ever had any contact with the Indians.

They, of course, believed they were savages.

"Oh no, they are a different culture, but they aren't to be considered savages. My father takes care of their dental needs, and I've been with him at their pow-wows. He is a blood brother of one of the chiefs." That really brought out many questions from the friends, and BethAnn was held in high esteem.

When dinner came, they were seated by the maitre d' at the same table as the night before, with the same waiters. He was familiar with Jakob's party. Jakob managed to have a dance with BethAnn, but two other boys were waiting to ask Jakob if they could dance with her.

Jenny Lynn spent most of her time by herself, but it was good because she rested a lot. She was generally sober but talked about the baby she would be having.

Time seemed to pass by slowly. Most of the passengers were older, and they sequestered themselves from the younger ones like Jakob and Geraldine. There were some French and German passengers, but most were businessmen who didn't seek other passengers.

Jakob met Lieutenant Bernhardt at 1100. He took him around the bridge and showed him all the different systems they used to operate the ship. Bernhardt told him about the propulsion of the vessel, which burned coal. A ship this size was quite formidable. He showed him the chart, which he used to show the progress of the ship. They were now approaching the midpoint of the voyage.

"As we approach England, I will go to a more detailed chart that includes England and our destination, Southampton. We are nearing the noon hour. The elevation of the sun at noon will tell us our latitude," said the lieutenant. "Our location on the chart is measured in latitude and longitude. Latitude is how far above the equator we are located, and longitude tells us how far west we are from Greenwich, England. Greenwich is the zero line. We are west of Greenwich, and that is figured as longitude west, and everything north of the equator is latitude north. I hope I haven't confused you. Look at the chart and see our last position.

"This instrument is a sextant. It has a telescope and two mirrors. I will find the sun with the telescope, which is seen on one of the mirrors. By moving one part of it, I will see the mirror image on the second mirror, which will move toward the horizon. When that mirror image of the sun hits the horizon, I will have measured the angle of the sun to the earth, which will be the latitude we are at." He showed Jakob the sextant, and Jakob did the measurement. Jakob smiled and said he needed more time to digest what the lieutenant had said. He laughed and repeated what he had said. He then did a calculation and put the numbers on the chart. Jakob studied what they had done. He told the lieutenant he would let him do the navigating. Jakob would be a grateful passenger. The confession made the lieutenant laugh.

That night Jakob and his group were invited to have dinner with the captain, Commodore Edward Bertram. There was a reception where they would meet him. He came dressed in an impeccable white uniform with gold braid and medals. His hat visor had a splash of gold braid. Each one met the captain and shook his hand, including Randy.

The gray beard and steel blue eyes of the captain looked down sternly at Randy. "Welcome aboard, young man. I see you have a nautical suit on. I hope one day you will become one of my officers."

Randy's eyes were opened wide. "Yes, Sir," he slowly said.

The captain gave a brief salute and looked up at the next passenger in line as Jakob pulled Randy away. They all smiled at him, surprised Randy said yes, sir. The table was set up in a different dining room, more lavish and ornate. Wine was poured with each course, and the captain stood up, welcomed all, and thanked them for coming. He pointed out the greatness of his ship and his pride in her.

Jakob sat next to a countess, whose name he immediately forgot, and was bored to death with her. Geraldine had a difficult time keeping a straight face as she saw poor Jakob cope with the countess.

As they were leaving, the Commodore made a point to address Randy, who gave him another Yes, Sir. BethAnn saw one of the boys she had danced with sitting at the captain's table. Geraldine had her dressed like a debutante. The event set up the evening as the highlight of the trip.

The next days were almost perfect. The weather held, except for one rainy and windy day. For little Randy, it was a great experience. He was impressed with the Commodore and asked Jakob what he had to do to become an officer on the ship.

The last night of the trip was always a special night with a special dinner and entertainment. Geraldine always attracted the attention of other passengers. Her English accent was enough to get inquires of her reason to travel to Ipswich. Some knew or heard of Sir Gerald Landry. He had made his mark in Parliament. Of course, she was addressed as Lady Geraldine.

They danced and sang, toasting with champagne and cheering. They sang Auld Lang Syne and wished their new-made friends health and happiness as they ended the evening.

Jakob awoke to hear the melodious sound in the companionway announcing breakfast was now being served. The door to their cabin opened, and the cabin boy drew back the drapes to bring in the new day.

"Coffee and juice are available in the sitting room," he said and left.

Jakob got up and put on his robe.

Geraldine lifted her head. "I guess it's time. I will be more motivated to get up with a kiss from my husband,"

Jakob laughed, went to the bed, and did what she requested. "I guess we're at anchor. I can see the Isle of Wight. I suppose we're waiting for the Pilot and tugs to take us up to Southampton. I'm going out and get some coffee," he said.

Opening the door to the sitting room, he was greeted by Randy and BethAnn. "What's going on, Daddy? Why aren't we moving? Is that Southampton over there?"

Jakob explained that they saw the Isle of Wight, seven miles from the Southampton docks. "We will take on a Pilot who will guide us there. He will be helped by tugs to take us up to the docks."

Geraldine came in time to fill the children in on the history of Southampton and to point out the white cliffs of the Isle of Wight. "You don't know it, but this is a very important and old area. Everything is old in England, and by old, I mean thousands of years. It's not like Sheridan, which is less than a hundred years."

They had their last breakfast on the ship and got their luggage together as the ship slowly moved to Southampton. There was a crowd of people on the docks waiting for the ship and much cheering and laughter. BethAnn and little Randy were now anxious to get off.

The ship first had to go through quarantine before anyone could debark. Then the first-class passengers were starting to move off the *Celtic* and go through immigration and customs. Having passed the rigor of customs, their baggage was now moved to the railway just off the dock. The train would take them into the city of Southampton and then on to London. BethAnn was impressed because they entered the seating from the outside, which was different from back home. They had small pieces of luggage that they stowed above the seats.

"BethAnn, you will see a lot of things different from Sheridan because we are now entering England," said Geraldine. It was a short stopover in Southampton, and they were off to London. BethAnn's eyes were glued to the window as she saw the brief countryside and the outskirts of London, a short two-hour train ride to a congested city.

There was a short stop for the train to Ipswich. Geraldine made the call home to make arrangements to be picked up. Everyone was excited because they were near to their destination, Landry Manor. Jenny Lynn was a different person as she got off the ship to the train and on the way to her home. She seemed happy and laughed as she talked about going home.

London was old, which they saw as they left the station. They saw commercial buildings and crowded narrow streets before they saw signs of rural areas. Finally, Ipswich looked very old, and the station platform was crowded. Their luggage was removed and placed on a cart.

Geraldine saw the driver next to a car and waved to him. He drove up to them. "Samson, so nice to see you."

Sampson was uniformed in a green suit with boots and a cap. "Lady Geraldine, it's been a long time since we've seen you, and you brought back our Lady Jenny Lynn. We are all so happy to have you back."

Geraldine introduced BethAnn and little Randy. He remembered Jakob and shook his hand. With all the luggage stored, they crowded into the car and drove off.

Jakob remembered Ipswich, and it looked the same as when he first saw it. He remembered the same pothole as they turned and the sheep which crowded the road.

Chapter 33
An Opportunity Declined

The road out of Ipswich to Landry Manor was mostly rural and bumpy. It was well-traveled, with very few needed repairs having been done. Horses and wagons and some cars and trucks cut deep ruts in it, and it was very rough to travel in some places. An occasional cow might wander on it, or someone moving his sheep across would slow people down.

Not much change from the last time I was in England, Jakob thought.

Sampson was a careful driver, and this was a newer car. Geraldine was excited and anxious to get to the home of her birth. "It's just over this hill," she said to BethAnn, "and you'll see Landry Manor."

A white-capped red brick wall with an open black iron gate could then be seen. On the wall, on the right side of the entrance, was a shiny bronze plaque with raised letters that read Landry Manor. Part of the wall was covered with dark green ivy, and various bushes were planted alongside. Entering the gate and several hundred yards ahead was the manor itself. The well-cared-for road curved its way toward the building. It was impressive, as BethAnn put it. Built of red bricks, like the red brick of the wall at the entrance, it was four stories, with the fourth story having dormers. There were chimneys placed near the crest of the roof. The entrance alcove was in the middle of the building with large, heavy wooden doors with black hinge straps and hinges. The doors were wide open.

"Who are those people standing there?" said BethAnn.

"That's the staff, who have come out to greet us," said Geraldine, "Oh, and there's my mama." The car stopped, and one of the men came forward and opened the doors. Jenny Lynn and Geraldine got out and ran to meet Lady Mary, who moved toward them with open arms and tears in her eyes. She put her arms around them, and they kissed. Jakob, BethAnn, and little Randy stood by Lady Mary until she turned toward them.

"Jakob, you came. It's so nice to see you." She kissed Jakob on both cheeks and hugged him. Then she looked at her grandchildren.

"Mama, this is BethAnn and Randy."

She put her arms out and hugged and kissed BethAnn and took Randy's hands, and then bent and kissed him. "You're my grandchildren. I'm so happy to see you," said a smiling Lady Mary. After the greetings, she took them to the people standing by the door. "This is my staff, who wish to welcome you. I think you have met all of them, Rutherford, except for my beautiful grandchildren, BethAnn and Randy. Mrs. Wrightson, aren't they just lovely? Mrs. Wrightson is in charge of the household. Look, these are my grandchildren. Aren't they wonderful? They came here all the way from Wyoming in the United States."

Then Lady Mary took Jenny Lynn in her arms and held her as they both cried, and she placed her hands on both sides of her face and kissed her. "Come, come, everyone, let's go inside. They have made a high tea for you."

BethAnn was first inside the large sitting room and looked up at the high ceiling and around. She sighed at the magnificence of the room. She viewed the big paintings, tapestries, and chandeliers and was awed by the staircase to the second floor.

Rutherford came out and announced, "My Lady Mary, High Tea is now being served."

Everyone started going into the dining room, and BethAnn said to Randy, "Come on, Randy, let's go in. I'm hungry."

Lady Mary, hearing BethAnn, said, "You poor people. I bet you haven't eaten since you left the ship. You all must be famished, but this will hold you over until dinner."

The High Tea had various crumpets, meats, and small sandwiches, snacks, and treats to go along with the tea, and all got enough on their plates to carry on till dinner.

Geraldine took BethAnn and Randy to their rooms and settled them in so they could nap before dinner because all were exhausted from a long day of travel. BethAnn had no trouble, but Randy was ready to do anything but sleep. He did succumb with Geraldine at his side

Naptime did help some. Geraldine and Jakob were refreshed, but Randy and BethAnn were ready to go full speed ahead. They all came down, and Rutherford suggested they go out on the veranda to the back of the Manor. Lady Mary and Jenny Lynn were already out there talking when they arrived.

The veranda was often used in warmer weather, and this English summer was quite warm. It faced the broad expanse of the manor. You could see the stables and the equipment buildings .as well as lots of trees and a creek in the distance.

The stable boy was exercising one of the horses, and he came up to the veranda. BethAnn immediately got up and went to the horse to pet and hug it.

The animal liked the attention, and Geraldine said to the stable boy, "Why don't you get off and let BethAnn take the reins? She'll walk her, and the two of them will get acquainted."

BethAnn smiled, took the reins, and started to walk the horse in the direction of the stables. It nickered as she followed BethAnn. When they stopped near the barn, she continued to pet and hug the horse, who liked the attention, and they walked back.

BethAnn looked at Geraldine. "Can I get on her? I think she likes me."

Geraldine smiled. "Go ahead. She's quite gentle. Help her, Archie."

BethAnn started to mount the horse. It moved a little, but BethAnn got on it and sat up straight. She began to walk her with Archie following close by.

Lady Mary was amazed by what she was seeing. "My goodness. I didn't realize that lovely child could ride."

BethAnn signaled the horse, and she started to walk faster as BethAnn moved toward the barn, turned around, and trotted back.

Geraldine told her to get off. She was all smiles and hugged her. "Honey, looks like you're all set for tomorrow. Archie, she'll ride Ginger. That's her name, isn't it?"

He nodded that it was. Randy went up to the horse and petted it.

"Randy, you want to get on?" said Geraldine.

Randy nodded his head. "Yes, can I?"

Archie picked him up and put him on the saddle. Randy was thrilled as BethAnn led the horse while Archie supported Randy in the saddle.

Jakob laughed. "Looks like you're going to have to get Randy a pony, Geraldine."

The group spent the rest of the afternoon talking and making plans for the coming days. They had to plan the memorial for Sir Randolph. His remains were at a mortuary in Ipswich. The army regiment commander would be coming when they set the date. Arrangements also had to be made with the rector at Trinity Church in Ipswich.

Lady Mary said she would be having a dinner party for Geraldine and her family on the weekend. She told them Lord Oliver Henry was aware Jakob and Geraldine were coming, so he would attend, as well as other close friends.

Lady Mary even talked about a possible fox hunt. "Oh my, it's getting toward dinner. We'll dine at seven," she said.

As they were leaving, Rutherford approached Jakob. "Doctor, will you be having a valet? I have Andrew, who would be excellent and available for you."

"No, not for dress, but I would like him to care for my clothes."

"It shall be done as you please. Just tell him what you may want" Rutherford moved off.

Geraldine met Jakob at the door to their bedroom. "I have the children settled, and we have this room for us, she said as she pushed him on the bed. Remember, we're married now." She hugged and kissed him, and Jakob willingly responded.

This bedroom was large and even had an attached bath and dressing room. Geraldine had a personal maid, which she shared with BethAnn.

Mrs. Wrightson's cooks made a sumptuous dinner. Lady Mary was so happy to have them. There was a grand piano in the corner of the large sitting room, which Geraldine went up to and played. Then she asked BethAnn if she would play something. BethAnn sat down and thought about what she might play. She decided on *Fur Elise* by Beethoven. She performed without sheet music.

"My, that young lady is talented," said Lady Mary.

The evening ended early, and as Geraldine tucked in Randy, he said, "I like my grandmother. She kisses and hugs me."

"Well, I kiss and hug you, don't I?"

Randy laughed. "I know, but you're my mother."

Later, as Jakob and Geraldine lay in bed, she recounted the day and talked about the children and their grandmother.

"I'm so glad we came. My mother is really so happy we're here," Geraldine said.

The rooster crowing awakened Jakob. It was just getting light. *There's that blasted bird again. I should have realized it would wake me.* He laid thinking about being in England and how different everything was here. *I couldn't live here. A vacation like this is one thing, but lords, ladies, valets. It's not natural. I'm not an Englishman. I could never live this way.* He couldn't fall back asleep, and the sun started to enter the room. *Geraldine is still asleep. I think I'll get up.*

He quietly put his robe on and was leaving when Geraldine began to move. "Jakob, what time is it? Are you getting up so early? I'm going to stay in bed for a while. You go ahead."

"Will you be having breakfast in bed?" said Jakob.

"No, I'll be down in a bit. I'll get the kids ready, and we'll come down for breakfast together."

He entered the dining room, and Rutherford was getting breakfast together. He poured Jakob coffee and gave him the newspaper. "Will Lady Geraldine be having breakfast in bed.?"

"No, Rutherford, she'll be down with the children, and we'll eat together." Jakob scanned through the newspaper and had his coffee until Geraldine and the children came down.

After breakfast, Geraldine suggested they take the horses out. "We'll see what's new around here."

"How about me, Mother? Can I go with you?" said Randy.

"No, Honey, Grandma said she wants to take care of you. She has some things she wants to show you."

Later, Lady Mary came down and took charge of Randy. She really took a fancy to him, and they walked off together.

Jakob, Geraldine, and BethAnn changed and came down in their riding clothes, Wyoming style. They walked to the stable where Archie had the horses ready. Jakob was amazed his horse seemed to remember him, and BethAnn's Ginger was waiting for her. She gave her a carrot which the horse relished. BethAnn had an amazing manner in her approach.

The ride was slow and took them to some far reaches of the Manor. They stopped at a spring and creek and had lunch. Everything was so green, and the birds were out. They came upon a shepherd boy. Geraldine got off the horse and talked with the boy.

"You're the Williams boy, aren't you?"

"Yes, Ma'am." His dog came up to Geraldine so she could pet it.

"I see you're doing a good job with your sheep. What's your dog's name?"

"His name is Freddie, and he really helps me keep my sheep from wandering away."

"I'm Lady Geraldine. Be sure to give my regards to your father and mother. I will try to stop by and see them if I can." She got up on her horse and waved goodbye to him.

"He's the son of one of our tenant farmers. They're nice people," she told them.

Their ride lasted most of the day. When they got home, they napped and then went out on the veranda.

Lady Mary was there already with Randy, who started telling them about his day with grandmother. "I never had such a good time as I had today with my grandson. That's right, I never had a grandchild. I took him with me to the Child Welfare Society, and the ladies enjoyed him so much. He told us all about the ranch in Wyoming and your home in Sheridan. I had a lovely time with him. Oh yes, I also took him to Barr & Roberts, and they will make a suit for him. You don't mind, do you?"

"Mama, why should I mind? He's your grandson."

"Of course he is, and I'll do whatever I want for the short time I have him with me."

It was obvious Lady Mary loved her grandson, and he liked it.

"Oh, I have some more news for you. Mary Sarah is coming to see you and to be at the memorial. I don't know if her husband is coming, but I wouldn't mind if he did."

Apparently, Mary Sarah had not been to Landry Manor since Sir Gerald's passing. All were surprised.

Before dinner, Geraldine prevailed on Robert to make his famous martinis. While he carefully concocted the delight, Jakob asked him how he made them.

Robert gave him detailed instructions and added, "I'm using Hayman's London Dry Gin."

As they imbibed the ambrosia, they talked about the next day's schedule. They decided to go into Ipswich and the historic waterfront.

Their dinner was a local favorite of Mrs. Wrightson's cook, Lizzi—Shepherd's Pie.

Following dinner, Lady Mary started teaching her grandson how to play checkers, and he really liked it. The others spent their evening talking about the current politics in England and the desire for women's voting rights.

The next morning Sampson took Geraldine, Jakob, and BethAnn into Ipswich. Lady Mary wanted Randy to spend the day with her, and Randy was happy to do so. Sampson took the rural road with its ruts and holes into the city. The city streets were in good repair, although some were cobblestone. It was an old city dating back centuries.

"There were Romans who spent time here as well as Anglo-Saxons. We have a museum with all kinds of artifacts in our history. The River Orwell, where it runs into the North Sea, was the gateway for those ancient visitors," said Geraldine. She pointed out the various historical points of Ipswich, which was in the county of Suffolk. "I've told you England was an old country. Let's find one of the oldest restaurants and have lunch. Sampson, drive us to Ipswich Seafood Limited, down on the docks."

"Oh no, Lady Geraldine, it's not a respectable place for you and your daughter," said Sampson.

"Oh, it's not that bad at this time of the day, and it does have the best soft shell crabs."

Sampson reluctantly took them down to the docks to a very old and dilapidated building used as a pub and restaurant. The inside wasn't much better than the outside.

Geraldine ordered, and the voluptuous waitress brought out baskets of crabs with a dipping sauce, a biscuit, and a pint to wash it down. They broke the crabs with their fingers to eat them. Jakob and BethAnn admitted they were very good. They left, filled with the crustacean delight, but aware the ambiance of Ipswich Seafood Limited could be improved.

"Geraldine, were you able to understand the waitress? I had a hard time. You seemed to understand her," said Jakob.

"Oh yes, it was her Suffolk dialect. Years ago, the people here used to talk in their own dialect. To those whom they think are outsiders, they sometimes do now to make fun of them. She didn't know I understood some of it."

They continued their historical tour of Ipswich and returned after a full day of sightseeing. Geraldine tried to give them a view of an important and historic town in England.

Returning to the manor, they freshened up before going out to sit on the veranda. Geraldine was surprised to see her sister Mary Sarah sitting with Lady Mary and Randy.

"Sarah! You've come. I didn't expect you so soon," said Geraldine.

They embraced, and tears were shed for her sister that she had not seen for years before Geraldine introduced Jakob and BethAnn.

Sarah, as she liked to be called, was younger than Geraldine and was an attractive dark-haired lady. She looked more like her mother than Geraldine but was tall and slim. She had many of Geraldine's mannerisms. There was a lot of talk about old times.

BethAnn had been left out of the conversation and was bored, so she asked to be excused. "I'd like to go to the stable to see Ginger and ride her. May I please, Mother?"

Geraldine smiled and nodded approval. "But don't go too far. You don't know your way around, so stay close."

Sarah told Geraldine about her life. She was now married to Percy

Jamison, a businessman. "Yes, he was divorced, but his wife had remarried shortly after the parting. That was five years before we married. We loved each other and had much in common. As you know, being a divorced man was not acceptable to our morals. Mama was opposed to my marriage, but she's finally decided she would accept my husband, which has me very happy. Percy will come on the weekend and be at the memorial."

Geraldine could see BethAnn in the distance as she rode Ginger. She finally rode up to the verandah and told them about all she had seen. She loved being on horseback.

Then she tried some of the exercises from dressage, and Ginger was able to do several. "Ginger is smart, Mother. I bet I could teach her more if we had the time."

Geraldine agreed. BethAnn rode back to the stable.

Sarah was impressed with BethAnn's horsemanship. "I was never good with horses," she said. You were, Geraldine. You and Papa rode together. I miss him a lot." She bowed her head.

Lady Mary made it known dinner was at seven. They went to their rooms to ready for dinner.

"Jakob, I'm so happy to see Sarah and that she had mended things with Mama. I know how Mama felt, but I also felt for Sarah. She is really very sweet, and this must have played hard on her emotionally. I'm anxious to meet her husband."

"Yes, I know what you mean. But do you know what really makes me feel good? BethAnn. She has shown her very best, and they all love her."

"Yes, and our Randy too. He's really taken to his grandmother."

Arrangements were made to have the memorial services for Sir Randolph Landry on Tuesday. The church service would be at eleven at the Trinity Church in Ipswich with the Rector Robert Henderson officiating. Afterward, the burial would be at the Trinity cemetery. Colonel Roy Howard of the HM Royal 18th Regiment will be in charge. Twelve riflemen would salute Captain Randolph Edward Landry.

People started to move into the church. The dark oak coffin with Captain Landry was placed in front of the altar. To the side of the coffin was an easel with a portrait of Captain Randolph in full uniform. As people came in, some approached the casket, hesitated, and touched it in reverence, and found a seat in a pew.

The church soon filled to capacity. On the left side in the front pew sat Lady Mary, Jenny Lynn, Mary Sarah, and Geraldine, with Jakob, BethAnn, and Randy. The women all wore black with short veils on their hats. On the other side of the church in the front pew sat Lord Oliver Henry, Lady Abigail, Lord George Robertson, Lady Susan, Sir Peter Colwell. The rest of the church was filled with a mixture of Members of Parliament, close friends, and acquaintances. Tenants of the manor and interested townsfolk sat at the back of the church. The colonel and his men marched in carrying the Union Flag and took places at the sides of the coffin.

Rector Roy began the service. He said words of praise for Randolph Edward. "He served God, his wife and family, his country, and the men, women, and children of Landry Manor."

Colonel Roy Howard, in his scarlet tunic, medals, and gold braid, praised Captain Landry's service. There were hymns, and it was over. The Union Flag was placed over the casket, and the men of the HM Royal Regiment took places on either side and marched forward, carrying it out of the church. It was placed on a carrier with a single horse. One of the men led the horse, and they moved to the cemetery.

They removed the casket, moved to the gravesite next to where Sir Gerald Landry was buried and stood to the coffin's side. After the rector said a prayer, the soldiers raised their rifles and fired a ten-gun salute. They lowered their rifles, and two of them came forward, lifted the flag from the casket, and carefully folded it. They handed the folded flag to the colonel, who moved to a seated Jenny Lynn, addressed her, and handed it to her. Then he saluted, and they all marched away.

Some came forward and placed flowers on the casket before it was lowered. Others gave their condolences to Jenny Lynn, whose cheeks were wet with tears, and Lady Mary, who lost her son in the terrible tragedy. Some came forward to Sarah and Geraldine. Some stayed and talked, while others just left.

Lunch would be served at Landry Manor. The doors of the manor were open, and the living area was filled with mourners. The veranda attracted some who went out to talk and have their wine and luncheon. Jakob spoke with many friends of Randolph Edward. He was a popular man, and those from the Parliament said they would miss his wisdom. Little Randy was the attraction to many. He was dressed in the suit Barr & Roberts made for him. He looked like a handsome young man.

Most had left when an important-looking man came up to Jakob and Geraldine. They conversed about Randolph Edward. He apparently knew him well because he talked about the things he had accomplished for Landry Manor.

He then suggested they sit in an alcove with a small table. "Please excuse me. I should have introduced myself. My name is Rex Jordan. Lady Geraldine, we met once when you were married to James Whitaker."

"Oh yes, I remember now. You're an attorney," said Geraldine.

"That's right. I have acted as solicitor for Sir Gerald almost from the very beginning when Queen Victoria knighted him. We made Landry Manor what it is today: a successful business. When Sir Gerald passed away, I helped his son take over the manor. He would have been Baron within the year if the terrible tragedy hadn't struck. He was knighted by the Queen, and she knew all about his military career and how well he managed Landry Manor. Now that he has gone, we must have a male heir to take over. Doctor Miller, Lady Geraldine, that heir is your son: Randolph Jakob Miller." Rex Jordan stopped talking, and his gray eyes looked directly at Jakob and Geraldine. Silence prevailed as he stared at them.

Geraldine was the first to speak. "I guess I should have known, but the thought didn't enter my mind. Jakob?"

"Yes, the thought didn't enter my mind either, but Randy is an American by birth."

"That doesn't matter," Jordan said. "He is still the heir. Obviously, he can't take over until he is of age. But when he is, and with Her Majesty's act, he will be the Baron of Landry Manor."

Jakob looked at Geraldine, who was still stunned by what she heard.

Thoughts whirled through Jakob's mind before he spoke again. His head shook slightly as if in disbelief. "Well, this sounds interesting. I don't know what Geraldine's thoughts are. Still, I am an American, and Randy was born an American. I, for one, would object to him leaving our country to live in England. It sounds like it might be a great opportunity, but I believe living in America is a greater one."

Rex looked at Jakob as if he didn't understand the opportunity he was overlooking. "You have to understand we would take care of his education. He would be enrolled in the finest prep schools and earn a degree at Cambridge. He would travel and do everything needed to make him a worthy baron. He could have a proper wife of means." He seemed to soul search Jakob for a long pause. "If you wish to hold your decision, we can wait. You may want to change your mind when he gets a little older."

Jakob smiled and said, "Mister Jordan, I won't give up my son for your Queen or anyone."

He looked at Geraldine, who spoke. "Mr. Jordan, I will agree with my husband. It may be a good opportunity, but he is right in not wanting to give up his son. If Randy was of age and he chose to do so, then it would be his decision. For now, this is a closed issue. We appreciate your desire to find a proper heir, but Randy will not be the one. However, you do have a possibility, and that is Jenny Lynn. She is pregnant by Randy Edward. If she has a boy, you may very well have an heir."

Rex smiled and thanked them for their time and that the offer would be open until he found a suitable heir. He picked up his case and left.

BethAnn and little Randy came into the room. They had been on the verandah. Randy looked up at Jakob, and he picked him up. Randy hugged him and kissed his cheek.

Jakob smiled. "I love you, son. What are you going to be when you grow up?"

His eyes grew big as he thought. "I don't know, Daddy, but I would like to be a baseball player."

Geraldine heard the answer and laughed. "Really, Randy?"

"Yes, Mother. That would be fun."

Geraldine smiled. "I guess it would be, and I bet you would be good."

He laughed and hugged Geraldine.

During the trip, they spent a great deal of time together, and that was good. Randy showed a loving personality to all he met. His grandmother would miss him when the Millers left for home.

Following the memorial, most of the visitors left. Oliver Henry and Abby spent time together with Jakob and Geraldine. Geraldine and James had lived with them for some time, so they developed a close relationship. Jakob was his dentist, and they immediately became friends. They felt Geraldine's marriage to Jakob was a good one for her. They also understood their reason for turning down little Randy's succession to be heir to Landry Manor.

"Giving up one's son was not in his best interests," said Oliver.

They now had an opportunity to meet Sarah's husband, Percy. They found him to be an interesting chap, as he would put it. He liked the idea of them visiting with Geraldine and Jakob at the ranch.

On the last days of their stay, Geraldine, BethAnn, and Jakob made visits to the various tenants of Landry Manor. Geraldine felt it was important to keep in communication with them. Farming was the business of the manor, and without it, the estate would not survive.

People in rural areas were starting to move to the cities for better wages, and the politics of England were beginning to change. The Labor Party was seeking recognition.

Geraldine and Jakob stopped at the Brothers farm. The boys remembered her when she helped them out. Dr. Bridges came to see their mother when she was sick, and she gave them the food they needed. Harry, their father, took on the raising of pigs, and his income increased significantly. Such things made being a tenant in Landry Manor a better life than going to the city.

Lady Mary invited a group of friends to dinner before the Millers left. Oliver Henry and Abby were house guests that stayed on. Ambassador Warren Wilson and his wife, Major Robertson, and Emma, Sarah and Percy, and Jenny Lynn's parents, the Herberts. The long table in the dining room was set with silver and glass and burning candelabra. Mrs. Wrightson had Lizzi prepare a fine dinner for the group. Footmen did the serving, and Rutherford poured the wine. The conversation was light, with most directed at the Millers.

When the dinner was over, the men broke for the traditional cigars and port. Jakob's cigar didn't stay lit very long, but the other men seemed to enjoy theirs. The conversation was mainly on the politics of the day. There was also talk of a possible war in Europe. Some felt there might be one, while others did not think they would be involved. Jakob thought there was a certain degree of envy for the United States, and some thought they might one day visit America. Jakob extended his invitation to those interested in the ranch. They were considering guests as an extension to people who might like to try ranching as a vacation. The idea of a dude ranch still floated around in their thinking.

The evening ended on a positive note, and all agreed that Jakob and his family should return sometime in the future. They all left except for the houseguests that would leave the next day.

Geraldine made sure Randy was bedded down. It had been a full day for him and BethAnn. They saw a different style of life on the trip to England. Jakob and Geraldine were ready to leave for Sheridan. The trip was enjoyable, but it was enough. They fell asleep recapping the past day.

Sampson took Lord Oliver and his wife to the train early, and they had their goodbyes. He would be taking the Millers later. They had to get all their things together and say their final goodbyes. Lady Mary was lamenting that they didn't stay long enough but was grateful they had come. Jenny Lynn thanked them for helping her in her time of need. She embraced Geraldine for all she had done for her.

Lady Mary then gave gifts to BethAnn and Randy, which she said couldn't be opened until they returned to Sheridan. She had enjoyed her grandchildren. Randy was especially proud of the suit Lady Mary had bought for him. She had also purchased a dress for BethAnn, who wore it at the last dinner. Lady Mary had tears in her eyes as she hugged all of them.

Sampson secured the baggage. Rutherford spoke for the staff, who all came out to wish them a pleasant and safe journey. The car doors closed, and Sampson started off to Ipswich and the train to London

"Bye, Grandmother," said Randy as he waved tearfully.

Chapter 34
Going Home

Sampson stopped at the Ipswich train station, unloaded the baggage to be checked in, and bid the Millers goodbye. There was a short wait, and the train arrived, and with its doors open, the Millers entered and took seats. The train was near capacity, and most seats were occupied, so seating was tight. Randy sat on Jakob's lap. A couple sitting across from them got up.

"I say, folks, we can move. No use you being uncomfortable and crowded. You have a good day." The gentleman tipped his hat, the lady smiled at them, and they left. Jakob thanked them, and he and Randy moved to the empty seats.

It was a two-hour ride to London's South Central Station, where they got off. Their luggage was put on a cart and taken to the Great Eastern Hotel, just across the street. This was an old but fine hotel where they checked in for the night. Lunch was at a small restaurant in the hotel that served local food specialties.

"Being in England, you have to try Bangers and Mash," said Geraldine. "They have especially good bangers here."

BethAnn looked at her. "Mother, what are bangers?"

Geraldine laughed, "Why, bangers are a type of sausage they serve with mashed potatoes. It's a food item served in most English-style restaurants. I think you will like it. Give it a try."

They ordered the bangers and found them acceptable but not quite as good as they had expected. The stay in London was just overnight, and they didn't have time to do much sightseeing. There were vendors in the vicinity of the hotel, which sold many different items. Flowers were a big item, but some sold all sorts of trinkets and even clothing. They checked out the various vendors but didn't find anything which interested them. The stay in the hotel was pleasant but short.

The next day it was a good breakfast, and shortly after, they would be taking the train to Southampton and the ship. Reservations were on the *HMS Oceanic*. This was the ship they had traveled on their previous trip to England. It was considered the fastest ship of the line. The *HMS Celtic* was a sister ship, so it was essentially the same, except not as fast.

The train made the stop in Southampton to discharge local passengers and then went to the docks where they boarded the *Oceanic*. Everyone was anxious to board because it meant they were going home, and home was Sheridan. They were still dressed in English-style clothes. Going through customs was easy, and the agent asked if they would be coming back.

"It will be some time before we will return. We enjoyed our England stay, but Sheridan, Wyoming is home for us," said Jakob.

"Blimey, you must be from the wild west," said the agent.

Jakob laughed and assured him it was not wild anymore. He laughed, and they moved on. There was an hour wait before they would board.

They were lucky to get a cabin on the promenade deck. A steward took them to their suite, which was located mid-ships. No owner's suite this time, but it was still very comfortable. The cabin boy introduced himself and told them he would make their trip pleasant. They could enter the deck from a door in the suite. There was a large window where they could look out on the ocean. Their luggage arrived, and they started to do some storing.

Randy and BethAnn were anxious to go on deck and see some of the ship. They walked out of the suite onto the deck. The *Oceanic* was filling up with passengers. BethAnn noticed a family with two girls who were just a few cabins away. They looked English.

The main dining room staircase was approached further aft of their suite. Jakob found a soda fountain nearby where Randy and BethAnn could get ice cream, which delighted them. Then, he came across a pub where they could go in for cocktails. There were already a few couples inside, and as they walked in, a waitress found them a table.

"Do you have a bartender who knows how to make a good martini?" asked Jakob.

The waitress smiled and answered. "I can assure you, sir, that Harold is an expert in martinis. He has an array of twenty different gins available. Certainly, you don't want a barbaric vodka, do you? He uses a gentleman's gin like Hayman's London Dry, and he won't make it dirty, but he will garnish it with a pure olive."

Jakob laughed. "Then I will order one for Lady Geraldine and myself on your recommendation."

She smiled and took the order, then returned with a silver serving dish with various nuts. Jakob and Geraldine chuckled as they waited for their martini, which came back carried on a silver tray. The voluptuous server carefully placed it in front of them.

"This, sir, is a martini," she said and smiled. "Ambrosia suitable for the gods.".

They looked at each other and carefully picked up the stemmed glass with two spired olives and a chilled martini. As they toasted, the waitress left.

"Careful, Geraldine, we don't want to disturb the gods. Sip it slowly. By golly, it is good!" Jakob said.

Geraldine held Jakob's hand. "You know, I love you more than ever, and I still remember the wonderful trip we had when we went to Landry Manor before we were married."

They talked about the trip and their love and how they looked for Geraldine's parents' approval to their marriage. Their reminiscing was interrupted by the long sounding of the ship's horn. BethAnn and Randy stood in front of them.

"I think we're getting ready to leave," said BethAnn. There's a lot of excitement on the decks, and people are throwing confetti and streamers to the people on the dock."

With another long blast of the ship's horn, they could start to feel the ship's movement. The Millers went to the starboard side and saw a tug with lines attached to the stern. It churned water along with the ship's engines and pulled the *Oceanic* away from the dock and toward the middle of the channel. At the bow, another tug pulled until the ship was mid-channel, and the ship's engines were moving it slowly forward. The tugs backed off, staying with the liner, which was now going forward under the direction of the Pilot, whose crew had intimate knowledge of the channel depth and possible underwater obstructions. As the ship passed the Isle of Wight, the Pilot could be seen leaving, and the *Oceanic* was now under the captain's control.

Randy watched all of this activity and questioned Jakob about the goings-on. He was excited, and Jakob was happy to know he was interested. "Papa, I have to know how to do this if I am going to be an officer on the ship."

Jakob was amazed he remembered what the Captain said to him when they met him at dinner. The ship was underway, and most of the people started going inside. Standing at the rail and looking back, you could see the Isle Wight, but the English shore still remained close. As they watched the land pass by, the *Oceana* drew farther from the coast, and soon only tall objects like chimneys could be discerned.

"Papa, can we go up to the bow. I want to see what it's like up there," said Randy.

"Sure, but we might get wet if we got too close. See the spray coming over it?"

"But we can be careful and not get too close," said Randy.

However, they did get too close, and a fine spray did sprinkle them until they moved back a little. Randy laughed as some drops of water got him.

Jakob noticed he really enjoyed being with Randy. It gave him a sense of love he had never felt. His BethAnn gave him enjoyment and a sense of pride and love, but Randy was different. Jakob didn't spend as much time with him as he had spent with BethAnn. Randy was home with Geraldine most of the time. But on the trip, he was with him more. They stood by the rail until most of England was no longer visible, and only the stark Atlantic was ahead. Looking back at the wings of the bridge, they watched the navigator taking celestial observations. The darkening sky had started to reveal stars.

"See the stars up there twinkling? The navigator is taking measurements of them, and that will tell him where we're at." Randy was a little confused, and Jakob tried to explain what he learned from the navigator on the *Celtic*.

"Look up there, Randy. See the stars that are becoming brighter as the sky gets darker. They have names, like Arcturus and Dubi, and there are planets like Venus and Mars." The more he told Randy, the more questions he asked. Lights on the distant shore started to blink on.

"It's getting dark, Randy. Let's go back into our cabin. We have to be ready for dinner." They walked back as Randy talked about all they had seen.

Geraldine ordered a personal maid to take care of her and BethAnn's needs. They were almost ready for dinner. She had a backless blue ankle-length gown on and looked beautiful, and BethAnn had a lighter blue gown. Geraldine started to dress her in more attractive young girl's clothes. No longer a teenager, BethAnn showed the beauty of a seventeen-year-old. BethAnn's blond hair was parted and tied to the side. Geraldine had Randy's suit ready for him, and Jakob wore his English dinner attire.

They left the cabin in style and stood at the bottom of the large staircase to the dining room to have their pictures taken by the ship's photographer.

"Doctor Miller, we're happy to have you and your family with us.

Lady Geraldine, I remember you sailed with us before. I have a table especially for you, and it will be near the dance floor. However, I'm going to make a suggestion for you. You might enjoy the company of another passenger and their family. Dr. Mallory and his family might be interesting people to dine with. They have two children about the same ages as yours. If you should be interested, just let me know. Roland will seat you."

They followed the waitperson to their table and sat down. The first to step forward was the wine steward, who helped them select the wine. He was followed by the waiter with the menu. After they ordered, Jakob asked Geraldine to the dance floor. The floor was not crowded, and they danced several dances.

The wine steward was waiting for them, so they sat down. Randy and BethAnn had fancy soft drinks, and Jakob tasted and accepted the steward's wine. Randy told them all about what he and Jakob had done near the bow of the ship.

Their dinner was exquisite. They all enjoyed lobster bisque, salad with garden varieties, and filet of sole almandine with a rice dish and creamed asparagus. The dessert was baked ice cream, which the waiters marched out in flames. They talked about the trip and Landry Manor, but they looked forward to Sheridan.

Geraldine and Jakob decided to dance and returned after several.

When they did, a young man approached Jakob. "Sir, may I ask you if it would be all right to dance with your daughter?"

Jakob smiled and looked at BethAnn. "BethAnn, would you like to dance with this young man?"

She smiled and nodded her head in approval.

The young man politely assisted her to the dance floor. His family sat at the adjacent table. Jakob nodded and smiled at them. He assumed they were the party the maitre d' talked about.

Later, they left the dining room and walked out on the deck. There was a brisk wind, and the sea was running several feet. The stars had an accompanying moon lighting the sky. Geraldine held Jakob and kissed him. They walked until Geraldine said, "Let's go to our room. I'm getting tired." They all agreed they had a full day.

Jakob was usually an early riser. He didn't need a rooster to wake him. Light from outside crept inside the cabin. He was happy to be going home. Then, thoughts about his Randy came up. *The idea he was an heir to Landry Manor might seem tempting. An English aristocrat, but the idea of trading one's country was not attractive. Why would we ever even consider it—exchanging being an American for that of being an English aristocrat.? His mother made the trade of being an aristocrat for being an American. There is no comparison to being an American!*

Geraldine was still sound asleep, so he thought he'd get up. He put on his robe and stepped out on the deck. He saw the navigator leave the bridge and the sky begin to lighten. He looked back and could see a bare tip of the sun starting to show on the horizon. A bright aura of rays reached from the sea, and then like an explosion, the sun came up in full glory. *Wow! I've never seen anything like this. The sky became awash in the sun's light.* He watched the sun ascend until it was completely visible. *I wish Geraldine and the kids had seen this.*

He could feel the motion of the ship as it passed through waves. The bow would rise and then fall, leaving a wash on the bow. There were a few others on the deck watching the sea. The birds that followed yesterday were no longer present. There was a chill in the air. The sun was now fully present and rising higher, and he started to feel its warmth. *I wonder if anybody is up yet.* And he decided to go in.

"I wondered where you went," said Geraldine. "Our cabin boy brought us some coffee and Danish."

Their day was spent largely resting, but BethAnn and Randy found friends to be with.

Geraldine made it known to the maitre d' they would like to have dinner with the family he described. Thus, they met the Mallorys. He was a doctor who practiced medicine in Southampton. They found them interesting, and their children made friends with BethAnn and Randy. The doctor talked with Jakob and was interested in medicine as was practiced in Sheridan. He spoke of his practice. He liked being a doctor but was not too happy with their hospital or dealings with the government. He didn't like the government interfering in medical treatment. They now had a form of socialized medicine. He was going to attend a medical convention in New York. They enjoyed their company and had some things in common.

They sat with the Mallorys for dinner and also met other passengers to associate with. It became a more interesting trip. Most were English and going to the United States for a vacation. Because they came from different parts of England, they often spoke differently. It was like visiting other parts of the United States. Southerners had different accents from people living in New England or Chicago.

On the fourth day out, they woke up to nasty weather. The sky was dark, and it was raining. Winds had picked up substantially, and the seas grew larger. No one went on deck, and most stayed in their cabins. Some took their meals in the main dining room, but the heavy seas made things difficult for the wait staff, and dinners were dropped, and glasses fell. There was music but no one danced. Jakob decided to go on deck to see what he could but came back quickly.

"The deck was awash at times, and the wind was very strong. Made it hard to walk, and I had to hold on to the rail. The wind driving the rain made my face sting. It was dangerous, so I came back in."

The storm got worse, and the ship slowed down. It rolled, so it was hard to walk, especially when a big wave hit. Passengers were warned not to go on deck, and meals could be brought to the cabin if they wanted. The children were afraid, but both Jakob and Geraldine told them not to worry.

On the third day, the storm subsided, and they were able to go on deck and have their meals in the main dining room. The entertainers did their routines but not without difficulty. The passengers took the discomforts and laughed at them. They joined in the singing.

Jakob awoke. It was the fourth day of bad weather, and he realized the storm was all but over. The seas were still high, but the rain and wind had subsided. Today they would be landing in New York harbor. You could see land ahead, and the ship should be able to dock by the afternoon. The sun burned bright, and people were coming out on deck without life jackets.

There was a full breakfast available, which made Randy and BethAnn happy. They liked the waffles with all the fruit and whipped cream. Standing at the rail, they saw the inspirational Statue of Liberty. Everybody was excited because they were almost there. They watched the pilot boat come out, and the pilot could be seen coming up the gangway. They had already said their goodbyes to their newfound friends, and their baggage was collected. The ship was now in quarantine. They had to indicate if there were sick passengers or a reason to prevent them from leaving. The ship maneuvered New York Harbor with tugs alongside. It slowly came into the dock, which was crowded with people waving and shouting.

Quarantine and immigration were aboard, and passengers were positioning themselves for departure. They disembarked and ended in line for customs, declared some of the items they brought back, and paid the duty. Getting a taxi was a problem, but they gathered their belongings and found one to take them to the Knickerbocker Hotel, where they would stay that night. The taxi ride was hectic as usual. Traffic in New York was heavy at this time of the day. The Knickerbocker Hotel was located in Times Square. Jakob thought it would be an interesting place to stay. They would only be there one night and leave for Sheridan the next day on the New York Central railroad. Randy and BethAnn were amazed at how high the buildings were.

They decided to eat in one of the restaurants in the hotel. Afterward, they walked down Broadway and saw some of the theaters. Their hotel room was pleasant but no comparison to the ship cabin. New York weather was hot, and the fans in their room didn't help much. They were glad to leave New York.

They boarded the New York Central train, which would take them to Chicago. Leaving New York's Grand Central Station, the train passed through a less desirable portion of the city. The tall buildings were now behind, and some more pleasant rural countryside showed out of their windows. Sheridan, Wyoming, was still a long distance away.

BethAnn took up with reading a book. Jakob thought buying a checker set would help Randy pass the time since his grandmother taught him how to play.

Geraldine had the ranch on her mind. The sale of horses had dropped considerably. English buyers had cut back, and getting the right horses was getting more difficult. Cattle ranching was big business, and she did some but didn't want to get bigger. She was giving more thought to guests. More dude ranches were starting up in Wyoming, and easterners liked the idea. It was a rustic atmosphere, and trail riding on horses could be enjoyable with mountains and streams for a background. After their dinner, it wasn't too hard to go to sleep.

They would change trains in Chicago. It was a very long distance before the train entered Sheridan. There were taxis now available to take them to their home. Loukes Street looked good to them, and they were greeted by Helen and Simba, who showed how much she missed them.

Chapter 35
Going Hunting

Returning from England, Jakob's first day at the office turned busy. BethAnn came to help him get the office ready. He was concerned the Ford might not start after standing for a month, but it immediately started. He parked it in front of the office. Patients had gotten used to seeing his car there, but Jakob wasn't expecting any today. He was surprised to find one waiting for him. He never knew how they found out he would be in, but there was usually one there. This time what really surprised him was that it was one of his old patients from Buffalo, Wyoming, George Hillman.

After Liz died, Jakob had busied himself and decided to expand his practice to Buffalo. They had no dentist there, and they needed one. BethAnn was just two, and he didn't want to leave her in Sheridan with Chucha, so he took her with him.

He had first met George when he took care of him in Sheridan, and they became friends. George came from Racine, Wisconsin. Racine was just about twenty miles from Milwaukee, so they had something in common.

George had encouraged Jakob to start a dental office in Buffalo because of the need and told him to bring BethAnn. "My wife would love to take care of her while you work in Buffalo. It might put a stop on her mooning over the grandchildren in Racine."

Mary Hillman fell in love with BethAnn and was like a grandmother to her. The practice there was successful, but Jakob was also busy in Sheridan. He couldn't handle both places, so he found a dentist to take over that office. He regretted giving it up because he lost contact with those people, but Sheridan took preference.

He hadn't seen George for many years. Now he came to see Jakob because he felt no one but Jakob could take care of him. The electric streetcar was now going to Buffalo, so his transportation was now possible. But he also brought bad news about Mary, who had passed away. He couldn't believe BethAnn had grown so big and broke down when he saw her because BethAnn had become his granddaughter. George was an old friend, and they talked at length until Jakob took him into his treatment room to take care of him.

BethAnn was cleaning up the office, and when the next patient came in, she put him at ease by talking with him while Jakob was with George. She liked to work there and always spoke to the people who came in. Jakob thought she might be interested in being a dentist when she graduated high school, so he encouraged her to come to the office. She did her cleaning and talked to the patient until Jakob finished George Hillman.

While she did her clean-up, Jakob took care of several more patients after George left. Later, George came back, and he went to lunch with Jakob.

Geraldine then came by and took BethAnn with her to lunch. She told BethAnn she thought it was time to start Randy riding. He was excited to go on the horse in England and liked it. He had no fears, so Geraldine thought it wasn't too early to try him on Nelly, who was smaller. BethAnn was already riding a more challenging Princess. She thought they could bring Princess from the ranch. It would mean building onto the stable because it was already too small. Besides, Princess needed a stall.

They talked about the horses, and BethAnn was really excited. She talked about working her to be a jumper, which Geraldine agreed would be a good idea. BethAnn had a way with horses, and Geraldine marveled at how she could do things with them. She thought it was a gift BethAnn had. But the subject changed, and BethAnn asked Geraldine if she could help her with a decision she was trying to make.

"I'll be graduating high school soon, and I have to make up my mind about what I want to do with my life. Some of my friends are already thinking about what they want to do. My friend Betty is talking about marrying her boyfriend. In fact, two other girls have boyfriends they talk about marrying. But I want to do something different with my life. I'll get married sometime when I meet the right man. I like horses and riding, but I don't want to spend my life in rodeos and things like that. I want to help people like Daddy does. But, I'm not sure I want to be a dentist. I would have to leave home for two years of dental school, and I don't want to go to Chicago. You and Daddy said I should attend college, but that would even be farther away. I like being home with my family." When they got home, the conversation continued.

BethAnn sat down. Simba jumped up next to her and put her head on her lap. "I was at the hospital with Daddy and saw him work there. I talked to the nurses who help people, and they said they liked their work. I could help people if I became a nurse. I think I would like that. The last time there, I saw Dr. Ross's son, Mark, there. He will graduate and be a doctor in two years. What do you think, Mother?"

Geraldine sighed. "You have given me a hard job. But I would like to help you. Have you talked this over with your father?"

"Not exactly, but I plan to do that," said BethAnn. "We've talked a little, but I have not yet settled on some things I've been thinking about. But he's a man, and you're a girl like me, so maybe you understand my feelings more."

"Thank you, Honey. I guess we girls do think different from boys."

They talked longer, and Geraldine realized that she had an important role in her daughter's life. They were closer friends than they had ever been.

That next weekend Raymond came to Sheridan and brought Princess with him. BethAnn hadn't seen her for several months, and the horse showed its affection to BethAnn when she saw her. She took her to the property they laid out as a training ground, and BethAnn worked with Princess. She directed Princess to go around and around in a circle. When she finally stopped and just stood there, the horse came up to her and followed her wherever BethAnn walked. It was a way of developing a bond with the horse. She treated the horse with apples and carrots, pets and hugs, and she talked with her. Then she put the blanket and saddle on Princess and mounted her. Princess followed every command BethAnn lovingly gave her. All the time she did her training Simba watched and followed her. Simba was a sheepherder and instinctively did what the horse did. BethAnn left the training ground with Princess, and Simba followed toward Little Goose Creek.

Geraldine watched them ride off and followed. They met at the creek and watched the birds. Before coming back together, she said, "Looks like you and Princess are getting along quite well. She seems to be bonded with you, and that's good. Now, all we have to do is get Randy riding Nelly. We can both teach him,"

"That would be fine. I hope Nelly takes to him since I won't be riding her much now that I have Princess. I hope Nelly won't mind because I do love her," said BethAnn.

Several new dentists started practices in town, but Jakob still remained busy. However, Sheridan continued to grow, so there was a need for more dentists and medical doctors. Jakob was in the Lucky Lady after he finished in the office. The Lady was always busy, and he was at the bar talking to some of his friends. Mayor Burns didn't show up very much now. He had retired from being the mayor. Ray Johnson, the pharmacist, wanted the job, so there was an election, and he was now mayor. He was younger and had some different ideas on running Sheridan. He had a business head, and his staff and the commissioners were mostly new to the office. Some of Burn's people stayed on. Jakob was one of them. There was also a new sheriff elected, although Sheridan also had a police force that handled mostly town work.

County sheriff Willard Wiley was at the bar talking to Jakob. "Glad you're back, Doc. Always nice to talk to you. You always have good ideas. Things are pretty quiet in the county. The old Hole in the Wall Gang seems to have disappeared. There's talk that Longabaugh and Cassidy went to Bolivia and were killed there, but some of the others are still around, and that's a concern."

Sheriff Wiley also spoke of the two rustlers Jakob had encountered. One was still in jail, and the other escaped and, to date, had not been found. He was the one who threatened to get Jakob. He had just disappeared. Some lawmen thought he may have been killed during the escape and never found.

There had not been a bank robbery in Sheridan for a long time. Wiley talked about some of the gangsters from the east who were something to be concerned with. Some of them were seen more in Montana than Wyoming.

"High crime is not that much of a problem. I'm more concerned with small crimes, which appear to be increasing. I'm especially concerned with a hobo encampment outside of town. Some of them come into town and prey on the housewives, asking for food or for work. This is frightening to the ladies, and they want me, as sheriff, to do something about it. There's always the problem of jurisdiction between me and the police."

Jakob's problem was that some of the hobos entered his office with toothaches or looking for work. Some would ask for money and even suggest something could happen if he didn't give it to them.

As he left his office and before he got into his car, one did come to him out of the dark.

"Doc, I was just wondering if you could help me out. I haven't found any work today, and I thought maybe you could help me out with a couple of bucks for dinner."

Jakob felt he was panhandling. "Tell you what I'll do. Across from the train station is a restaurant. I'm going there. I'll stop and buy you a good meal. I know Andrew, who owns it. I'll tell him you'll stop by. He'll even throw in a piece of pie."

"Look, Doc, I don't want a piece of that pie. I want a piece of your poke." He pulled out a knife and lunged at Jakob. Jakob stepped aside, and the hobo passed him with the blade shining. The door to the office was not yet closed, and Jakob ducked inside and opened the drawer where he kept his personal weapon. As he took it out, the man came in and, seeing Jakob with it, immediately turned around and ran. Jakob pursued him out of the office, but he was already some distance ahead. Jakob fired into the air to let him know he wasn't kidding but didn't pursue him. Some people heard the shot and came running to find out what had happened.

"Good thing you had your gun handy, Doc. I heard that guy had pulled the same stunt on a couple of others, and they paid him off. Stop at the police station and tell them what happened, so they know what's going on."

Jakob did go to the police station and made them aware of what had happened. They said others had reported similar incidents and hoped that maybe he had scared him off for good.

Jakob decided not to tell Geraldine about his event but did warn the ladies not to cooperate with a panhandler if he approached the house. He was also happy to have Simba around. She was protective when it came to strangers and made enough noise when they approached the house. A coyote once approached the horse stable and found Simba a tough caretaker. Funny though, when patients came by, she was more tolerant.

It was a Saturday afternoon when cowboys came into Sheridan to let off steam. Jakob was in his office when Zeke came in with a couple of his beat-up friends from Riley's Bad Bar. Needless to say, it must have been a real donnybrook. Not Zeke this time, but two of his friends had facial lacerations and fractured teeth. Jakob took the worst first and removed four broken teeth and sutured a split lip. Hector, their Mexican friend, lost only two teeth but also the tip of his tongue. Fortunately, they both still had some money left to pay for the fees. Zeke thanked Jakob for caring for his friends and told him he was well satisfied with his false teeth.

"Zeke, you know, we never did set a date to go elk hunting, remember? I made you those teeth, and you were going to take my dad and me hunting, remember? That was the deal. You were to provide everything: guns, food, pack animals, and your expert guiding, remember? Well, I figure we should set a date. It will be for my father and me, remember? This time no bears."

"Yep, Doc, I remember. When you fixin' to go?"

"How about two weeks from today? My father will come from Milwaukee. He's a good bird hunter but never got a big animal like an elk. If he gets one, I know he'll tell his friends about the great guide he had in Sheridan, and you will get some business. How does that sound, Zeke?"

"Sounds good to me, Doc. I'll get things together, and we'll leave at sunup two weeks from today. I know jess where they be, and we'll get him a big one and you too, Doc. They make good eatin' in the winter. Now, we got's a good butcher here. Ole Herman, the German, really knows how to handle the game. He makes a great sausage too."

"Okay, then we're on. I'll have my dad here and ready. Well, now maybe you should get these guys back to the hotel or wherever they're staying. Be a good idea if they put some ice on for the swelling. On fifteen minutes and off a half-hour."

"Okay if they have a short one if it hurts?"

"Well, maybe just one," said Jakob. "And Zeke, don't forget. No bears this time."

Zeke laughed, and they left.

The rest of the day was quiet, so he decided to call his dad and tell him about the hunting trip. It took a while before the call went through.

"And Dad, he'll provide everything, the guns, food, and everything we might need. Yes, Dad, he's the guide who got me the elk whose antlers are in my office. No, Dad, I told him we didn't want any bears. Yes he does understand, Dad." Jakob smiled when he hung up. His dad was wary about the possibility of bears. *But then again, you never know what you'll run into out in the Bighorns, but at least now I would be smart enough to be wary.*

He came home and drove up to the garage. Geraldine, BethAnn, and Randy were in the yard. Randy was smiling as he sat high in the saddle on Nelly with the others looking on. Jakob watched as Randy talked to Nelly and moved the reins. Nelly started to walk. When Randy saw Jakob, he turned Nelly, who came up to him and stopped.

"Hi, Daddy. I'm riding Nelly." He laid forward on her neck, hugged her, then sat up straight, turned her around, and went back to Geraldine and BethAnn. This was quite an achievement for him. BethAnn got up on Princess and started out toward the road, with Randy and Nelly following. He watched as they went down Loukes Street to the end. The two stayed there talking and turned around, and came back to Jakob

"Hey, Daddy, did you see? I can ride Nelly. Now I can go out riding with the rest of you." He was thrilled with his achievement. "Look, I can get off." He brought his right leg back and slid to the ground but a little unsteady. He hugged Nelly and held the reins while Nelly nuzzled him.

"Okay, Randy, now you have to lead her back to her stall, and don't forget to feed and water her."

He later came back to Jakob with smiles and hugged him. "Are you proud of me, Daddy?"

Jakob reached down and hugged him. "I sure am. You're right. We can now all go riding together."

Jakob was truly proud of Randy because he wasn't sure he would take to riding Nelly. They went into the house and announced to Helen and Wanda Randy's achievement.

"Tomorrow, we're going to town and get Randy his riding boots and Stetson," said Geraldine.

"I did good, didn't I?" said Randy. Simba came up to him and licked him as Randy hugged her. Dinner was all about Randy and the horse.

Later, Jakob told Geraldine about the date he had set to go hunting with his dad and Zeke.

His dad called later and talked with Jakob. "Mother has decided to come with me." He laughed and continued. "No, she doesn't want to go with us, but she thought it might be a good time to visit you and especially the grandchildren. So, I'm really excited about the trip. Tell me what I should bring with me? I'll bring my hunting clothes and jacket, and you can let me know if there might be anything else."

Jakob told Geraldine and the children the news, and they were excited grandmother was coming to visit.

For the next two weeks, everyone was excited about Jakob's parents coming and Jakob getting ready to go hunting. Randy and BethAnn spent a lot of time riding. She took him to some of the spots she liked to visit but not too far. Sometimes they went with Daisy Ross, who had become a good rider. Mark, her brother, a medical student, was home for a short break and went riding with them.

Jakob had been in touch with Zeke, and it was all arranged for the hunting trip. Zeke's two friends Jakob took care of were well on their way to healing and talked to Jakob about making bridges. Their current appearance didn't look very good with the loss of so many front teeth.

The parents came in on the Burlington Missouri train Thursday at 2:30 pm. There was a lot of excitement, and they brought gifts for both BethAnn and Randy and Geraldine and Jakob. They would be staying at the Sheridan Inn, where they were well known. Helen had been making all kinds of special treats for them and planned a sumptuous dinner. They were amazed by how much the kids had grown. Especially BethAnn, who was now a young lady. Randy had to show them his achievement of being able to ride a horse. Margarete, of course, was concerned for his safety.

"Don't worry, Grandmother. Nelly is very gentle, and I am very careful," said Randy, but grandmother did worry.

On Friday, Zeke met with Jakob and his father, Bob, at the office, and the final plans were gone over. Zeke gave Jakob all kinds of accolades for his dentistry so his father could be proud of him. The next meeting would be at the Sheridan Inn at sunup in the dining room.

"I git evertin' reddy for us'n to go," said Zeke.

Chapter 36
A Successful Hunt

When Zeke said for them to be ready before sunrise, he really meant it. Jakob rode up to the Sheridan Inn and tied his horse to the rail. Zeke was already there and had everything ready for the elk hunting trip. His buckboard was loaded with everything they would need, as well as the packhorse. Jakob thought about his father riding a horse. He wasn't sure he had ever ridden. Living and practicing dentistry in Milwaukee, there was no need for a horse there anymore. He had owned a car for several years. It was one of the first in Milwaukee, and there was always good public transportation, so there was no need for horses. *I don't think mother ever rode a horse either. Good thing Zeke brought the buckboard. Dad could ride a horse if he had to but certainly not to the hunting area.*

Zeke and Bob were already in the dining room having coffee. As Jakob arrived, Lukas put out the eggs, bacon, fried potatoes, and toast. Zeke was all wound up and talking about the hunt to Bob.

He told Jakob where they would be heading. "You might as well ride in the buckboard with us till we gits to the place where we might see some elk. And then you can take to yer hoss."

The buckboard didn't move too fast, and so it took well into the day before they were in the foothills of the Bighorns. The sun was up with a few clouds and a pretty good but cool breeze. It took a while until it warmed up.

They entered a wooded area and saw some birds and even some smaller animals. In one open place, they came on some buzzards circling in the distance. As it got more hilly, the buckboard slowed down some more. Jakob decided to take to his horse and ease up on the load. It would also give his horse some good exercise. In one area, they saw some antelope in the distance.

"From here on, we might start seein' elk or deer," said Zeke. "You's not interested in deer, are ya? They's plenty 'round here. We git to a plain soon, and sometimes they's buffalo there."

They made it to the plain, and it was late, so Zeke decided to stay on the outskirts overnight. "This be a good spot to stay t'night."

He gathered some wood and started a fire. They sat close around the fire because it had begun to cool off. A light breeze came off the plain. Zeke then put together some grub and coffee. First, he broke out a bottle and passed it around. "This'll warm yer innards," he said. Zeke always kept the conversation going, talking about how things used to be in Sheridan and around the Goose Creek Valley.

Stars appeared in the sky as they ate, and the noises in the night were now being heard. Finishing up with the grub, the bedrolls were brought out, and they decided to turn in. This was to be a new experience for Bob, sleeping in the open. He and Jakob were on one side of the fire and Zeke on the other, snoring away.

"You know, Dad, I'm thinking, this is the first time we've done anything like this. I always meant to, but it seems I never got around to doing it. I hope you get an elk. There's no guarantee, but we'll try. It's nice to be with you like this."

"I agree, Jakob. It's good being together. I'm beginning to see why you like living out here in the remoteness and the beauty of the mountains and the vast plains. I can't ever remember seeing so many stars."

They quietly talked until they ran out of words and fell asleep.

The howling of a coyote woke Jakob, and he saw Zeke putting wood on the fire. More thoughts of his dad came to his mind, and he fell back asleep. The sky was just starting to lighten, and Jakob awoke. He heard the horses rustling and snorting but couldn't fall back asleep.

Bob quietly said, "Jakob, are you up? I'm getting up to use the pot. No problem."

Jakob saw him get up and go behind a bush. Coming back, he saw the fire was getting low, and he put some wood on it and went back to his bedroll as the fire flared and started up again. Neither one fell back asleep, and now Zeke was up and putting on the coffee pot and starting breakfast.

"Best you guys git up now. I'm starting breakfast. I want to git going soon. On the other side of this'un, there be another clearing where we can usual find some elk. They don't stick around long. So we best git thar afore they leave."

The hot coffee felt good, and then the bacon and eggs really hit the spot. They also finished up some beans that were left from the night before.

They got ready, put out the fire, and moved on closer to the second clearing. "Best we leave our horses here. Git yer guns reddy, and we kin walk the rest of the way. It's a fir piece, but they's got good ears, so we don't want to spook 'em."

The sun was up now, but it was shivering cold as they quietly moved through a rocky area. Zeke led the way. A hawk graced the sky up high. An occasional prairie dog could be seen poking its head above the ground. Zeke turned around and put a finger across his mouth. They could see a clearing ahead. He stopped and motioned them forward to view the full meadow. It was large, and on the far side, a herd of elk grazed.

"They's fir away. Too fir to git a good shot. We jes wait and see if they git closer."

The elk were moving toward the hunters, but it was slow. Zeke was worried they might see something to spook them and move out of range.

Finally, Zeke said, looking at Bob, "What you say, Doc? You think you can take one? How good a shot are ya? This is different from bird huntin', I knows. Doc, Jake could do it, but he say you git first shot."

"Oh, I've done target shooting. I see one I believe I can hit." He carefully aimed his rifle and pulled the trigger. The sound of the shot reverberated, and the herd scattered. The elk dropped, but it looked like it was trying to get up.

"Quick, take another shot Dad," said Jakob. Bob shot again, and the elk was motionless. They got up and ran toward the downed animal.

"Doc, you got him good, and he's a good'un. I be goin' fer the pack hoss. You jes stay here and keep your eyes open. I don't think a b'ar is around, but watch out."

He left, and they examined the elk, being wary there was no bear around.

"Good shot, Dad. I thought you got him on the first round, but I believe it might have started to move when you fired the first time," Jakob said. "It didn't take too long, and the buzzards are flying high above." Jakob kept his eyes moving over the area, but no bear showed up.

Zeke finally pulled up with the buckboard and horses and proceeded to butcher the elk. "He gonna make some good eatin' when we git him over to Herman. Ya gonna keep the rack, or do ya want the head too? We kin git that fixed too."

It took a while for Zeke to get the elk ready for them to get loaded on the buckboard. They crossed the clearing and went some distance without finding any more elk. It was late in the afternoon, and they came on a stream.

"This be a good spot fer the night," said Zeke, and he broke out his cooking utensils and gathered up some wood to start a fire.

They watered the horses and fed them while he was getting the grub ready.

"I'm gonna cut us some steaks to fry up," said Zeke, and he began to carve some from the carcass. Carrying the bloodied steaks to the stream, he washed them and put them in a large frying pan. He broke out the bottle of whiskey and passed it around. The sun was going down, and the air was cooling off, so the whiskey shot felt good.

"That elk is a big'un, and you gonna get lotsa meat." Zeke buried some potatoes in the embers, and the steaks were fried up. A can of beans was heated up along with a pot of coffee. The dinner was now ready. The steaks were done to perfection. Except, when they put their fork in them, they were mighty tough. Tasty, but tough. They had to be chewed and chewed and chewed. Jakob looked at Zeke as he chewed and chewed the steaks with his dentures.

"Tell you what, Doc. Ya think you could sharpen ma teeth for me?"

Jakob watched as Zeke worked on that elk steak as best as he could. "Sorry, Zeke, you just have to cut the meat as fine as you can. There's no sharpening of those teeth."

"Gol dern, Doc, makes eatin' a tough job."

Bob laughed.

After finishing their elk steaks and the rest of the vittles, they were ready to turn in for the night. The fire was prepared with plenty of wood to feed it and their bedrolls laid out.

Bob looked over at Jakob. "This was some day, son. I wondered if I would get an elk. Thanks for giving me the opportunity. Sorry, you didn't get one. Wait till I tell the bunch at the country club about my experience."

They quietly chattered and finally fell asleep. There were the sounds of the night, and the horses were restless. A coyote howling nearby kept them nervous. They both awakened at different times to feed the fire.

Morning came too soon, and breakfast was some flapjacks Zeke made along with eggs. Zeke was a pretty good cook. Cleaning up the site and putting out the fire, they started off and traveled most of the day without seeing any elk. Jakob didn't realize it, but Zeke had them going in circles. Other animals were seen, but they were interested in another elk.

"Looks like they plumb disappeared, Doc," said Zeke. "We can stay out another day if'n you want, but I'm not sure we git another elk. What say we head home? We can make it by dark."

It was accepted by Jakob and Bob, who were satisfied with one elk. They had a good time and felt it was worthwhile. They made it to town and stopped to see Herman Stein, the butcher, who thought it was a nice elk and would give them plenty of roasts and steaks as well as sausages.

"I'll get the elk head and rack mounted and have it shipped to Milwaukee," Herman told them. Before they left, Bob gave him his home address to ensure it was delivered to the right place.

Jakob and his dad got home safe and sound. Simba heard them arrive and announced to everyone the hunters had returned. Randy was first to greet them.

"We wondered if you'd be back today," said Geraldine. "Did you get an elk?"

"We sure did. Grandfather Bob got him, and he's a beaut," said Jakob.

Zeke carefully unloaded their belongings, and he was on his way.

Helen set the table for Bob and Jakob, and they told the story of the hunting trip. Margarete was surprised Bob got the elk. "Where's it at, and what are you going to do with it?"

Bob informed her that it was being butchered and would be shipped to Milwaukee later. "I'm having some sausage made, which we'll barbeque at the country club outing. The head and antlers are for the den," said Bob.

Margaret looked horrified as everyone laughed. They stayed on for several days and were treated to Sheridan living. Their stay was enjoyed—especially by the grandchildren. As they were boarding the train to go back home, Margarete admitted they enjoyed coming to Wyoming, and added that Bob could display the elk trophy in the garage.

Chapter 37
Jakob Plays Hero

Jakob had just opened his office when an excited Doc Kelly came in.

"Jake, they had a ruckus over in the Cowboy Saloon last night. It put four in the hospital in bad shape. They all have busted faces, and one of them might have a broken jaw. A couple of broken arms and some fingers, and I don't know what else, but I think you should go over and take a look. I'm on my way, so we might as well go together."

"Kelly, you always bring me such good news when I've been gone a few days. My folks just left yesterday for Milwaukee after a very nice visit. I went elk hunting with my dad, and he had a great time, and now you bring me this."

"Oh, I didn't know you went hunting. Did you get an elk?"

"I didn't, but my dad did get a nice one. You think it's a fractured mandible on one of them?" said Jakob.

"I'm not sure, but one of the doctors told me he thought it was fractured, and they did some x-rays, so you better take a look. Nobody else around here can do fractures, so let's go."

"You want to come with me? Because I'll drive over," said Jakob.

"No, I'll take my nag and meet you there."

Jakob arrived first and went into the x-ray room and found the ones of Willy George. "Hmm, fractured mandible, sure enough, but so are a bunch of teeth," said Jakob.

Kelly arrived, and they went in to see a cowboy who looked like a horse kicked him in the face. His face was swollen with other lacerations, some that had been sutured. He could hardly open his mouth.

"Let's get rid of some of these broken teeth first," said Jakob. "I may still be able to use some teeth to wire to. Is there anyone around to give anesthesia?"

"There's a nurse who's been trained."

They transferred the patient to surgery and did the anesthesia. Jakob removed the broken teeth and roots and stabilized the fracture as best as he could. He would get him back in a couple of days when the swelling was down and do the wiring.

"All this has happened because of a disagreement of some sort. Liquor was probably involved, and all this leads to permanent disfigurements," said Jakob.

"You know, Jake, these guys will never learn. Every Saturday, they come to town to have a good time, and they end up in the hospital."

"They should close up that Cowboy Saloon if they can't keep the peace."

"I agree, but it seems inevitable," said Kelly.

"Kelly, I got to get back to the office. I'll look in on this guy with the fracture tomorrow and see how he's doing."

Jakob left and stopped at the post office for his mail before going on. It was near lunchtime when he arrived at the office. Passing the bank next to his office, he looked in the window. There were quite a few people there, including Jozef, but he saw one with a bandana over his face and a gun in hand. Then he saw two others with guns drawn and people on the floor. *Oh my gosh. The bank is being robbed!*

He parked and quickly opened his office and took up the telephone to call the sheriff. The phone rang and rang, but no answer came, and so he called the police station. It was finally answered, and he told them the bank was being robbed. Someone there said they knew and had already sent men. Not knowing what else he could do, he took his gun out of the drawer and went to the door. Then he heard firing out in the street, a lot of it. There was screaming and shouting.

"Drop those guns." Looking out of the partially opened door, he could see two men on horses firing and others behind a big flowerpot firing at the sheriff and his deputies out in the street. One was on the ground, and Sheriff Willard just got hit and went down. Jakob could hear him screaming in pain and saw blood. He was only twenty or thirty feet away and holding his leg and thrashing. The other deputy was about twenty feet from Willard.

Jakob opened the door to his office and ducked behind his car before venturing out into the street. Someone was still firing at Willard when Jakob got to him. Actually, he was firing at Jakob. Seeing a lot of blood coming from Willard's leg, Jakob tore his shirt off and placed some of it over the wound with pressure to stop the bleeding, but the compress was soaked with blood, and it still continued. He realized he had to tourniquet the injury, so he quickly took off his belt and tightened it until the bleeding stopped. Willard was moaning and seemed to go unconscious. The policemen arrived, and all four of the bandits were on their horses and riding away.

Willard stopped bleeding, so Jakob went to the deputy, unconscious and bleeding heavily from his shoulder. Someone came up to Jakob and gave him his shirt, which Jakob tore and placed over the wound with pressure to stop the bleeding. The police left, pursuing the bandits, and people came up to Jakob as he tended the sheriff and deputy. It was then Jakob felt pain and saw bleeding in his left arm. He had been hit and didn't realize it. Someone put a towel over the forearm and held it tightly. Jakob started to get dizzy and almost lost consciousness as the two guys picked him up and put him on a buggy which hurried to the hospital.

He regained consciousness with Kelly standing over him. The room was filled with doctors and nurses tending Jakob and the sheriff and deputy. Kelly cleaned the arm of blood and applied a compress to it while they took an x-ray. It seemed like forever, but they finally came out with the x-ray.

"Jake, this looks like a flesh wound. There's no bullet. You lucked out. Boy, are you lucky. I'll just clean it up and suture it." Looking sternly at Jakob, he said, "What the hell were you doing out there with all the shooting going on? You're lucky you didn't get yourself killed."

"I don't know. I just saw Willard on the ground and bleeding like hell. He could have bled to death right there."

"You're right. They're giving him a transfusion right now. Poor Leroy, he's on the table, and Ross and Hudell are looking for the slug. He has a fifty-fifty chance of making it. You may have saved both their lives."

Jakob was quiet. He felt a little dizzy. He realized he could have been killed, and the thought took hold of him as he laid on the table in the emergency room. Then he heard Geraldine in the background, begging the nurse to let her see him. Tears flowed down her cheeks as she came forward and saw Jakob lying there, pale and quiet. He saw her and weakly smiled.

"I'm oka,y honey. I'm okay," he tried to reassure her as Geraldine held his face, kissing him. "I"m okay, really."

"Oh, Jakob! I was so afraid I lost you when I heard what happened. They said you're going to be all right. BethAnn wants to come in. She's frantic. Is it okay?"

"Sure, tell the nurse."

Kelly was there with BethAnn, who buried her face in Jakob's chest. She held him and sobbed.

"Daddy, I love you so. You've got to be all right."

Jakob weakly smiled. "Honey, I am going to be all right. Don't worry."

"You want to stay here the night, Jake? I don't think you have to. Just take it easy and leave the sling on your arm. Why don't you just rest for a couple of hours? The nurse will bring you some tea. Geraldine and your daughter can stay here with you. I'm going to check in on Willard and the deputy and then go over to the Lady and have one for you and me. If you need me, give a holler." Kelly left.

The nurses brought them tea, and they sat and talked till Jakob dozed off. In a couple of hours, the nurse came back. She shook Jakob a little. "Are you all right, doctor?"

Jakob's eyes opened, and he smiled. "Yes, I'm all right. I guess it was the morphine that knocked me out."

The nurse just shook her head and left again.

"Let's go, Honey," he said to Geraldine. "I'm hungry. Maybe you can make me something to eat."

BethAnn and Geraldine helped him get up, and they left the hospital. BethAnn drove the buggy home. Helen and Randy were waiting for him. News traveled fast. They already knew what had happened. Helen quickly made them something to eat. As they sat at the table, Helen poured them a glass of wine.

"This will help settle your nerves, Pan." This was the first time she called him Pan, just like Chucha used to, and she laughed and said some other words they did not understand. "When I heard what happened to you, I thought about my Walter and prayed for you. My prayers were answered. You are all right."

Randy sat on Jakob's lap and hugged and kissed him. He saw his bandaged arm supported by a sling and was careful not to disturb it. It was late now, and they were all tired from a stressful day. One by one, they left for bed, with Geraldine and Jakob following. She laid close to him, being grateful his injury was not too severe.

Jakob's eyes opened, and he could smell the coffee brewing in the kitchen. Simba was moving around as Helen got breakfast ready. Geraldine, lying close to him, was softly slumbering. He had no reason to get up now. His arm was hurting some, especially if he moved it, so he thought he wouldn't go to the office. With the sling on, he couldn't do much as far as dentistry was concerned. His thoughts came back to yesterday afternoon. *I was sure Willard would bleed to death when I saw the blood flowing in spurts. I just knew a major artery was ruptured, and the deputy was lying motionless. I thought he was a goner. I heard the shooting, but I didn't know it could be at me. I still don't remember when I got hit. Thank goodness the police arrived when they did because the bank robbers stopped shooting, and that's when I knew I had been hit. Then they left.*

He laid thinking over and over those moments he was in the open, exposed to the gunfire. He felt the warmness of Geraldine next to him and could smell the fragrance from her hair, and he felt so good. Thoughts of Randy and BethAnn added to his feeling of security.

Then Geraldine started to move. She lifted her head and kissed his forehead and then his lips. "You awake?" she said quietly.

"Yes, I've been awake for some time. I've been thinking about you and the kids and how much I love you and how important you are to me."

She cuddled up closer to him, and they quietly laid there until they heard the children in the kitchen and the dog scurrying around.

"Well, looks like it's time to join the family," said Jakob as he kissed Geraldine, and they got out of bed.

Randy and BethAnn were at the table starting their breakfast when Jakob and Geraldine came into the kitchen. Simba ran up to Jakob and put her paws on him. He petted her and brushed her off. Both children hugged Jakob and Geraldine.

"Hey, Dad, how long will you have to have that sling on your arm? We won't be able to play catch, will we?" said Randy.

"I don't know. Not too long, I hope. I'll see if I can use my arm when I go to the office. If it hurts too much and I can't use it to work, I'll have to take it easy. Right now, it hurts some but not as much as I thought it would."

"Daddy, were you scared when they were shooting at you?" said BethAnn.

"You know, Honey, I didn't even think about that. The sheriff on the ground was my focus. I hope he will be all right. I hope they got the bullet out." There was a knock on the door, and Helen went to answer.

It was Kelly, who bolted in and went to the kitchen. "Well, how's our hero doing today?"

"Kelly, cut it out. I'm no hero. You would have done the same thing I did if you were in my position."

"I don't know what I would have done, Jake. When something like that happens, you, um, you act instinctively. And I believe you did just that. I guess it happened to me on several occasions, but you did it. Yes, you did it, and I respect you for it. Now, don't get a big head about it. Think you can go down to the hospital? I stopped by and saw Willy. He doesn't look any better. We can put it off a couple of days, can't we? It's going to be hard getting into his mouth to put on the arch bars."

"Okay, we'll wait a couple of days."

"You should be able to use that arm by then. Oh yes, Willard and the deputy are doing okay. They got the slug out of the deputy. It was in deep, and Willard's slug nicked the bone. He could end up with a limp, but he'll be okay. He could have ended up in a puddle of blood if you hadn't helped him. Hey, what are those cakes with the jelly on them? They look good."

"Oh, Helen," said Geraldine, "Give our guest of honor here a coffee and one of your special cakes. Sit over here, Doctor."

Kelly sat down with them, and they talked about the bank robbery. Then there was another knock on the door. Helen opened it, and Jozef came in.

"Doc, I just had to stop by and see how you were doing. I find it hard to believe that we had a robbery. As near as I can tell, they got away with about $10,000.00. I really was concerned for the people in the bank, but thank God no one got hurt. They screamed and frightened the people. I was afraid one might shoot someone."

They talked about the robbery, and Jozef and Kelly left. Others stopped by to express their concern for Jakob but left, knowing he was all right.

Following breakfast, Jakob got dressed. Some of his neighbors stopped by to see how he was doing, and he then sat around and talked to Randy. They played ball with Simba, who would play forever if you let her. It was almost noon, and boredom set in. Geraldine was busy, and Jakob had his fill of rest.

"Geraldine, why don't you take me to the office? I left the car there when they took me to the hospital. I can maybe make an arch bar for my fracture case and do a couple of other things in the lab. Then I'll bring the car home."

"I thought you were going to rest after the ordeal," said Geraldine.

"Well, I've rested the morning. I could rest in the office too."

Geraldine smiled; "Okay, I didn't think you could just rest for even one full day."

Geraldine got the buggy ready, and they were off. She left him at the office, and Jakob walked into the emptiness. He sat in his lab and tried bending the arch bar, but the sling prevented movement of his left hand, so he took off the sling and tried again. Although the injury was above the hand, any movement of his fingers was difficult and painful. He realized he would not be able to work, at least for now. *Now, what can I do?* At that time, a patient came into his office.

"Hi, Doc. Heard you got shot. Must not have been too bad. Maybe you can help me. I got this tooth here that's killing me. Why don't you just yank it out?"

"I can't do it, Jack. I have only one arm to use, and I need both to take out a tooth."

"Gosh, Doc, it's killing me. What am I going to do?" Jakob, realizing he was in pain, told him to sit in the chair. Jakob looked at the offending tooth.

"Tell you what I can do. I'll put some eugenol in the cavity and seal it in with temporary cement. That should keep the pain down for a while. You can put some cold packs on it."

Jack smiled after Jakob had finished. "That feels great, Doc. It don't hurt at all. Take your time. I'll stop by in a couple of days."

Jakob decided to leave the office lest others might stop by for treatment. He went to the hospital to see his fracture case and make sure the jaw was still stabilized. He saw the swelling was going down, and maybe he could do the fracture in a couple of days. That done, he decided to see Willard and the deputy.

Willard was awake and propped up. He was doing pretty good and thanked Jakob for saving him. "Gosh Doc, if you weren't there, they would be putting me in the ground. I shore don't know how to thank you enough. Lying there on the ground, I thought I was a goner. The leg hurts, but they give me stuff, and it's starting to feel better."

Jakob left and looked in on the deputy. He was asleep, but the nurse said he was doing better but very weak.

It was nearly noon, so he decided to drive over to the Lucky Lady, visit Andy Meeks, and have some lunch. Getting the car started was not easy, but he managed to use the injured arm with difficulty and a lot of pain. The Lucky Lady was quiet as Jakob walked in. Several saw him and came up to Jakob to commend him for his heroic act.

"Doc, you are something else. You have guts I would never have believed," said Andy.

"Come on, Andy. I really don't have the guts you say."

"You went to Willard while they were shooting."

"I saw Willard out there on the ground and bleeding. I had to help him. I know Willard and take care of his four kids. I never thought about the fact that I was in danger."

"Doc, I don't know about you."

"Hey, the reason I'm here is I thought we might go over to Lee Chang for lunch."

Andy called Harry, who took over, and they went to Lee Chang. They talked at length about the robbery and Jakob's hunting trip and had a good lunch. He left for home because he realized he was handicapped with his arm in a sling, so there was no use going to the office.

Randy was waiting for him with hopes they could play catch. He worked to be a pitcher on the Elk's Club team and was doing well with Jakob coaching him. On the backside of the garage, Jakob mounted a small galvanized tub, and Randy used it to practice pitching. He was getting most of the pitches straight in the tub. Simba was acting as a catcher. Randy would throw, and Simba would bring the ball back to him. Jakob was now working with him to throw a curveball. However, throwing a ball was difficult for him with the sling on, so he watched Randy and instructed him. They did that until Randy's arm got tired.

After several days, Jakob took off the sling and started using the arm, but it still hurt, so he went back to wearing it.

Chapter 38
Jakob Becomes a Legend

Jakob may have taken off the sling too soon. His arm still pained him. It got red and started to swell. He also noticed he had trouble raising his wrist. Kelly came to take a look at it and thought infection had developed. Jakob was in trouble. They tried cold packs at first and then hot packs. The swelling localized, and they finally decided to open it and drain it. Then the swelling started to come down. The arm felt better, but Jakob could not practice dentistry yet. They decided the ulnar nerve had been damaged, and the wrist had to be supported, so he wore a splint and exercised it as best as possible.

It took a while before Jakob's life could get back to normal. Someone would always bring up his heroic venture, and he appreciated their comments. However, it got to the point where he wanted to get beyond it. But so many of the patients and people who knew him were proud of what he had done.

Jakob was proud of what he had been doing in his profession, and he also liked living in Sheridan, so he took part in the city affairs. He still went to city meetings, but because Sheridan was now a commissioner elected government, he took part as an interested citizen. Sheridan was growing, and with growth, there were those ever-present growth pains. They never did capture the bank robbers Jakob happened on that October day. Still, crime in Sheridan was pretty much under control.

Winter was now around the corner, and most activities went inside. BethAnn and Geraldine still did some riding, weather permitting. Princess, BethAnn's horse was being trained. Randy often went riding with them on the trails if they were not too difficult. BethAnn also had other friends like Daisy Ross, who rode with her. They had a riding club of sorts, and it was a good activity for the young people in Sheridan. Sometimes they performed at rodeos. Princess already had developed into a good jumping horse.

BethAnn was a busy young lady. She was now near graduation with her school activities, and boys were knocking at the Miller door.

BethAnn found her piano an important part of her life, but it was being squeezed for time. Jakob still liked her going with him to the office on Saturday.

It was a late Wednesday afternoon when some Crow Indians entered the office. They carried in a little girl who was crying because she was in pain. Poor little thing was about ten years old and emaciated. Unfortunately, she had been treated by the shaman for the pain in her mouth for some time, according to the interpreter who usually came along. BethAnn saw her first and tried to talk to her, but she was very upset and not cooperative. She had pain, and there was no way anyone could allay it.

Jakob picked her up and gently placed her in his chair. He managed to get her to open her mouth, and he saw that her teeth were mostly decayed. The inside of her mouth was also inflamed with some white patches. The shaman evidently gave her something which caused a burn of the tissues. Jakob talked to the little thing, hoping to gain her confidence, and she finally stopped sobbing and crying. He had a mouthwash which was mildly astringent to comfort the pain. Then he showed her how to hold it in her mouth to relieve the burning sensation, and then her mouth felt better. He had her do this for some time, and then she could hold it open so Jakob could see her teeth and find which tooth was giving her pain. There was one that showed an exposed nerve. He tried using an injection of Novocain, but it didn't seem to work well for some reason. He had a paste which he put on a cotton pellet and carefully sealed it in the tooth. It didn't take very long, and the pain subsided. He left it in the tooth and instructed the woman to bring the child back the next day. He impressed on her the need to use the mouthwash and not let the shamans touch the child. She was better, and the Indians seemed satisfied. They left with Jakob telling them to be sure to come back the next day.

Other patients often grumbled when they saw Jakob was treating Indians. However, the day finished for Jakob on a positive note when another patient commended Jakob for helping to take care of them.

The next day had almost ended, and the child he took care of the previous day did not return as Jakob instructed. Jakob had placed a treatment in the child's tooth, which had to be replaced after twenty-four hours. Unfortunately, the Indians were not very dependable with keeping appointments, so Jakob decided to wait until the following day and see if they brought the child in.

It was almost noon on the next day. She had not been brought in, and there was no way to contact them. *I had better go out to the village, see the child, and change that dressing. Leaving it in too long could cause necrosis of the bone.* It was a very strong chemical, and he felt it must be taken out. He decided to go to the Crow reservation and see the child. He stopped at the Lucky Lady to see Andy Meeks.

"Let's get some lunch at Grand Ma's place Andy," he said.

Andy always obliged and asked Harry to take over for him.

As they had their lunch, Jakob asked, "How'd you like to go with me to the Crow reservation, Andy?"

"You're kidding me, aren't you, Jake?"

"No, I got a kid I have to see. You've never been out there, have you? It would be a good experience for you to see it."

"Okay, Jake, you got me. But are you sure it's safe?"

"Of course it's safe. We'll stop back at the Lady, and you can tell Harry to take care of the place while you're gone."

In about an hour and a half, they were outside the reservation with a group of the Indians on horses whooping and hollering a welcome for them. They recognized Jakob. He stopped at Chief Medicine Crow's teepee. The chief was outside when he heard all the noise. He welcomed Jakob but was concerned as to why Jakob was there.

Jakob first introduced Andy, who was dumbfounded and tried some small talk with the chief. Jakob then told Medicine Crow he wanted to see the child he had taken care of the other day. It took a while before they found her. Jakob sat her on a large rock near the teepee and took out his instrument kit. He proceeded to remove the dressing he had placed in the tooth. She fidgeted a little but was cooperative. He then used his instrument to clean out the tooth. She was perfectly comfortable. He noticed the inflammation inside her mouth had disappeared. Then he placed another cotton pellet with some different medication back into the tooth and sealed it.

The interpreter said the child was in no pain, so they decided not to go back to Jakob's office. He then told her they must bring her back the next day. The child seemed happy and ran off with other children who had been watching.

Jakob saw the chief's wife standing next to him. He hadn't seen her since he treated her for a bad case of ulcerative gingivitis. He asked her to sit on the same rock the girl sat on and proceeded to examine her. The Chief and other tribe members looked on. Jakob told the chief she was better but needed more treatment, and she should come back to his office. The chief said they would come, and then he asked Jakob to stay with them overnight. Jakob talked with him and told him he had to leave to take care of other patients but thanked him and said he would return another time. They promptly left because it was getting late.

Coming back, Andy was amazed by Jakob's apparent friendship with Chief Medicine Crow, and Jakob talked about how the Indians should be respected. Andy had never had any contact with them and couldn't believe how well they treated Jakob.

They entered Sheridan at dark, and Jakob left Andy at the Lucky Lady. As he was leaving, Andy turned around and said, "Doc, I just can't believe how well those people respected and treated you."

It was almost ten when Jakob opened the door to his house.

Geraldine was frantic. "Jakob. What happened? Where have you been? When you didn't come for dinner, I went to the office, and you weren't there. Then I went to the Lucky Lady, and they said you had left with Andy Meeks somewhere."

Jakob apologized and went on to explain what he had done and why. He apologized again for not informing her.

The next day Jakob saw the Indian girl and took care of her needs, which were many. His care of those people was limited to mainly emergency work. Other dentists in Sheridan followed Jakob's lead and cared for them, but they only sought help when they were in pain.

Thanksgiving Day was approaching, and the business community in Sheridan would try to make it a special holiday. They planned on decorating Sheridan and having special events. A group of businessmen met at the Sheridan Inn for a social lunch and a business meeting in the ornate bar room. Lucas made them a special lunch. They talked about what was important to Sheridan. Over the years, they met and set up different programs for Sheridan's betterment. Sometimes the meetings would recognize the achievements of its members.

This day the sheriff, Willard, limped in as well as Mayor Johnson and former mayor Burns. There was some joking as well as serious talk.

Mayor Johnson started the discussion. "Gentlemen, the other day I was in the Lucky Lady and, as we often do, stood at the bar with Andy Meeks and some others and just yak yakked. You get to know what's going on in town at the Lady, like whose wife is cheating on who and stuff like that," which brought on some laughing. "But I heard something about one of our members you should be aware of. Who was it? You all know him. Jake Miller. He's sitting over there."

The group all turned and looked at Jakob, who felt a little uneasy.

"Andy talked about going with him last week to the Crow Indian reservation to take care of a little Indian girl. Now, why would a man in his right mind do something like that?. And why would someone go all the way out to the reservation to take care of a little girl?"

The group chuckled.

"He was welcomed by Chief Medicine Crow. Andy thought Jake was a blood brother of the chief. Is that true, Jake?"

Jakob, though somewhat uneasy, nodded and said, "I am."

"We all know Jake takes care of the tribe when they need him, but to go out to the reservation to care for one of them is something else. This is the same guy who went through a hail of bullets to save one of us here. Yes, they were shooting when he went to Willard's aid and saved him from bleeding to death. He saved his life. What kind of a guy would do that? A guy who one day would be a special citizen in Sheridan and act as a guide to the President of the United States. A guy who takes part in our yearly events like the Sheridan Fair and the Elk Club's baseball. Oh, there's too many things to mention. This guy's a legend; Jake Miller. How do we keep up with him?"

There was laughter and side remarks by others in the room.

By this time, Jakob didn't know what to do or say. The room had become crowded, and he received applause. He was asked to speak, and he thanked them, but he stumbled and finally said he didn't deserve the praise.

"When I came to Sheridan, all I wanted to do was be a good dentist. You guys are making too big a thing out of this. I think all of you have worked to make Sheridan better."

Epilogue

Four years later...

The story of Jakob and Geraldine continues. BethAnn decides to follow in her father's footsteps and becomes a dentist. Jakob takes her to Chicago, where she is accepted in a Chicago College of Dental Surgery class. It is the school Jakob graduated from. She does well and graduates with a degree in Doctor of Dental Surgery. While attending school, BethAnn runs into Mark Ross, the son of Dr. Frederick Ross, in the medical bookstore in Chicago. His medical school, Rush Medical, is next door to the Chicago College of Dental Surgery. The two of them had met in Sheridan while BethAnn was riding horses with Mark's sister Daisy. Their chance meeting leads to a subsequent date, and they eventually fell in love. They marry when he graduates in June.

Randy Jakob, who is now nine, rides Nelly to baseball practice. He's on the Elk's junior baseball team that Jakob coaches. He was once asked what he wanted to be when he grew up, and his answer was to be a baseball player. Simba usually follows him to practice and becomes the team mascot, retrieving baseballs for the team. Jakob finds coaching young ballplayers very gratifying. Dentistry can be stressful, but coaching the kids is satisfying. He looks forward to BethAnn being his partner in the office.

Geraldine continues to bring her English ways to Sheridan, and she loves her work in the Sheridan Library. She and BethAnn find as much time together as they can. Riding with BethAnn is limited because of school, so Geraldine gives her time to teach other girls to ride. She and Jakob have a great marriage. They are inseparable and find time to spend at the ranch. Geraldine and the Allens decide to convert it to a dude ranch. Each year they plan to take more guests. The Homerdings are in charge of the operation, and their boy helps with the horses. Geraldine's desire for another child fails, and she resigns herself to being a mother to Randy Jakob and BethAnn.

Off in England, there are changes at Landry Manor. Jenny Lynn has a baby boy she names Gerald Randolph. He will be the next Baron of Landry Manor. The solicitor is in contact with Geraldine about Randy before naming Gerald Randolph the heir of Landry Manor. The young Jenny Lynn will find a suitable husband in William McDonald, whose parents are Sir Henry McDonald and Rose Ann. They are fine English stock.

Lady Mary has not forgotten young Randy. She remembers him and sends gifts and cards to him. She hopefully looks forward to another visit from the Millers.

Life in Sheridan has been enjoyable and successful for the Millers, and they look forward to their children's successes. But on the horizon is a period of anxiety. A terrible World War has erupted in Europe that will include the United States, and peace will be denied for some years to come.

THE END

Acknowledgments

No author can write a book without the help of others. This author relied on a number of people for assistance. Without the efforts of a knowledgeable editing team, I am sure the book would not be publishable. Thanks to Sue Eller and Kate Poitevin for their expertise.

My knowledge of Sheridan, Wyoming, came from several books. "In the Shadow of the Bighorns" by Cynde Gorgen, from the Sheridan Historical Society, was invaluable. I found a copy of "Sagebrush Dentist" by Herman Gastrell to give me an idea of what early dentistry was in Sheridan. I thank the Sheridan library for their help. Assistance from Andrea Matlak, American Dental Association Library, gave me further historical knowledge of early dentistry.

Knowledge and research into English aristocracy came from several books.

I thank those who took the time to read my book and give me valuable assistance: Lois Rubens, Donna Odean, Patsy Porter, Candace Rouse, and John Woods.

Books by Stan Parks

Jakob's Ladies

Jakob's Legacy

and coming soon...

The Uncommon Man

Books are available at amazon.com and in select bookstores.
We hope you enjoyed reading Jakob's Legacy. *Before you go, please leave a review on Amazon or Goodreads.*
Thank you.

About the Author

Stan Parks

Stanley C. (Stan) Parks was born in Chicago, Illinois, and attended Loyola University, Chicago and the University of Notre Dame. He was a teacher at Loyola University Dental School, and Assistant Professor at Northwestern University School of Dentistry.

He served as a naval officer in WW II—a navigator in the Pacific theater. Among many accomplishments, he served as a director at the Illinois division of the American Cancer Society, past president of both the Aurora, Illinois Lions, and Fort Myers, Florida Kiwanis. He was a mission volunteer as a dentist in Guatemala and has been a Safe Boating instructor, an actor on stage and television, a sculptor, and an author. He has written two novels: *Jakob's Ladies* and *Jakob's Legacy*, both of which are available on Amazon.com and at select bookstores. Stan is also a member of the Spokane Authors & Self-Publishers group in Spokane, Washington.